Hannibal
of
Carthage

Hannibal
of
Carthage

Edited and Introduced by
Lindsay Powell

General Editor: Jake Jackson

**FLAME TREE
PUBLISHING**

This is a FLAME TREE Book

FLAME TREE PUBLISHING
6 Melbray Mews
Fulham, London SW6 3NS
United Kingdom
www.flametreepublishing.com

First published 2023
Copyright © 2023 Flame Tree Publishing Ltd

23 25 27 26 24
1 3 5 7 9 8 6 4 2

ISBN: 978-1-80417-330-5

The classic text in this book derives from *Hannibal (Makers of History)* by Jacob
Abbott, published by Harper & Brothers Publishers, New York and London, 1901; in
addition to extracts from: *The Histories of Polybius*, Vol. I of the Loeb Classical Library
edition, English translation by H.J. Edwards, 1922; *The History of Rome* by Livy, English
translation by Rev. Canon Roberts, published by E. P. Dutton and Co., New York, 1912;
and *The Foreign Wars* by Appian, English translation by Horace White, published by The
MacMillan Company, New York, 1899.

Printed and bound in the UK by Clays Ltd, Elcograf S.p.A

Contents

Contemporary Perspectives

Series Foreword

STRETCHING BACK to the oral traditions of thousands of years ago, tales of heroes and disaster, creation and conquest have been told by many different civilizations in many different ways. Their impact sits deep within our culture even though the detail in the tales themselves are a loose mix of historical record, transformed narrative and the distortions of hundreds of storytellers.

Today the language of mythology lives with us: our mood is jovial, our countenance is saturnine, we are narcissistic and our modern life is hermetically sealed from others. The nuances of myths and legends form part of our daily routines and help us navigate the world around us, with its half truths and biased reported facts.

The nature of a myth is that its story is already known by most of those who hear it, or read it. Every generation brings a new emphasis, but the fundamentals remain the same: a desire to understand and describe the events and relationships of the world. Many of the great stories are archetypes that help us find our own place, equipping us with tools for self-understanding, both individually and as part of a broader culture.

For Western societies it is Greek mythology that speaks to us most clearly. It greatly influenced the mythological heritage of the ancient Roman civilization and is the lens through which we still see the Celts, the Norse and many of the other great peoples and religions. The Greeks themselves learned much from their neighbours, the Egyptians, an older culture that became weak with age and incestuous leadership.

It is important to understand that what we perceive now as mythology had its own origins in perceptions of the divine and the rituals of the sacred. The earliest civilizations, in the crucible of the Middle East, in the Sumer of the third millennium BC, are the source to which many of the mythic archetypes can be traced. As humankind collected together in cities for the first time, developed writing and industrial scale agriculture, started to irrigate the rivers and attempted to control rather than be at the mercy of its environment, humanity began to write down its tentative explanations of natural events, of floods and plagues, of disease.

Early stories tell of Gods (or god-like animals in the case of tribal societies such as African, Native American or Aboriginal cultures) who are crafty and use their wits to survive, and it is reasonable to suggest that these were the first rulers of the gathering peoples of the earth, later elevated to god-like status with the distance of time. Such tales became more political as cities vied with each other for supremacy, creating new Gods, new hierarchies for their pantheons. The older Gods took on primordial roles and became the preserve of creation and destruction, leaving the new gods to deal with more current, everyday affairs. Empires rose and fell, with Babylon assuming the mantle from Sumeria in the 1800s BC, then in turn to be swept away by the Assyrians of the 1200s BC; then the Assyrians and the Egyptians were subjugated by the Greeks, the Greeks by the Romans and so on, leading to the spread and assimilation of common themes, ideas and stories throughout the world.

The survival of history is dependent on the telling of good tales, but each one must have the 'feeling' of truth, otherwise it will be ignored. Around the firesides, or embedded in a book or a computer, the myths and legends of the past are still the living materials of retold myth, not restricted to an exploration of origins. Now we have devices and global communications that give us unparalleled access to a diversity of traditions. We can find out about Indigenous American, Indian, Chinese and tribal African mythology in a way that was denied to our ancestors, we can find connections, match the archaeology, religion and the mythologies of the world to build a comprehensive image of the human adventure.

The great leaders of history and heroes of literature have also adopted the mantle of mythic experience, because the stories of historical figures – Cyrus the Great, Alexander, Genghis Khan – and mytho-poetic warriors such as Beowulf achieve a cultural significance that transcends their moment in the chronicles of humankind. Myth, history and literature have become powerful, intwined instruments of perception, with echoes of reported fact and symbolic truths that convey the sweep of human experience. In this series of books we are glad to share with you the wonderful traditions of the past.

Jake Jackson
General Editor

Introduction to Hannibal

HANNIBAL BARCA OF CARTHAGE (247–*c*. 183–81 BCE), son of Hamilcar, has been described as Ancient Rome's greatest enemy and its worst nightmare. While he lived, the Romans unreservedly despised him, but in death the Romans reluctantly respected him. Today he is mostly known for his audacious march over the Alps with a herd of elephants. Military professionals and history buffs know him for his extraordinary victories – most famously at Cannae (216 BCE) where he deployed a tactical manoeuvre that generals ever since have many times sought to emulate on their own battlefields. What became of him thereafter has faded from popular memory – and undeservedly so. Hannibal was a leader in the truest sense and his life, achievements and legend deserve study.

The first part of this book is a lightly edited version of *Hannibal* in the *Makers of History* series written by Jacob Abbott in 1876 and published in 1901. His work drew upon contemporary scholarship, which was then extensive, and his personal study of extant works by Greek and Roman historians. Extracts from some of those ancient texts translated from the Greek or Latin that describe key events are also included in this book.

The Ancient Sources and Historians

In researching *Hannibal*, Jacob Abbott had access to good English translations of the ancient sources – it is made clear in the preface that he has 'endeavoured to avail himself of the best sources of information'; indeed, he specifically mentions one of the authors by name in the text.

Everything that is known today about Hannibal comes from accounts recorded by his enemies or by foreign commentators. Hannibal was a learned man who is known to have written books, some of which were published during his lifetime. In his biography of Hannibal, the Roman historian Cornelius Nepos (*c*. 110–*c*. 25/24 BCE) says: 'And that great man, although busied with such great wars, devoted some time to letters; for there are several books of his, written in Greek, among them one, addressed to the Rhodians, on the deeds of Cnaeus Manlius Volso in Asia'. Sadly, nothing written by Hannibal – or indeed about him by his fellow Carthaginians – now survives from the Ancient World.

Many ancient historians wrote about Hannibal; very few of those accounts survive. The most important extant source is *The Histories* written by Polybius of Megalopolis (*c.* 200–*c.* 118 BCE). Of the 40 books making up the complete work just five exist in part or in whole. Sometimes called *World History*, it is a narrative history, a weaving together of stories, based both on facts gleaned from chronicles and official reports, and from people he interviewed who had knowledge of the events he described. Starting with the year 264 BCE and ending in 146 BCE, Polybius focuses on the 53 years in which Rome became the 'superpower' of his day. It was a phenomenon the contemporary Greek-speaking world sought to understand. For Polybius the turning point was the First Punic War, which he called 'the longest and most severely contested war in history'. Books 3 through 11 and 14 through 15 of *The Histories* cover the Second Punic War. Polybius was held as a hostage in Rome, then served as a client to the Scipio family, which leads some to doubt his impartiality.

Titus Livius (59 BCE–17 CE), the formidable Roman historian known to English speakers as Livy, is the other important source of information about Hannibal; he is 'the great Roman historian' to which Abbott refers. Livy's epic work called *From the Foundation of the City* – that is, the city of Rome – covers the period 753–9 BCE. Nowadays often called *The History of Rome*, it is an erudite weaving together of stories, both tales derived from legend and traditional interpretations, and facts gleaned from chronicles and official reports (he specifically mentions Fabius), as well as Polybius. Of the 142 books making up the complete work, just 35 survive in part or in whole. Books 21 through 39 cover Hannibal's lifetime. The equally highly regarded Roman historian P. Cornelius Tacitus (*c.* 56–*c.* 120 CE) remarked that, 'Titus Livius [was] pre-eminently famous for eloquence and truthfulness'. As he was writing about events some two centuries after they happened, however, he must be read with this fact in mind.

Julius Florus (*c.* 74–*c.* 130 CE) wrote about the three Punic Wars in his *Epitome of Roman History*, a summary of all of Rome's wars from the city's foundation onwards spanning the next 700 years, based on Livy.

Cornelius Nepos wrote a *Life of Hannibal* (extracted above) in a book on great generals from foreign lands. His account provides several personal details not recorded elsewhere.

Plutarch (*c*. 46–after 119 CE) included vignettes about Hannibal in his *Life of Fabius Maximus*, *Life of Flamininus* and *Life of Marcellus* – three of the profiles in his series of biographical portraits entitled *The Parallel Lives*.

Appian of Alexandria (*c*. 95–*c*. 165 CE), a lawyer, wrote the *Roman History* in 24 books, and *The Foreign Wars*, the latter describing Rome's global conflicts including those in which Hannibal fought.

Pausanias (*c*. 110–*c*. 180 CE), the travel writer, included anecdotes about Hannibal specific to places he visited in his *Description of Greece*.

To both the Greek and Roman writers, the Carthaginians were barbarians – they did not speak their languages and they were foreign to them in every way. To excuse his victories over them and to valorize their own achievements, Roman historians exaggerated Hannibal's talents; they often did so when writing about non-Roman rebel leaders (like Arminius or Boudica or Vercingetorix) who audaciously fought against them, initially with success. Hannibal was portrayed as clever, inspiring and wily, yet also cruel, avaricious and treacherous. To the Romans who managed relations with their neighbours through carefully worded treaties, the Carthaginians did not play by the rules. *Punica fides* ('Punic faith') came to mean the exact opposite, a term for treachery. Thus, getting to know the *real* Hannibal is difficult: our sources are partial and partisan.

Hannibal's Appearance

There is only one portrait bust which is generally accepted to be of Hannibal Barca. It is now in the collections of the Quirinal Palace in Rome. Carved from a block of white marble, the head is tilted to the right, both eyes gazing upwards into the distance. That Hannibal had a powerful gaze was a fact remarked upon by Livy; this is captured in the bust.

The bust shows a man wearing an Attic-style helmet with a peaked decorative *fronton* but no cheek plates. The helmet reveals a thick line of hair along the forehead. Curls run down the sides of the handsome face, forming a moustache and a beard around the cheeks and chin. The nose is long and straight. The shoulders and chest are covered with a cloak pinned at the right shoulder with a large, round, domed brooch. Hints of a tunic and a cuirass show from underneath. Fringed *pteryges* (the edge strips of an arming doublet) are exposed on the upper right and left arms.

Some believe that the bust was made for a wealthy man to decorate his house in Capua, Campania where it was reportedly found. Capua, an Italian ally, reneged on its treaty with Rome in 216 BCE and welcomed Hannibal, who made it his headquarters. It was here in 211 BCE that the Romans finally defeated Hannibal, discussed by Abbott in Chapter X. 'Capua was Hannibal's Cannae', as the Roman historian Florus states.

Hannibal's Genius at Warfighting

The origins of the First Punic War are explained by Abbott in Chapter I. In essence, it was a war that had happened by accident, one which neither adversary had wanted to wage. Hamilcar Barca ('The Thunderbolt') led the Carthaginian side. He proved to be an able commander-in-chief, winning his own battles; it was his less able generals who finally lost the war. Hamilcar himself died fighting in 229/28 BCE. In the wake of the defeat of Carthage, Hannibal – (*Hnb'l* in ancient Punic) which means 'He Who Is Favoured by Baal', the Phoenician god of fertility, weather and war – was raised with a deep hatred of the Romans (Chapter II). In 221 BCE, aged just 26, Hannibal assumed command of all Carthaginian forces in the Iberian Peninsula. He decided upon an invasion of Italy. Hannibal's march across the Ebro River and siege of Saguntum (a city under Roman protection) provoked war with Rome – the Second Punic War.

Hannibal's expeditionary army was a coalition of different nationalities and capabilities. His order of battle comprised: cavalry from Mauretania and Numidia in North Africa with a reputation as the finest mounted troops in the West; lightly armed infantry from Libya skilled in ambushing and raiding; infantry from various Gallic tribes, fighting with long slashing swords and spears; mercenary soldiers from the Iberian Peninsula fighting with the *gladius*, a short stabbing and thrusting weapon; and slingers from the Balearic Islands practised in throwing stones over distance but with deadly accuracy. There was also a small contingent of armed men drafted from Campania, Italy. Polybius mentions that Hannibal left the Iberian

Peninsula in June 218 BCE with 50,000 infantry and 9,000 cavalry; Livy counts 90,000 infantry and 12,000 cavalry. Hannibal's challenge was to lead this motley force and deploy it effectively against an army fighting on its home ground. Through hardships and victories, he succeeded in building an army that was immensely loyal to him.

The army fielded by the Romans was very different. It was a citizen militia. Free-born Roman citizens were picked by lot to serve for a campaign season in the ranks of two legions (from the Latin *legio*, 'levy'), each of 4,200–4,500 infantry (not 4,000 as Abbott asserts) and 300 cavalry. The legion was subdivided into *manipuli* ('maniples' or 'companies') comprising two *centuriae* ('centuries'), commanded by the senior of the two centurions. There were maniples of three different kinds of soldiers: *hastati*, lightly armed, relatively inexperienced troops, forming the front battle line; *principes*, better equipped and more experienced soldiers forming the second line, to whom the *hastati* would fall back if overwhelmed; and *triarii*, heavily armed soldiers, battle-hardened from several campaigns, held in reserve at the rear. The army was supplemented with infantry and cavalry from Italian allies (*socii*), obliged by treaty with Rome to provide manpower in wartime when called upon.

During the Second Punic War, between 215 and 205 BCE, there were generally seven, but never fewer than four, two-legion army groups stationed every year in the Italian Peninsula. In 212 BCE, the Romans raised and deployed 25 legions as well as a large fleet. Roman armed forces then numbered some 200,000 men – an immense investment in men and matériel. With them Rome conducted military operations simultaneously, from the Iberian Peninsula to the Italian Peninsula, from North Africa to the Greek Islands.

The fighting season ran from early spring through late summer. At the close of the campaign, Roman soldiers returned to their urban homes or farms. It was an army of motivated amateurs, not professionals. The Roman force pitched against Hannibal was led by non-professionals too. Consuls – the two most senior magistrates elected annually by the Roman people to their offices – were imbued with *imperium* ('power') to command military units. Thus, at the start of each year new commanders would be appointed to lead the campaign, sometimes executing military strategies quite different from those of their predecessors (compare Caius Flaminius to Quintus Fabius Maximus) or even their contemporaries (compare Lucius Aemilius Paullus to Caius Terrentius Varro).

Hannibal is now widely regarded as a military genius and ranked among the very best generals in recorded history. Based on analysis of his campaigns, the secrets to his success in warfare were his effective use of informers and spies to gather field intelligence, his clever ruses and unpredictable battle tactics, and the smart way he deployed his cavalry.

Hannibal's great skill as a tactical field commander was first demonstrated at the Battle of the Tagus (220 BCE). There he overcame the four-to-one numerical superiority of his Iberian adversary by tricking the enemy into following his retreat across the river, then forcing them on to a narrow crossing where they were slaughtered. In 218 BCE, he moved his army over the Alps in just 15 days *in winter* to surprise the Romans. Once in Italy he confronted them in four great battles (discussed in Chapters VI, VII, VIII and IX). At Ticinus (late November 218 BCE) he used his cavalry to devastating effect – a tactic he repeated at Trebia (22/23 December 218 BCE), where he also forced the Romans to cross the frigid river. At Trasimene (21 June 217 BCE), Hannibal exploited the cover of mist or fog above the lake to hide his army and entrap, ambush and annihilate the Roman army sent to intercept him. At Cannae (2 August 216 BCE) Hannibal famously used the double envelopment manoeuvre, or pincer movement, to encircle the Roman army, which his men then cut down.

For 15 years Hannibal waged a war throughout Italy, besieging cities and winning over Rome's allies. Remarkably, he never actually attacked the city of Rome. Quintus Fabius Maximus *Verrucosus* ('Warty'), nicknamed *Cunctator* ('the Delayer'), was appointed dictator in 217 BCE after the defeat at Lake Trasimene to lead Rome through its existential crisis. He adopted a strategy of evasion and attrition, avoiding direct contact with Hannibal to wear him down and buy time for the Romans to recover their strength (Chapter VIII) – a cautious military doctrine even now called 'Fabianism' or Fabian strategy.

Hannibal's Roman opponent was able to sustain losses and recruit more men to replace casualties; it was much more difficult for Hannibal. Yet he took great, and at times reckless, risks with his men and suffered terrible casualties – as much as half of his army died just on the march over the Alps. His luck ran out completely when he met his match in Publius Cornelius Scipio, often called 'Rome's greatest general'. Scipio had learned how to fight Hannibal head on. Abbott notes that Scipio 'at last, arose greater than Hannibal' (Chapter XI) when he finally defeated Rome's nemesis at Zama (19 October 202 BCE), earning him the honorary war title *Africanus* ('the African').

As great a military leader as he was, Hannibal could not finally defeat his Roman enemy; he could win battles, but he lost the war. Indeed, Livy reports the Numidian cavalry commander Marhabal as saying: 'The gods have not given all their gifts to one man. You know how to win victory, Hannibal, you do not how to use it'.

His plan to retaliate against Rome using an army and navy provided by Antiochus III of Syria failed when he was defeated at sea off Side, Pamphylia and the king lost on land at Magnesia in 190 BCE. Hannibal had more luck fighting for King Prusias of Bithynia, beating Eumenes II of Pergamum in a naval battle in 184 BCE.

Hannibal's March Over the Alps

Rome's victory in the First Punic War, which Abbott discusses in Chapter I, led to Carthage surrendering Sicily, proffering a huge indemnity and losing its naval capability. In the Second Punic War, Hannibal audaciously chose to take the war to Italy by land. That meant traversing the Alps (which Abbott describes in Chapter V). It would be no easy task. For his research, Polybius travelled the route himself, having interviewed survivors of the invasion around 60 or 70 years after the event. Centuries since, historians and explorers have attempted to plot the actual route taken by Hannibal over the Alps in 218 BCE.

Based on Polybius's descriptions, and from other ancient sources, the consensus is that four routes through the Alps were available to Hannibal: two track north, going over the Col du Mont Cenis or the Col de Clapier; one goes through the centre of the mountain range over the Col de Montgenèvre; and a route to the south runs over the Col de la Traversette.

The Col de la Traversette, which rises to 3,000 metres (9,843 feet) above sea level, makes it the highest – and the most difficult – route to navigate. In 2004, geologist Bill Mahaney from the Department of Geography at York University, Toronto studied aerial and satellite surveys, which revealed that only the Col de la Traversette had rock deposits and frozen ground that most closely matched Polybius's description.

Seven years later, Mahaney assembled a team with microbiologist Chris Allen of Queen's University Belfast and historian Eve MacDonald of Cardiff University. They knew that a full-grown horse should eat about 5.4 to 6.8 kilogrammes (12–15 pounds) of hay a day to stay healthy, while an adult elephant can consume up to

136 kilogrammes (300 pounds) of food per day. Hannibal had some 10,000 pack animals, 6,000–12,000 cavalry and up to 40 elephants. The researchers had a theory that traces of *clostridia* in the dung dropped by Hannibal's animals could still be present in the soil. To prove it, they had to find a layer of earth contaminated with the bacteria, which could be dated to the time of the ancient expedition.

They knew that as Hannibal's army marched into the uplands, the column would have stretched an estimated 32 kilometres (20 miles) through the mountain range. Polybius mentions that Hannibal and his elephants regrouped and rested along the way. The researchers therefore located a peat bog – an 'alluvial floodplain' – some 500 metres (1,640 feet) below the Col de la Traversette, which could have been the first place with sufficient available pasture for Hannibal's animals. They took soil core samples and studied them back at their lab.

In March 2016 the researchers published their findings in the academic journal *Archaeometry*. About 40 centimetres below the surface they had discovered a 'mass animal deposition based on disrupted bedding' – a churned up and compacted layer of soil. Radiocarbon dating confirmed it was disturbed around 218 BCE ± 60 years. Chemical analysis found high levels of molecules associated with *clostridia*. In their paper they 'propose that the highly abnormal churned up (bioturbated) bed was contaminated by the passage of Hannibal's animals, possibly thousands, feeding and watering at the site, during the early stage of Hannibal's invasion of Italia (218 BCE).' They believe they *have* found compelling evidence that Hannibal crossed the Alps via the Col de la Traversette. Perhaps archaeological excavations at the site or along the presumed route of the march will one day produce artefacts, such as Carthaginian military equipment, to validate the claim.

Hannibal's Elephants

Hannibal's story is inextricably linked to elephants. At the outset of his campaign, he had up to 40 of them (37 according to Polybius). Elephants were an intrinsic part of Carthaginian culture. A silver coin struck at a mint in Spain around 237–209 BCE by Hannibal's father, Hamilcar, depicts an elephant in profile on the reverse. It shows a rider in a hooded cloak sitting on the animal's back. He holds a goad and directs the elephant to move forward. All of the animal's distinctive features are perfectly reproduced in the image – so well, in fact, that the particular species of elephant can be identified. The large, rounded ear, the outward-pointing tusks and the dip in the back identifies this as an African bush or savanna elephant (*Loxodonta africana*). Although no longer present in North Africa and only found south of the Sahara Desert, in Hannibal's day there was a remnant population of African bush elephants located closer to Carthage in the Atlas Mountains.

Then, as now, African elephants were the largest animals walking the Earth. A fully grown bush elephant's shoulder height is 3.4 metres (11 feet), its length 5.8–7.3 metres (19–24 feet) and its weight may be 5,440 kilogrammes (6 tons). Its mobile bulk made the elephant ideal for ancient warfare, where the animal itself was the war machine, terrifying to men on the ground – especially ones, like the Romans, who had never been charged by an elephant on a battlefield. It was used to smash through massed formations and as a platform to launch missiles and pick off individual enemy combatants. Whether Hannibal's war elephants carried a *howdah* (a turreted wooden structure) to carry an archer or a spear thrower is debated. Hannibal used his elephants with great destructive effect at the Battle of the Tagus (220 BCE).

Managing his squadron of giant beasts on the long journey to Italy, however, posed a significant logistical challenge for Hannibal. It took nearly two weeks just for his men and elephants to cross the Rhône River *en route* to the Alps, as Abbott discusses in Chapter IV. On the journey through the Alpine passes, he lost all but one elephant. The survivor was often ridden by Hannibal himself, sitting on a red cloth; it was named Surus ('the Syrian') and may have been a Western Asiatic or Syrian elephant (*Elephas maximus asurus*). It took part in the Battle of Ticinus (218 BCE), and Hannibal rode it in triumph when he took Capua.

Hannibal's Eye Injury

An active frontline commander, Hannibal thrust himself into harm's way. Mentioned by Abbott in Chapter VII, while campaigning in the Italian Peninsula, Hannibal lost vision in one eye. The injury occurred in the spring of 217 BCE. According to Polybius, 'Hannibal himself on the sole remaining elephant got across [the marshes of the Arno River] with much difficulty and suffering, being in great pain from a severe attack of *ophthalmia* (Greek οφθαλμια), which finally led to the loss of one eye as he had no time to stop and apply any treatment to it, the circumstances rendering that impossible'. Having assessed the reported symptoms, Justin T. Denholm of the University of Melbourne and Patrick N. Hunt of Stanford University 'suggest that a keratitis from waterborne organisms, such as *Pseudomonas* spp. or *Acanthamoeba* spp., might provide the best answer to this ancient enigma' (*Emerging Infectious Diseases*, January 2021). Keratitis is an inflammation of the cornea: to avoid loss of vision, urgent medical attention is necessary.

Hannibal's Death

At the end of the Second Punic War, Hannibal went into voluntary exile to avoid capture (Chapter XI). He initially found sanctuary with Antiochus III of the Seleucid Empire. When the Romans reached an accord with Antiochus, Hannibal fled to Crete. He then found refuge with Prusias I ('the Lame') of Bithynia. When the Romans reached an accord with Prusias, Hannibal determined not to fall into Roman hands.

How he died is unclear. According to Pausanias, he may have died from a wound to a finger caused when unsheathing his sword while he was seated on his horse, which became infected and led to a fatal fever. Another version reported by Appian suggests he was poisoned by Prusias. Yet another version found in Livy's and Cornelius Nepos's accounts – and the one which Abbott relates – suggests Hannibal evaded capture by a Roman delegation sent to the court of Prusias by poisoning himself.

When he died is also disputed – even at the time Cornelius Nepos wrote his *Life of Hannibal* in the first century BCE. Nepos explained that: 'For Atticus has recorded in his *Annals* that [Hannibal] died in the consulate of Marcus Claudius Marcellus and Quintus Fabius Labeo [183 BCE]; Polybius, under Lucius Aemilius Paulus and Cnaeus Baebius Tamphilus [182 BCE]; and Sulpicius Blitho, in the time of Publius Cornelius Cethegus and Marcus Baebius Tamphilus [181 BCE]'. It is a reminder that there are many uncertainties and unknowns in ancient history.

Hannibal's grave at Libyssa in Bithynia (modern Gebze, Turkey) could still be visited in the time of Pliny the Elder (23–79 CE). Its location is now unknown. In 1981 a memorial dedicated to him was set up inside the circular Tübitak campus in Gebze. His head – based on the bust in the Quirinal Palace, Rome – was carved in high relief by sculptor Nejat Özatay on a large rock of pudding stone weighing 25 tons.

Hannibal's Legend

As Hannibal beat each Roman army sent against him, his fame grew. Ironically, it was the Romans themselves who were mainly responsible for propagating Hannibal's legend. Plutarch described the Carthaginian as 'Hannibal the African, a most inveterate enemy of Rome'. The Roman writer Cornelius Nepos wrote in his biography of Hannibal, 'If it be true, as no one doubts, that the Roman People have surpassed all other nations in valour, it must be admitted that Hannibal excelled all other commanders in skill as much as the Roman People are superior to all nations in bravery'. In *Stratagemata*, a book of military stratagems collated by Sextus Julius Frontinus (35–c. 103 CE), the Roman author records more clever ruses of Hannibal than of any other single commander.

In his *Epitome*, Julius Florus refers to Hannibal's military actions poetically as four 'storms' or 'thunderbolts' – an indication, perhaps, of how daring and threatening they were perceived to be by the Romans. He writes of how Hannibal's army 'burst its way through the midst of the Alps and swooped down upon Italy from those snows of fabulous heights like a missile hurled from the skies'. Florus shows that three centuries after he invaded Italy, the Romans were still curious about the Carthaginian commander. As long as Romans were able to write about their past, Hannibal was part of *their* foundation story: victory over him was seen as validation of Rome's destiny to rule the known world.

In later ages, the Carthaginian leader had admirers among military leaders. Napoleon Bonaparte was one. In 1788 he read a volume of ancient history written by Abbé Rollin and made notes about Hannibal from it. Louis Lemercier reported a conversation he had had with Napoleon in 1800 in which he recalled the First Consul saying Hannibal 'was the greatest captain in the world'. He chose Hannibal over others because 'even when abandoned and betrayed by Carthage, the city that he served, he always kept himself going in enemy land by his own resources, and he managed to create for himself fresh troops from the foreign peoples he met on his way'. Napoleon kept a portrait bust of Hannibal over his fireplace. It was paired with a bust of Scipio. The cast bronze image of Hannibal was not ancient but made in Naples in the seventeenth century; it is now in the collections of the Museum of Antiquities at the University of Saskatchewan, Canada.

In the twentieth century, US Army General George S. Patton Jr. (a.k.a. 'Blood and Guts') had enjoyed reading about ancient and modern military history since childhood. The story of Hannibal especially resonated with him. A believer in reincarnation, it is reported that Patton was convinced that he been Hannibal in a previous life. During the Persian Gulf War (1990–91), US Army General Stormin' Norman Schwarzkopf, who regarded Hannibal as a personal hero, hoped to repeat Cannae – 'his favorite battle' – and encircle and then annihilate the army of Saddam Hussein.

Military academies, from Sandhurst to West Point, still teach officers about Hannibal's stratagems and tactics for possible application to modern battle spaces. Students of history, too, continue to try to understand how a young man from North Africa became, for a while, Ancient Rome's most challenging adversary. As Abbott's book shows, two millennia on, Hannibal's legend endures and enthrals.

Lindsay Powell (Introduction, editor) is a historian and author. He writes about conflicts, commanders and campaigns of the Late Roman Republic and Early Roman Empire. He edited, and wrote the introduction for, the volume *Julius Caesar* in this series for Flame Tree Publishing. His critically acclaimed books include the biographies *Marcus Agrippa*, *Eager for Glory*, *Germanicus* and *Bar Kokhba*, as well as the military histories *Augustus at War*, *Roman Soldier versus Germanic Warrior, 1st Century AD* and *The Bar Kokhba War, AD 132–136*. He is news editor of *Ancient History* and *Ancient Warfare* magazines. His articles have also appeared in *Military History, Strategy and Tactics* and *Desperta Ferro* magazines. Lindsay is a regular guest on the *Ancient Warfare* and *History Hit* podcasts. He is a 10-year veteran of the Ermine Street Guard, the world's leading Roman army re-enactment society. He has a BSc (Hons) in managerial and administrative studies from Aston University, England. He divides his time between Austin, Texas and Wokingham, England.

Hannibal the Carthaginian

WHAT FOLLOWS is the text of *Hannibal* by Jacob Abbott published in 1901 (some editions were also entitled *Hannibal the Carthaginian*). It was one of 22 historical biographies he wrote over a busy career. Each is a complete account of the life and deeds of his famous subject, brim full of enthralling stories of growing up, and of an extraordinary career in adulthood, often establishing a legend that persists after death. Spanning the Ancient World to the Renaissance, his biographical studies included Alexander the Great, Cleopatra, Julius Caesar, Genghis Khan, Nero, Peter the Great and William the Conqueror.

Jacob Abbott was born on 14 November 1803 in Hallowell, Maine in the United States of America. Graduating from Bowdoin College in 1820, he went on to study at Andover Theological Seminary and then taught at Portland Academy. From 1825 he was a professor at Amhurst College, teaching mathematics and natural philosophy. Over the next 20 years he moved to other schools, becoming principal of the Mount Vernon School for Boys in New York City (1845–48).

A prolific author, Abbott wrote some 180 books and co-authored or edited 31 more. His *Rollo* books about a fictional boy, his associates and their escapades were his most popular works. Abbott's books of history and biography helped educate and inform generations of Americans. They provided his young readers with studies not just of history, but of people of character. Having related an episode in his subject's story, he often adds a moralizing comment as a life lesson to his reader, a practice from which modern biographers refrain.

Abbott's biography of Hannibal Barca is essentially sound. He sets Hannibal in his time, beginning with the military struggle between Carthage and Rome. He tells his subject's life story chronologically, drawing upon the ancient sources – primarily Livy – to share anecdotes and interesting details, which make Hannibal's life story human and compelling. While Abbott presents Hannibal as a great military hero, he concludes that the war the Carthaginian incited was reckless and unnecessary, its cost in blood and treasure an immense price to pay for what was, in the end, a failed endeavour.

Jacob Abbott died on 31 October 1879 in Farmington, Maine, aged 75. During his lifetime he had been a witness to profound changes in the world. As the British Empire reached its zenith, the fledgling United States went through its own growth pains, surviving the War of 1812, then suffering a wrenching Civil War (1861–65) and negotiating a fraught Reconstruction (1865–77) to address the inequities of slavery, while its people spread from the East Coast to the West in search of gold. The Union had developed into a wealthy industrial nation able to compete with the Europeans. Abbott's writings are part of the American story too.

Chapter I
The First Punic War, 280–249 BCE

Hannibal – Rome and Carthage

HANNIBAL WAS A CARTHAGINIAN GENERAL. He acquired his great distinction as a warrior by his desperate contests with the Romans. Rome and Carthage grew up together on opposite sides of the Mediterranean Sea. For about 100 years they waged against each other most dreadful wars. There were three of these wars. Rome was successful in the end, and Carthage was entirely destroyed.

There was no real cause for any disagreement between these two nations. Their hostility to each other was mere rivalry and spontaneous hate. They spoke a different language; they had a different origin; and they lived on opposite sides of the same sea. So they hated and devoured each other.

Tyre – Founding of Carthage – Its Commercial Spirit – New Carthage

Carthage was originally founded by a colony from this city of Tyre, and it soon became a great commercial and maritime power like its mother. The Carthaginians built ships, and with them explored all parts of the Mediterranean Sea. They visited all the nations on these coasts, purchased the commodities they had to sell, carried them to other nations and sold them at great advances. They soon began to grow rich and powerful. They hired soldiers to fight their battles and began to take possession of the islands of the Mediterranean, and, in some instances, of points on the mainland. For example, in Spain: some of their ships, going there, found that the natives had silver and gold, which they obtained from veins of ore near the surface of the ground.

At first the Carthaginians obtained this gold and silver by selling the natives commodities of various kinds, which they had procured in other countries; paying, of course, to the producers only a very small price compared with what they required the Spaniards to pay them. Finally, they took possession of that part of

Spain where the mines were situated and worked the mines themselves. They dug deeper; they employed skilful engineers to make pumps to raise the water, which always accumulates in mines, and prevents their being worked to any great depth unless the miners have a considerable degree of scientific and mechanical skill. They founded a city here, which they called New Carthage – *Nova Carthago*. They fortified and garrisoned this city, and made it the centre of their operations in Spain. This city is called Carthagena to this day.

Ships and Army – Numidia – Balearic Isles

Thus, the Carthaginians did everything by power of money. They extended their operations in every direction, each new extension bringing in new treasures, and increasing their means of extending them more. They had, besides the merchant vessels which belonged to private individuals, great ships of war belonging to the state. These vessels were called galleys, and were rowed by oarsmen, tier above tier, there being sometimes four and five banks of oars. They had armies, too, drawn from different countries, in various troops, according as different nations excelled in the different modes of warfare. For instance, the Numidians, whose country extended in the neighbourhood of Carthage on the African coast, were famous for their horsemen. There were great plains in Numidia, and good grazing, and it was, consequently, one of those countries in which horses and horsemen naturally thrive. On the other hand, the natives of the Balearic Isles, now called Majorca, Minorca and Ivica, were famous for their skill as slingers. So the Carthaginians, in making up their forces, would hire bodies of cavalry in Numidia, and of slingers in the Balearic Isles; and, for reasons analogous, they got excellent infantry in Spain.

The Sling

The tendency of the various nations to adopt and cultivate different modes of warfare was far greater, in those ancient times, than now. The Balearic Isles, in fact, received their name from the Greek word *ballein*, which means to throw with a sling. The youth there were trained to perfection in the use of this weapon from a very early age. It is said that mothers used to practice the plan of putting the bread for their boys' breakfast on the branches of trees, high above their heads, and not allow them to have their food to eat until they could bring it down with a stone thrown from a sling.

The Government of Carthage – The Aristocracy

Thus, the Carthaginian power became greatly extended. The whole government, however, was exercised by a small body of wealthy and aristocratic families at home. It depended on commercial greatness, combined with hereditary family distinction. The aristocracy of Carthage controlled and governed everything. None but its own sons could ordinarily obtain office or power. The great mass of inhabitants were kept in a state of servitude and vassalage. This state of things operated then very unjustly and hardly for those who were thus debased; but the result was that a very efficient and energetic government was created. The government of an oligarchy makes sometimes a very rich and powerful state, but a discontented and unhappy people.

Geographical Relations of the Carthaginian Empire

Imagine a great and rich city with piers, docks and extensive warehouses for the commerce, and temples and public edifices of splendid architecture for the religious and civil service of the state, and elegant mansions and palaces for the wealthy aristocracy, and walls and towers for the defence of the whole. Then imagine a back country, extending for some 100 miles into the interior of Africa, fertile and highly cultivated, producing great stores of corn, wine and rich fruits of every description. Imagine the islands of Sicily, of Corsica, Sardinia and the Baleares, and conceive of them as rich and prosperous countries, and all under the Carthaginian rule. See in the imagination, the city of Carthagena, with its fortifications, its army and the gold and silver mines, with thousands and thousands of slaves toiling in them. Imagine fleets of ships going continually along the shores of the Mediterranean, from country to country, cruising back and forth to Tyre, to Cyprus, to Egypt, to Sicily, to Spain, carrying corn, flax, purple dyes, spices, perfumes, precious stones, ropes and sails for ships and gold and silver, and then periodically returning to Carthage, to add the profits they had made to the vast treasures of wealth already accumulated there.

Rome and the Romans – Their Character

Rome itself was very differently situated. Rome had been built by some wanderers from Troy, and it grew, for a long time, silently and slowly, by a sort of internal principle of life and energy. One region after another of the Italian peninsula was merged in the Roman state. They formed a population which was, in the main, stationary and agricultural. They tilled the fields; they hunted the wild beasts; they raised great flocks and herds. They possessed a very refined and superior organization, which, in its development, gave rise to a character of firmness, energy and force, both of body and mind, which has justly excited the admiration of mankind. The Carthaginians had sagacity – the Romans called it cunning – and activity, enterprise and wealth. Their rivals, on the other hand, were characterized by genius, courage and strength, giving rise to a certain calm and indomitable resolution and energy, which has since, in every age, been strongly associated, in the minds of men, with the very word Roman.

Progress of Carthage and Rome

The progress of nations was much slower in ancient days than now, and these two rival empires continued their gradual growth and extension, each on its own side of the great sea which divided them, for *500 years*, before they came into collision. At last, however, the collision came. It originated in the following way:

Origin of the First Punic War

The island of Sicily is separated from the mainland by a narrow strait called the Strait of Messina. This strait derives its name from the town of Messina, which is situated upon it, on the Sicilian side. Opposite Messina, on the Italian side, there was a town named Rhegium. Now it happened that both these towns had been taken possession of by lawless bodies of soldiery. The Romans came and delivered Rhegium, and punished the soldiers who had seized it very severely. The Sicilian authorities advanced to the deliverance of Messina. The troops there, finding themselves thus threatened, sent to the Romans to say that if they, the Romans, would come and protect them, they would deliver Messina into their hands.

Rhegium and Messina – A Perplexing Question

The question, what answer to give to this application, was brought before the Roman senate, and caused them great perplexity. It seemed very inconsistent to take sides with the rebels of Messina when they had punished so severely those of Rhegium.

Still the Romans had been, for a long time, becoming very jealous of the growth and extension of the Carthaginian power. Here was an opportunity of meeting and resisting it. The Sicilian authorities were about calling for direct aid from Carthage to recover the city, and the affair would probably result in establishing a large body of Carthaginian troops within sight of the Italian shore, and at a point where it would be easy for them to make hostile incursions into the Roman territories. In a word, it was a case of what is called political necessity; that is to say, a case in which the *interests* of one of the parties in a contest were so strong that all considerations of justice, consistency and honour are to be sacrificed to the promotion of them. Instances of this kind of political necessity occur very frequently in the management of public affairs in all ages of the world.

The Romans Determine to Build a Fleet

The contest for Messina was, after all, however, considered by the Romans merely as a pretext, or rather as an occasion, for commencing the struggle which they had long been desirous of entering upon. They evinced their characteristic energy and greatness in the plan which they adopted at the outset. They knew very well that the power of Carthage rested mainly on her command of the seas, and that they could not hope successfully to cope with her till they could meet and conquer her on her own element. In the meantime, however, they had not a single ship and not a single sailor, while the Mediterranean was covered with Carthaginian ships and seamen. Not at all daunted by this prodigious inequality, the Romans resolved to begin at once the work of creating for themselves a naval power.

Preparations

The preparations consumed some time; for the Romans had not only to build the ships, they had first to learn how to build them. They took their first lesson from a Carthaginian galley which was cast away in a storm upon the coast of Italy. They seized this galley, collected their carpenters to examine it and set woodmen at work to fell trees and collect materials for imitating it. The carpenters studied their model very carefully, measured the dimensions of every part and observed the manner in which the various parts were connected and secured together. The heavy shocks which vessels are exposed to from the waves makes it necessary to secure great strength in the construction of them; it is surprising that the Romans could succeed at all in such a sudden and hasty attempt at building them.

Training the Oarsmen – The Roman Fleet Puts to Sea

They did, however, succeed. While the ships were building, officers appointed for the purpose were training men, on shore, to the art of rowing them. Benches, like the seats which the oarsman would occupy in the ships, were arranged on the ground, and the intended seamen were drilled every day in the movements and action of rowers. The result was that in a few months after the building of the ships was commenced, the Romans had a fleet of 100 galleys of five banks of oars ready. They remained in harbour with them for some time, to give the oarsmen the opportunity to see whether they could row on the water as well as on the land, and then boldly put to sea to meet the Carthaginians.

Grappling Irons – Courage and Resolution of the Romans

There was one part of the arrangements made by the Romans in preparing their fleets which was strikingly characteristic of the determined resolution which marked all their conduct. They constructed machines containing grappling irons, which they mounted on the prows of their vessels. These engines were so contrived, that the moment one of the ships containing them should encounter a vessel of the enemy, the grappling irons would fall upon the deck of the latter, and hold the two firmly together, so as to prevent the possibility of either escaping from the other. The idea that they themselves should have any wish to withdraw from the encounter seemed entirely out of the question. Their only fear was that the Carthaginian seamen would employ their superior skill and experience in naval manoeuvres in making their escape.

Mankind have always regarded the action of the Romans, in this case, as one of the most striking examples of military courage and resolution which the history of war has ever recorded. An army of landsmen come down to the seashore, and, without scarcely having ever seen a ship, undertake to build a fleet, and go out to attack a power whose navies covered the sea, and made her the sole and acknowledged mistress of it. They seize a wrecked galley of their enemies for their model; they build 100 vessels like it; they practice manoeuvres for a short time in port; and then go forth to meet the fleets of their powerful enemy, with grappling machines to hold them, fearing nothing but the possibility of their escape.

Success of the Romans – The Rostral Column

The result was as might have been expected. The Romans captured, sunk, destroyed, or dispersed the Carthaginian fleet which was brought to oppose them. They took the prows of the ships which they captured and conveyed them to Rome, and built what is called a *rostral pillar* of them. A rostral pillar is a column ornamented with such beaks or prows, which were, in the Roman language, called *rostra*. This column was nearly destroyed by lightning about 50 years afterward, but it was repaired and rebuilt again, and it stood then for many centuries, a very striking and appropriate monument of this extraordinary naval victory. The Roman commander in this case was the consul Duilius. The rostral column was erected in honour of him. In digging among the ruins of Rome, there was found what was supposed to be the remains of this column, about 300 years ago.

Government of Rome

The Romans now prepared to carry the war into Africa itself. Of course it was easy, after their victory over the Carthaginian fleet, to transport troops across the sea to the Carthaginian shore. The Roman commonwealth was governed at this time by a senate, who made the laws, and by two supreme executive officers, called consuls. They thought it was safer to have two chief magistrates than one, as each of the two would naturally be a check upon the other. The result was, however, that mutual jealousy involved them often in disputes and quarrels. It is thought better, in modern times, to have but one chief magistrate in the state, and to provide other modes to put a check upon any disposition he might evince to abuse his powers.

The Consuls

The Roman consuls, in time of war, took command of the armies. The name of the consul upon whom it devolved to carry on the war with the Carthaginians, after this first great victory, was Regulus, and his name has been celebrated in every age, on account of his extraordinary adventures in this campaign, and his untimely fate. How far the story is strictly true it is now impossible to ascertain, but the following is the story, as the Roman historians relate it:

Story of Regulus – He is Made Consul

At the time when Regulus was elected consul he was a plain man, living simply on his farm, maintaining himself by his own industry, and evincing no ambition or pride. His fellow citizens, however, observed those qualities of mind in him which they were accustomed to admire, and made him consul. He left the city and took command of the army. He enlarged the fleet to more than 300 vessels. He put 140,000 men on board and sailed for Africa. One or two years had been spent in making these preparations, which time the Carthaginians had improved in building new ships; so that, when the Romans set sail, and were moving along the coast of Sicily, they soon came in sight of a larger Carthaginian fleet assembled to oppose them. Regulus advanced to the contest. The Carthaginian fleet was beaten as before. The ships which were not captured or destroyed made their escape in all directions, and Regulus went on, without further opposition, and landed his forces on the Carthaginian shore. He encamped as soon as he landed, and sent back word to the Roman senate asking what was next to be done.

Regulus Marches Against Carthage

The senate, considering that the great difficulty and danger, viz., that of repulsing the Carthaginian fleet, was now past, ordered Regulus to send home nearly all the ships and a very large part of the army, and with the rest to commence his march toward Carthage. Regulus obeyed: he sent home the troops which had been ordered home, and with the rest began to advance upon the city.

His Difficulties

Just at this time, however, news came out to him that the farmer who had had the care of his land at home had died, and that his little farm, on which rested his sole reliance for the support of his family, was going to ruin. Regulus accordingly sent to the senate, asking them to place someone else in command of the army, and to allow him to resign his office, that he might go home and take care of his wife and children. The senate sent back orders that he should go on with his campaign, and promised to provide support for his family, and to see that someone was appointed to take care of his land. This story is thought to illustrate the extreme simplicity and plainness of all the habits of life among the Romans in those days. It certainly does so, if it is true. It is, however, very extraordinary, that a man who was entrusted by such a commonwealth, with the command of a fleet of 130 vessels, and an army of a 140,000 men, should have a family at home dependent for subsistence on the hired cultivation of seven acres of land. Still, such is the story.

Successes of Regulus – Arrival of Greeks – The Romans Put to Flight

Regulus advanced toward Carthage, conquering as he came. The Carthaginians were beaten in one field after another, and were reduced, in fact, to the last extremity, when an occurrence took place which turned the scale. This occurrence was the arrival of a large body of troops from Greece, with a Grecian general at their head. These were troops which the Carthaginians had hired to fight for them, as was the case with the rest of their army. But these were *Greeks*, and the Greeks were of the same race, and possessed the same qualities, as the Romans.

The newly arrived Grecian general evinced at once such military superiority, that the Carthaginians gave him the supreme command. He marshalled the army, accordingly, for battle. He had 100 elephants in the van. They were trained to rush forward and trample down the enemy. He had the Greek phalanx in the centre, which was a close, compact body of many thousand troops, bristling with long, iron-pointed spears, with which the men pressed forward, bearing everything before them. Regulus was, in a word, ready to meet Carthaginians, but he was not prepared to encounter Greeks. His army was put to flight, and he was taken prisoner. Nothing could exceed the excitement and exultation in the city when they saw Regulus and 500 other Roman soldiers, brought captive in. A few days before, they had been in consternation at the imminent danger of his coming in as a ruthless and vindictive conqueror.

Regulus a Prisoner

The Roman senate were not discouraged by this disaster. They fitted out new armies, and the war went on, Regulus being kept all the time at Carthage as a close prisoner. At last the Carthaginians authorized him to go to Rome as a sort of commissioner, to propose to the Romans to exchange prisoners and to make peace. They exacted from him a solemn promise that if he was unsuccessful he would return. The Romans had taken many of the Carthaginians prisoners in their naval combats, and held them captive at Rome. It is customary, in such cases, for the belligerent nations to make an exchange, and restore the captives on both sides to their friends and home. It was such an exchange of prisoners as this which Regulus was to propose.

Regulus Before the Roman Senate

When Regulus reached Rome, he refused to enter the city, but he appeared before the senate without the walls, in a very humble garb and with the most subdued and unassuming demeanour. He was no longer, he said, a Roman officer, or even citizen, but a Carthaginian prisoner, and he disavowed all right to direct, or even to counsel, the Roman authorities in respect to the proper course to be pursued. His opinion was, however, he said, that the Romans ought not to make peace or to exchange prisoners. He himself and the other Roman prisoners were old and infirm, and not worth the exchange; and, moreover, they had no claim whatever on their country, as they could only have been made prisoners in consequence of want of courage or patriotism to die in their country's cause. He said that the Carthaginians were tired of the war, and that their resources were exhausted, and that the Romans ought to press forward in it with renewed vigour, and leave himself and the other prisoners to their fate.

Result of His Mission – Death of Regulus

The senate came very slowly and reluctantly to the conclusion to follow this advice. They, however, all earnestly joined in attempting to persuade Regulus that he was under no obligation to return to Carthage. His promise, they said, was extorted by the circumstances of the case, and was not binding. Regulus, however, insisted on keeping his faith with his enemies. He sternly refused to see his family, and, bidding the senate farewell, he returned to Carthage. The Carthaginians, exasperated at his having himself interposed to prevent the success of his mission, tortured him for some time in the most cruel manner, and finally put him to death. One would think that he ought to have counselled peace and an exchange of prisoners, and he ought not to have refused to see his unhappy wife and children; but it was certainly very noble in him to refuse to break his word.

Conclusion of the War

The war continued for some time after this, until, at length, both nations became weary of the contest, and peace was made. The following is the treaty which was signed. It shows that the advantage, on the whole, in this First Punic War, was on the part of the Romans:

'There shall be peace between Rome and Carthage. The Carthaginians shall evacuate all Sicily. They shall not make war upon any allies of the Romans. They shall restore to the Romans, without ransom, all the prisoners which they have taken from them, and pay them within 10 years 3,200 talents of silver.'

The war had continued 24 years.

Chapter II
Hannibal at Saguntum, 234–218 BCE

Parentage of Hannibal

THE NAME OF HANNIBAL'S FATHER was Hamilcar. He was one of the leading Carthaginian generals. He occupied a very prominent position, both on account of his rank, wealth and high family connections at Carthage, and also on account of the great military energy which he displayed in the command of the armies abroad. He carried on the wars which the Carthaginians waged in Africa and in Spain after the conclusion of the war with the Romans, and he longed to commence hostilities with the Romans again.

Character of Hamilcar – Religious Ceremonies

At one time, when Hannibal was about nine years of age, Hamilcar was preparing to set off on an expedition into Spain, and, as was usual in those days, he was celebrating the occasion with games, spectacles and various religious ceremonies. It has been the custom in all ages of the world, when nations go to war with each other, for each side to take measures for propitiating the favour of Heaven. Christian nations at the present day do it by prayers offered in each country for the success of their own arms. Heathen nations do it by sacrifices, libations and offerings. Hamilcar had made arrangements for such sacrifices, and the priests were offering them in the presence of the whole assembled army.

Hannibal's Famous Oath of Enmity to Rome

Young Hannibal, then about nine years of age, was present. He was a boy of great spirit and energy, and he entered with much enthusiasm into the scene. He wanted to go to Spain himself with the army, and he came to his father and began to urge his request. His father could not consent to this. He was too young to endure the privations and fatigues of such an enterprise. However, his father brought him to one of the altars, in the presence of the other officers of the army, and made him lay his hand upon the consecrated victim, and swear that, as soon as he was old enough, and had it in his power, he would make war upon the Romans. This was done, no doubt, in part to amuse young Hannibal's mind, and to relieve his disappointment in not being able to go to war at that time, by promising him a great and mighty enemy to fight at some future day. Hannibal remembered it, and longed for the time to come when he could go to war against the *Romans*.

Hamilcar in Spain

Hamilcar bade his son farewell and embarked for Spain. He was at liberty to extend his conquests there in all directions west of the river Iberus, a river flowing southeast into the Mediterranean Sea. Its name, Iberus, has been gradually changed, in modern times, to Ebro. By the treaty with the Romans the Carthaginians were not to cross the Iberus. They were also bound by the treaty not to molest the people of Saguntum, a city lying between the Iberus and the Carthaginian dominions. Saguntum was in alliance with the Romans and under their protection.

Hasdrubal – Death of Hamilcar – Hannibal Sent for to Spain

Hamilcar was, however, very restless and uneasy at being obliged thus to refrain from hostilities with the Roman power. He began, immediately after his arrival in Spain, to form plans for renewing the war. He had under him, as his principal lieutenant, a young man who had married his daughter. His name was Hasdrubal. With Hasdrubal's aid, he went on extending his conquests in Spain, and strengthening his position there, and gradually maturing his plans for renewing war with the Romans, when at length he died. Hasdrubal succeeded him. Hannibal was now, probably, about 21 or 22 years old, and still in Carthage. Hasdrubal sent to the Carthaginian government a request that Hannibal might receive an appointment in the army, and be sent out to join him in Spain.

Opposition of Hanno

On the subject of complying with this request there was a great debate in the Carthaginian senate. In all cases where questions of government are controlled by *votes*, it has been found, in every age, that *parties* will always be formed, of which the two most prominent will usually be nearly balanced one against the other. Thus, at this time, though the Hamilcar family were in power, there was a very strong party in Carthage in opposition to them. The leader of this party in the senate, whose name was Hanno, made a very earnest speech against sending Hannibal. He was too young, he said, to be of any service. He would only learn the vices and follies of the camp, and thus become corrupted and ruined. 'Besides,' said Hanno, 'at this rate, the command of our armies in Spain is getting to be a sort of hereditary right. Hamilcar was not a king, that his authority should thus descend first to his son-in-law and then to his son; for this plan of making Hannibal,' he said, 'while yet scarcely arrived at manhood, a high officer in the army, is only a stepping-stone to the putting of the forces wholly under his orders, whenever, for any reason, Hasdrubal shall cease to command them.'

Hannibal Sets Out for Spain

The Roman historian, through whose narrative we get our only account of this debate, says that, though these were good reasons, yet strength prevailed, as usual, over wisdom, in the decision of the question. They voted to send Hannibal, and he set out to cross the sea to Spain with a heart full of enthusiasm and joy.

Favourable Impression on the Army – Character of Hannibal

A great deal of curiosity and interest was felt throughout the army to see him on his arrival. The soldiers had been devotedly attached to his father, and they were all ready to transfer this attachment at once to the son, if he should prove worthy of it. It was very evident, soon after he reached the camp, that he was going to prove himself thus worthy. He entered at once into the duties of his position with a degree of energy, patience and self-denial which attracted universal attention, and made him a universal favourite. He dressed plainly; he assumed no airs; he sought for no pleasures or indulgences, nor demanded any exemption from the dangers and privations which the common soldiers had to endure. He ate plain food, and slept, often in his military cloak, on the ground, in the midst of the soldiers on guard; and in battle he was always foremost to press forward into the contest, and the last to leave the ground when the time came for repose. The Romans say that, in addition to these qualities, he was inhuman and merciless when in open warfare with his foes, and cunning and treacherous in every other mode of dealing with them. It is very probable that he was so. Such traits of character were considered by soldiers in those days, as they are now, virtues in themselves, though vices in their enemies.

He is Elevated to the Supreme Command

However this may be, Hannibal became a great and universal favourite in the army. He went on for several years increasing his military knowledge, and widening and extending his influence, when at length, one day, Hasdrubal was suddenly killed by a ferocious native of the country whom he had by some means offended. As soon as the first shock of this occurrence was over, the leaders of the army went in pursuit of Hannibal, whom they brought in triumph to the tent of Hasdrubal, and instated him at once in the supreme command, with one consent and in the midst of universal acclamations. As soon as news of this event reached Carthage, the government there confirmed the act of the army, and Hannibal thus found himself suddenly but securely invested with a very high military command.

The River Iberus

His eager and restless desire to try his strength with the Romans received a new impulse by his finding that the power was now in his hands. Still the two countries were at peace. They were bound by solemn treaties to continue so. The river Iberus (Ebro) was the boundary which separated the dominions of the two nations from each other in Spain, the territory east of that boundary being under the Roman power, and that on the west under that of the Carthaginians; except that Saguntum, which was on the western side, was an ally of the Romans, and the Carthaginians were bound by the treaty to leave it independent and free.

Hannibal Seeks a War with the Romans

Hannibal could not, therefore, cross the Iberus or attack Saguntum without an open infraction of the treaty. He, however, immediately began to move toward Saguntum and to attack the nations in the immediate vicinity of it. If he wished to get into a war with the Romans, this was the proper way to promote it; for, by advancing thus into the immediate vicinity of the capital of their allies, there was great probability that disputes would arise which would sooner or later end in war.

Stratagem of Hannibal – Great Battle in the River Tagus – Victory of Hannibal

The Romans say that Hannibal was cunning and treacherous, and he certainly did display, on some occasions, a great degree of adroitness in his stratagems. In one instance in these preliminary wars, he gained a victory over an immensely superior force in a very remarkable manner.

He was returning from an inroad upon some of the northern provinces, laden and encumbered with spoil, when he learned that an immense army, consisting, it was said, of 100,000 men, were coming down upon his rear. There was a river at a short distance before him. Hannibal pressed on and crossed the river by a ford, the water being, perhaps, about three feet deep. He secreted a large body of cavalry near the bank of the stream and pushed on with the main body of the army to some little distance from the river, so as to produce the impression upon his pursuers that he was pressing forward to make his escape. The enemy, thinking that they had no time to lose, poured down in great numbers into the stream from various points along the banks; and, as soon as they had reached the middle of the current, and were wading laboriously, half submerged, with their weapons held above their heads, so as to present as little resistance as possible to the water, the horsemen of Hannibal rushed in to meet and attack them. The horsemen had, of course, greatly the advantage; for, though their horses were in the water, they were themselves raised above it, and their limbs were free, while their enemies were half submerged, and, being encumbered by their arms and by one another, were nearly helpless. They were immediately thrown into complete confusion and were overwhelmed and carried down by the current in great numbers. Some of them succeeded in landing below, on Hannibal's side; but, in the meantime, the main body of his army had returned, and was ready to receive them, and they were trampled underfoot by the elephants, which it was the custom to employ, in those days, as a military force.

As soon as the river was cleared, Hannibal marched his own army across it, and attacked what remained of the enemy on their own side. He gained a complete victory, which was so great and decisive that he secured by it possession of the whole country west of the Iberus, except Saguntum, and Saguntum itself began to be seriously alarmed.

Saguntum

The Saguntines sent ambassadors to Rome to ask the Romans to interpose and protect them from the dangers which threatened them. These ambassadors made diligent efforts to reach Rome as soon as possible, but they were too late. On some pretext or other, Hannibal contrived to raise a dispute between the city and one of the neighbouring tribes, and then, taking sides with the tribe, he advanced to attack the city. The Saguntines prepared for their defence, hoping soon to receive succours from Rome. They strengthened and fortified their walls, while Hannibal began to move forward great military engines for battering them down.

Hannibal Attacks It

Hannibal knew very well that by his hostilities against this city he was commencing a contest with Rome itself, as Rome must necessarily take part with her ally. In fact, there is no doubt that his design was to bring on a general war between the two great nations. He began with Saguntum for two reasons: first, it would not be safe for him to cross the Iberus, and advance into the Roman territory, leaving so wealthy and powerful a city in his rear; and then, in the second place, it was easier for him to find pretexts for getting indirectly into a quarrel with Saguntum, and throwing the odium of a declaration of war on Rome, than to persuade the Carthaginian state to renounce the peace and themselves commence hostilities. There was, as has been already stated, a very strong party at Carthage opposed to Hannibal, who would, of course, resist any measures tending to a war with Rome, for they would consider such a war as opening a vast field for gratifying Hannibal's ambition. The only way, therefore, was to provoke a war by aggressions on the Roman allies, to be justified by the best pretexts he could find.

Progress of the Siege – Hannibal Wounded – Hannibal Recovers

Saguntum was a very wealthy and powerful city. It was situated about a mile from the sea. The attack upon the place, and the defence of it by the inhabitants, went on for some time with great vigour. In these operations, Hannibal exposed himself to great danger. He approached, at one time, so near the wall, in superintending the arrangements of his soldiers and the planting of his engines, that a heavy javelin, thrown from the parapet, struck him on the thigh. It pierced the flesh and inflicted so severe a wound that he fell immediately, and was borne away by the soldiers. It was several days before he was free from the danger incurred by the loss of blood and the fever which follows such a wound. During all this time his army were in a great state of excitement and anxiety and suspended their active operations. As soon, however, as Hannibal was found to be decidedly convalescent, they resumed them again, and urged them onward with greater energy than before.

The Falarica

The weapons of warfare in those ancient days were entirely different from those which are now employed, and there was one, described by an ancient historian as used by the Saguntines at this siege, which might almost come under the modern denomination of firearms. It was called the *falarica*. It was a sort of javelin, consisting of a shaft of wood, with a long point of iron. This point was said to be three feet long. This javelin was to be thrown at the enemy either from the hand of the soldier or by an engine. The leading peculiarity of it was, however, that, near to the pointed end, there were wound around the wooden shaft long bands of *tow*, which were saturated with pitch and other combustibles, and this inflammable band was set on fire just before the javelin was thrown. As the missile flew on its way, the wind fanned the flames, and made them burn so fiercely, that when the javelin struck the shield of the soldier opposing it, it could not be pulled out, and the shield itself had to be thrown down and abandoned.

Arrival of the Roman Ambassadors

While the inhabitants of Saguntum were vainly endeavouring to defend themselves against their terrible enemy by these and similar means, their ambassadors, not knowing that the city had been attacked, had reached Rome, and had laid before the Roman senate their fears that the city would be attacked, unless they adopted vigorous and immediate measures to prevent it. The Romans resolved to send ambassadors to Hannibal to demand of him what his intentions were, and to warn him against any acts of hostility against Saguntum. When these Roman ambassadors arrived on the coast, near to Saguntum, they found that hostilities had commenced, and that the city was hotly besieged. They were at a loss to know what to do.

Hannibal's Policy

It is better for a rebel not to hear an order which he is determined beforehand not to obey. Hannibal, with an adroitness which the Carthaginians called sagacity, and the Romans treachery and cunning, determined not to see these messengers. He sent word to them, at the shore, that they must not attempt to come to his camp, for the country was in such a disturbed condition that it would not be safe for them to land; and besides, he could not receive or attend to them, for he was too much pressed with the urgency of his military works to have any time to spare for debates and negotiations.

Hannibal Sends Ambassadors to Carthage

Hannibal knew that the ambassadors, being thus repulsed, and having found, too, that the war had broken out, and that Saguntum was actually beset and besieged by Hannibal's armies, would proceed immediately to Carthage to demand satisfaction there. He knew, also, that Hanno and his party would very probably espouse the cause of the Romans, and endeavour to arrest his designs. He accordingly sent his own ambassadors to Carthage, to exert an influence in his favour in the Carthaginian senate, and endeavour to urge them to reject the claims of the Romans, and allow the war between Rome and Carthage to break out again.

The Roman Ambassadors

The Roman ambassadors appeared at Carthage and were admitted to an audience before the senate. They stated their case, representing that Hannibal had made war upon Saguntum in violation of the treaty, and had refused even to receive the communication which had been sent him by the Roman senate through them. They demanded that the Carthaginian government should disavow his acts, and deliver him up to them, in order that he might receive the punishment which his violation of the treaty, and his aggressions upon an ally of the Romans, so justly deserved.

Parties in the Carthaginian Senate – Hanno Proposes to Give Up Hannibal

The party of Hannibal in the Carthaginian senate were, of course, earnest to have these proposals rejected with scorn. The other side, with Hanno at their head, maintained that they were reasonable demands. Hanno, in a very energetic and powerful speech, told the senate that he had warned them not to send Hannibal into Spain. He had foreseen that such a hot and turbulent spirit as his would involve them in inextricable difficulties with the Roman power. Hannibal had, he said, plainly violated the treaty. He had invested and besieged Saguntum, which they were solemnly bound not to molest, and they had nothing to expect in return but that the Roman legions would soon be investing and besieging their own city. In the meantime, the Romans, he added, had been moderate and forbearing. They had brought nothing to the charge of the Carthaginians. They accused nobody but Hannibal, who, thus far, alone was guilty. The Carthaginians, by disavowing his acts, could save themselves from the responsibility of them. He urged, therefore, that an embassage of apology should be sent to Rome, that Hannibal should be deposed and delivered up to the Romans, and that ample restitution should be made to the Saguntines for the injuries they had received.

Defence of Hannibal's Friends

On the other hand, the friends of Hannibal urged in the Carthaginian senate their defence of the general. They reviewed the history of the transactions in which the war had originated, and showed, or attempted to show, that the Saguntines themselves commenced hostilities, and that consequently they, and not Hannibal, were responsible for all that followed; that, under those circumstances, the Romans ought not to take their part, and if they did so, it proved that they preferred the friendship of Saguntum to that of Carthage; and that it would be cowardly and dishonourable in the extreme for them to deliver the general whom they had placed in power, and who had shown himself so worthy of their choice by his courage and energy, into the hands of their ancient and implacable foes.

Hannibal Triumphant – Saguntum Falls

Thus Hannibal was waging at the same time two wars, one in the Carthaginian senate, where the weapons were arguments and eloquence, and the other under the walls of Saguntum, which was fought with battering rams and fiery javelins. He conquered in both.

The senate decided to send the Roman ambassadors home without acceding to their demands, and the walls of Saguntum were battered down by Hannibal's engines. The inhabitants refused all terms of compromise, and resisted to the last, so that, when the victorious soldiery broke over the prostrate walls, and poured into the city, it was given up to them to plunder, and they killed and destroyed all that came in their way. The disappointed ambassadors returned to Rome with the news that Saguntum had been taken and destroyed by Hannibal, and that the Carthaginians, far from offering any satisfaction for the wrong, assumed the responsibility of it themselves, and were preparing for war.

Thus Hannibal accomplished his purpose of opening the way for waging war against the Roman power. He prepared to enter into the contest with the utmost energy and zeal. The conflict that ensued lasted 17 years, and is known in history as the Second Punic War. It was one of the most dreadful struggles between rival and hostile nations which the gloomy history of mankind exhibits to view. The events that occurred will be described in the subsequent chapters.

Chapter III
Opening of the Second Punic War, 217 BCE

Fall of Hanno's Party

WHEN THE TIDE once turns in any nation in favour of war, it generally rushes on with great impetuosity and force, and bears all before it. It was so in Carthage in this instance. The party of Hanno were thrown entirely into the minority and silenced, and the friends and partisans of Hannibal carried not only the government, but the whole community with them, and everybody was eager for war. This was owing, in part, to the natural contagiousness of the martial spirit, which, when felt by one, catches easily, by sympathy, in the heart of another. It is a fire which, when once it begins to burn, spreads in every direction, and consumes all that comes in its way.

Power of Hannibal – Desperate Valour of the Saguntines

Besides, when Hannibal gained possession of Saguntum, he found immense treasures there, which he employed, not to increase his own private fortune, but to strengthen and confirm his civil and military power. The Saguntines did everything they could to prevent these treasures from falling into his hands. They fought desperately to the last, refused all terms of surrender, and they became so insanely desperate in the end, that, according to the narrative of Livy, when they found that the walls and towers of the city were falling in, and that all hope of further defence was gone, they built an enormous fire in the public streets, and heaped upon it all the treasures which they had time to collect that fire could destroy, and then that many of the principal inhabitants leaped into the flames themselves, in order that their hated conquerors might lose their prisoners as well as their spoils.

Hannibal's Disposition of the Spoils – Hannibal Chosen One of the Suffetes

Notwithstanding this, however, Hannibal obtained a vast amount of gold and silver, both in the form of money and of plate, and also much valuable merchandise, which the Saguntine merchants had accumulated in their palaces and warehouses. He used all this property to strengthen his own political and military position. He paid his soldiers all the arrears due to them in full. He divided among them a large additional amount as their share of the spoil. He sent rich trophies home to Carthage, and presents, consisting of sums of money, jewellery and gems, to his friends there, and to those whom he wished to make his friends. The result of this munificence, and of the renown which his victories in Spain had procured for him, was to raise him to the highest pinnacle of influence and honour. The Carthaginians chose him one of the *suffetes*.

Nature of the Office

The suffetes were the supreme executive officers of the Carthaginian commonwealth. The government was, as has been remarked before, a sort of aristocratic republic, and republics are always very cautious about entrusting power, even executive power, to any one man. As Rome had *two* consuls, reigning jointly, so the Carthaginians chose annually two *suffetes*, as they were called at Carthage, though the Roman writers call them indiscriminately suffetes, consuls and kings. Hannibal was now advanced to this dignity; so that, in conjunction with his colleague, he held the supreme civil authority at Carthage, besides being invested with the command of the vast and victorious army in Spain.

Great Excitement at Rome – Fearful Anticipations

When news of these events – the siege and destruction of Saguntum, the rejection of the demands of the Roman ambassadors, and the vigorous preparations making by the Carthaginians for war – reached Rome, the whole city was thrown into consternation. The senate and the people held tumultuous and disorderly assemblies, in which the events which had occurred, and the course of proceeding which it was incumbent on the Romans to take, were discussed with much excitement and clamour. The Romans were, in fact, afraid of the Carthaginians. The campaigns of Hannibal in Spain had impressed the people with a strong sense of the remorseless and terrible energy of his character; they at once concluded that his plans would be formed for marching into Italy, and they even anticipated the danger of his bringing the war up to the very gates of the city, so as to threaten *them* with the destruction which he had brought upon Saguntum. The event showed how justly they appreciated his character.

Since the conclusion of the First Punic War, there had been peace between the Romans and Carthaginians for about a quarter of a century. During all this time both nations had been advancing in wealth and power, but the Carthaginians had made much more rapid progress than the Romans. The Romans had, indeed, been very successful at the onset in the former war, but in the end the Carthaginians had proved themselves their equal. They seemed, therefore, to dread now a fresh encounter with these powerful foes, led on, as they were now to be, by such a commander as Hannibal.

New Embassy to Carthage – Warm Debates – Fruitless Negotiations

They determined, therefore, to send a second embassy to Carthage, with a view of making one more effort to preserve peace before actually commencing hostilities. They accordingly elected five men from among the most influential citizens of the state – men of venerable age and of great public consideration – and commissioned them to proceed to Carthage and ask once more whether it was the deliberate and final decision of the Carthaginian senate to avow and sustain the action of Hannibal. This solemn embassage set sail.

They arrived at Carthage. They appeared before the senate. They argued their cause, but it was, of course, to deaf and unwilling ears. The Carthaginian orators replied to them, each side attempting to throw the blame of the violation of the treaty on the other. It was a solemn hour, for the peace of the world, the lives of hundreds of thousands of men, and the continued happiness or the desolation and ruin of vast regions of country, depended on the issue of the debate. Unhappily, the breach was only widened by the discussion. 'Very well,' said the Roman commissioners, at last, 'we offer you peace or war, which do you choose?' 'Whichever you please,' replied the Carthaginians; 'decide for yourselves.' 'War, then,' said the Romans, 'since it must be so.' The conference was broken up, and the ambassadors returned to Rome.

The Ambassadors Return – Reply of the Volscians

They returned, however, by the way of Spain. Their object in doing this was to negotiate with the various kingdoms and tribes in Spain and in France, through which Hannibal would have to march in invading Italy, and endeavour to induce them to take sides with the Romans. They were too late, however, for Hannibal had contrived to extend and establish his influence in all that region too strongly to be shaken; so that, on one pretext or another, the Roman proposals were all rejected.

There was one powerful tribe, for example, called the Volscians. The ambassadors, in the presence of the great council of the Volscians, made known to them the probability of war, and invited them to ally themselves with the Romans. The Volscians rejected the proposition with a sort of scorn. 'We see,' said they, 'from the fate of Saguntum, what is to be expected to result from an alliance with the Romans. After leaving that city defenceless and alone in its struggle against such terrible danger, it is in vain to ask other nations to trust to your protection. If you wish for new allies, it will be best for you to go where the story of Saguntum is not known.' This answer of the Volscians was applauded by the other nations of Spain, as far as it was known, and the Roman ambassadors, despairing of success in that country, went on into Gaul, which is the name by which the country now called France is known in ancient history.

Council of Gauls

On reaching a certain place which was a central point of influence and power in Gaul, the Roman commissioners convened a great martial council there. The spectacle presented by this assembly was very imposing, for the warlike counsellors came to the meeting armed completely and in the most formidable manner, as if they were coming to a battle instead of a consultation and debate. The venerable ambassadors laid the subject before them. They descanted largely on the power and greatness of the Romans, and on the certainty that they should conquer in the approaching contest, and they invited the Gauls to espouse their cause, and to rise in arms and intercept Hannibal's passage through their country, if he should attempt to effect one.

Tumultuous Scene - Repulse of the Ambassadors

The assembly could hardly be induced to hear the ambassadors through; and, as soon as they had finished their address, the whole council broke forth into cries of dissent and displeasure, and even into shouts of derision. Order was at length restored, and the officers, whose duty it was to express the sentiments of the assembly, gave for their reply that the Gauls had never received anything but violence and injuries from Rome, or anything but kindness and goodwill from Carthage; and that they had no idea of being guilty of the folly of bringing the impending storm of Hannibal's hostility upon their own heads, merely for the sake of averting it from their ancient and implacable foes. Thus, the ambassadors were everywhere repulsed. They found no friendly disposition toward the Roman power till they had crossed the Rhône.

Hannibal's Kindness to His Soldiers

Hannibal began now to form his plans, in a very deliberate and cautious manner, for a march into Italy. He knew well that this was an expedition of such magnitude and duration as to require beforehand the most careful and well-considered arrangements, both for the forces which were to go, and for the states and communities which were to remain. The winter was coming on. His first measure was to dismiss a large portion of his forces, that they might visit their homes. He told them that he was intending some great designs for the ensuing spring, which might take them to a great distance, and keep them for a long time absent from Spain, and he would, accordingly, give them the intervening time to visit their families and their homes, and to arrange their affairs. This act of kind consideration and confidence renewed the attachment of the soldiers to their commander, and they returned to his camp in the spring not only with new strength and vigour, but with redoubled attachment to the service in which they were engaged.

He Matures His Designs

Hannibal, after sending home his soldiers, retired himself to New Carthage, is further west than Saguntum, where he went into winter quarters, and devoted himself to the maturing of his designs. Besides the necessary preparations for his own march, he had to provide for the government of the countries that he should leave. He devised various and ingenious plans to prevent the danger of insurrections and rebellions while he was gone. One was, to organize an army for Spain out of soldiers drawn from *Africa*, while the troops which were to be employed to garrison Carthage, and to sustain the government there, were taken from Spain. By thus changing the troops of the two countries, each country was controlled by a foreign soldiery, who were more likely to be faithful in their obedience to their commanders, and less in danger of sympathizing with the populations which they were respectively employed to control, than if each had been retained in its own native land.

Hannibal's Plan for the Government of Spain in His Absence

Hannibal knew very well that the various states and provinces of Spain, which had refused to ally themselves with the Romans and abandon him, had been led to do this through the influence of his presents or the fear of his power, and that if, after he had penetrated into Italy, he should meet with reverses, so as to diminish very much their hope of deriving benefit from his favour or their fear of his power, there would be great danger of defections and revolts. As an additional security against this, he adopted the following ingenious plan. He enlisted a body of troops from among all the nations of Spain that were in alliance with him, selecting the young men who were enlisted as much as possible from families of consideration and influence, and this body of troops, when organized and officered, he sent into Carthage, giving the nations and tribes from which they were drawn to understand that he considered them not only as soldiers serving in his armies, but as *hostages*, which he should hold as security for the fidelity and obedience of the countries from which they had come. The number of these soldiers was 4,000.

Hannibal's Brother Hasdrubal – He is Left in Charge of Spain

Hannibal had a brother, whose name, as it happened, was the same as that of his brother-in-law, Hasdrubal. It was to him that he committed the government of Spain during his absence. The soldiers provided for him were, as has been already stated, mainly drawn from Africa. In addition to the foot soldiers, he provided him with a small body of horse. He left with him, also, 14 elephants. And as he thought it not improbable that the Romans might, in some contingency during his absence, make a descent upon the Spanish coast from the sea, he built and equipped for him a small fleet of about 60 vessels, 50 of which were of the first class. In modern times, the magnitude and efficiency of a ship is estimated by the number of guns she will carry; then, it was the number of banks of oars. Fifty of Hasdrubal's ships were *quinqueremes*, as they were called, that is, they had five banks of oars.

Preparations of the Romans – Their Plan for the War

The Romans, on the other hand, did not neglect their own preparations. Though reluctant to enter upon the war, they still prepared to engage in it with their characteristic energy and ardour, when they found that it could not be averted. They resolved on raising two powerful armies, one for each of the consuls. The plan was, with one of these to advance to meet Hannibal, and with the other to proceed to Sicily, and from Sicily to the African coast, with a view of threatening the Carthaginian capital. This plan, if successful, would compel the Carthaginians to recall a part or the whole of Hannibal's army from the intended invasion of Italy to defend their own African homes.

The Roman Fleet

The force raised by the Romans amounted to about 70,000 men. About a third of these were Roman soldiers, and the remainder were drawn from various nations dwelling in Italy and in the islands of the Mediterranean Sea which were in alliance with the Romans. Of these troops 6,000 were cavalry. Of course, as the Romans intended to cross into Africa, they needed a fleet. They built and equipped one, which consisted of 220 ships of the largest class, that is, quinqueremes, besides a number of smaller and lighter vessels for services requiring speed. There were vessels in use in those times larger than the quinqueremes. Mention is occasionally made of those which had six and even seven banks of oars. But these were only employed as the flagships of commanders, and for other purposes of ceremony and parade, as they were too unwieldy for efficient service in action.

Drawing Lots – Religious Ceremonies

Lots were then drawn in a very solemn manner, according to the Roman custom on such occasions, to decide on the assignment of these two armies to the respective consuls. The one destined to meet Hannibal on his way from Spain, fell to a consul named Cornelius Scipio. The name of the other was Sempronius. It devolved on him, consequently, to take charge of the expedition destined to Sicily and Africa. When all the arrangements were thus made, the question was finally put, in a very solemn and formal manner, to the Roman people for their final vote and decision. 'Do the Roman people decide and decree that war shall be declared against the Carthaginians?' The decision was in the affirmative. The war was then proclaimed with the usual imposing ceremonies. Sacrifices and religious celebrations followed, to propitiate the favour of the gods, and to inspire the soldiers with that kind of courage and confidence which the superstitious, however wicked, feel when they can imagine themselves under the protection of heaven. These shows and spectacles being over, all things were ready.

Hannibal's March

In the meantime, Hannibal was moving on, as the spring advanced, toward the banks of the Iberus, that frontier stream, the crossing of which made him an invader of what was, in some sense, Roman territory. He boldly passed the stream, and moved forward along the coast of the Mediterranean, gradually approaching the Pyrenees, which form the boundary between France and Spain. His soldiers hitherto did not know what his plans were. It is very little the custom *now* for military and naval commanders to communicate to their men much information about their designs, and it was still less the custom then; and besides, in those days, the common soldiers had no access to those means of information by which news of every sort is now so universally diffused. Thus, though all the officers of the army, and well-informed citizens, both in Rome and Carthage, anticipated and understood Hannibal's designs, his own soldiers, ignorant and degraded, knew nothing except that they were to go on some distant and dangerous service. They, very likely, had no idea whatever of Italy or of Rome, or of the magnitude of the possessions, or of the power held by the vast empire which they were going to invade.

The Pyrenees – Discontent in Hannibal's Army – Hannibal's Address

When, however, after traveling day after day they came to the foot of the Pyrenees and found that they were really going to pass that mighty chain of mountains, and for this purpose were actually entering its wild and gloomy defiles, the courage of some of them failed, and they began to murmur. The discontent and alarm were, in fact, so great, that one corps, consisting of about 3,000 men, left the camp in a body, and moved back toward their homes. On inquiry, Hannibal found that there were 10,000 more who were in a similar state of feeling. His whole force consisted of over 100,000. And now what does the reader imagine that Hannibal would do in such an emergency? Would he return in pursuit of these deserters, to recapture and destroy them as a terror to the rest? or would he let them go, and attempt by words of conciliation and encouragement to confirm and save those that yet remained? He did neither.

He called together the 10,000 discontented troops that were still in his camp, and told them that, since they were afraid to accompany his army, or unwilling to do so, they might return. He wanted none in his service who had not the courage and the fortitude to go on wherever he might lead. He would not have the faint-hearted and the timid in his army. They would only be a burden to load down and impede the courage and energy of the rest. So saying, he gave orders for them to return, and with the rest of the army, whose resolution and ardour were redoubled by this occurrence, he moved on through the passes of the mountains.

Hannibal's Sagacity

This act of Hannibal, in permitting his discontented soldiers to return, had all the effect of a deed of generosity in its influence upon the minds of the soldiers who went on. We must not, however, imagine that it was prompted by a spirit of generosity at all. It was policy. A seeming generosity was, in this case, exactly what was wanted to answer his ends. Hannibal was mercilessly cruel in all cases where he imagined that severity was demanded. It requires great sagacity sometimes in a commander to know when he must punish, and when it is wisest to overlook and forgive. Hannibal, possessed this sagacity in a very high degree; and it was, doubtless, the exercise of that principle alone which prompted his action on this occasion.

The Pyrenees Passed

Thus Hannibal passed the Pyrenees. The next difficulty that he anticipated was in crossing the River Rhône.

Chapter IV
The Passage of the Rhône, 217 BCE

Difficulties Anticipated – Reconnoitring Party

HANNIBAL, AFTER HE had passed the Pyrenees, did not anticipate any new difficulty until he should arrive at the Rhône. He knew very well that that was a broad and rapid river, and that he must cross it near its mouth, where the water was deep and the banks low; and, besides, it was not impossible that the Romans who were coming to meet him, under Cornelius Scipio, might have reached the Rhône before he should arrive there, and be ready upon the banks to dispute his passage. He had sent forward, therefore, a small detachment in advance, to reconnoitre the country and select a route to the Rhône, and if they met with no difficulties to arrest them there, they were to go on till they reached the Alps, and explore the passages and defiles through which his army could best cross those snow-covered mountains.

Some Tribes Reduced – Alarm of the Gauls

It seems that before he reached the Pyrenees – that is, while he was upon the Spanish side of them – some of the tribes through whose territories he had to pass undertook to resist him, and he, consequently, had to attack them and reduce them by force; and then, when he was ready to move on, he left a guard in the territories thus conquered to keep them in subjection. Rumours of this reached Gaul. The Gauls were alarmed for their own safety. They had not intended to oppose Hannibal so long as they supposed that he only wished for a safe passage through their country on his way to Italy; but now, when they found, from what had occurred in Spain, that he was going to conquer the countries he traversed as he passed along, they became alarmed. They seized their arms, and assembled in haste at Ruscino, and began to devise measures of defence. Ruscino was the same place as that in which the Roman ambassadors met the great council of the Gauls on their return to Italy from Carthage.

The Alps – Difficulty of Their Passage

While this great council, or, rather, assembly of armies, was gathering at Ruscino, full of threats and anger, Hannibal was at Illiberis, a town at the foot of the Pyrenean Mountains. He seems to have had no fear that any opposition which the Gauls could bring to bear against him would be successful, but he dreaded the delay. He was extremely unwilling to spend the precious months of the early summer in contending with such foes as they, when the road to Italy was before him. Besides, the passes of the Alps, which are difficult and laborious at any time, are utterly impracticable except in the months of July and August. At all other seasons they are, or were in those days, blocked up with impassable snows. In modern times roads have been made, with galleries cut through the rock, and with the exposed places protected by sloping roofs projecting from above, over which storms sweep and avalanches slide without injury; so that now the intercourse of ordinary travel between France and Italy, across the Alps, is kept up, in some measure, all the year. In Hannibal's time, however, the mountains could not be traversed except in the summer months, and if it had not been that the result justified the undertaking, it would have been considered an act of inexcusable rashness and folly to attempt to cross with an army at all.

Hannibal's Message to the Gauls

Hannibal had therefore no time to lose, and that circumstance made this case one of those in which forbearance and a show of generosity were called for, instead of defiance and force. He accordingly sent messengers to the council at Ruscino to say, in a very complaisant and affable manner, that he wished to see and confer with their princes in person, and that, if they pleased, he would advance for this purpose toward Ruscino; or they might, if they preferred, come on toward him at Illiberis, where he would await their arrival. He invited them to come freely into his camp, and said that he was ready, if they were willing to receive him, to go into theirs, for he had come to Gaul as a friend and an ally, and wanted nothing but a free passage through their territory. He had made a resolution, he said, if the Gauls would but allow him to keep it, that there should not be a single sword drawn in his army until he got into Italy.

Success of His Policy

The alarm and the feelings of hostility which prevailed among the Gauls were greatly allayed by this message. They put their camp in motion and went on to Illiberis. The princes and high officers of their armies went to Hannibal's camp and were received with the highest marks of distinction and honour. They were loaded with presents, and went away charmed with the affability, the wealth and the generosity of their visitor. Instead of opposing his progress, they became the conductors and guides of his army. They took them first to Ruscino, which was, as it were, their capital, and thence, after a short delay, the army moved on without any further molestation toward the Rhône.

Cornelius Scipio – He Embarks His Army – Both Armies on the Rhône

In the meantime, the Roman consul Scipio, having embarked the troops destined to meet Hannibal in 60 ships at the mouth of the Tiber, set sail for the mouth of the Rhône. The men were crowded together in the ships, as armies necessarily must be when transported by sea. They could not go far out to sea, for, as they had no compass in those days, there were no means of directing the course of navigation, in case of storms or cloudy skies, except by the land. The ships accordingly made their way slowly along the shore, sometimes by means of sails and sometimes by oars, and, after suffering for some time the hardships and privations incident to such a voyage – the seasickness and the confinement of such swarming numbers in so narrow a space bringing every species of discomfort in their train – the fleet entered the mouth of the Rhône.

The officers had no idea that Hannibal was near. They had only heard of his having crossed the Iberus. They imagined that he was still on the other side of the Pyrenees. They entered the Rhône by the first branch they came to – for the Rhône, like the Nile, divides near its mouth, and flows into the sea by several separate channels – and sailed without concern up to Marseilles, imagining that their enemy was still hundreds of miles away, entangled, perhaps, among the defiles of the Pyrenees. Instead of that, he was safely encamped upon the banks of the Rhône, a short distance above them, quietly and coolly making his arrangements for crossing it.

Exploring Party

When Cornelius got his men upon the land, they were too much exhausted by the sickness and misery they had endured upon the voyage to move on to meet Hannibal without some days for rest and refreshment. Cornelius, however, selected 300 horsemen who were able to move, and sent them up the river on an exploring expedition, to learn the facts in respect to Hannibal, and to report them to him. Dispatching them accordingly, he remained himself in his camp, reorganizing and recruiting his army, and awaiting the return of the party that he had sent to explore.

Feelings of the Gauls in Respect to Hannibal

Although Hannibal had thus far met with no serious opposition in his progress through Gaul it must not, on that account, be supposed that the people, through whose territories he was passing, were really friendly to his cause, or pleased with his presence among them. An army is always a burden and a curse to any country that it enters, even when its only object is to pass peacefully through. The Gauls assumed a friendly attitude toward this dreaded invader and his horde only because they thought that by so doing he would the sooner pass and be gone. They were too weak, and had too few means of resistance to attempt to stop him; and, as the next best thing that they could do, resolved to render him every possible aid to hasten him on. This continued to be the policy of the various tribes until he reached the river. The people on the *further* side of the river, however, thought it was best for them to resist. They were nearer to the Roman territories, and, consequently, somewhat more under Roman influence. They feared the resentment of the Romans if they should, even passively, render any co-operation to Hannibal in his designs; and, as they had the broad and rapid river between them and their enemy, they thought there was a reasonable prospect that, with its aid, they could exclude him from their territories altogether.

The Gauls Beyond the River Oppose Hannibal's Passage

Thus it happened that, when Hannibal came to the stream, the people on one side were all eager to promote, while those on the other were determined to prevent his passage, both parties being animated by the same desire to free their country from such a pest as the presence of an army of 90,000 men; so that Hannibal stood at last upon the banks of the river, with the people on his side of the stream waiting and ready to furnish all the boats and vessels that they could command, and to render every aid in their power in the embarkation, while those on the other were drawn up in battle array, rank behind rank, glittering with weapons, marshalled so as to guard every place of landing, and lining with pikes the whole extent of the shore, while the peaks of their tents, in vast numbers, with banners among them floating in the air, were to be seen in the distance behind them. All this time, the 300 horsemen which Cornelius had dispatched were slowly and cautiously making their way up the river from the Roman encampment below.

Preparations for Crossing the River – Boat Building

After contemplating the scene presented to his view at the river for some time in silence, Hannibal commenced his preparations for crossing the stream. He collected first all the boats of every kind which could be obtained among the Gauls who lived along the bank of the river. These, however, only served for a beginning, and so he next got together all the workmen and all the tools which the country could furnish, for several miles around, and went to work constructing more. The Gauls of that region had a custom of making boats of the trunks of large trees. The tree, being felled and cut to the proper length, was hollowed out with hatchets and adzes, and then, being turned bottom upward, the outside was shaped in such a

57

manner as to make it glide easily through the water. So convenient is this mode of making boats, that it is practiced, in cases where sufficiently large trees are found, to the present day. Such boats are now called canoes.

Rafts

There were plenty of large trees on the banks of the Rhône. Hannibal's soldiers watched the Gauls at their work, in making boats of them, until they learned the art themselves. Some first assisted their new allies in the easier portions of the operation, and then began to fell large trees and make the boats themselves. Others, who had less skill or more impetuosity chose not to wait for the slow process of hollowing the wood, and they, accordingly, would fell the trees upon the shore, cut the trunks of equal lengths, place them side by side in the water, and bolt or bind them together so as to form a raft. The form and fashion of their craft was of no consequence, they said, as it was for one passage only. Anything would answer, if it would only float and bear its burden over.

The Enemy Look on in Silence

In the meantime, the enemy upon the opposite shore looked on, but they could do nothing to impede these operations. If they had had artillery, such as is in use at the present day, they could have fired across the river, and have blown the boats and rafts to pieces with balls and shells as fast as the Gauls and Carthaginians could build them. In fact, the workmen could not have built them under such a cannonading; but the enemy, in this case, had nothing but spears, arrows and stones, to be thrown either by the hand or by engines far too weak to send them with any effect across such a stream. They had to look on quietly, therefore, and allow these great and formidable preparations for an attack upon them to go on without interruption. Their only hope was to overwhelm the army with their missiles, and prevent their landing, when they should reach the bank at last in their attempt to cross the stream.

Difficulties of Crossing a River

If an army is crossing a river without any enemy to oppose them, a moderate number of boats will serve, as a part of the army can be transported at a time, and the whole gradually transferred from one bank to the other by repeated trips of the same conveyances. But when there is an enemy to encounter at the landing, it is necessary to provide the means of carrying over a very large force at a time; for if a small division were to go over first alone, it would only throw itself, weak and defenceless, into the hands of the enemy. Hannibal, therefore, waited until he had boats, rafts and floats enough constructed to carry over a force all together sufficiently numerous and powerful to attack the enemy with a prospect of success.

Hannibal's Tactics – His Stratagem

The Romans, as we have already remarked, say that Hannibal was cunning. He certainly was not disposed to trust in his battles to simple superiority of bravery and force, but was always contriving some stratagem to increase the chances of victory. He did so in this case.

He kept up for many days a prodigious parade and bustle of building boats and rafts in sight of his enemy, as if his sole reliance was on the multitude of men that he could pour across the river at a single transportation, and he thus kept their attention closely riveted upon these preparations. All this time, however, he had another plan in course of execution. He had sent a strong body of troops secretly up the river, with orders to make their way stealthily through the forests and cross the stream some few miles above. This force was intended to move back from the river, as soon as it should cross the stream, and come down upon the enemy in the rear, so as to attack and harass them there at the same time that Hannibal was crossing with the main body of the army. If they succeeded in crossing the river safely, they were to build a fire in the woods, on the other side, in order that the column of smoke which should ascend from it might serve as a signal of their success to Hannibal.

Detachment Under Hanno – Success of Hanno – The Signal

This detachment was commanded by an officer named Hanno – of course a very different man from Hannibal's great enemy of that name in Carthage. Hanno set out in the night, moving back from the river, in commencing his march, so as to be entirely out of sight from the Gauls on the other side. He had some guides, belonging to the country, who promised to show him a convenient place for crossing. The party went up the river about 25 miles. Here they found a place where the water spread to a greater width, and where the current was less rapid, and the water not so deep. They got to this place in silence and secrecy, their enemies below not having suspected any such design. As they had, therefore, nobody to oppose them, they could cross much more easily than the main army below.

They made some rafts for carrying over those of the men that could not swim, and such munitions of war as would be injured by the wet. The rest of the men waded till they reached the channel, and then swam, supporting themselves in part by their bucklers, which they placed beneath their bodies in the water. Thus they all crossed in safety. They paused a day, to dry their clothes and to rest, and then moved cautiously down the river until they were near enough to Hannibal's position to allow their signal to be seen. The fire was then built, and they gazed with exultation upon the column of smoke which ascended from it high into the air.

Passage of the River

Hannibal saw the signal, and now immediately prepared to cross with his army. The horsemen embarked in boats, holding their horses by lines, with a view of leading them into the water so that they might swim in company with the boats. Other horses, bridled and accoutred, were put into large flat-bottomed boats, to be taken across dry, in order that they might be all ready for service at the instant of landing. The most vigorous and efficient portion of the army were, of course, selected for the first passage, while all those who, for any cause, were weak or disabled, remained behind, with the stores and munitions of war, to be transported afterward, when the first passage should have been affected. All this time the enemy, on the opposite shore, were getting their ranks in array, and making everything ready for a furious assault upon the invaders the moment they should approach the land.

Scene of Confusion – Attack of Hanno – Flight of the Gauls

There was something like silence and order during the period while the men were embarking and pushing out from the land, but as they advanced into the current, the loud commands, shouts and outcries increased more and more, and the rapidity of the current and of the eddies by which the boats and rafts were hurried down the stream, or whirled against each other, soon produced a terrific scene of tumult and confusion. As soon as the first boats approached the land, the Gauls assembled to oppose them rushed down upon them with showers of missiles, and with those unearthly yells which barbarous warriors always raise in going into battle, as a means both of exciting themselves and of terrifying their enemy. Hannibal's officers urged the boats on, and endeavoured, with as much coolness and deliberation as possible, to affect a landing.

It is perhaps doubtful how the contest would have ended, had it not been for the detachment under Hanno, which now came suddenly into action. While the Gauls were in the height of their excitement, in attempting to drive back the Carthaginians from the bank, they were thunderstruck at hearing the shouts and cries of an enemy behind them, and, on looking around, they saw the troops of Hanno pouring down upon them from the thickets with terrible impetuosity and force. It is very difficult for an army to fight both in front and in the rear at the same time. The Gauls, after a brief struggle, abandoned the attempt any longer to oppose Hannibal's landing. They fled down the river and back into the interior, leaving Hanno in secure possession of the bank while Hannibal and his forces came up at their leisure out of the water, finding friends instead of enemies to receive them.

Transportation of the Elephants – Manner of Doing It

The remainder of the army, together with the stores and munitions of war, were next to be transported, and this was accomplished with little difficulty now that there was no enemy to disturb their operations. There was one part of the force, however, which occasioned some trouble and delay. It was a body of elephants which formed a part of the army. How to get these unwieldy animals across so broad and rapid a river was a question of no little difficulty. There are various accounts of the manner in which Hannibal accomplished the object, from which it would seem that different methods were employed.

One mode was as follows: the keeper of the elephants selected one more spirited and passionate in disposition than the rest, and contrived to tease and torment him so as to make him angry. The elephant advanced toward his keeper with his trunk raised to take vengeance. The keeper fled; the elephant pursued him, the other elephants of the herd following, as is the habit of the animal on such occasions.

The keeper ran into the water as if to elude his pursuer, while the elephant and a large part of the herd pressed on after him. The man swam into the channel, and the elephants, before they could check themselves, found that they were beyond their depth. Some swam on after the keeper, and crossed the river, where they were easily secured. Others, terrified, abandoned themselves to the current, and were floated down, struggling helplessly as they went, until at last they grounded upon shallows or points of land, whence they gained the shore again, some on one side of the stream and some on the other.

A New Plan — Huge Rafts

This plan was thus only partially successful, and Hannibal devised a more effectual method for the remainder of the troop. He built an immensely large raft, floated it up to the shore, fastened it there securely, and covered it with earth, turf and bushes, so as to make it resemble a projection of the land. He then caused a second raft to be constructed of the same size, and this he brought up to the outer edge of the other, fastened it there by a temporary connection, and covered and concealed it as he had done the first. The first of these rafts extended 60 metres (200 feet) from the shore, and was 15 metres (50 feet) broad. The other, that is, the outer one, was only a little smaller. The soldiers then contrived to allure and drive the elephants over these rafts to the outer one, the animals imagining that they had not left the land. The two rafts were then disconnected from each other, and the outer one began to move with its bulky passengers over the water, towed by a number of boats which had previously been attached to its outer edge.

The Elephants Got Safely Over

As soon as the elephants perceived the motion, they were alarmed, and began immediately to look anxiously this way and that, and to crowd toward the edges of the raft which was conveying them away. They found themselves hemmed in by water on every side and were terrified and thrown into confusion. Some were crowded off into the river and were drifted down until they landed below. The rest soon became calm, and allowed themselves to be quietly ferried across the stream, when they found that all hope of escape and resistance were equally vain.

The Reconnoitring Parties – The Detachments Meet – A Battle Ensues

In the meantime, while these events were occurring, the troop of 300, which Scipio had sent up the river to see what tidings he could learn of the Carthaginians, were slowly making their way toward the point where Hannibal was crossing; and it happened that Hannibal had sent down a troop of 500, when he first reached the river, to see if they could learn any tidings of the Romans. Neither of the armies had any idea how near they were to the other. The two detachments met suddenly and unexpectedly on the way. They were sent to explore, and not to fight; but as they were nearly equally matched, each was ambitious of the glory of capturing the others and carrying them prisoners to their camp. They fought a long and bloody battle. A great number were killed, and in about the same proportion on either side. The Romans say *they* conquered. We do not know what the Carthaginians said, but as both parties retreated from the field and went back to their respective camps, it is safe to infer that neither could boast of a very decisive victory.

Chapter V
Hannibal Crosses the Alps, 217 BCE

The Alps

IT IS DIFFICULT for anyone who has not actually seen such mountain scenery as is presented by the Alps to form any clear conception of its magnificence and grandeur. Hannibal had never seen the Alps, but the world was filled then, as now, with their fame.

Their Sublimity and Grandeur – Perpetual Cold in the Upper Regions of the Atmosphere

Some of the leading features of sublimity and grandeur which these mountains exhibit result mainly from the perpetual cold which reigns upon their summits. This is owing simply to their elevation. In every part of the earth, as we ascend from the surface of the ground into the atmosphere, it becomes, for some mysterious reason or other, more and more cold as we rise, so that over our heads, wherever we are, there reigns, at a distance of two or three miles above us, an intense and perpetual cold.

It is from this region of perpetual cold that hail descend upon us in the midst of summer, and snow is continually forming and falling there; but the light and fleecy flakes melt before they reach the earth, so that, while the hail has such solidity and momentum that it forces its way through, the snow dissolves, and falls upon us as a cool and refreshing rain. Rain cools the air around us and the ground, because it comes from cooler regions of the air above.

Now it happens that not only the summits, but extensive portions of the upper declivities of the Alps, rise into the region of perpetual winter. Of course, ice congeals continually there, and the snow which forms falls to the ground as snow and accumulates in vast and permanent stores. The summit of Mount Blanc is covered with a bed of snow of enormous thickness, which is almost as much a permanent geological stratum of the mountain as the granite which lies beneath it.

Avalanches – Their Terrible Force

Of course, during the winter months, the whole country of the Alps, valley as well as hill, is covered with snow. In the spring the snow melts in the valleys and plains, and higher up it becomes damp and heavy with partial melting, and slides down the declivities in vast avalanches, which sometimes are of such enormous magnitude, and descend with such resistless force, as to bring down earth, rocks and even the trees of the forest in their train. On the higher declivities, however, and over all the rounded summits, the snow still clings to its place, yielding but very little to the feeble beams of the sun, even in July.

The Glaciers – Motion of the Ice

There are vast ravines and valleys among the higher Alps where the snow accumulates, being driven into them by winds and storms in the winter, and sliding into them, in great avalanches, in the spring. These vast depositories of snow become changed into ice below the surface; for at the surface there is a continual melting, and the water, flowing down through the mass, freezes below. Thus there are valleys, or rather ravines, some of them two or three miles wide and 10 or 15 miles long, filled with ice, transparent, solid and blue, hundreds of feet in depth. They are called *glaciers*. And what is most astonishing in respect to these icy accumulations is that, though the ice is perfectly compact and solid, the whole mass is found to be continually in a state of slow motion down the valley in which it lies, at the rate of about a foot in 24 hours.

By standing upon the surface and listening attentively, we hear, from time to time, a grinding sound. The rocks which lie along the sides are pulverized, and are continually moving against each other and falling; and then, besides, which is a more direct and positive proof still of the motion of the mass, a mark may be set up upon the ice, as has been often done, and marks corresponding to it made upon the solid rocks on each side of the valley, and by this means the fact of the motion, and the exact rate of it, may be fully ascertained.

Crevices and Chasms

Thus these valleys are really and literally rivers of ice, rising among the summits of the mountains, and flowing, slowly it is true, but with a continuous and certain current, to a sort of mouth in some great and open valley below. Here the streams which have flowed over the surface above and descended into the mass through countless crevices and chasms, into which the traveller looks down with terror, concentrate and issue from under the ice in a turbid torrent, which comes out from a vast archway made by the falling in of masses which the water has undermined. This lower end of the glacier sometimes presents a perpendicular wall hundreds of feet in height; sometimes it crowds down into the fertile valley, advancing in some unusually cold summer into the cultivated country, where, as it slowly moves on, it plows up the ground, carries away the orchards and fields, and even drives the inhabitants from the villages which it threatens. If the next summer proves warm, the terrible monster slowly draws back its frigid head, and the inhabitants return to the ground it reluctantly evacuates, and attempt to repair the damage it has done.

Situation of the Alps – Roads Over the Alps

The Alps lie between France and Italy, and the great valleys and the ranges of mountain land lie in such a direction that they must be *crossed* in order to pass from one country to the other. These ranges are, however, not regular. They are traversed by innumerable chasms, fissures and ravines; in some places they rise in vast rounded summits and swells, covered with fields of spotless snow; in others they tower in lofty, needle-like peaks, which even the chamois cannot scale, and where scarcely a flake of snow can find a place of rest.

Around and among these peaks and summits, and through these frightful defiles and chasms, the roads twist and turn, in a zigzag and constantly ascending course, creeping along the most frightful precipices, sometimes beneath them and sometimes on the brink, penetrating the darkest and gloomiest defiles, skirting the most impetuous and foaming torrents, and at last, perhaps, emerging upon the surface of a glacier, to be lost in interminable fields of ice and snow, where countless brooks run in glassy channels, and crevasses yawn, ready to take advantage of any slip which may enable them to take down the traveller into their bottomless abysses.

Beauty of the Alpine Scenery

And yet, notwithstanding the awful desolation which reigns in the upper regions of the Alps, the lower valleys, through which the streams finally meander out into the open plains, and by which the traveller gains access to the sublimer scenes of the upper mountains, are inexpressibly verdant and beautiful. They are fertilized by the deposits of continual inundations in the early spring, and the sun beats down into them with a genial warmth in summer, which brings out millions of flowers, of the most beautiful forms and colours, and ripens rapidly the broadest and richest fields of grain. Cottages, of every picturesque and beautiful form, tenanted by the cultivators, the shepherds and the herdsmen, crown every little swell in the bottom of the valley, and cling to the declivities of the mountains which rise on either hand. Above them eternal forests of firs and pines wave, feathering over the steepest and most rocky slopes with their sombre foliage. Still higher, grey precipices rise and spires and pinnacles, far grander and more picturesque, if not so symmetrically formed, than those constructed by man. Between these there is seen, here and there, in the background, vast towering masses of white and dazzling snow, which crown the summits of the loftier mountains beyond.

Hannibal Determines to Cross the Alps

Hannibal's determination to carry an army into Italy by way of the Alps, instead of transporting them by galleys over the sea, has always been regarded as one of the greatest undertakings of ancient times. He hesitated for some time whether he should go down the Rhône, and meet and give battle to Scipio, or whether he should leave the Roman army to its course and proceed himself directly toward the Alps and Italy.

The officers and soldiers of the army, who had now learned something of their destination and of their leader's plans, wanted to go and meet the Romans. They dreaded the Alps. They were willing to encounter a military foe, however formidable, for this was a danger that they were accustomed to and could understand; but their imaginations were appalled at the novel and awful images they formed of falling down precipices of ragged rocks, or of gradually freezing, and being buried half alive, during the process, in eternal snows.

Hannibal's Speech to His Army

Hannibal, when he found that his soldiers were afraid to proceed, called the leading portions of his army together, and made them an address. He remonstrated with them for yielding now to unworthy fears, after having successfully met and triumphed over such dangers as they had already incurred. 'You have surmounted the Pyrenees,' said he, 'you have crossed the Rhône. You are now actually in sight of the Alps, which are the very gates of access to the country of the enemy. What do you conceive the Alps to be? They are nothing but high mountains, after all. Suppose they are higher than the Pyrenees, they do not reach to the skies; and, since they do not, they cannot be insurmountable. They *are* surmounted, in fact, every day; they are even inhabited and cultivated, and travellers continually pass over them to and fro. And what a single man can do, an army can do, for an army is only a large number of single men. In fact, to a soldier, who has nothing to carry with him but the implements of war, no way can be too difficult to be surmounted by courage and energy.'

Its Effects – His Army Follows

After finishing his speech, Hannibal, finding his men reanimated and encouraged by what he had said, ordered them to go to their tents and refresh themselves, and prepare to march on the following day. They made no further opposition to going on. Hannibal did not, however, proceed at once directly toward the Alps. He did not know what the plans of Scipio might be, who, it will be recollected, was below him, on the Rhône, with the Roman army. He did not wish to waste his time and his strength in a contest with Scipio in Gaul, but to press on and get across the Alps into Italy as soon as possible. And so, fearing lest Scipio should strike across the country, and intercept him if he should attempt to go by the most direct route, he determined to move northwardly, up the river Rhône, until he should get well into the interior, with a view of reaching the Alps ultimately by a more circuitous journey.

Scipio Moves After Hannibal – Sad Vestiges

It was, in fact, the plan of Scipio to come up with Hannibal and attack him as soon as possible; and, accordingly, as soon as his horsemen, or, rather, those who were left alive after the battle had returned and informed him that Hannibal and his army were near, he put his camp in motion and moved rapidly up the river. He arrived at the place where the Carthaginians had crossed a few days after they had gone. The spot was in a terrible state of ruin and confusion. The grass and herbage were trampled down for the circuit of a mile, and all over the space were spots of black and smouldering remains, where the campfires had been kindled. The tops and branches of trees lay everywhere around, their leaves withering in the sun, and the groves and forests were encumbered with limbs, rejected trunks and trees felled and left where they lay. The shore was lined far down the stream with ruins of boats and rafts, with weapons which had been lost or abandoned, and with the bodies of those who had been drowned in the passage or killed in the contest on the shore. These and numerous other vestiges remained but the army was gone.

Perplexity of Scipio – He Sails Back to Italy

There were, however, upon the ground groups of natives and other visitors who had come to look at the spot now destined to become so memorable in history. From these men Scipio learned when and where Hannibal had gone. He decided that it was useless to attempt to pursue him. He was greatly perplexed to know what to do. In the casting of lots, Spain had fallen to him, but now that the great enemy whom he had come forth to meet had left Spain altogether, his only hope of intercepting his progress was to sail back into Italy and meet him as he came down from the Alps into the great valley of the Po. Still, as Spain had been assigned to him as his province, he could not well entirely abandon it. He accordingly sent forward the largest part of his army into Spain, to attack the forces that Hannibal had left there, while he himself, with a smaller force, went down to the seashore and sailed back to Italy again. He expected to find Roman forces in the valley of the Po, with which he hoped to be strong enough to meet Hannibal as he descended from the mountains, if he should succeed in effecting a passage over them.

Hannibal Approaches the Alps

In the meantime, Hannibal went on, drawing nearer and nearer to the ranges of snowy summits which his soldiers had seen for many days in their eastern horizon. These ranges were very resplendent and grand when the sun went down in the west, for then it shone directly upon them. As the army approached nearer and nearer to them, they gradually withdrew from sight and disappeared, being concealed by intervening summits less lofty, but nearer. As the soldiers went on, however, and began to penetrate the valleys, and draw near to the awful chasms and precipices among the mountains, and saw the turbid torrents descending from them, their fears revived. It was, however, now too late to retreat. They pressed forward, ascending continually, till their road grew extremely precipitous and insecure, threading its way through almost impassable defiles, with rugged cliffs overhanging them, and snowy summits towering all around.

A Dangerous Defile – The Army Encamps

At last they came to a narrow defile through which they must necessarily pass, but which was guarded by large bodies of armed men assembled on the rocks and precipices above, ready to hurl stones and weapons of every kind upon them if they should attempt to pass through. The army halted. Hannibal ordered them to encamp where they were, until he could consider what to do. In the course of the day he learned that the mountaineers did not remain at their elevated posts during the night, on account of the intense cold and exposure, knowing, too, that it would be impossible for an army to traverse such a pass as they were attempting to guard without daylight to guide them, for the road, or rather pathway, which passes through these defiles, follows generally the course of a mountain torrent, which flows through a succession of frightful ravines and chasms, and often passes along on a shelf or projection of the rock, hundreds and sometimes thousands of feet from the bed of the stream, which foams and roars far below. There could, of course, be no hope of passing safely by such a route without the light of day.

The Mountaineers – Hannibal's Stratagem

The mountaineers, therefore, knowing that it was not necessary to guard the pass at night – its own terrible danger being then a sufficient protection – were accustomed to disperse in the evening, and descend to regions where they could find shelter and repose, and to return and renew their watch in the morning. When Hannibal learned this, he determined to anticipate them in getting up upon the rocks the next day, and, in order to prevent their entertaining any suspicion of his design, he pretended to be making all the arrangements for encamping for the night on the ground he had taken. He accordingly pitched more tents, and built, toward evening, a great many fires, and he began some preparations indicating that it was his intention the next day to force his way through the pass. He moved forward a strong detachment up to a point near the entrance to the pass, and put them in a fortified position there, as if to have them all ready to advance when the proper time should arrive on the following day.

Its Success – Astonishment of the Mountaineers

The mountaineers, seeing all these preparations going on, looked forward to a conflict on the morrow, and, during the night, left their positions as usual, to descend to places of shelter. The next morning, however, when they began, at an early hour, to ascend to them again, they were astonished to find all the lofty rocks, cliffs and shelving projections which overhung the pass, covered with Carthaginians. Hannibal had aroused a strong body of his men at the earliest dawn, and led them up, by steep climbing, to the places which the mountaineers had left, so as to be there before them. The mountaineers paused, astonished, at this spectacle, and their disappointment and rage were much increased on looking down into the valley below and seeing there the remainder of the Carthaginian army quietly moving through the pass in a long train, safe apparently from any molestation, since friends, and not enemies, were now in possession of the cliffs above.

Terrible Conflict in the Defile – Attack of Hannibal

The mountaineers could not restrain their feelings of vexation and anger, but immediately rushed down the declivities which they had in part ascended and attacked the army in the defile. An awful scene of struggle and confusion ensued. Some were killed by weapons or by rocks rolled down upon them. Others, contending together, and struggling desperately in places of very narrow foothold, tumbled headlong down the rugged rocks into the torrent below; and horses, laden with baggage and stores, became frightened and unmanageable, and crowded each other over the most frightful precipices.

Hannibal, who was above, on the higher rocks, looked down upon this scene for a time with the greatest anxiety and terror. He did not dare to descend himself and mingle in the affray, for fear of increasing the confusion. He soon found, however, that it was absolutely necessary for him to interpose, and he came down as rapidly as possible, his detachment with him. They descended by oblique and zigzag paths, wherever they could get footing among the rocks, and attacked the mountaineers with great fury. The result was, as he had feared, a great increase at first of the confusion and the slaughter. The horses were more and more terrified by the fresh energy of the combat, and by the resounding of louder shouts and cries, which were made doubly terrific by the echoes and reverberations of the mountains. They crowded against each other, and fell, horses and men together, in masses, over the cliffs to the rugged rocks below, where they lay in confusion, some dead, and others dying, writhing helplessly in agony, or vainly endeavouring to crawl away.

The Mountaineers Defeated – The Army Pauses to Refresh

The mountaineers were, however, conquered and driven away at last, and the pass was left clear. The Carthaginian column was restored to order. The horses that had not fallen were calmed and quieted. The baggage which had been thrown down was gathered up, and the wounded men were placed on litters, rudely constructed on the spot, that they might be borne on to a place of safety. In a short time, all were ready to move on, and the march was accordingly recommenced. There was no further difficulty. The column advanced in a quiet and orderly manner until they had passed the defile. At the extremity of it they came to a spacious fort belonging to the natives. Hannibal took possession of this fort and paused for a little time there to rest and refresh his men.

Scarcity of Food

One of the greatest difficulties encountered by a general in conducting an army through difficult and dangerous roads, is that of providing food for them. An army can transport its own food only a very little way. Men traveling over smooth roads can only carry provisions for a few days, and where the roads are as difficult and dangerous as the passes of the Alps, they can scarcely carry any. The commander must, accordingly, find subsistence in the country through which he is marching. Hannibal had, therefore, now not only to look out for the safety of his men, but their food was exhausted, and he must take immediate measures to secure a supply.

Herds and Flocks Upon the Mountains

The lower slopes of lofty mountains afford usually abundant sustenance for flocks and herds. The showers which are continually falling there, and the moisture which comes down the sides of the mountains through the ground keep the turf perpetually green, and sheep and cattle love to pasture upon it; they climb to great heights, finding the herbage finer and sweeter the higher they go. Thus the inhabitants of mountain ranges are almost always shepherds and herdsmen. Grain can be raised in the valleys below, but the slopes of the mountains, though they produce grass to perfection, are too steep to be tilled.

Foraging Parties

As soon as Hannibal had got established in the fort, he sent around small bodies of men to seize and drive in all the cattle and sheep that they could find. These men were, of course, armed, in order that they might be prepared to meet any resistance which they might encounter. The mountaineers, however, did not attempt to resist them. They felt that they were conquered, and they were accordingly disheartened and discouraged. The only mode of saving their cattle which was left to them was to drive them as fast as they could into concealed and inaccessible places. They attempted to do this, and while Hannibal's parties were ranging up the valleys all around them, examining every field, barn and sheepfold that they could find, the wretched and despairing inhabitants were flying in all directions, driving the cows and sheep, on which their whole hope of subsistence depended, into the fastnesses of the mountains. They urged them into wild thickets, and dark ravines and chasms, and over dangerous glaciers, and up the steepest ascents, wherever there was the readiest prospect of getting them out of the plunderer's way.

Collecting Cattle

These attempts, however, to save their little property were but very partially successful. Hannibal's marauding parties kept coming home, one after another, with droves of sheep and cattle before them, some larger and some smaller, but making up a vast amount in all. Hannibal subsisted his men three days on the food thus procured for them. It requires an enormous store to feed 90,000 or 100,000 men, even for three days; besides, in all such cases as this, an army always waste and destroy far more than they really consume.

Progress of the Army

During these three days, the army was not stationary but was moving slowly on. The way, though still difficult and dangerous, was at least open before them, as there was now no enemy to dispute their passage. So they went on, rioting upon the abundant supplies they had obtained, and rejoicing in the double victory they were gaining, over the hostility of the people and the physical dangers and difficulties of the way. The poor mountaineers returned to their cabins ruined and desolate, for mountaineers who have lost their cows and their sheep have lost their all.

Cantons – An Embassage – Hostages

The Alps are not all in Switzerland. Some of the most celebrated peaks and ranges are in a neighbouring state called Savoy. The whole country is, in fact, divided into small states, called *cantons* at the present day, and similar political divisions seem to have existed in the time of the Romans. In his march onward from the pass which has been already described, Hannibal, accordingly, soon approached the confines of another canton.

As he was advancing slowly into it, with the long train of his army winding up with him through the valleys, he was met at the borders of this new state by an embassage sent from the government of it. They brought with them fresh stores of provisions, and a number of guides. They said that they had heard of the terrible destruction which had come upon the other canton in consequence of their effort to oppose his progress, and that they had no intention of renewing so vain an attempt. They came, therefore, they said, to offer Hannibal their friendship and their aid. They had brought guides to show the army the best way over the mountains, and a present of provisions; and to prove the sincerity of their professions they offered Hannibal hostages. These hostages were young men and boys, the sons of the principal inhabitants, whom they offered to deliver into Hannibal's power, to be kept by him until he should see that they were faithful and true in doing what they offered.

Hannibal's Suspicions

Hannibal was so accustomed to stratagem and treachery himself, that he was at first very much at a loss to decide whether these offers and professions were honest and sincere, or whether they were only made to put him off his guard. He thought it possible that it was their design to induce him to place himself under their direction, so that they might lead him into some dangerous defile or labyrinth of rocks, from which he could not extricate himself, and where they could attack and destroy him. He, however, decided to return them a favourable answer, but to watch them very carefully, and to proceed under their guidance with the utmost caution and care.

He accepted of the provisions they offered and took the hostages. These last he delivered into the custody of a body of his soldiers, and they marched on with the rest of the army. Then, directing the new guides to lead the way, the army moved on after them. The elephants went first, with a moderate force for their protection preceding and accompanying them. Then came long trains of horses and mules, loaded with military stores and baggage, and finally the foot soldiers followed, marching irregularly in a long column. The whole train must have extended many miles, and must have appeared from any of the eminences around like an enormous serpent, winding its way tortuously through the wild and desolate valleys.

Treachery of the Mountaineers – They Attack Hannibal – The Elephants

Hannibal was right in his suspicions. The embassage was a stratagem. The men who sent it had laid an ambuscade in a very narrow pass, concealing their forces in thickets and in chasms, and in nooks and corners among the rugged rocks, and when the guides had led the army well into the danger, a sudden signal was given, and these concealed enemies rushed down upon them in great numbers, breaking into their ranks, and renewing the scene of terrible uproar, tumult and destruction which had been witnessed in the other defile. One would have thought that the elephants, being so unwieldy and so helpless in such a scene, would have been the first objects of attack. But it was not so. The mountaineers were afraid of them. They had never seen such animals before, and they felt for them a mysterious awe, not knowing what terrible powers such enormous beasts might be expected to wield. They kept away from them, therefore, and from the horsemen, and poured down upon the head of the column of foot soldiers which followed in the rear.

Hannibal's Army Divided

They were quite successful at the first onset. They broke through the head of the column and drove the rest back. The horses and elephants, in the meantime, moved forward, bearing the baggage with them, so that the two portions of the army were soon entirely separated. Hannibal was behind, with the soldiers. The mountaineers made good their position, and, as night came on, the contest ceased, for in such wilds as these no one can move at all, except with the light of day. The mountaineers, however, remained in their place, dividing the army, and Hannibal continued, during the night, in a state of great suspense and anxiety, with the elephants and the baggage separated from him and apparently at the mercy of the enemy.

Hannibal's Attack on the Mountaineers – They Embarrass His March

During the night Hannibal made vigorous preparations for attacking the mountaineers the next day. As soon as the morning light appeared, he made the attack, and he succeeded in driving the enemy away, so far, at least, as to allow him to get his army together again. He then began once more to move on. The mountaineers, however, hovered about his way, and did all they could to molest and embarrass his march. They concealed themselves in ambuscades and attacked the Carthaginians as they passed. They rolled stones down upon them, or discharged spears and arrows from eminences above; and if any of Hannibal's army became, from any reason, detached from the rest, they would cut off their retreat, and then take them prisoners or destroy them. Thus they gave Hannibal a great deal of trouble. They harassed his march continually, without presenting at any point a force which he could meet and encounter in battle.

Of course, Hannibal could no longer trust to his guides, and he was obliged to make his way as he best could, sometimes right, but often wrong, and exposed to a thousand difficulties and dangers, which those acquainted with the country might have easily avoided. All this time the mountaineers were continually attacking him, in bands like those of robbers, sometimes in the van, and sometimes in the rear, wherever the nature of the ground or the circumstances of the marching army afforded them an opportunity.

Hannibal's Indomitable Perseverance

Hannibal persevered, however, through all these discouragements, protecting his men as far as it was in his power, but pressing earnestly on, until in nine days he reached the summit. By the summit, however, is not meant the summit of the mountains, but the summit of the *pass*, that is, the highest point which it was necessary for him to attain in going over. In all mountain ranges there are depressions, which are in Switzerland called *necks*, and the pathways and roads over the ranges lie always in these. In America, such a depression in a ridge of land, if well marked and decided, is called a *notch*. Hannibal attained the highest point of the *col*, by which he was to pass over, in nine days after the great battle. There were, however, of course, lofty peaks and summits towering still far above him.

He Encamps – Return of Straggling Parties

He encamped here two days to rest and refresh his men. The enemy no longer molested him. In fact, parties were continually coming into the camp, of men and horses, that had got lost, or had been left in the valleys below. They came in slowly, some wounded, others exhausted and spent by fatigue and exposure. In some cases, horses came in alone. They were horses that had slipped or stumbled, and fallen among the rocks, or had sunk down exhausted by their toil, and had thus been left behind, and afterward, recovering their strength, had followed on, led by a strange instinct to keep to the tracks which their companions had made, and thus they rejoined the camp at last in safety.

Dreary Scenery of the Summit – Storms in the Mountains

In fact, one great reason for Hannibal's delay at his encampment on or near the summit of the pass was to afford time for all the missing men to join the army again that had the power to do so. Had it not been for this necessity, he would doubtless have descended some distance, at least, to a more warm and sheltered position before seeking repose.

A gloomier and more desolate resting place than the summit of an Alpine pass can scarcely be found. The bare and barren rocks are entirely destitute of vegetation, and they have lost, besides, the sublime and picturesque forms which they assume further below. They spread in vast, naked fields in every direction around the spectator, rising in gentle ascents, bleak and dreary, the surface whitened as if bleached by the perpetual rains. Storms are, in fact, almost perpetual in these elevated regions. The vast cloud which, to the eye of the shepherd in the valley below, seems only a fleecy cap, resting serenely upon the summit, or slowly floating along the sides, is really a driving mist, or cold and stormy rain, howling dismally over interminable fields of broken rocks, as if angry that it can make nothing grow upon them, with all its watering. Thus there are seldom distant views to be obtained, and everything near presents a scene of simple dreariness and desolation.

A Dreary Encampment – Landmarks

Hannibal's soldiers thus found themselves in the midst of a dismal scene in their lofty encampment. There is one special source of danger, too, in such places as this, which the lower portions of the mountains are less exposed to, and that is the entire obliteration of the pathway by falls of snow. It seems almost absurd to speak of pathway in such regions, where there is no turf to be worn, and the boundless fields of rocks, ragged and hard, will take no trace of footsteps. There are, however, generally some faint traces of way, and where these fail entirely the track is sometimes indicated by small piles of stones, placed at intervals along the line of route. An unpractised eye would scarcely distinguish these little landmarks, in many cases, from accidental heaps of stones which lie everywhere around. They, however, render a very essential service to the guides and to the mountaineers, who have been accustomed to conduct their steps by similar aids in other portions of the mountains.

A Snowstorm

But when snow begins to fall, all these and every other possible means of distinguishing the way are soon entirely obliterated. The whole surface of the ground, or, rather, of the rocks, is covered, and all landmarks disappear. The little monuments become nothing but slight inequalities in the surface of the snow, undistinguishable from a thousand others. The air is thick and murky, and shuts off alike all distant prospects, and the shape and conformation of the land that is near; the bewildered traveller has not even the stars to guide him, as there is nothing but dark, falling flakes, descending from an impenetrable canopy of stormy clouds, to be seen in the sky.

The Army Resumes Its March

Hannibal encountered a snowstorm while on the summit of the pass, and his army were very much terrified by it. It was now November. The army had met with so many detentions and delays that their journey had been protracted to a late period. It would be unsafe to attempt to wait until this snow should melt again. As soon, therefore, as the storm ended, and the clouds cleared away, so as to allow the men to see the general features of the country around, the camp was broken up and the army put in motion. The soldiers marched through the snow with great anxiety and fear. Men went before to explore the way, and to guide the rest by flags and banners which they bore. Those who went first made paths, of course, for those who followed behind, as the snow was trampled down by their footsteps. Notwithstanding these aids, however, the army moved on very laboriously and with much fear.

Hannibal Among the Pioneers – First Sight of Italy – Joy of the Army

At length, however, after descending a short distance, Hannibal, perceiving that they must soon come in sight of the Italian valleys and plains which lay beyond the Alps, went forward among the pioneers, who had charge of the banners by which the movements of the army were directed, and, as soon as the open country began to come into view, he selected a spot where the widest prospect was presented, and halted his army there to let them take a view of the beautiful country which now lay before them.

The Alps are very precipitous on the Italian side. The descent is very sudden, from the cold and icy summits, to a broad expanse of the most luxuriant and sunny plains. Upon these plains, which were spread out in a most enchanting landscape at their feet, Hannibal and his soldiers now looked down with exultation and delight. Beautiful lakes, studded with still more beautiful islands, reflected the beams of the sun. An endless succession of fields, in sober autumnal colours, with the cottages of the laborers and stacks of grain scattered here and there upon them, and rivers meandering through verdant meadows, gave variety and enchantment to the view.

Hannibal's Speech – Fatigues of the March

Hannibal made an address to his officers and men, congratulating them on having arrived, at last, so near to a successful termination of their toils. 'The difficulties of the way,' he said, 'are at last surmounted, and these mighty barriers that we have scaled are the walls, not only of Italy, but of Rome itself. Since we have passed the Alps, the Romans will have no protection against us remaining. It is only one battle, when we get down upon the plains, or at most two, and the great city itself will be entirely at our disposal.'

The whole army were much animated and encouraged, both by the prospect which presented itself to their view, and by the words of Hannibal. They prepared for the descent, anticipating little difficulty; but they found, on recommencing their march, that their troubles were by no means over. The mountains are far steeper on the Italian side than on the other, and it was extremely difficult to find paths by which the elephants and the horses, and even the men, could safely descend. They moved on for some time with great labour and fatigue, until, at length, Hannibal, looking on before, found that the head of the column had stopped, and the whole train behind was soon jammed together, the ranks halting along the way in succession, as they found their path blocked up by the halting of those before them.

New Difficulties – March Over the Glacier

Hannibal sent forward to ascertain the cause of the difficulty and found that the van of the army had reached a precipice down which it was impossible to descend. It was necessary to make a circuit in hopes of finding some practicable way of getting down. The guides and pioneers went on, leading the army after them, and soon got upon a glacier which lay in their way. There was fresh snow upon the surface, covering the ice and concealing the *crevasses*, as they are termed – that is, the great cracks and fissures which extend in the glaciers down through the body of the ice. The army moved on, trampling down the new snow, and making at first a good roadway by their footsteps; but very soon the old ice and snow began to be trampled *up* by the hoofs of the horses and the heavy tread of such vast multitudes of armed men. It softened to a great depth and made the work of toiling through it an enormous labour. Besides, the surface of the ice and snow sloped steeply, and the men and beasts were continually falling or sliding down and getting swallowed up in avalanches which their own weight set in motion, or in concealed crevasses where they sank to rise no more.

A Formidable Barrier – Hannibal Cuts His Way Through the Rocks

They, however, made some progress, though slowly, and with great danger. They got below the region of the snow, but here they encountered new difficulties in the abruptness and ruggedness of the rocks, and in the zigzag and tortuous direction of the way. At last, they came to a spot where their further progress appeared to be entirely cut off by a large mass of rock, which it seemed necessary to remove in order to widen the passage sufficiently to allow them to go on.

The Roman historian says that Hannibal removed these rocks by building great fires upon them, and then pouring on vinegar, which opened seams and fissures in them, by means of which the rocks could be split and pried to pieces

with wedges and crowbars. On reading this account, the mind naturally pauses
to consider the probability of its being true. As they had no gunpowder in those
days, they were compelled to resort to some such method as the one above
described for removing rocks. There are some species of rock which are easily
cracked and broken by the action of fire. Others resist it. There seems, however,
to be no reason obvious why vinegar should materially assist in the operation.
Besides, we cannot suppose that Hannibal could have had, at such a time and
place, any very large supply of vinegar on hand. On the whole, it is probable that,
if any such operation was performed at all, it was on a very small scale, and the
results must have been very insignificant at the time, though the fact has since
been greatly celebrated in history.

The Army in Safety on the Plains of Italy

In coming over the snow, and in descending the rocks immediately below,
the army, and especially the animals connected with it, suffered a great deal
from hunger. It was difficult to procure forage for them of any kind. At length,
however, as they continued their descent, they came first into the region of
forests, and soon after to slopes of grassy fields descending into warm and
fertile valleys. Here the animals were allowed to stop and rest and renew their
strength by abundance of food. The men rejoiced that their toils and dangers
were over, and, descending easily the remainder of the way, they encamped at
last safely on the plains of Italy.

Chapter VI
Hannibal in the North of Italy, 217 BCE

Miserable Condition of the Army – Its Great Losses

WHEN HANNIBAL'S ARMY FOUND themselves on the plains of
Italy, and sat down quietly to repose, they felt the effects of their
fatigues and exposures far more sensibly than they had done

under the excitement which they naturally felt while actually upon the mountains. They were, in fact, in a miserable condition. Hannibal told a Roman officer whom he afterward took prisoner that more than 30,000 perished on the way in crossing the mountains; some in the battles which were fought in the passes, and a greater number still, probably, from exposure to fatigue and cold, and from falls among the rocks and glaciers, and diseases produced by destitution and misery. The remnant of the army that was left on reaching the plain were emaciated, sickly, ragged and spiritless; far more inclined to lie down and die than to go on and undertake the conquest of Italy and Rome.

Feelings of Hannibal's Soldiers

After some days, however, they began to recover. Although they had been half-starved among the mountains, they had now plenty of wholesome food. They repaired their tattered garments and their broken weapons. They talked with one another about the terrific scenes through which they had been passing, and the dangers which they had surmounted, and thus, gradually strengthening their impressions of the greatness of the exploits they had performed, they began soon to awaken in each other's breasts an ambition to go on and undertake the accomplishment of other deeds of daring and glory.

Plans of Scipio

We left Scipio with his army at the mouth of the Rhône, about to set sail for Italy with a part of his force, while the rest of it was sent on toward Spain. Scipio sailed along the coast by Genoa, and thence to Pisa, where he landed. He stopped a little while to recoup his soldiers after the voyage, and in the meantime sent orders to all the Roman forces then in the north of Italy to join his standard. He hoped in this way to collect a force strong enough to encounter Hannibal. These arrangements being made, he marched to the northward as rapidly as possible. He knew in what condition Hannibal's army had descended from the Alps, and wished to attack them before they should have time to recover from the effects of their privations and sufferings. He reached the Po before he saw anything of Hannibal.

The Armies Approach Each Other

Hannibal, in the meantime, was not idle. As soon as his men were in a condition to move, he began to act upon the tribes that he found at the foot of the mountains, offering his friendship to some, and attacking others. He thus conquered those who attempted to resist him, moving, all the time, gradually southward toward the Po. That river has numerous branches, and among them is one named the Ticinus. It was on the banks of this river that the two armies at last came together.

Feelings of Hannibal and Scipio

Both generals must have felt some degree of solicitude in respect to the result of the contest which was about to take place. Scipio knew very well Hannibal's terrible efficiency as a warrior, and he was himself a general of great distinction, and a *Roman*, so that Hannibal had no reason to anticipate a very easy victory. Whatever doubts or fears, however, general officers may feel on the eve of an engagement, it is always considered very necessary to conceal them entirely from the men, and to animate and encourage the troops with a most undoubting confidence that they will gain the victory.

Both Hannibal and Scipio, accordingly, made addresses to their respective armies – at least so say the historians of those times – each one expressing to his followers the certainty that the other side would easily be beaten. The speech attributed to Scipio was somewhat as follows:

Address of Scipio to the Roman Army

'I wish to say a few words to you, soldiers, before we go into battle. It is, perhaps, scarcely necessary. It certainly would not be necessary if I had now under my command the same troops that I took with me to the mouth of the Rhône. They knew the Carthaginians there, and would not have feared them here. A body of our horsemen met and attacked a larger body of theirs, and defeated them. We then advanced with our whole force toward their encampment, in order to give them battle. They, however, abandoned the ground and retreated before we reached the spot, acknowledging, by their flight, their own fear, and our superiority. If you had been with us there, and had witnessed these facts, there would have been no need that I should say anything to convince you now how easily you are going to defeat this Carthaginian foe.

'We have had a war with this same nation before. We conquered them then, both by land and sea; and when, finally, peace was made, we required them to pay us tribute, and we continued to exact it from them for 20 years. They are a conquered nation; and now this miserable army has forced its way insanely over the Alps, just to throw itself into our hands. They meet us reduced in numbers, and exhausted in resources and strength. More than half of their army perished in the mountains, and those that survive are weak, dispirited, ragged and diseased. And yet they are compelled to meet us. If there was any chance for retreat, or any possible way for them to avoid the necessity of a battle, they would avail themselves of it. But there is not. They are hemmed in by the mountains, which are now, to them, an impassable wall, for they have not strength to scale them again.

'They are not real enemies; they are the mere remnants and shadows of enemies. They are wholly disheartened and discouraged, their strength and energy, both of soul and body, being spent and gone, through the cold, the hunger and the squalid misery they have endured. Their joints are benumbed, their sinews stiffened and their forms emaciated. Their armour is shattered and broken, their horses are lamed and all their equipment worn out and ruined, so that really what most I fear is that the world will refuse us the glory of the victory, and say that it was the Alps that conquered Hannibal, and not the Roman army.

'Easy as the victory is to be, however, we must remember that there is a great deal at stake in the contest. It is not merely for glory that we are now about to contend. If Hannibal conquers, he will march to Rome, and our wives, our children and all that we hold dear will be at his mercy. Remember this, and go into the battle feeling that the fate of Rome itself is depending upon the result.'

Hannibal's Ingenious Method of Introducing His Speech – Curious Combat – Effect on the Army

An oration is attributed to Hannibal, too, on the occasion of this battle. He showed, however, his characteristic ingenuity and spirit of contrivance in the way in which he managed to attract strong attention to what he was going to say, by the manner in which he introduced it.

He formed his army into a circle, as if to witness a spectacle. He then brought into the centre of this circle a number of prisoners that he had taken among the Alps – perhaps they were the hostages which had been delivered to him, as related in the preceding chapter. Whoever they were, however, whether hostages or captives taken in the battles which had been fought in the defiles, Hannibal had brought them with his army down into Italy, and now introducing them into the centre of the circle which the army formed, he threw down before them such arms as they were accustomed to use in their native mountains, and asked them whether they would be willing to take those weapons and fight each other, on condition that each one who killed his antagonist should be restored to his liberty, and have a horse and armour given him, so that he could return home with honour.

The barbarous monsters said readily that they would, and seized the arms with the greatest avidity. Two or three pairs of combatants were allowed to fight. One of each pair was killed, and the other set at liberty according to the promise of Hannibal. The combats excited the greatest interest, and awakened the strongest enthusiasm among the soldiers who witnessed them. When this effect had been sufficiently produced, the rest of the prisoners were sent away, and Hannibal addressed the vast ring of soldiery as follows:

Hannibal's Speech to His Army

'I have intended, soldiers, in what you have now seen, not merely to amuse you, but to give you a picture of your own situation. You are hemmed in on the right and left by two seas, and you have not so much as a single ship upon either of them. Then there is the Po before you and the Alps behind. The Po is a deeper, and more rapid and turbulent river than the Rhône; and as for the Alps, it was with the utmost difficulty that you passed over them when you were in full strength and vigour; they are an insurmountable wall to you now. You are therefore shut in, like our prisoners, on every side, and have no hope of life and liberty but in battle and victory.

His Words of Encouragement

'The victory, however, will not be difficult. I see, wherever I look among you, a spirit of determination and courage which I am sure will make you conquerors. The troops which you are going to contend against are mostly fresh recruits, that know nothing of the discipline of the camp, and can never successfully confront such war-worn veterans as you. You all know each other well, and me. I was, in fact, a pupil with you for many years, before I took the command. But Scipio's forces are strangers to one another and to him, and, consequently, have no common bond of sympathy; and as for Scipio himself, his very commission as a Roman general is only six months old.

Hannibal's Promises

'Think, too, what a splendid and prosperous career victory will open before you. It will conduct you to Rome. It will make you masters of one of the most powerful and wealthiest cities in the world. Thus far you have fought your battles only for glory or for dominion; now, you will have something more substantial to reward your success. There will be great treasures to be divided among you if we conquer, but if we are defeated, we are lost. Hemmed in as we are on every side, there is no place that we can reach by flight. There is, therefore, no such alternative as flight left to us. We *must conquer.'*

His Real Feelings

It is hardly probable that Hannibal could have really and honestly felt all the confidence that he expressed in his harangues to his soldiers. He must have had some fears. In fact, in all enterprises undertaken by man, the indications of success, and the hopes based upon them, will fluctuate from time to time, and cause his confidence in the result to ebb and flow, so that bright anticipations of success and triumph will alternate in his heart with feelings of discouragement and despondency. This effect is experienced by all; by the energetic and decided as well as by the timid and the faltering. The former, however, never allow these fluctuations of hope and fear to influence their action. They consider well the substantial grounds for expecting success before commencing their undertaking, and then go steadily forward, under all aspects of the sky – when it shines and when it rains – until they reach the end. The inefficient and undecided can act only under the stimulus of present hope. The end they aim at must be visible before them all the time. If for a moment it passes out of view, their motive is gone, and they can do no more, until, by some change in circumstances, it comes in sight again.

Hannibal's Energy and Decision – His Steady Resolution and Unfaltering Courage

Hannibal was energetic and decided. The time for him to consider whether he would encounter the hostility of the Roman empire, aroused to the highest possible degree, was when his army was drawn up upon the banks of the Iberus, before they crossed it. The Iberus was his Rubicon. That line once overstepped, there was to be no further faltering. The difficulties, which arose from time to time to throw a cloud over his prospects, only seemed to stimulate him to fresh energy, and to awaken a new, though still a calm and steady resolution. It was so at the Pyrenees; it was so at the Rhône; it was so among the Alps, where the difficulties and dangers would have induced almost any other commander to have returned; and it was still so, now that he found himself shut in on every hand by the stern boundaries of Northern Italy, which he could not possibly hope again to pass, and the whole disposable force of the Roman empire, commanded, too, by one of *the consuls*, concentrated before him. The imminent danger produced no faltering, and apparently no fear.

Movements of Scipio

The armies were not yet in sight of each other. They were, in fact, yet on opposite sides of the river Po. The Roman commander concluded to march his troops across the river, and advance in search of Hannibal, who was still at some miles' distance. After considering the various means of crossing the stream, he decided finally on building a bridge.

Scipio's Bridge Over the Po – The Army Crosses the River

Military commanders generally throw some sort of a bridge across a stream of water lying in their way, if it is too deep to be easily forded, unless, indeed, it is so wide and rapid as to make the construction of the bridge difficult or impracticable. In this latter case they cross as well as they can by means of boats and rafts, and by swimming. The Po, though not a very large stream at this point, was too deep to be forded, and Scipio accordingly built a bridge.

The soldiers cut down the trees which grew in the forests along the banks, and after trimming off the tops and branches, they rolled the trunks into the water. They placed these trunks side by side, with others, laid transversely and pinned down, upon the top. Thus they formed rafts, which they placed in a line across the stream, securing them well to each other and to the banks. This made the foundation for the bridge, and after this foundation was covered with other materials, so as to make the upper surface a convenient roadway, the army were conducted across it, and then a small detachment of soldiers was stationed at each extremity of it as a guard.

Such a bridge as this answers a very good temporary purpose, and in still water, as, for example, over narrow lakes or very sluggish streams, where there is very little current, a floating structure of this kind is sometimes built for permanent service. Such bridges will not, however, stand on broad and rapid rivers liable to floods. The pressure of the water alone, in such cases, would very much endanger all the fastenings; and in cases where driftwood or ice is brought down by the stream, the floating masses, not being able to pass under the bridge, would accumulate above it, and would soon bear upon it with so enormous a pressure that nothing could withstand its force. The bridge would be broken away, and the whole accumulation – bridge, driftwood and ice – would be borne irresistibly down the stream together.

Hannibal's Warlike Operations

Scipio's bridge, however, answered very well for his purpose. His army passed over it in safety. When Hannibal heard of this, he knew that the battle was at hand. Hannibal was himself at this time about five miles distant. While Scipio was at work upon the bridge, Hannibal was employed, mainly, as he had been all the time since his descent from the mountains, in the subjugation of the various petty nations and tribes north of the Po. Some of them were well disposed to join his standard. Others were allies of the Romans, and wished to remain so. He made treaties and sent help to the former, and dispatched detachments of troops to intimidate and subdue the latter. When, however, he learned that Scipio had crossed the river, he ordered all these detachments to come immediately in, and he began to prepare in earnest for the contest that was impending.

He Concentrates His Army – Hannibal Promises His Soldiers Lands

He called together an assembly of his soldiers and announced to them finally that the battle was now nigh. He renewed the words of encouragement that he had spoken before, and in addition to what he then said, he now promised the soldiers rewards in land in case they proved victorious. 'I will give you each a farm,' said he, 'wherever you choose to have it, either in Africa, Italy, or Spain. If, instead of the land, any of you shall prefer to receive rather an equivalent in money, you shall have the reward in that form, and then you can return home and live with your friends, as before the war, under circumstances which will make you objects of envy to those who remained behind. If any of you would like to live in Carthage, I will have you made free citizens, so that you can live there in independence and honour.'

Ratifying a Promise

But what security would there be for the faithful fulfilment of these promises? In modern times such security is given by bonds, with pecuniary penalties, or by the deposit of titles to property in responsible hands. In ancient days they managed differently. The promiser bound himself by some solemn and formal mode of adjuration, accompanied, in important cases, with certain ceremonies, which were supposed to seal and confirm the obligation assumed. In this case, Hannibal brought a lamb in the presence of the assembled army. He held it before them with his left hand, while with his right he grasped a heavy stone. He then called aloud upon the gods, imploring them to destroy him as he was about to slay the lamb, if he failed to perform faithfully and fully the pledges that he had made. He then struck the poor lamb a heavy blow with the stone. The animal fell dead at his feet, and Hannibal was thenceforth bound, in the opinion of the army, by a very solemn obligation indeed, to be faithful in fulfilling his word.

Omens

The soldiers were greatly animated and excited by these promises, and were in haste to have the contest come on. The Roman soldiers, it seems, were in a different mood of mind. Some circumstances had occurred which they considered as bad omens, and they were very much dispirited and depressed by them. It is astonishing that men should ever allow their minds to be affected by such wholly accidental occurrences as these were. One of them was this: a wolf came into their camp, from one of the nearby forests, and after wounding several men, made his escape again. The other was more trifling still. A swarm of bees flew into the encampment, and lighted upon a tree just over Scipio's tent. This was considered, for some reason or other, a sign that some calamity was going to befall them, and the men were accordingly intimidated and disheartened. They consequently looked forward to the battle with uneasiness and anxiety, while the army of Hannibal anticipated it with eagerness and pleasure.

The Battle – Scipio Wounded – The Romans Driven Back Across the River

The battle came on, at last, very suddenly, and at a moment when neither party were expecting it. A large detachment of both armies were advancing toward the position of the other, near the river Ticinus, to reconnoitre, when they met, and the battle began.

Hannibal advanced with great impetuosity, and sent, at the same time, a detachment around to attack his enemy in the rear. The Romans soon began to fall into confusion; the horsemen and foot soldiers got entangled together; the men were trampled upon by the horses, and the horses were frightened by the men. In the midst of this scene, Scipio received a wound. A consul was a dignitary of very high consideration. He was, in fact, a sort of semi-king. The officers, and all the soldiers, so fast as they heard that the consul was wounded, were terrified and dismayed, and the Romans began to retreat.

Scipio had a young son, named also Scipio, who was then about 20 years of age. He was fighting by the side of his father when he received his wound. He protected his father, got him into the centre of a compact body of cavalry, and moved slowly off the ground, those in the rear facing toward the enemy and beating them back, as they pressed on in pursuit of them. In this way they reached their camp. Here they stopped for the night. They had fortified the place, and, as night was coming on, Hannibal thought it not prudent to press on and attack them there. He waited for the morning. Scipio, however, himself wounded and his army discouraged, thought it not prudent for him to wait until the morning.

At midnight he put his whole force in motion on a retreat. He kept the campfires burning and did everything else in his power to prevent the Carthaginians observing any indications of his departure. His army marched secretly and silently until they reached the river. They recrossed it by the bridge they had built, and then, cutting away the fastenings by which the different rafts were held together, the structure was at once destroyed, and the materials of which it was composed floated away, a mere mass of ruins, down the stream. From the Ticinus they floated, we may imagine, into the Po, and thence down the Po into the Adriatic Sea, where they drifted about upon the waste of waters until they were at last, one after another, driven by storms upon the sandy shores.

Chapter VII
The Apennines, 217 BCE

Hannibal Pursues the Romans – He Takes Some Prisoners

AS SOON AS HANNIBAL was apprised in the morning that Scipio and his forces had left their ground, he pressed on after them, very earnest to overtake them before they should reach the river. But he was too late. The main body of the Roman army had got over. There was, however, a detachment of a few hundred men, who had been left on Hannibal's side of the river to guard the bridge until all the army should have passed, and then to help in cutting it away. They had accomplished this before Hannibal's arrival, but had not had time to contrive any way to get across the river themselves. Hannibal took them all prisoners.

Revolt of Some Gauls from the Romans

The condition and prospects of both the Roman and Carthaginian cause were entirely changed by this battle, and the retreat of Scipio across the Po. All the nations of the north of Italy, who had been subjects or allies of the Romans, now turned to Hannibal. They sent embassies into his camp, offering him their friendship and alliance. In fact, there was a large body of Gauls in the Roman camp, who were fighting under Scipio at the battle of Ticinus, who deserted his standard immediately afterward, and came over in a mass to Hannibal. They made this revolt in the night, and, instead of stealing away secretly, they raised a prodigious tumult, killed the guards, filled the encampment with their shouts and outcries, and created for a time an awful scene of terror.

Hannibal received them, but he was too sagacious to admit such a treacherous horde into his army. He treated them with great consideration and kindness, and dismissed them with presents, that they might all go to their respective homes, charging them to exert their influence in his favour among the tribes to which they severally belonged.

Hannibal Crosses the River

Hannibal's soldiers, too, were very much encouraged by the commencement they had made. The army made immediate preparations for crossing the river. Some of the soldiers built rafts, others went up the stream in search of places to ford. Some swam across. They could adopt these or any other modes in safety, for the Romans made no stand on the opposite bank to oppose them, but moved rapidly on, as fast as Scipio could be carried. His wounds began to inflame and were extremely painful.

Dismay of the Romans – Sempronius Recalled to Italy

In fact, the Romans were dismayed at the danger which now threatened them. As soon as news of these events reached the city, the authorities there sent a dispatch immediately to Sicily to recall the other consul. His name was Sempronius. It will be recollected that, when the lots were cast between him and Scipio, it fell to Scipio to proceed to Spain, with a view to arresting Hannibal's march, while Sempronius went to Sicily and Africa. The object of this movement was to threaten and attack the Carthaginians at home, in order to distract their attention and prevent their sending any fresh forces to aid Hannibal, and, perhaps, even to compel them to recall him from Italy to defend their own capital. But now that Hannibal had not only passed the Alps, but had also crossed the Po, and was marching toward Rome – Scipio himself disabled, and his army flying before him – they were obliged at once to abandon the plan of threatening Carthage. They sent with all dispatch an order to Sempronius to hasten home and assist in the defence of Rome.

Sufferings of Scipio from His Wound – He is Joined by Sempronius

Sempronius was a man of a very prompt and impetuous character, with great confidence in his own powers, and very ready for action. He came immediately into Italy, recruited new soldiers for the army, put himself at the head of his forces, and marched northward to join Scipio in the valley of the Po. Scipio was suffering great pain from his wounds, and could do but little toward directing the operations of the army. He had slowly retreated before Hannibal, the fever and pain of his wounds being greatly exasperated by the motion of traveling. In this manner he arrived at the Trebia, a small stream flowing northward into the Po. He crossed this stream, and finding that he could not go any further, on account of the torturing pain to which it put him to be moved, he halted his army, marked out an encampment, threw up fortifications around it and prepared to make a stand. To his great relief, Sempronius soon came up and joined him here.

The Roman Commanders Disagree

There were now two generals. Napoleon used to say that one bad commander was better than two good ones, so essential is it to success in all military operations to secure that promptness, confidence and decision which can only exist where action is directed by one single mind. Sempronius and Scipio disagreed as to the proper course to be pursued. Sempronius wished to attack Hannibal immediately. Scipio was in favour of delay. Sempronius attributed Scipio's reluctance to give battle to the dejection of mind and discouragement produced by his wound, or to a feeling of envy lest he, Sempronius, should have the honour of conquering the Carthaginians, while he himself was helpless in his tent. On the other hand, Scipio thought Sempronius inconsiderate and reckless, and disposed to rush heedlessly into a contest with a foe whose powers and resources he did not understand.

Skirmishes – Sempronius Eager for a Battle

In the meantime, while the two commanders were thus divided in opinion, some skirmishes and small engagements took place between detachments from the two armies, in which Sempronius thought that the Romans had the advantage. This excited his enthusiasm more and more, and he became extremely desirous to bring on a general battle. He began to be quite out of patience with Scipio's caution and delay. The soldiers, he said, were full of strength and courage, all eager for the combat, and it was absurd to hold them back on account of the feebleness of one sick man. 'Besides,' said he, 'of what use can it be to delay any longer? We are as ready to meet the Carthaginians now as we shall ever be. There is no *third* consul to come and help us; and what a disgrace it is for us Romans, who in the former war led our troops to the very gates of Carthage, to allow Hannibal to bear sway over all the north of Italy, while we retreat gradually before him, afraid to encounter now a force that we have always conquered before.'

Hannibal's Stratagem

Hannibal was not long in learning, through his spies, that there was this difference of opinion between the Roman generals, and that Sempronius was full of a presumptuous sort of ardour, and he began to think that he could contrive some plan to draw the latter out into battle under circumstances in which he would have to act at a great disadvantage. He did contrive such a plan. It succeeded admirably; and the case was one of those numerous instances which occurred in the history of Hannibal, of successful stratagem, which led the Romans to say that his leading traits of character were treachery and cunning.

Details of Hannibal's Scheme

Hannibal's plan was, in a word, an attempt to draw the Roman army out of its encampment on a dark, cold and stormy night in December, and get them into the river. This river was the Trebia. It flowed north into the Po, between the Roman and Carthaginian camps. His scheme, in detail, was to send a part of his army over the river to attack the Romans in the night or very early in the morning. He hoped that by this means Sempronius would be induced to come out of his camp to attack the Carthaginians. The Carthaginians were then to fly and recross the river, and Hannibal hoped that Sempronius would follow, excited by the ardour of pursuit. Hannibal was then to have a strong reserve of the army, that had remained all the time in warmth and safety, to come out and attack the Romans with unimpaired strength and vigour, while the Romans themselves would be benumbed by the cold and wet, and disorganized by the confusion produced in crossing the stream.

The Ambuscade – Two Thousand Chosen Men

A part of Hannibal's reserve was to be placed in an ambuscade. There were some meadows near the water, which were covered in many places with tall grass and bushes. Hannibal went to examine the spot and found that this shrubbery was high enough for even horsemen to be concealed in it. He determined to place 1,000 foot soldiers and 1,000 horsemen here, the most efficient and courageous in the army. He selected them in the following manner:

Hannibal's Manner of Choosing Them

He called one of his lieutenant generals to the spot, explained somewhat of his design to him, and then asked him to go and choose from the cavalry and the infantry, 100 each, the best soldiers he could find. This 200 were then assembled, and Hannibal, after surveying them with looks of approbation and pleasure, said, 'Yes, you are the men I want, only, instead of 200, I need 2,000. Go back to the army, and select and bring to me, each of you, nine men like yourselves.' It is easy to be imagined that the soldiers were pleased with this commission, and that they executed it faithfully. The whole force thus chosen was soon assembled, and stationed in the thickets above described, where they lay in ambush ready to attack the Romans after they should pass the river.

Hannibal also made arrangements for leaving a large part of his army in his own camp, ready for battle, with orders that they should partake of food and refreshments, and keep themselves warm by the fires until they should be called upon. All things being thus ready, he detached a body of horsemen to cross the river and see if they could provoke the Romans to come out of their camp and pursue them.

'Go,' said Hannibal, to the commander of this detachment, 'pass the stream, advance to the Roman camp, assail the guards, and when the army forms and comes out to attack you, retreat slowly before them back across the river.'

Attack on the Roman Camp – Success of Hannibal's Stratagem – Sempronius Crosses the River

The detachment did as it was ordered to do. When they arrived at the camp, which was soon after break of day – for it was a part of Hannibal's plan to bring the Romans out before they should have had time to breakfast – Sempronius, at the first alarm, called all the soldiers to arms, supposing that the whole Carthaginian force was attacking them. It was a cold and stormy morning, and the atmosphere being filled with rain and snow, but little could be seen. Column after column of horsemen and of infantry marched out of the camp. The Carthaginians retreated. Sempronius was greatly excited at the idea of so easily driving back the assailants, and, as they retreated, he pressed on in pursuit of them.

As Hannibal had anticipated, he became so excited in the pursuit that he did not stop at the banks of the river. The Carthaginian horsemen plunged into the stream in their retreat, and the Romans, foot soldiers and horsemen together, followed on. The stream was usually small, but it was now swelled by the rain which had been falling all the night. The water was, of course, intensely cold. The horsemen got through tolerably well, but the foot soldiers were all thoroughly drenched and benumbed; and as they had not taken any food that morning, and had come forth on a very sudden call, and without any sufficient preparation, they felt the effects of the exposure in the strongest degree. Still they pressed on. They ascended the bank after crossing the river, and when they had formed again there, and were moving forward in pursuit of their still flying enemy, suddenly the whole force of Hannibal's reserves, strong and vigorous, just from their tents and their fires, burst upon them. They had scarcely recovered from the astonishment and the shock of this unexpected onset, when the 2,000 concealed in the ambuscade came sallying forth in the storm, and assailed the Romans in the rear with frightful shouts and outcries.

Situation of the Roman Army – Terrible Conflict

All these movements took place very rapidly. Only a very short period elapsed from the time that the Roman army, officers and soldiers, were quietly sleeping in their camp, or rising slowly to prepare for the routine of an ordinary day, before they found themselves all drawn out in battle array some miles from their encampment and surrounded and hemmed in by their foes. The events succeeded each other so rapidly as to appear to the soldiers like a dream; but very soon their wet and freezing clothes, their limbs benumbed and stiffened, the sleet which was driving along the plain, the endless lines of Carthaginian infantry, hemming them in on all sides, and the columns of horsemen and of elephants charging upon them, convinced them that their situation was one of dreadful reality.

The calamity, too, which threatened them was of vast extent, as well as imminent and terrible; for, though the stratagem of Hannibal was very simple in its plan and management, still he had executed it on a great scale, and had brought out the whole Roman army. There were, it is said, about 40,000 that crossed the river, and about an equal number in the Carthaginian army to oppose them. Such a body of combatants covered, of course, a large extent of ground, and the conflict that ensued was one of the most terrible scenes of the many that Hannibal assisted in enacting.

Utter Defeat of the Romans

The conflict continued for many hours, the Romans getting more and more into confusion all the time. The elephants of the Carthaginians, that is, the few that now remained, made great havoc in their ranks, and finally, after a combat of some hours, the whole army was broken up and fled, some portions in compact bodies, as their officers could keep them together, and others in hopeless and inextricable confusion. They made their way back to the river, which they reached at various points up and down the stream. In the meantime, the continued rain had swollen the waters still more, the lowlands were overflowed, the deep places concealed, and the broad expanse of water in the centre of the stream whirled in boiling and turbid eddies, whose surface was roughened by the December breeze, and dotted everywhere with the drops of rain still falling.

Scene After the Battle

When the Roman army was thoroughly broken up and scattered, the Carthaginians gave up the further prosecution of the contest. They were too wet, cold and exhausted themselves to feel any ardour in the pursuit of their enemies. Vast numbers of the Romans, however, attempted to recross the river, and were swept down and destroyed by the merciless flood, whose force they had not strength enough remaining to withstand. Other portions of the troops lay hid in lurking-places to which they had retreated, until night came on, and then they made rafts on which they contrived to float themselves back across the stream. Hannibal's troops were too wet, cold and exhausted to go out again into the storm, and so they were unmolested in these attempts. Notwithstanding this, however, great numbers of them were carried down the stream and lost.

Various Battles of Hannibal – Scarcity of Food

It was now December, too late for Hannibal to attempt to advance much further that season, and yet the way before him was open to the Apennines, by the defeat of Sempronius, for neither he nor Scipio could now hope to make another stand against him till they should receive new re-enforcements from Rome. During the winter months Hannibal had various battles and adventures, sometimes with portions and detachments of the Roman army, and sometimes with the native tribes. He was sometimes in great difficulty for want of food for his army, until at length he bribed the governor of a castle, where a Roman granary was kept, to deliver it up to him, and after that he was well supplied.

The natives of the country were, however, not at all well disposed toward him, and in the course of the winter they attempted to impede his operations, and to harass his army by every means in their power. Finding his situation uncomfortable, he moved on toward the south, and at length determined that, inclement as the season was, he would cross the Apennines.

Valley of the Arno

The great valley of the Po extends across the whole north of Italy. The valley of the Arno and of the Umbro lies south of it, separated from it by a part of the Apennine chain. This southern valley was Etruria. Hannibal decided to attempt to pass over the mountains into Etruria. He thought he should find there a warmer climate, and inhabitants more well-disposed toward him, besides being so much nearer Rome.

Crossing the Apennines – Terrific Storm – Death of the Elephants

Though Hannibal conquered the Alps, the Apennines conquered him. A very violent storm arose just as he reached the most exposed place among the mountains. It was intensely cold, and the wind blew the hail and snow directly into the faces of the troops, so that it was impossible for them to proceed. They halted and turned their backs to the storm, but the wind increased more and more, and was attended with terrific thunder and lightning, which filled the soldiers with alarm, as they were at such an altitude as to be themselves enveloped in the clouds from which the peals and flashes were emitted.

Unwilling to retreat, Hannibal ordered the army to encamp on the spot, in the best shelter they could find. They attempted, accordingly, to pitch their tents, but it was impossible to secure them. The wind increased to a hurricane. The tent poles were unmanageable, and the roof material was carried away from its fastenings, and sometimes split or blown into rags by its flapping in the wind. The poor elephants, that is, all that were left of them from previous battles and exposures, sunk down under this intense cold and died. One only remained alive.

Hannibal's Uneasiness

Hannibal ordered a retreat, and the army went back into the valley of the Po. But Hannibal was ill at ease here. The natives of the country were very weary of his presence. His army consumed their food, ravaged their country and destroyed all their peace and happiness. Hannibal suspected them of a design to poison him or assassinate him in some other way. He was continually watching and taking precautions against these attempts. He had a great many different dresses made to be used as disguises, and false hair of different colours and fashion, so that he could alter his appearance at pleasure. This was to prevent any spy or assassin who might come into his camp from identifying him by any description of his dress and appearance. Still, notwithstanding these precautions, he was ill at ease, and at the very earliest practicable period in the spring he made a new attempt to cross the mountains, and was now successful.

He Crosses the Apennines

On descending the southern declivities of the Apennines, he learned that a new Roman army, under a new consul, was advancing toward him from the south. He was eager to meet this force, and was preparing to press forward at once by the nearest way. He found, however, that this would lead him across the lower part of the valley of the Arno, which was here very broad, and, though usually passable, was now overflowed in consequence of the swelling of the waters of the river by the melting of the snows upon the mountains. The whole country was now, in fact, a vast expanse of marshes and fens.

Perilous March – Hannibal's Sickness

Still, Hannibal concluded to cross it, and, in the attempt, he involved his army in difficulties and dangers as great, almost, as he had encountered upon the Alps. The waters were rising continually; they filled all the channels and spread over extended plains. They were so turbid, too, that everything beneath the surface was concealed, and the soldiers wading in them were continually sinking into deep and sudden channels and into bogs of mire, where many were lost. They were all exhausted and worn out by the wet and cold, and the long continuance of their exposure to it. They were four days and three nights in this situation, as their progress was, of course, extremely slow.

The men, during all this time, had scarcely any sleep, and in some places the only way by which they could get any repose was to lay their arms and their baggage in the standing water, so as to build, by this means, a sort of couch or platform on which they could lie. Hannibal himself was sick too. He was attacked with a violent inflammation of the eyes, and the sight of one of them was in the end destroyed. He was not, however, so much exposed as the other officers; for there was one elephant left of all those that had commenced the march in Spain, and Hannibal rode this elephant during the four days' march through the water. There were guides and attendants to precede him, for the purpose of finding a safe and practicable road, and by their aid, with the help of the animal's sagacity, he got safely through.

Chapter VIII
The Dictator Fabius, 216 BCE

Alarm at Rome – The Consul Flaminius

IN THE MEANTIME, while Hannibal was thus rapidly making his way toward the gates of Rome, the people of the city became more and more alarmed, until at last a general feeling of terror pervaded all the ranks of society. Citizens and soldiers were struck with one common dread. They had raised a new army and put it under the command of a new consul, for the terms of service of the others had expired. Flaminius was the name of this new commander, and he was moving northward at the head of his forces at the time that Hannibal was conducting his troops with so much labour and difficulty through the meadows and morasses of the Arno.

Another Stratagem – Confidence of Flaminius

This army was, however, no more successful than its predecessors had been. Hannibal contrived to entrap Flaminius by a stratagem, as he had entrapped Sempronius before. There is in the eastern part of Etruria, near the mountains, a lake called Lake Trasimene. It happened that this lake extended so near to the base of the mountains as to leave only a narrow passage between – a passage but little wider than was necessary for a road. Hannibal contrived to station a detachment of his troops in ambuscade at the foot of the mountains, and others on the declivities above, and then in some way or other to entice Flaminius and his army through the defile. Flaminius was, like Sempronius, ardent, self-confident and vain. He despised the power of Hannibal, and thought that his success hitherto had been owing to the inefficiency or indecision of his predecessors. For his part, his only anxiety was to encounter him, for he was sure of an easy victory. He advanced, therefore, boldly and without concern into the pass of Trasimene, when he learned that Hannibal was encamped beyond it.

Complete Rout of the Romans

Hannibal had established an encampment openly on some elevated ground beyond the pass, and as Flaminius and his troops came into the narrowest part of the defile, they saw this encampment at a distance before them, with a broad plain beyond the pass intervening. They supposed that the whole force of the enemy was there, not dreaming of the presence of the strong detachments which were hid on the slopes of the mountains above them and were looking down upon them at that very moment from behind rocks and bushes. When, therefore, the Romans had got through the pass, they spread out upon the plain beyond it, and were advancing to the camp, when suddenly the secreted troops burst forth from their ambuscade, and, pouring down the mountains, took complete possession of the pass, and attacked the Romans in the rear, while Hannibal attacked them in the van. Another long, desperate and bloody contest ensued. The Romans were beaten at every point, and, as they were hemmed in between the lake, the mountain and the pass, they could not retreat; the army was, accordingly, almost wholly cut to pieces. Flaminius himself was killed.

Effects of the Battle

The news of this battle spread everywhere, and produced the strongest sensation. Hannibal sent dispatches to Carthage announcing what he considered his final victory over the great foe, and the news was received with the greatest rejoicings. At Rome, on the other hand, the news produced a dreadful shock of disappointment and terror. It seemed as if the last hope of resisting the progress of their terrible enemy was gone, and that they had nothing now to do but to sink down in despair and await the hour when his columns should come pouring in through the gates of the city.

Panic of the Romans – Their Superstitious Fears

The people of Rome were, in fact, prepared for a panic, for their fears had been increasing and gathering strength for some time. They were very superstitious in those ancient days in respect to signs and omens. A thousand trifling occurrences, which would, at the present day, be considered of no consequence whatever, were then considered bad signs, auguring terrible calamities; and, on occasions like these, when calamities seemed to be impending, everything was noticed, and circumstances, which would not have been regarded at all at ordinary times, were reported from one to another, the stories being exaggerated as they spread, until the imaginations of the people were filled with mysterious but invincible fears. So universal was the belief in these prodigies and omens, that they were sometimes formally reported to the senate, committees were appointed to inquire into them, and solemn sacrifices were offered to 'expiate them', as it was termed, that is, to avert the displeasure of the gods, which the omens were supposed to foreshadow and portend.

Omens and Bad Signs

A very curious list of these omens was reported to the senate during the winter and spring in which Hannibal was advancing toward Rome. An ox from the cattle market had got into a house, and, lósing his way, had climbed up into the third story, and, being frightened by the noise and uproar of those who followed him, ran out of a window and fell down to the ground. A light appeared in the sky in the form of ships. A temple was struck with lightning. A spear in the hand of a statue of Juno, a celebrated goddess, shook, one day, of itself. Apparitions of men in white garments were seen in a certain place. A wolf came into a camp and snatched the sword of a soldier on guard out of his hands, and ran away with it. The sun one day looked smaller than usual. Two moons were seen together in the sky. This was in the daytime, and one of the moons was doubtless a halo or a white cloud. Stones fell out of the sky at a place called Picenum. This was one of the most dreadful of all the omens, though it is now known to be a common occurrence.

Curious Transformations

These omens were all, doubtless, real occurrences, more or less remarkable, it is true, but, of course, entirely unmeaning in respect to their being indications of impending calamities. There were other things reported to the senate which must have originated almost wholly in the imaginations and fears of the observers. Two shields, it was said, in a certain camp, sweated blood. Some people were reaping, and bloody ears of grain fell into the basket. This, of course, must have been wholly imaginary, unless, indeed, one of the reapers had cut his fingers with the sickle. Some streams and fountains became bloody; and, finally, in one place in the country, some goats turned into sheep. A hen, also, became a cock, and a cock changed to a hen.

Their Influence – Importance Attached to These Stories

Such ridiculous stories would not be worthy of a moment's attention now, were it not for the degree of importance attached to them then. They were formally reported to the Roman senate, the witnesses who asserted that they had seen them were called in and examined, and a solemn debate was held on the question what should be done to avert the supernatural influences of evil which the omens expressed. The senate decided to have three days of expiation and sacrifice, during which the whole people of Rome devoted themselves to the religious observances which they thought calculated to appease the wrath of Heaven. They made various offerings and gifts to the different gods, among which one was a golden thunderbolt of 50 pounds' weight, manufactured for Jupiter, whom they considered the thunderer.

Feverish Excitement at Rome – News of the Battle

All these things took place before the battle at Lake Trasimene, so that the whole community were in a feverish state of excitement and anxiety before the news from Flaminius arrived. When these tidings at last came, they threw the whole city into utter consternation. Of course, the messenger went directly to the senate-house to report to the government, but the story that such news had arrived soon spread about the city, and the whole population crowded into the streets and public squares, all eagerly asking for the tidings.

An enormous throng assembled before the senate-house calling for information. A public officer appeared at last, and said to them in a loud voice, 'We have been defeated in a great battle.' He would say no more. Still rumours spread from one to another, until it was generally known throughout the city that Hannibal had conquered the Roman army again in a great battle, that great numbers of the soldiers had fallen or been taken prisoners and that the consul himself was slain.

Gatherings of the People – Arrival of Stragglers

The night was passed in great anxiety and terror, and the next day, and for several of the succeeding days, the people gathered in great numbers around the gates, inquiring eagerly for news of every one that came in from the country. Pretty soon scattered soldiers and small bodies of troops began to arrive, bringing with them information of the battle, each one having a different tale to tell, according to his own individual experience in the scene.

Whenever these men arrived, the people of the city, and especially the women who had husbands or sons in the army, crowded around them, overwhelming them with questions, and making them tell their tale again and again, as if the intolerable suspense and anxiety of the hearers could not be satisfied. The intelligence was such as in general to confirm and increase the fears of those who listened to it; but sometimes, when it made known the safety of a husband or a son, it produced as much relief and rejoicing as it did in other cases terror and despair. That maternal love was as strong an impulse in those rough days as it is in the more refined and cultivated periods of the present age, is evinced by the fact that two of these Roman mothers, on seeing their sons coming suddenly into their presence, alive and well, when they had heard that they had fallen in battle, were killed at once by the shock of surprise and joy, as if by a blow.

Appointment of a Dictator – Fabius

In seasons of great and imminent danger to the commonwealth, it was the custom of the Romans to appoint what they called a *dictator*, that is, a supreme executive, who was clothed with absolute and unlimited powers; and it devolved on him to save the state from the threatened ruin by the most prompt and energetic action. This case was obviously one of the emergencies requiring such a measure. There was no time for deliberations and debates; for deliberations and debates, in periods of such excitement and danger, become disputes, and end in tumult and uproar. Hannibal was at the head of a victorious army, ravaging the country which he had already conquered, and with no obstacle between him and the city itself. It was an emergency calling for the appointment of a *dictator*. The people made choice of a man of great reputation for experience and wisdom, named Fabius, and placed the whole power of the state in his hands. All other authority was suspended, and everything was subjected to his sway. The whole city, with the life and property of every inhabitant, was placed at his disposal; the army and the fleets were also under his command, even the consuls being subject to his orders.

Measures of Fabius – Religious Ceremonies

Fabius accepted the vast responsibility which his election imposed upon him, and immediately began to take the necessary measures. He first made arrangements for performing solemn religious ceremonies to expiate the omens and propitiate the gods. He brought out all the people in great convocations, and made them take vows, in the most formal and imposing manner, promising offerings and celebrations in honour of the various gods, at some future time, in case these divinities would avert the threatening danger. It is doubtful, however, whether Fabius, in doing these things, really believed that they had any actual efficiency, or whether he resorted to them as a means of calming and quieting the minds of the people and producing that composure and confidence which always results from a hope of the favour of Heaven. If this last was his object, his conduct was eminently wise.

Minucius – Supreme Authority of a Dictator

Fabius, also, immediately ordered a large levy of troops to be made. His second in command, called his *Master of Horse*, was directed to make this levy, and to assemble the troops at a place called Tibur, a few miles east of the city. There was always a Master of Horse appointed to attend upon and second a dictator. The name of this officer in the case of Fabius was Minucius. Minucius was as ardent, prompt and impetuous as Fabius was cool, prudent and calculating. He levied the troops and brought them to their place of rendezvous. Fabius went out to take the command of them.

One of the consuls was coming to join him, with a body of troops which he had under his command. Fabius sent word to him that he must come without any of the insignia of his authority, as all his authority, semi-regal as it was in ordinary times, was superseded and overruled in the presence of a dictator. A consul was accustomed to move in great state on all occasions. He was preceded by 12 men (*lictores*), bearing badges and insignia (*fasces*), to impress the army and the people with a sense of the greatness of his dignity. To see, therefore, a consul divested of all these marks of his power, and coming into the dictator's presence as any other officer would come before an acknowledged superior, made the army of Fabius feel a very strong sense of the greatness of their new commander's dignity and power.

Proclamation of Fabius

Fabius then issued a proclamation, which he sent by proper messengers into all the region of country around Rome, especially to that part toward the territory which was in possession of Hannibal. In this proclamation he ordered all the people to abandon the country and the towns which were not strongly fortified, and to seek shelter in the fortresses, forts and fortified cities. They were commanded, also, to lay waste the country which they should leave, and destroy all the property, and especially all the provisions, which they could not take to their places of refuge. This being done,

Fabius placed himself at the head of the forces which he had got together, and moved on, cautiously and with great circumspection, in search of his enemy.

Progress of Hannibal

In the meantime, Hannibal had crossed over to the eastern side of Italy, and had passed down, conquering and ravaging the country as he went, until he got considerably south of Rome. He seems to have thought it not quite prudent to advance to the actual attack of the city after the Battle of Lake Trasimene; for the vast population of Rome was sufficient, if rendered desperate by his actually threatening the capture and pillage of the city, to overwhelm his army entirely. So he moved to the eastward, and advanced on that side until he had passed the city, and thus it happened that Fabius had to march to the southward and eastward in order to meet him. The two armies came in sight of each other quite on the eastern side of Italy, very near the shores of the Adriatic Sea.

Policy of Fabius – He Declines Fighting

The policy which Fabius resolved to adopt was not to give Hannibal battle but to watch him and wear his army out by fatigue and delays. He kept, therefore, near him, but always posted his army on advantageous ground, which all the defiance and provocations of Hannibal could not induce him to leave. When Hannibal moved, which he was soon compelled to do to procure provisions, Fabius would move too, but only to post and entrench himself in some place of security as before. Hannibal did everything in his power to bring Fabius to battle, but all his efforts were unavailing.

Hannibal's Danger – Stratagem of the Fiery Oxen

In fact, he himself was at one time in imminent danger. He had got drawn, by Fabius's good management, into a place where he was surrounded by mountains, upon which Fabius had posted his troops, and there was only one defile which offered any egress, and this, too, Fabius had strongly guarded. Hannibal resorted to his usual resource, cunning and stratagem, for means of escape.

He collected a herd of oxen. He tied fagots across their horns, filling the fagots with pitch, so as to make them highly combustible. In the night on which he was going to attempt to pass the defile, he ordered his army to be ready to march through, and then had the oxen driven up the hills around on the further side of the Roman detachment which was guarding the pass. The fagots were then lighted on the horns of the oxen. They ran about, frightened and infuriated by the fire, which burned their horns to the quick, and blinded them with the sparks which fell from it. The leaves and branches of the forests were set on fire. A great commotion was thus made, and the guards, seeing the moving lights and hearing the tumult, supposed that the Carthaginian army were upon the heights, and were coming down to attack them. They turned out in great hurry and confusion to meet the imaginary foe, leaving the pass unguarded, and, while they were pursuing the bonfires on the oxen's heads into all sorts of dangerous and impracticable places, Hannibal quietly marched his army through the defile and reached a place of safety.

Unpopularity of Fabius

Although Fabius kept Hannibal employed and prevented his approaching the city, still there soon began to be felt a considerable degree of dissatisfaction that he did not act more decidedly. Minucius was continually urging him to give Hannibal battle and, not being able to induce him to do so, he was continually expressing his discontent and displeasure. The army sympathized with Minucius. He wrote home to Rome too, complaining bitterly of the dictator's inefficiency. Hannibal learned all this by means of his spies, and other sources of information, which so good a contriver as he has always at command. Hannibal was, of course, very much pleased to hear of these dissensions, and of the unpopularity of Fabius. He considered such an enemy as he – so prudent, cautious and watchful – as a far more dangerous foe than such bold and impetuous commanders as Flaminius and Minucius, whom he could always entice into difficulty, and then easily conquer.

Hannibal's Sagacity

Hannibal thought he would render Minucius a little help in making Fabius unpopular. He found out from some Roman deserters that the dictator possessed a valuable farm in the country, and he sent a detachment of his troops there, with orders to plunder and destroy the property all around it, but to leave the farm of Fabius untouched and in safety. The object was to give to the enemies of Fabius at Rome occasion to say that there was secretly a good understanding between him and Hannibal, and that he was kept back from acting boldly in defence of his country by some corrupt bargain which he had traitorously made with the enemy.

Plots Against Fabius

These plans succeeded. Discontent and dissatisfaction spread rapidly, both in the camp and in the city. At Rome they made an urgent demand upon Fabius to return, ostensibly because they wished him to take part in some great religious ceremonies, but really to remove him from the camp, and give Minucius an opportunity to attack Hannibal. They also wished to devise some method, if possible, of depriving him of his power. He had been appointed for six months, and the time had not yet nearly expired: but they wished to shorten, or, if they could not shorten, to limit and diminish his power.

He Goes to Rome – Minucius Risks a Battle

Fabius went to Rome, leaving the army under the orders of Minucius, but commanding him positively not to give Hannibal battle, nor expose his troops to any danger, but to pursue steadily the same policy which he himself had followed. He had, however, been in Rome only a short time before tidings came that Minucius had fought a battle and gained a victory. There were boastful and ostentatious letters from Minucius to the Roman senate, lauding the exploit which he had performed.

Speech of Fabius

Fabius carefully examined the accounts. He compared one thing with another, and satisfied himself of what afterward proved to be the truth, that Minucius had gained no victory at all. He had lost 5,000 or 6,000 men, and Hannibal had lost no more, and Fabius showed that no advantage had been gained. He urged upon the senate the importance of adhering to the line of policy he had pursued, and the danger of risking everything, as Minucius had done, on the fortunes of a single battle. Besides, he said, Minucius had disobeyed his orders, which were distinct and positive, and he deserved to be recalled.

In saying these things Fabius irritated and exasperated his enemies more than ever. 'Here is a man,' said they, 'who will not only not fight the enemies whom he is sent against himself, but he will not allow anybody else to fight them. Even at this distance, when his second in command has obtained a victory, he will not admit it, and endeavours to curtail the advantages of it. He wishes to protract the war, that he may the longer continue to enjoy the supreme and unlimited authority with which we have intrusted him.'

Fabius Returns to the Army – He is Deprived of the Supreme Power

The hostility to Fabius at last reached such a pitch, that it was proposed in an assembly of the people to make Minucius his equal in command. Fabius, having finished the business which called him to Rome, did not wait to attend to the discussion of this question, but left the city, and was proceeding on his way to join the army again when he was overtaken with a messenger bearing a letter informing him that the decree had passed, and that he must thenceforth consider Minucius as his colleague and equal. Minucius was, of course, extremely elated at this result. 'Now,' said he, 'we will see if something cannot be done.'

Division of Power

The first question was, however, to decide on what principle and in what way they should share their power. 'We cannot both command at once,' said Minucius. 'Let us exercise the power in alternation, each one being in authority for a day, or a week, or a month, or any other period that you prefer.'

'No,' replied Fabius, 'we will not divide the time, we will divide the men. There are four legions. You shall take two of them, and the other two shall be mine. I can thus, perhaps, save half the army from the dangers in which I fear your impetuosity will plunge all whom you have under your command.'

Ambuscade of Hannibal – Hannibal's Success

This plan was adopted. The army was divided, and each portion went, under its own leader, to its separate encampment. The result was one of the most curious and extraordinary occurrences that is recorded in the history of nations.

Hannibal, who was well informed of all these transactions, immediately felt that Minucius was in his power. He knew that he was so eager for battle that it would be easy to entice him into it, under almost any circumstances that he himself might choose to arrange. Accordingly, he watched his opportunity when there was a good place for an ambuscade near Minucius's camp, and lodged 5,000 men in it in such a manner that they were concealed by rocks and other obstructions to the view. There was a hill between this ground and the camp of Minucius. When the ambuscade was ready, Hannibal sent up a small force to take possession of the top of the hill, anticipating that Minucius would at once send up a stronger force to drive them away. He did so. Hannibal then sent up more as a re-enforcement. Minucius, whose spirit and pride were now aroused, sent up more still, and thus, by degrees, Hannibal drew out his enemy's whole force, and then, ordering his own troops to retreat before them, the Romans were drawn on, down the hill, till they were surrounded by the ambuscade. These hidden troops then came pouring out upon them, and in a short time the Romans were thrown into utter confusion, flying in all directions before their enemies, and entirely at their mercy.

Fabius Comes to the Rescue – Speech of Minucius

All would have been irretrievably lost had it not been for the interposition of Fabius. He received intelligence of the danger at his own camp, and marched out at once with all his force, and arrived upon the ground so opportunely, and acted so efficiently, that he at once completely changed the fortune of the day. He saved Minucius and his half of the army from utter destruction. The Carthaginians retreated in their turn, Hannibal being entirely overwhelmed with disappointment and vexation at being thus deprived of his prey.

History relates that Minucius had the candour and good sense, after this, to acknowledge his error, and yield to the guidance and direction of Fabius. He called his part of the army together when they reached their camp, and addressed them thus: 'Fellow soldiers, I have often heard it said that the wisest men are those who possess wisdom and sagacity themselves, and, next to them, those who know how to perceive and are willing to be guided by the wisdom and sagacity of others; while they are fools who do not know how to conduct themselves, and will not be guided by those who do. We will not belong to this last class; and since it is proved that we are not entitled to rank with the first, let us join the second. We will march to the camp of Fabius, and join our camp with his, as before. We owe to him, and also to all his portion of the army, our eternal gratitude for the nobleness of spirit which he manifested in coming to our deliverance, when he might so justly have left us to ourselves.'

The Roman Army Again United

The two legions repaired, accordingly, to the camp of Fabius, and a complete and permanent reconciliation took place between the two divisions of the army. Fabius rose very high in the general esteem by this transaction. The term of his dictatorship, however, expired soon after this, and as the danger from Hannibal was now less imminent, the office was not renewed, but consuls were chosen as before.

Character of Fabius – His Integrity

The character of Fabius has been regarded with the highest admiration by all mankind. He evinced a very noble spirit in all that he did. One of his last acts was a very striking proof of this. He had bargained with Hannibal to pay a certain sum of money as ransom for a number of prisoners which had fallen into his hands, and whom Hannibal, on the faith of that promise, had released. Fabius believed that the Romans would readily ratify the treaty and pay the amount; but they demurred, being displeased, or pretending to be displeased, because Fabius had not consulted them before making the arrangement. Fabius, in order to preserve his own and his country's faith unsullied, sold his farm to raise the money. He did thus most certainly protect and vindicate his own honour, but he can hardly be said to have saved that of the people of Rome.

Chapter IX
The Battle of Cannae, 215 BCE

Interest Excited by the Battle of Cannae

THE BATTLE OF CANNAE was the last great battle fought by Hannibal in Italy. This conflict has been greatly celebrated in history, not only for its magnitude, and the terrible desperation with which it was

fought, but also on account of the strong dramatic interest which the circumstances attending it are fitted to excite. This interest is perhaps, however, quite as much due to the peculiar skill of the ancient historian who narrates the story, as to the events themselves which he records.

Various Military Operations – State of the Public Mind at Rome

It was about a year after the close of the dictatorship of Fabius that this battle was fought. That interval had been spent by the Roman consuls who were in office during that time in various military operations, which did not, however, lead to any decisive results. In the meantime, there were great uneasiness, discontent and dissatisfaction at Rome. To have such a dangerous and terrible foe, at the head of 40,000 men, infesting the vicinity of their city, ravaging the territories of their friends and allies and threatening continually to attack the city itself, was a continual source of anxiety and vexation. It mortified the Roman pride, too, to find that the greatest armies they could raise, and the ablest generals they could choose and commission, proved wholly unable to cope with the foe. The most sagacious of them, in fact, had felt it necessary to decline the contest with him altogether.

The Plebeians and Patricians – The Consuls Aemilius and Varro

This state of things produced a great deal of ill humour in the city. Party spirit ran very high; tumultuous assemblies were held; disputes and contentions prevailed, and mutual criminations and recriminations without end. There were two great parties formed: that of the middling classes on one side, and the aristocracy on the other. The former were called the Plebeians, the latter the Patricians. The division between these two classes was very great and very strongly marked.

There was, in consequence of it, infinite difficulty in the election of consuls. At last the consuls were chosen, one from each party. The name of the patrician was Paulus Aemilius. The name of the plebeian was Varro. They were inducted into office, and were thus put jointly into possession of a vast power, to wield which with any efficiency and success would seem to require union and harmony in those who held it, and yet Aemilius and Varro were inveterate and implacable political foes. It was often so in the Roman government. The consulship was a double-headed monster, which spent half its strength in bitter contests waged between its members.

A New Army Raised

The Romans determined now to make an effectual effort to rid themselves of their foe. They raised an enormous army. It consisted of eight legions. The Roman legion was an army of itself. It contained ordinarily 4,000 foot soldiers and a troop of 300 horsemen. It was very unusual to have more than two or three legions in the field at a time. The Romans, however, on this occasion, increased the number of the legions, and also augmented their size, so that they contained, each, 5,000 infantry and 400 cavalry. They were determined to make a great and last effort to defend their city and save the commonwealth from ruin. Aemilius and Varro prepared to take command of this great force, with very strong determinations to make it the means of Hannibal's destruction.

Self-Confidence of Varro

The characters of the two commanders, however, as well as their political connections, were very dissimilar, and they soon began to manifest a very different spirit, and to assume a very different air and bearing, each from the other. Aemilius was a friend of Fabius, and approved of his policy. Varro was for greater promptness and decision. He made great promises, and spoke with the utmost confidence of being able to annihilate Hannibal at a blow. He condemned the policy of Fabius in attempting to wear out the enemy by delays. He said it was a plan of the aristocratic party to protract the war in order to put themselves in high offices and perpetuate their importance and influence. The war might have been ended long ago, he said; and he would promise the people that he would now end it, without fail, the very day that he came in sight of Hannibal.

Caution of Aemilius – Views of Aemilius

As for Aemilius, he assumed a very different tone. He was surprised, he said, that any man could pretend to decide before he had even left the city, and while he was, of course, entirely ignorant, both of the condition of their own army, and of the position, designs and strength of the enemy, how soon and under what circumstances it would be wise to give him battle. Plans must be formed in adaptation to circumstances, as circumstances cannot be made to alter to suit plans. He believed that they should succeed in the encounter with Hannibal, but he thought that their only hope of success must be based on the exercise of prudence, caution and sagacity; he was sure that rashness and folly could only lead in future, as they had always done in the past, to discomfiture and ruin.

Counsel of Fabius – Conversation Between Fabius and Aemilius

It is said that Fabius, the former dictator, conversed with Aemilius before his departure for the army, and gave him such counsel as his age and experience, and his knowledge of the character and operations of Hannibal, suggested to his mind.

'If you had a colleague like yourself,' said he, 'I would not offer you any advice; you would not need it. Or, if you were yourself like your colleague, vain, self-conceited and presumptuous, then I would be silent; counsel would be thrown away upon you. But as it is, while you have great judgment and sagacity to guide you, you are to be placed in a situation of extreme difficulty and peril. If I am not mistaken, the greatest difficulty you will have to encounter will not be the open enemy you are going to meet upon the field. You will find, I think, that Varro will give quite as much trouble as Hannibal. He will be presumptuous, reckless and headstrong. He will inspire all the rash and ardent young men in the army with his own enthusiastic folly, and we shall be very fortunate if we do not yet see the terrible and bloody scenes of Lake Trasimene acted again.

'I am sure that the true policy for us to adopt is the one which I marked out. That is always the proper course for the invaded to pursue with invaders, where there is the least doubt of the success of a battle. We grow strong while Hannibal grows continually weaker by delay. He can only prosper so long as he can fight battles and perform brilliant exploits. If we deprive him of this power, his strength will be continually wasting away, and the spirit and courage of his men waning. He has now scarce a third part of the army which he had when he crossed the Iberus, and nothing can save this remnant from destruction if we are wise.'

Resolution of Aemilius

Aemilius said, in reply to this, that he went into the contest with very little of encouragement or hope. If Fabius had found it so difficult to withstand the turbulent influences of his Master of Horse, who was his subordinate officer, and, as such, under his command, how could *he* expect to restrain his colleague, who was entitled, by his office, to full equality with him. But, notwithstanding the difficulties which he foresaw, he was going to do his duty, and abide by the result; and if the result should be unfavourable, he should seek for death in the conflict, for death by Carthaginian spears was a far lighter evil, in his view, than the displeasure and censures of his countrymen.

The Consuls Join the Army

The consuls departed from Rome to join the army, Aemilius attended by a moderate number of men of rank and station, and Varro by a much larger train, though it was formed of people of the lower classes of society. The army was organized, and the arrangements of the encampments perfected. One ceremony was that of administering an oath to the soldiers, as was usual in the Roman armies at the commencement of a campaign. They were made to swear that they would not desert the army, that they would never abandon the post at which they were stationed in fear or in flight, nor leave the ranks except for the purpose of taking up or recovering a weapon, striking an enemy or protecting a friend. These and other arrangements being completed, the army was ready for the field. The consuls made a different arrangement in respect to the division of their power from that adopted by Fabius and Minucius. It was agreed between them that they would exercise their common authority alternately, each for a day.

Situation of Hannibal – Scarcity of Food

In the meantime, Hannibal began to find himself reduced to great difficulty in obtaining provisions for his men. The policy of Fabius had been so far successful as to place him in a very embarrassing situation, and one growing more and more embarrassing every day. He could obtain no food except what he got by plunder, and there was now very little opportunity for that, as the inhabitants of the country had carried off all the grain and deposited it in strongly fortified towns; and though Hannibal had great confidence in his power to cope with the Roman army in a regular battle on an open field, he had not strength sufficient to reduce citadels or attack fortified camps. His stock of provisions had become, therefore, more and more nearly exhausted, until now he had a supply for only 10 days, and he saw no possible mode of increasing it.

Sufferings of Hannibal's Troops

His great object was, therefore, to bring on a battle. Varro was ready and willing to give him battle, but Aemilius, or, to call him by his name in full, Paulus Aemilius, which is the appellation by which he is more frequently known, was very desirous to persevere in the Fabian policy until the 10 days had expired, after which he knew that Hannibal must be reduced to extreme distress, and might have to surrender at once to save his army from actual famine. In fact, it was said that the troops were on such short allowance as to produce great discontent, and that a large body of Spaniards were preparing to desert and go over together to the Roman camp.

Defeat of a Foraging Party

Things were in this state, when, one day, Hannibal sent out a party from his camp to procure food, and Aemilius, who happened to hold the command that day, sent out a strong force to intercept them. He was successful. The Carthaginian detachment was routed. Nearly 2,000 men were killed, and the rest fled, by any roads they could find, back to Hannibal's camp. Varro was very eager to follow them there, but Aemilius ordered his men to halt. He was afraid of some trick or treachery on the part of Hannibal, and was disposed to be satisfied with the victory he had already won.

Hannibal's Pretended Abandonment of His Camp

This little success, however, only inflamed Varro's ardour for a battle, and produced a general enthusiasm in the Roman army; and, a day or two afterward, a circumstance occurred which raised this excitement to the highest pitch.

Some reconnoitrers, who had been stationed within sight of Hannibal's camp to watch the motions and indications there, sent in word to the consuls that the

Carthaginian guards around their encampment had all suddenly disappeared, and that a very extraordinary and unusual silence reigned within. Parties of the Roman soldiers went up gradually and cautiously to the Carthaginian lines, and soon found that the camp was deserted, though the fires were still burning and the tents remained. This intelligence, of course, put the whole Roman army into a fever of excitement and agitation. They crowded around the consuls' pavilions, and clamorously insisted on being led on to take possession of the camp, and to pursue the enemy. 'He has fled,' they said, 'and with such precipitation that he has left the tents standing and his fires still burning. Lead us on in pursuit of him.'

Mission of Statilius

Varro was as much excited as the rest. He was eager for action. Aemilius hesitated. He made particular inquiries. He said they ought to proceed with caution. Finally, he called up a certain prudent and sagacious officer, named Statilius, and ordered him to take a small body of horsemen, ride over to the Carthaginian camp, ascertain the facts exactly, and report the result. Statilius did so. When he reached the lines he ordered his troops to halt, and took with him two horsemen on whose courage and strength he could rely, and rode in. The three horsemen rode around the camp and examined everything with a view of ascertaining whether Hannibal had really abandoned his position and fled, or whether some stratagem was intended.

The Stratagem Discovered – Chagrin of Hannibal and the Romans

When he came back, he reported to the army that, in his opinion, the desertion of the camp was not real, but a trick to draw the Romans into some difficulty. The fires were the largest on the side toward the Romans, which indicated that they were built to deceive. He saw money, too, and other valuables strewed about upon the ground, which appeared to him much more like a bait set in a trap, than like property abandoned by fugitives as incumbrances to flight.

Varro was not convinced; and the army, hearing of the money, were excited to a greater eagerness for plunder. They could hardly be restrained. Just then, however, two slaves that had been taken prisoners by the Carthaginians some time before, came into the Roman camp. They told the consuls that the whole Carthaginian force was hid in ambush very near, waiting for the Romans to enter their encampment, when they were going to surround them and cut them to pieces. In the bustle and movement attendant on this plan, the slaves had escaped. Of course, the Roman army were now satisfied. They returned, chagrined and disappointed, to their own quarters, and Hannibal, still more chagrined and disappointed, returned to his.

Hannibal soon found, however, that he could not remain any longer where he was. His provisions were exhausted, and he could obtain no more. The Romans would not come out of their encampment to give him battle on equal terms, and they were too strongly intrenched to be attacked where they were. He determined, therefore, to evacuate that part of the country, and move, by a sudden march, into Apulia.

Apulia

Apulia was on the eastern side of Italy. The river Aufidus runs through it, having a town named Cannae near its mouth. The region of the Aufidus was a warm and sunny valley, which was now waving with ripening grain. Being further south than the place where he had been, and more exposed to the influence of the sun, Hannibal thought that the crops would be sooner ripe, and that, at least, he should have a new field to plunder.

Hannibal Marches into Apulia – The Romans Follow Him

He accordingly decided now to leave his camp in earnest and move into Apulia. He made the same arrangements as before, when his departure was a mere pretence. He left tents pitched and fires burning, but marched his army off the ground by night and secretly, so that the Romans did not perceive his departure; and the next day, when they saw the appearances of silence and solitude about the camp, they suspected another deception, and made no move themselves. At length, however, intelligence came that the long columns of Hannibal's army had been seen already far to the eastward, and moving on as fast as possible, with all their baggage. The

Romans, after much debate and uncertainty, resolved to follow. The eagles of the Apennines looked down upon the two great moving masses, creeping slowly along through the forests and valleys, like swarms of insects, one following the other, led on by a strange but strong attraction, drawing them toward each other when at a distance but kept asunder by a still stronger repulsion when near.

The New Encampments – Dissensions Between the Consuls

The Roman army came up with that of Hannibal on the river Aufidus, near Cannae, and the two vast encampments were formed with all the noise and excitement attendant on the movements of two great armies posting themselves on the eve of a battle, in the neighbourhood of each other. In the Roman camp, the confusion was greatly aggravated by the angry disputes which immediately arose between the consuls and their respective adherents as to the course to be pursued. Varro insisted on giving the Carthaginians immediate battle. Aemilius refused. Varro said that he must protest against continuing any longer these inexcusable delays, and insist on a battle. He could not consent to be responsible any further for allowing Italy to lie at the mercy of such a scourge. Aemilius replied that if Varro did precipitate a battle, he himself protested against his rashness, and could not be, in any degree, responsible for the result. The various officers took sides, some with one consul and some with the other, but most with Varro. The dissension filled the camp with excitement, agitation and ill will.

Flight of the Inhabitants

In the meantime, the inhabitants of the country into which these two vast hordes of ferocious, though restrained and organized, combatants had made such a sudden irruption, were flying as fast as they could from the awful scene which they expected was to ensue. They carried from their villages and cabins what little property could be saved, and took the women and children away to retreats and strongholds, wherever they imagined they could find temporary concealment or protection. The news of the movement of the two armies spread throughout the country, carried by hundreds of refugees and messengers, and all Italy, looking on with suspense and anxiety, awaited the result.

Manoeuvres

The armies manoeuvred for a day or two, Varro, during his term of command, making arrangements to promote and favour an action, and Aemilius, on the following day, doing everything in his power to prevent it. In the end, Varro succeeded. The lines were formed and the battle must be begun. Aemilius gave up the contest now, and while he protested earnestly against the course which Varro pursued, he prepared to do all in his power to prevent a defeat, since there was no longer a possibility of avoiding a collision.

The Battle of Cannae

The battle began, and the reader must imagine the scene, since no pen can describe it. Fifty thousand men on one side and 80,000 on the other, at work hard and steadily, for six hours, killing each other by every possible means of destruction – stabs, blows, struggles, outcries, shouts of anger and defiance and screams of terror and agony, all mingled together, in one general din, which covered the whole country for an extent of many miles, all together constituted a scene of horror of which none but those who have witnessed great battles can form any adequate idea.

Another Stratagem

It seems as if Hannibal could do nothing without stratagem. In the early part of this conflict, he sent a large body of his troops over to the Romans as deserters. They threw down their spears and bucklers as they reached the Roman lines, in token of surrender. The Romans received them, opened a passage for them through into the rear, and ordered them to remain there. As they were apparently unarmed, they left only a very small guard to keep them in custody. The men had, however, daggers concealed about their dress, and, watching a favourable moment, in the midst of the battle, they sprang to their feet, drew out their weapons, broke away from their guard and attacked the Romans in the rear at a moment when they were so pressed by the enemy in front that they could scarcely maintain their ground.

Defeat of the Romans – Aemilius Wounded

It was evident before many hours that the Roman forces were everywhere yielding. From slowly and reluctantly yielding they soon began to fly. In the flight, the weak and the wounded were trampled underfoot by the throng who were pressing on behind them, or were dispatched by wanton blows from enemies as they passed in pursuit of those who were still able to fly.

In the midst of this scene, a Roman officer named Lentulus, as he was riding away, saw before him at the roadside another officer wounded, sitting upon a stone, faint and bleeding. He stopped when he reached him, and found that it was the consul Aemilius. He had been wounded in the head with a sling, and his strength was almost gone. Lentulus offered him his horse, and urged him to take it and fly. Aemilius declined the offer. He said it was too late for his life to be saved, and that, besides, he had no wish to save it. 'Go on, therefore, yourself,' said he, 'as fast as you can. Make the best of your way to Rome. Tell the authorities there, from me, that all is lost, and they must do whatever they can themselves for the defence of the city. Make all the speed you can, or Hannibal will be at the gates before you.'

Death of Aemilius – Escape of Varro – Condition of the Battlefield

Aemilius sent also a message to Fabius, declaring to him that it was not his fault that a battle had been risked with Hannibal. He had done all in his power, he said, to prevent it, and had adhered to the policy which Fabius had recommended to the last. Lentulus having received these messages, and perceiving that the Carthaginians were close upon him in pursuit, rode away, leaving the consul to his fate. The Carthaginians came on, and, on seeing the wounded man, they thrust their spears into his body, one after another, as they passed, until his limbs ceased to quiver.

As for the other consul, Varro, he escaped with his life. Attended by about 70 horsemen, he made his way to a fortified town not very remote from the battlefield, where he halted with his horsemen, and determined that he would attempt to rally there the remains of the army.

The Carthaginians, when they found the victory complete, abandoned the pursuit of the enemy, returned to their camp, spent some hours in feasting and rejoicing and then laid down to sleep. They were, of course, well exhausted by the intense exertions of the day. On the field where the battle had been fought, the wounded lay all night mingled with the dead, filling the air with cries and groans, and writhing in their agony.

The Wounded and Dying – The Roman and Carthaginian Soldier

Early the next morning the Carthaginians came back to the field to plunder the dead bodies of the Romans. The whole field presented a most shocking spectacle to the view. The bodies of horses and men lay mingled in dreadful confusion as they had fallen, some dead, others still alive, the men moaning, crying for water and feebly struggling from time to time to disentangle themselves from the heaps of carcasses under which they were buried.

The deadly and inextinguishable hate which the Carthaginians felt for their foes not having been appeased by the slaughter of 40,000 of them, they beat down and stabbed these wretched lingerers wherever they found them, as a sort of morning pastime after the severer labours of the preceding day. This slaughter, however, could hardly be considered a cruelty to the wretched victims of it, for many of them bared their breasts to their assailants, and begged for the blow which was to put an end to their pain.

In exploring the field, one Carthaginian soldier was found still alive, but imprisoned by the dead body of his Roman enemy lying upon him. The Carthaginian's face and ears were shockingly mangled. The Roman, having fallen upon him when both were mortally wounded, had continued the combat with his teeth when he could no longer use his weapon, and had died at last, binding down his exhausted enemy with his own dead body.

Immense Plunder

The Carthaginians secured a vast amount of plunder. The Roman army was full of officers and soldiers from the aristocratic ranks of society, and their arms and their dress were very valuable. The Carthaginians obtained some bushels of gold rings from their fingers, which Hannibal sent to Carthage as a trophy of his victory.

Chapter X
Scipio, 215–201 BCE

Reason of Hannibal's Success — The Scipios

THE TRUE REASON why Hannibal could not be arrested in his triumphant career seems not to have been because the Romans did not pursue the right kind of policy toward him, but because, thus far, they had no general who was his equal. Whoever was sent against him soon proved to be his inferior. Hannibal could outmanoeuvre them all in stratagem and could conquer them on the field.

There was, however, now destined to appear a man capable of coping with Hannibal. It was young Scipio, the one who saved the life of his father at the battle of Ticinus. This Scipio, though the son of Hannibal's first great antagonist of that name, is commonly called, in history, the elder Scipio; for there was another of his name after him, who was greatly celebrated for his wars against the Carthaginians in Africa. These last two received from the Roman people the surname of Africanus, in honour of their African victories, and the one who now comes upon the stage was called Scipio Africanus the elder, or sometimes simply the elder Scipio. The deeds of the Scipio who attempted to stop Hannibal at the Rhône and upon the Po were so wholly eclipsed by his son, and by the other Scipio who followed him, that the former is left out of view and forgotten in designating and distinguishing the others.

Fragments of the Roman Army — Scipio Elected Commander

Our present Scipio first appears upon the stage, in the exercise of military command, after the battle of Cannae. He was a subordinate officer and on the day following the battle he found himself at a place called Canusium, which was at a short distance from Cannae, on the way toward Rome, with a number of other officers of his own rank, and with broken masses and detachments of the army coming in from time to time, faint, exhausted and in despair. The rumour was that both consuls were killed. These fragments of the army had, therefore, no one to command them. The officers met together, and unanimously agreed to make Scipio their commander in the emergency, until some superior officer should arrive, or they should get orders from Rome.

Scipio's Energy

An incident here occurred which showed, in a striking point of view, the boldness and energy of the young Scipio's character. At the very meeting in which he was placed in command, and when they were overwhelmed with perplexity and care, an officer came in, and reported that in another part of the camp there was an assembly of officers and young men of rank, headed by a certain Metellus, who had decided to give up the cause of their country in despair, and that they were making arrangements to proceed immediately to the seacoast, obtain ships and sail away to seek a new home in some foreign lands, considering their cause in Italy as utterly lost and ruined. The officer proposed that they should call a council and deliberate what was best to do.

Case of Metellus

'Deliberate!' said Scipio; 'this is not a case for deliberation, but for action. Draw your swords and follow me.' So saying, he pressed forward at the head of the party to the quarters of Metellus. They marched boldly into the apartment where he and his friends were in consultation. Scipio held up his sword, and in a very solemn manner pronounced an oath, binding himself not to abandon his country in this the hour of her distress, nor to allow any other Roman citizen to abandon her. If he should be guilty of such treason, he called upon Jupiter, by the most dreadful imprecations, to destroy him utterly, house, family, fortune, soul and body.

Metellus Yields

'And now, Metellus, I call upon you,' said he, 'and all who are with you, to take the same oath. You must do it, otherwise you have got to defend yourselves against these swords of ours, as well as those of the Carthaginians.' Metellus and his party yielded. Nor was it wholly to fear that they yielded. It was to the influence of hope quite as much as to that of fear. The courage, energy and martial ardour which Scipio's conduct evinced awakened a similar spirit in them, and made them hope again that possibly their country might yet be saved.

Consternation at Rome

The news of the awful defeat and destruction of the Roman army flew swiftly to Rome, and produced universal consternation. The whole city was in an uproar. There were soldiers in the army from almost every family, so that every woman and child throughout the city was distracted by the double agitation of inconsolable grief at the death of their husband or their father slain in the battle, and of terrible fear that Hannibal and his raging followers were about to burst in through the gates of the city to murder them. The streets of the city, and especially the Forum, were thronged with vast crowds of men, women and children, who filled the air with loud lamentations, and with cries of terror and despair.

The Senate Adjourns

The magistrates were not able to restore order. The senate actually adjourned, that the members of it might go about the city and use their influence and their power to produce silence at least, if they could not restore composure. The streets were finally cleared. The women and children were ordered to remain at home. Armed patrols were put on guard to prevent tumultuous assemblies forming. Men were sent off on horseback on the road to Canusium and Cannae, to get more accurate intelligence and then the senate assembled again, and began to consider, with as much of calmness as they could command, what was to be done.

Hannibal Refuses to March to Rome – Makes His Headquarters at Capua

The panic at Rome was, however, in some measure, a false alarm, for Hannibal, contrary to the expectation of all Italy, did not go to Rome. His generals urged him very strongly to do so. Nothing could prevent, they said, his gaining immediate possession of the city. But Hannibal refused to do this. Rome was strongly fortified and had an immense population. His army, too, was much weakened by the battle of

Cannae, and he seems to have thought it most prudent not to attempt the reduction of Rome until he should have received reinforcements from home. It was now so late in the season that he could not expect such reinforcements immediately, and he accordingly determined to select some place more accessible than Rome and make it his headquarters for the winter. He decided in favour of Capua, which was a large and powerful city one or 200 miles southeast of Rome.

Hannibal, in fact, conceived the design of retaining possession of Italy and of making Capua the capital of the country, leaving Rome to itself, to decline, as under such circumstances it inevitably must, to the rank of a second city. Perhaps he was tired of the fatigues and hazards of war, and having narrowly escaped ruin before the battle of Cannae, he now resolved that he would not rashly incur any new dangers.

It was a great question with him whether he should go forward to Rome, or attempt to build up a new capital of his own at Capua. The question which of these two he ought to have done was a matter of great debate then, and it has been discussed a great deal by military men in every age since his day. Right or wrong, Hannibal decided to establish his own capital at Capua, and to leave Rome, for the present, undisturbed.

Hannibal Sends Mago to Carthage

He, however, sent immediately to Carthage for reinforcements. The messenger whom he sent was one of his generals named Mago. Mago made the best of his way to Carthage with his tidings of victory and his bushel of rings, collected, as has been already said, from the field of Cannae. The city of Carthage was greatly excited by the news which he brought. The friends and patrons of Hannibal were elated with enthusiasm and pride, and they taunted and reproached his enemies with the opposition to him they had manifested when he was originally appointed to the command of the army of Spain.

Mago's Speech — The Bag of Rings

Mago met the Carthaginian senate, and in a very spirited and eloquent speech he told them how many glorious battles Hannibal had fought, and how many victories he had won. He had contended with the greatest generals that the Romans could bring against him, and had conquered them all. He had slain, he said, in all, over 200,000 men. All Italy was now subject to his power; Capua was his capital, and Rome had fallen. He concluded by saying that Hannibal was in need of considerable additional supplies of men, money and provisions, which he did not doubt the Carthaginians would send without any unnecessary delay. He then produced before the senate the great bag of rings which he had brought, and poured them upon the pavement of the senate-house as a trophy of the victories which he had been announcing.

Debate in the Carthaginian Senate

This would, perhaps, have all been very well for Hannibal if his friends had been contented to have left the case where Mago left it; but some of them could not resist the temptation of taunting his enemies, and especially Hanno, who, as will be recollected, originally opposed his being sent to Spain. They turned to him, and asked him triumphantly what he thought now of his factious opposition to so brave a warrior. Hanno rose. The senate looked toward him and were profoundly silent, wondering what he would have to reply. Hanno, with an air of perfect ease and composure, spoke somewhat as follows:

The Speech of Hanno in the Carthaginian Senate

'I should have said nothing, but should have allowed the senate to take what action they pleased on Mago's proposition if I had not been particularly addressed. As it is, I will say that I think now just as I always have thought. We are plunged into a most costly and most useless war, and are, as I conceive, no nearer the end of it now than ever, notwithstanding all these boasted successes. The emptiness of them is clearly shown by the inconsistency of Hannibal's pretensions as to what he has done, with the demands that he makes in respect to what he wishes us to do.

'He says he has conquered all his enemies, and yet he wants us to send him more soldiers. He has reduced all Italy – the most fertile country in the world – to subjection, and reigns over it at Capua, and yet he calls upon us for corn. And then, to crown all, he sends us bushels of gold rings as a specimen of the riches he has obtained by plunder, and accompanies the offering with a demand for new supplies of money. In my opinion, his success is all illusive and hollow. There seems to be nothing substantial in his situation except his necessities, and the heavy burdens upon the state which these necessities impose.'

Progress of the War

Notwithstanding Hanno's sarcasms, the Carthaginians resolved to sustain Hannibal, and to send him the supplies that he needed. They were, however, long in reaching him. Various difficulties and delays occurred. The Romans, though they could not dispossess Hannibal from his position in Italy, raised armies in different countries, and waged extended wars with the Carthaginians and their allies, in various parts of the world, both by sea and land.

Enervation of Hannibal's Army

The result was that Hannibal remained 15 or 16 years in Italy, engaged, during all this time, in a lingering struggle with the Roman power, without ever being able to accomplish any decisive measures. During this period, he was sometimes successful and victorious, and sometimes he was very hard pressed by his enemies. It is said that his army was very much enervated and enfeebled by the comforts and luxuries they enjoyed at Capua.

Capua was a very rich and beautiful city, and the inhabitants of it had opened their gates to Hannibal of their own accord, preferring, as they said, his alliance to that of the Romans. The officers – as the officers of an army almost always do, when they find themselves established in a rich and powerful city, after the fatigues of a long and honourable campaign – gave themselves up to festivities and rejoicing, to games, shows and entertainments of every kind, which they soon learned infinitely to prefer to the toil and danger of marches and battles.

Decline of the Carthaginian Power

Whatever may have been the cause, there is no question about the fact that, from the time Hannibal and his army got possession of their comfortable quarters in Capua, the Carthaginian power began gradually to decline. As Hannibal determined to make that city the Italian capital instead of Rome, he, of course, when established there, felt in some degree settled and at home, and was less interested than he had been in plans for attacking the ancient capital. Still, the war went on; many battles were fought, many cities were besieged, the Roman power gaining ground all the time, though not, however, by any very decisive victories.

Marcellus

In these contests there appeared, at length, a new Roman general named Marcellus, and, either on account of his possessing a bolder and more active temperament, or else in consequence of the change in the relative strength of the two contending powers, he pursued a more aggressive policy than Fabius had thought it prudent to attempt. Marcellus was, however, cautious and wary in his enterprises, and he laid his plans with so much sagacity and skill that he was almost always successful. The Romans applauded very highly his activity and ardour, without, however, forgetting their obligations to Fabius for his caution and defensive reserve. They said that Marcellus was the *sword* of their commonwealth, as Fabius had been its *shield*.

Success of the Romans – Siege of Capua

The Romans continued to prosecute this sort of warfare, being more and more successful the longer they continued it, until, at last, they advanced to the very walls of Capua, and threatened it with a siege. Hannibal's entrenchments and fortifications were too strong for them to attempt to carry the city by a sudden assault, nor were the Romans even powerful enough to invest the place entirely, so as completely to shut their enemies in. They, however, encamped with a large army in the neighbourhood, and assumed so threatening an attitude as to keep Hannibal's forces within in a state of continual alarm. And, besides the alarm, it was very humiliating and mortifying to Carthaginian pride to find the very seat of their power, as it were, shut up and overawed by an enemy over whom they had been triumphing themselves so short a time before, by a continued series of victories.

Hannibal's Attack on the Roman Camp – He Marches to Rome

Hannibal was not himself in Capua at the time that the Romans came to attack it. He marched, however, immediately to its relief, and attacking the Romans in his turn, endeavoured to compel them to *raise the siege*, as it is technically termed, and retire. They had, however, so entrenched themselves in the positions that they had taken, and the assaults with which he encountered them had lost so much of their former force, that he could accomplish nothing decisive. He then left the ground with his army and marched himself toward Rome. He encamped in the vicinity of the city, and threatened to attack it; but the walls, castles and towers with which Rome, as well as Capua, was defended, were too formidable, and the preparations for defence too complete, to make it prudent for him really to assail the city. His object was to alarm the Romans and compel them to withdraw their forces from his capital that they might defend their own.

Preparations for a Battle – Prevented by Storms

There was, in fact, some degree of alarm awakened, and in the discussions which took place among the Roman authorities, the withdrawal of their troops from Capua was proposed; but this proposal was overruled; even Fabius was against it. Hannibal was no longer to be feared. They ordered back a small detachment from Capua, and added to it such forces as they could raise within the city, and then advanced to give Hannibal battle.

The preparations were all made, it is said, for an engagement, but a violent storm came on, so violent as to drive the combatants back to their respective camps. This happened, the great Roman historian gravely says, two or three times in succession; the weather immediately becoming serene again, each time, as soon as the respective generals had withdrawn their troops from the intended fight. Something like this may perhaps have occurred, though the fact doubtless was that both parties were afraid, each of the other, and were disposed to avail themselves of any excuse to postpone a decisive conflict. There was a time when Hannibal had not been deterred from attacking the Romans even by the most tempestuous storms.

Sales at Auction

Thus, though Hannibal did, in fact, in the end, get to the walls of Rome, he did nothing but threaten when he was there, and his encampment near the city can only be considered as a bravado. His presence seems to have excited very little apprehension within the city. The Romans had, in fact, before this time, lost their terror of the Carthaginian arms.

To show their contempt of Hannibal, they sold, at public auction, the land on which he was encamped, while he was upon it besieging the city, and it brought the usual price. The bidders were, perhaps, influenced somewhat by a patriotic spirit, and by a desire to taunt Hannibal with an expression of their opinion that his occupation of the land would be a very temporary encumbrance. Hannibal, to revenge himself for this taunt, put up for sale at auction, in his own camp, the shops of one of the principal streets of Rome, and they were bought by his officers with great spirit. It showed that a great change had taken place in the nature of the contest between Carthage and Rome, to find these vast powers, which were a few years before grappling each other with such destructive and terrible fury on the Po and at Cannae, now satisfying their declining animosity with such squibbing as this.

Hasdrubal Crosses the Alps

When the other modes by which Hannibal attempted to obtain reinforcements failed, he made an attempt to have a second army brought over the Alps under the command of his brother Hasdrubal. It was a large army, and in their march they experienced the same difficulties, though in a much lighter degree, that Hannibal had himself encountered. And yet, of the whole mighty mass which set out from Spain, nothing reached Hannibal except his brother's *head*. The circumstances of the unfortunate termination of Hasdrubal's attempt were as follows:

When Hasdrubal descended from the Alps, rejoicing in the successful manner in which he had surmounted those formidable barriers, he imagined that all his difficulties were over. He dispatched couriers to his brother Hannibal, informing him that he had scaled the mountains, and that he was coming on as rapidly as possible to his aid.

Livius and Nero – Division of the Provinces

The two consuls in office at this time were named, the one Nero, and the other Livius. To each of these, as was usual with the Roman consuls, was assigned a particular province, and a certain portion of the army to defend it, and the laws enjoined it upon them very strictly not to leave their respective provinces, on any pretext whatever, without authority from the Roman Legislature. In this instance Livius had been assigned to the northern part of Italy, and Nero to the southern. It devolved upon Livius, therefore, to meet and give battle to Hasdrubal on his descent from the Alps, and to Nero to remain in the vicinity of Hannibal, to thwart his plans, oppose his progress and, if possible, conquer and destroy him, while his colleague prevented his receiving the expected reinforcements from Spain.

The Intercepted Letters – Nero's Perplexity

Things being in this state, the couriers whom Hasdrubal sent with his letters had the vigilance of both consuls to elude before they could deliver them into Hannibal's hands. They did succeed in passing Livius, but they were intercepted by Nero. The patrols who seized these messengers brought them to Nero's tent. Nero opened and read the letters. All Hasdrubal's plans and arrangements were detailed in them very fully, so that Nero perceived that, if he were at once to proceed to the northward with a strong force, he could render his colleague such aid as, with the knowledge of Hasdrubal's plans, which he had obtained from the letters, would probably enable them to defeat him; whereas, if he were to leave Livius in ignorance and alone, he feared that Hasdrubal would be successful in breaking his way through, and in ultimately effecting his junction with Hannibal. Under these circumstances, he was, of course, very earnestly desirous of going northward to render the necessary aid, but he was strictly forbidden by law to leave his own province to enter that of his colleague without an authority from Rome, which there was not now time to obtain.

Laws of Military Discipline – Their Strictness and Severity

The laws of military discipline are very strict and imperious, and in theory they are never to be disobeyed. Officers and soldiers, of all ranks and gradations, must obey the orders which they receive from the authority above them, without looking at the consequences, or deviating from the line marked out on any pretext whatever. It is, in fact, the very essence of military subordination and efficiency, that a command, once given, suspends all exercise of judgment or discretion on the part of the one to whom it is addressed; and a good general or a good government would prefer generally that harm should be done by a strict obedience to commands, rather than a benefit secured by an unauthorized deviation from them. It is a good principle, not only in war, but in all those cases in social life where men have to act in concert, and yet wish to secure efficiency in action.

Plan of Nero

Nero, after much anxious deliberation, concluded that the emergency in which he found himself placed was one requiring him to take the responsibility of disobedience. He did not, however, dare to go northward with all his forces, for that would be to leave southern Italy wholly at the mercy of Hannibal. He selected, therefore, from his whole force, which consisted of 40,000 men, 7,000 or 8,000 of the most efficient and trustworthy; the men on whom he could most securely rely, both in respect to their ability to bear the fatigues of a rapid march, and the courage and energy with which they would meet Hasdrubal's forces in battle at the end of it. He was, at the time when Hasdrubal's letters were intercepted, occupying a spacious and well-situated camp. This he enlarged and strengthened, so that Hannibal might not suspect that he intended any diminution of the forces within. All this was done very promptly, so that, in a few hours after he received the intelligence on which he was acting, he was drawing off secretly, at night, a column of 6,000 or 8,000 men, none of whom knew at all where they were going.

A Night March

He proceeded as rapidly as possible to the northward, and, when he arrived in the northern province, he contrived to get into the camp of Livius as secretly as he had got out from his own. Thus, of the two armies, the one where an accession of force was required was greatly strengthened at the expense of the other, without either of the Carthaginian generals having suspected the change.

Livius and Nero Attack Hasdrubal

Livius was rejoiced to get so opportune a reinforcement. He recommended that the troops should all remain quietly in camp for a short time, until the newly arrived troops could rest and recuperate themselves a little after their rapid and fatiguing march; but Nero opposed this plan, and recommended an immediate battle. He knew the character of the men that he had brought, and he was, besides, unwilling to risk the dangers which might arise in his own camp, in southern Italy, by too long an absence from it. It was decided, accordingly, to attack Hasdrubal at once, and the signal for battle was given.

Hasdrubal Orders a Retreat – Butchery of His Army – Hasdrubal's Death

It is not improbable that Hasdrubal would have been beaten by Livius alone, but the additional force which Nero had brought made the Romans altogether too strong for him. Besides, from his position in the front of the battle, he perceived, from some indications that his watchful eye observed, that a part of the troops attacking him were from the southward; and he inferred from this that Hannibal had been defeated, and that, in consequence of this, the whole united force of the Roman army was arrayed against him. He was disheartened and discouraged, and soon ordered a retreat. He was pursued by the various divisions of the Roman army, and the retreating columns of the Carthaginians were soon thrown into complete confusion. They became entangled among rivers and lakes; and the guides who had undertaken to conduct the army, finding that all was lost, abandoned them and fled, anxious only to save their own lives.

The Carthaginians were soon pent up in a position where they could not defend themselves, and from which they could not escape. The Romans showed them no mercy, but went on killing their wretched and despairing victims until the whole army was almost totally destroyed. They cut off Hasdrubal's head, and Nero sat out the very night after the battle to return with it in triumph to his own encampment. When he arrived, he sent a troop of horse to throw the head over into Hannibal's camp, a ghastly and horrid trophy of his victory.

Hannibal was overwhelmed with disappointment and sorrow at the loss of his army, bringing with it, as it did, the destruction of all his hopes. 'My fate is sealed,' said he; 'all is lost. I shall send no more news of victory to Carthage. In losing Hasdrubal my last hope is gone.'

Progress of the Roman Arms – Successes of Scipio

While Hannibal was in this condition in Italy, the Roman armies, aided by their allies, were gaining gradually against the Carthaginians in various parts of the world, under the different generals who had been placed in command by the Roman senate. The news of these victories came continually home to Italy, and encouraged and animated the Romans, while Hannibal and his army, as well as the people who were in alliance with him, were disheartened and depressed by them.

Scipio was one of these generals commanding in foreign lands. His province was Spain. The news which came home from his army became more and more exciting, as he advanced from conquest to conquest, until it seemed that the whole country was going to be reduced to subjection. He overcame one Carthaginian general after another until he reached New Carthage, which he besieged and conquered, and the Roman authority was established fully over the whole land.

Scipio then returned in triumph to Rome. The people received him with acclamations. At the next election they chose him consul. On the allotment of provinces, Sicily fell to him, with power to cross into Africa if he pleased. It devolved on the other consul to carry on the war in Italy more directly against Hannibal. Scipio levied his army, equipped his fleet and sailed for Sicily.

Scipio in Africa

The first thing that he did on his arrival in his province was to project an expedition into Africa itself. He could not, as he wished, face Hannibal directly, by marching his troops into the south of Italy, for this was the work allotted to his colleague. He could, however, make an incursion into Africa, and even threaten Carthage itself, and this, with the boldness and ardour which marked his character, he resolved to do.

Carthage Threatened

He was triumphantly successful in all his plans. His army, imbibing the spirit of enthusiasm which animated their commander, and confident of success, went on, as his forces in Spain had done, from victory to victory. They conquered cities, they overran provinces, they defeated and drove back all the armies which the Carthaginians could bring against them, and finally they awakened in the streets and dwellings of Carthage the same panic and consternation which Hannibal's victorious progress had produced in Rome.

A Truce

The Carthaginians being now, in their turn, reduced to despair, sent ambassadors to Scipio to beg for peace, and to ask on what terms he would grant it and withdraw from the country. Scipio replied that *he* could not make peace. It rested with the

Roman senate, whose servant he was. He specified, however, certain terms which he was willing to have proposed to the senate, and, if the Carthaginians would agree to them, he would grant them a *truce*, that is, a temporary suspension of hostilities, until the answer of the Roman senate could be returned.

Hannibal Recalled

The Carthaginians agreed to the terms. They were very onerous. The Romans say that they did not really mean to abide by them, but acceded for the moment in order to gain time to send for Hannibal. They had great confidence in his resources and military power, and thought that, if he were in Africa, he could save them. At the same time, therefore, that they sent their ambassadors to Rome with their propositions for peace, they dispatched expresses to Hannibal, ordering him to embark his troops as soon as possible, and, abandoning Italy, to hasten home, to save, if it was not already too late, his native city from destruction.

When Hannibal received these messages, he was overwhelmed with disappointment and sorrow. He spent hours in extreme agitation, sometimes in a moody silence, interrupted now and then by groans of despair, and sometimes uttering loud and angry curses, prompted by the exasperation of his feelings. He, however, could not resist. He made the best of his way to Carthage. The Roman senate, at the same time, instead of deciding on the question of peace or war, which Scipio had submitted to them, referred the question back to him. They sent commissioners to Scipio, authorizing him to act for them, and to decide himself alone whether the war should be continued or closed, and if to be closed, on what conditions.

Hannibal Raises a New Army – The Romans Capture His Spies

Hannibal raised a large force at Carthage, joining with it such remains of former armies as had been left after Scipio's battles, and he went forth at the head of these troops to meet his enemy. He marched five days, going, perhaps, 75 or 100 miles from Carthage, when he found himself approaching Scipio's camp. He sent out spies to reconnoitre. The patrols of Scipio's army seized these spies and brought them to the general's tent, as they supposed, for execution. Instead of punishing them,

Scipio ordered them to be led around his camp, and to be allowed to see everything they desired. He then dismissed them, that they might return to Hannibal with the information they had obtained.

Interview Between Hannibal and Scipio

Of course, the report which they brought in respect to the strength and resources of Scipio's army was very formidable to Hannibal. He thought it best to make an attempt to negotiate a peace rather than to risk a battle, and he accordingly sent word to Scipio requesting a personal interview. Scipio acceded to this request, and a place was appointed for the meeting between the two encampments.

To this spot the two generals repaired at the proper time, with great pomp and parade, and with many attendants. They were the two greatest generals of the age in which they lived, having been engaged for 15 or 20 years in performing, at the head of vast armies, exploits which had filled the world with their fame. Their fields of action had, however, been widely distant, and they met personally now for the first time. When introduced into each other's presence, they stood for some time in silence, gazing upon and examining one another with intense interest and curiosity, but not speaking a word.

Negotiations

At length, however, the negotiation was opened. Hannibal made Scipio proposals for peace. They were very favourable to the Romans, but Scipio was not satisfied with them. He demanded still greater sacrifices than Hannibal was willing to make. The result, after a long and fruitless negotiation, was, that each general returned to his camp and prepared for battle.

The Last Battle – Defeat of the Carthaginians

In military campaigns, it is generally easy for those who have been conquering to go on to conquer: so much depends upon the expectations with which the contending armies go into battle. Scipio and his troops expected to conquer. The Carthaginians expected to be beaten. The result corresponded. At the close of the day on which the battle was fought, 40,000 Carthaginians were dead and dying upon the ground, as many more were prisoners in the Roman camp, and the rest, in broken masses, were flying from the field in confusion and terror, on all the roads which led to Carthage. Hannibal arrived at the city with the rest, went to the senate, announced his defeat and said that he could do no more. 'The fortune which once attended me,' said he, 'is lost forever, and nothing is left to us but to make peace with our enemies on any terms that they may think fit to impose.'

Chapter XI
Hannibal, a Fugitive and an Exile, 200–182 BCE

Hannibal's Conquests

HANNIBAL'S LIFE was like an April day. Its brightest glory was in the morning. The setting of his sun was darkened by clouds and showers. Although for 15 years the Roman people could find no general capable of maintaining the field against him, Scipio conquered him at last, and all his brilliant conquests ended, as Hanno had predicted, only in placing his country in a far worse condition than before.

Peaceful Pursuits – The Danger of a Spirit of Ambition and Conquest

In fact, as long as the Carthaginians confined their energies to useful industry, and to the pursuits of commerce and peace, they were prosperous, and they increased in wealth, influence and honour every year. Their ships went everywhere, and were everywhere welcome. All the shores of the Mediterranean were visited by their merchants, and the comforts and the happiness of many nations and tribes were promoted by the very means which they took to swell their own riches and fame. All might have gone on so for centuries longer, had not military heroes arisen with appetites for a more piquant sort of glory.

Hannibal's father was one of the foremost of these. He began by conquests in Spain and encroachments on the Roman jurisdiction. He inculcated the same feelings of ambition and hate in Hannibal's mind which burned in his own. For many years, the policy which they led their countrymen to pursue was successful. From being useful and welcome visitors to all the world, they became the masters and the curse of a part of it. So long as Hannibal remained superior to any Roman general that could be brought against him, he went on conquering. But at last Scipio arose, greater than Hannibal. The tide was then turned, and all the vast conquests of half a century were wrested away by the same violence, bloodshed and misery with which they had been acquired.

Gradual Progress of Scipio's Victories

We have described the exploits of Hannibal, in making these conquests, in detail, while those of Scipio, in wresting them away, have been passed over very briefly, as this is intended as a history of Hannibal, and not of Scipio. Still, Scipio's conquests were made by slow degrees, and they consumed a long period of time.

He but about 18 years of age at the battle of Cannae, soon after which his campaigns began, and he was 30 when he was made consul, just before his going into Africa. He was thus 15 or 18 years in taking down the vast superstructure of power which Hannibal had raised, working in regions away from Hannibal and Carthage during all this time, as if leaving the great general and the great city for the last. He was, however, so successful in what he did, that when, at length, he advanced to the attack of Carthage everything else was gone. The Carthaginian power had become a mere hollow shell, empty and vain, which required only one great final blow to affect its absolute demolition. In fact, so far spent and gone were all the Carthaginian resources, that the great city had to summon the great general to its aid the moment it was threatened, and Scipio destroyed them both together.

Severe Conditions of Peace Exacted by Scipio

And yet Scipio did not proceed so far as literally and actually to destroy them. He spared Hannibal's life, and he allowed the city to stand; but the terms and conditions of peace which he exacted were such as to put an absolute and perpetual end to Carthaginian dominion.

By these conditions, the Carthaginian state was allowed to continue free and independent, and even to retain the government of such territories in *Africa* as they possessed before the war; but all their foreign possessions were taken away; and even in respect to Africa, their jurisdiction was limited and curtailed by very hard restrictions. Their whole navy was to be given to the Romans except 10 small ships of three banks of oars, which Scipio thought the government would need for the purposes of civil administration. These they were allowed to retain. Scipio did not say what he should do with the remainder of the fleet; it was to be unconditionally surrendered to him. Their elephants of war were also to be all given up, and they were to be bound not to train any more. They were not to appear at all as a military power in any other quarter of the world but Africa, and they were not to make war in Africa except by previously making known the occasion for it to the Roman people, and obtaining their permission. They were also to pay to the Romans a very large annual tribute for 50 years.

Debates in the Carthaginian Senate

There was great distress and perplexity in the Carthaginian councils while they were debating these cruel terms. Hannibal was in favour of accepting them. Others opposed. They thought it would be better still to continue the struggle, hopeless as it was, than to submit to terms so ignominious and fatal.

Hannibal was present at these debates, but he found himself now in a very different position from that which he had been occupying for 30 years as a victorious general at the head of his army. He had been accustomed there to control and direct everything. In his councils of war, no one spoke but at his invitation, and no opinion was expressed but such as he was willing to hear.

In the Carthaginian senate, however, he found the case very different. There, opinions were freely expressed, as in a debate among equals, Hannibal taking his place among the rest, and counting only as one. And yet the spirit of authority and command which he had been so long accustomed to exercise, lingered still, and made him very impatient and uneasy under contradiction. In fact, as one of the speakers in the senate was rising to animadvert upon and oppose Hannibal's views, he undertook to pull him down and silence him by force. This proceeding awakened immediately such expressions of dissatisfaction and displeasure in the assembly as to show him very clearly that the time for such domineering was gone. He had, however, the good sense to express the regret he soon felt at having so far forgotten the duties of his new position, and to make an ample apology.

Terms of Peace Complied With – Surrender of the Elephants and Ships

The Carthaginians decided at length to accede to Scipio's terms of peace. The first instalment of the tribute was paid. The elephants and the ships were surrendered. After a few days, Scipio announced his determination not to take the ships away with him, but to destroy them there. Perhaps this was because he thought the ships would be of little value to the Romans, on account of the difficulty of manning them. Ships, of course, are useless without seamen, and many nations in modern times, who could easily build a navy, are debarred from doing it, because their population does not furnish sailors in sufficient numbers to man and navigate it.

It was probably, in part, on this account that Scipio decided not to take the Carthaginian ships away, and perhaps he also wanted to show to Carthage and to the world that his object in taking possession of the national property of his foes was not to enrich his own country by plunder, but only to deprive ambitious soldiers of the power to compromise any longer the peace and happiness of mankind by expeditions for conquest and power. However this may be, Scipio determined to destroy the Carthaginian fleet, and not to convey it away.

Scipio Burns the Carthaginian Fleet – Feelings of the Spectators

On a given day, therefore, he ordered all the galleys to be got together in the bay opposite to the city of Carthage and to be burned. There were 500 of them, so that they constituted a large fleet, and covered a large expanse of the water. A vast concourse of people assembled upon the shores to witness the grand conflagration. The emotion which such a spectacle was of itself calculated to excite was greatly heightened by the deep but stifled feelings of resentment and hate which agitated every Carthaginian breast. The Romans, too, as they gazed upon the scene from their encampment on the shore, were agitated as well, though with different emotions. Their faces beamed with an expression of exultation and triumph as they saw the vast masses of flame and columns of smoke ascending from the sea, proclaiming the total and irretrievable ruin of Carthaginian pride and power.

Scipio Sails to Rome – His Reception

Having thus fully accomplished his work, Scipio set sail for Rome. All Italy had been filled with the fame of his exploits in thus destroying the ascendency of Hannibal. The city of Rome had now nothing more to fear from its great enemy. He was shut up, disarmed and helpless, in his own native state, and the terror which his presence in Italy had inspired had passed forever away. The whole population of Rome, remembering the awful scenes of consternation and terror which the city had so often endured, regarded Scipio as a great deliverer. They were eager to receive and welcome him on his arrival.

When the time came and he approached the city, vast throngs went out to meet him. The authorities formed civic processions to welcome him. They brought crowns, garlands and flowers, and hailed his approach with loud and prolonged acclamations of triumph and joy. They gave him the name of *Africanus*, in honour of his victories. This was a new honour – giving to a conqueror the name of the country that he had subdued; it was invented specially as Scipio's reward, the deliverer who had saved the empire from the greatest and most terrible danger by which it had ever been assailed.

Hannibal's Position and Standing at Carthage

Hannibal, though fallen, retained still in Carthage some portion of his former power. The glory of his past exploits still invested his character with a sort of halo, which made him an object of general regard, and he still had great and powerful friends. He was elevated to high office and exerted himself to regulate and improve the internal affairs of the state. In these efforts he was not, however, very successful. The historians say that the objects which he aimed to accomplish were good, and that the measures for effecting them were, in themselves, judicious; but, accustomed as he was to the authoritative and arbitrary action of a military commander in camp, he found it hard to practice that caution and forbearance, and that deference for the opinion of others, which are so essential as means of influencing men in the management of the civil affairs of a commonwealth. He made a great many enemies, who did everything in their power, by plots and intrigues, as well as by open hostility, to accomplish his ruin.

Orders from Rome – Hannibal's Mortification

His pride, too, was extremely mortified and humbled by an occurrence which took place very soon after Scipio's return to Rome. There was some occasion of war with a neighbouring African tribe, and Hannibal headed some forces which were raised in the city for the purpose, and went out to prosecute it. The Romans, who took care to have agents in Carthage to keep them acquainted with all that occurred, heard of this, and sent word to Carthage to warn the Carthaginians that this was contrary to the treaty, and could not be allowed. The government, not willing to incur the risk of another visit from Scipio, sent orders to Hannibal to abandon the war and return to the city.

Hannibal was compelled to submit; but after having been accustomed, as he had been, for many years, to bid defiance to all the armies and fleets which Roman power could, with their utmost exertion, bring against him, it must have been very hard for such a spirit as his to find itself stopped and conquered now by a word. All the force they could command against him, even at the very gates of their own city, was once impotent and vain. Now, a mere message and threat, coming across the distant sea, seeks him out in the remote deserts of Africa, and in a moment deprives him of all his power.

Years passed away, and Hannibal, though compelled outwardly to submit to his fate, was restless and ill at ease. His scheming spirit, spurred on now by the double stimulus of resentment and ambition, was always busy, vainly endeavouring to discover some plan by which he might again renew the struggle with his ancient foe.

Syria and Phoenicia – King Antiochus

It will be recollected that Carthage was originally a commercial colony from Tyre, a city on the eastern shores of the Mediterranean Sea. The countries of Syria and Phoenicia were in the vicinity of Tyre. They were powerful commercial communities, and they had always retained very friendly relations with the Carthaginian commonwealth. Ships passed continually to and fro, and always, in case of calamities or disasters threatening one of these regions, the inhabitants naturally looked to the other for refuge and protection, Carthage looking upon Phoenicia as its mother, and Phoenicia regarding Carthage as her child.

Now there was, at this time, a very powerful monarch on the throne in Syria and Phoenicia, named Antiochus. His capital was Damascus. He was wealthy and powerful, and was involved in some difficulties with the Romans. Their conquests, gradually extending eastward, had approached the confines of Antiochus's realms, and the two nations were on the brink of war.

Hannibal's Intrigues with Antiochus

Things being in this state, the enemies of Hannibal at Carthage sent information to the Roman senate that he was negotiating and plotting with Antiochus to combine the Syrian and Carthaginian forces against them, and thus plunge the world into another general war. The Romans accordingly determined to send an embassage to the Carthaginian government, and to demand that Hannibal should be deposed from his office, and given up to them a prisoner, in order that he might be tried on this charge.

Embassy from Rome

These commissioners came, accordingly, to Carthage, keeping, however, the object of their mission a profound secret, since they knew very well that if Hannibal should suspect it he would make his escape before the Carthaginian senate could decide upon the question of surrendering him. Hannibal was, however, too wary for them. He contrived to learn their object, and immediately resolved on making his escape. He knew that his enemies in Carthage were numerous and powerful, and that the animosity against him was growing stronger and stronger. He did not dare, therefore, to trust to the result of the discussion in the senate, but determined to fly.

Flight of Hannibal

He had a small castle or tower on the coast, about 150 miles southeast of Carthage. He sent there by an express, ordering a vessel to be ready to take him to sea. He also made arrangements to have horsemen ready at one of the gates of the city at nightfall. During the day he appeared freely in the public streets, walking with an unconcerned air, as if his mind was at ease, and giving to the Roman ambassadors, who were watching his movements, the impression that he was not meditating an escape. Toward the close of the day, however, after walking leisurely home, he immediately made preparations for his journey. As soon as it was dark he went to the gate of the city, mounted the horse which was provided for him, and fled across the country to his castle. Here he found the vessel ready which he had ordered. He embarked, and put to sea.

Island of Cercina – Stratagem of Hannibal – He Sails for Syria

There is a small island called Cercina at a little distance from the coast. Hannibal reached this island on the same day that he left his tower. There was a harbour here, where merchant ships were accustomed to come in. He found several Phoenician vessels in the port, some bound to Carthage. Hannibal's arrival produced a strong sensation here, and, to account for his appearance among them, he said he was going on an embassy from the Carthaginian government to Tyre.

He was now afraid that some of these that were about setting sail for Carthage might carry the news back of his having been seen at Cercina, and, to prevent this, he contrived, with his characteristic cunning, the following plan. He sent around to all the shipmasters in the port, inviting them to a great entertainment which he was to give, and asked, at the same time, that they would lend him the mainsails of their ships, to make a great awning with, to shelter the guests from the dews of the night. The shipmasters, eager to witness and enjoy the convivial scene which Hannibal's proposal promised them, accepted the invitation, and ordered their mainsails to be taken down. Of course, this confined all their vessels to port.

In the evening, the company assembled under the vast tent, made by the mainsails, on the shore. Hannibal met them, and remained with them for a time. In the course of the night, however, when they were all in the midst of their carousing, he stole away, embarked on board a ship and set sail, and, before the shipmasters could awake from the deep and prolonged slumbers which followed their wine, and rig their mainsails to the masts again, Hannibal was far out of reach on his way to Syria.

Excitement at Carthage – Hannibal Safe at Ephesus

In the meantime, there was a great excitement produced at Carthage by the news which spread everywhere over the city, the day after his departure, that he was not to be found. Great crowds assembled before his house. Wild and strange rumours circulated in explanation of his disappearance, but they were contradictory and impossible, and only added to the universal excitement. This excitement continued until the vessels at last arrived from Cercina, and made the truth known. Hannibal was himself, however, by this time, safe beyond the reach of all possible pursuit. He was sailing prosperously, so far as outward circumstances were concerned, but dejected and wretched in heart, toward Tyre. He landed there in safety, and was kindly received. In a few days he went into the interior, and, after various wanderings, reached Ephesus, where he found Antiochus, the Syrian king.

Carthaginian Deputies – The Change of Fortune

As soon as the escape of Hannibal was made known at Carthage, the people of the city immediately began to fear that the Romans would consider them responsible for it, and that they should thus incur a renewal of Roman hostility. In order to avert this danger, they immediately sent a deputation to Rome, to make known the fact of Hannibal's flight, and to express the regret they felt on account of it, in hopes thus to save themselves from the displeasure of their formidable foes.

It may at first view seem very ungenerous and ungrateful in the Carthaginians to abandon their general in this manner, in the hour of his misfortune and calamity, and to take part against him with enemies whose displeasure he had incurred only in their service and in executing their will. And this conduct of the Carthaginians would have to be considered as not only ungenerous, but extremely inconsistent, if it had been the same individuals that acted in the two cases. But it was not. The men and the influences which now opposed Hannibal's projects and plans had opposed them always and from the beginning; only, so long as he went on successfully and well, they were in the minority, and Hannibal's adherents and friends controlled all the public action of the city. But, now that the bitter fruits of his ambition and of his totally unjustifiable encroachments on the Roman territories and Roman rights began to be realized, the party of his friends was overturned, the power reverted to the hands of those who had always opposed him, and in trying to keep him down when he was once fallen, their action, whether politically right or wrong, was consistent with itself, and cannot be considered as at all subjecting them to the charge of ingratitude or treachery.

Hannibal's Unconquerable Spirit – His New Plans

One might have supposed that all Hannibal's hopes and expectations of ever again coping with his great Roman enemy would have been now effectually and finally destroyed, and that henceforth he would have given up his active hostility and would have contented himself with seeking some refuge where he could spend the remainder of his days in peace, satisfied with securing, after such dangers and escapes, his own personal protection from the vengeance of his enemies. But it is hard to quell and subdue such indomitable perseverance and energy as his. He was very little inclined yet to submit to his fate.

As soon as he found himself at the court of Antiochus, he began to form new plans for making war against Rome. He proposed to the Syrian monarch to raise a naval force and put it under his charge. He said that if Antiochus would give him 100 ships and 10,000 or 12,000 men, he would take the command of the expedition in person, and he did not doubt that he should be able to recover his lost ground, and once more humble his ancient and formidable enemy. He would go first, he said, with his force to Carthage, to get the co-operation and aid of his countrymen there in his new plans. Then he would make a descent upon Italy, and he had no doubt that he should soon regain the ascendency there which he had formerly held.

Hannibal Sends a Secret Messenger to Carthage

Hannibal's design of going first to Carthage with his Syrian army was doubtless induced by his desire to put down the party of his enemies there, and to restore the power to his adherents and partisans. In order to prepare the way the more effectually for this, he sent a secret messenger to Carthage, while his negotiations with Antiochus were going on, to make known to his friends there the new hopes which he began to cherish, and the new designs which he had formed. He knew that his enemies in Carthage would be watching very carefully for any such communication; he therefore wrote no letters, and committed nothing to paper which, on being discovered, might betray him. He explained, however, all his plans very fully to his messenger, and gave him minute and careful instructions as to his manner of communicating them.

The Placards

The Carthaginian authorities were indeed watching very vigilantly, and intelligence brought to them, by their spies, of the arrival of this stranger. They immediately took measures for arresting him. The messenger, who was himself as vigilant as they, got intelligence of this in his secret lurking-place in the city, and determined immediately to fly. He, however, first prepared some papers and placards, which he posted up in public places, in which he proclaimed that Hannibal was far from considering himself finally conquered; that he was, on the contrary, forming new plans for putting down his enemies in Carthage, resuming his former ascendency there, and carrying fire and sword again into the Roman territories; and, in the meantime, he urged the friends of Hannibal in Carthage to remain faithful and true to his cause.

Excitement Produced by Them

The messenger, after posting his placards, fled from the city in the night, and went back to Hannibal. Of course, the occurrence produced considerable excitement in the city. It aroused the anger and resentment of Hannibal's enemies, and awakened new encouragement and hope in the hearts of his friends. Further than this, however, it led to no immediate results. The power of the party which was opposed to Hannibal was too firmly established at Carthage to be very easily shaken. They sent information to Rome of the coming of Hannibal's emissary to Carthage, and of the result of his mission, and then everything went on as before.

Roman Commissioners – Supposed Interview of Hannibal and Scipio – Hannibal's Opinion of Alexander and Pyrrhus

In the meantime, the Romans, when they learned where Hannibal had gone, sent two or three commissioners there to confer with the Syrian government in respect to their intentions and plans, and watch the movements of Hannibal. It was said that Scipio himself was joined to this embassy, and that he actually met Hannibal at Ephesus, and had several personal interviews and conversations with him there. Some ancient historian gives a particular account of one of these interviews, in which the conversation turned, as it naturally would do between two such distinguished commanders, on military greatness and glory.

Scipio asked Hannibal whom he considered the greatest military hero that had ever lived. Hannibal gave the palm to Alexander the Great, because he had penetrated, with comparatively a very small number of Macedonian troops, into such remote regions, conquered such vast armies, and brought so boundless an empire under his sway. Scipio then asked him who he was inclined to place next to Alexander. He said Pyrrhus. Pyrrhus was a Greek, who crossed the Adriatic Sea, and made war, with great success, against the Romans. Hannibal said that he gave the second rank to Pyrrhus because he systematized and perfected the art of war, and also because he had the power of awakening a feeling of personal attachment to himself on the part of all his soldiers, and even of the inhabitants of the countries that he conquered, beyond any other general that ever lived. Scipio then asked Hannibal who came next in order, and he replied that he should give the third rank to himself. 'And if,' added he, 'I had conquered Scipio, I should consider myself as standing above Alexander, Pyrrhus and all the generals that the world ever produced.'

Anecdotes

Various other anecdotes are related of Hannibal during the time of his first appearance in Syria, all indicating the very high degree of estimation in which he was held, and the curiosity and interest that were everywhere felt to see him. On one occasion, it happened that a vain and self-conceited orator, who knew little of war but from his own theoretic speculations, was haranguing an assembly where Hannibal was present, being greatly pleased with the opportunity of displaying his powers before so distinguished an auditor. When the discourse was finished, they asked Hannibal what he thought of it. 'I have heard,' said he, in reply, 'many old dotards in the course of my life, but this is, verily, the greatest dotard of them all.'

Hannibal's Efforts Prove Vain – Antiochus Agrees to Give Him Up

Hannibal failed, notwithstanding all his perseverance, in obtaining the means to attack the Romans again. He was unwearied in his efforts, but, though the king sometimes encouraged his hopes, nothing was ever done. He remained in this part of the world for 10 years, striving continually to accomplish his aims, but every year he found himself farther from the attainment of them than ever. The hour of his good fortune and of his prosperity were obviously gone. His plans all failed, his influence declined, his name and renown were fast passing away. At last, after long and fruitless contests with the Romans, Antiochus made a treaty of peace with them, and, among the articles of this treaty, was one agreeing to give up Hannibal into their power.

Hannibal's Treasures

Hannibal resolved to fly. The place of refuge which he chose was the island of Crete. He found that he could not long remain here. He had, however, brought with him a large amount of treasure, and when about leaving Crete again, he was uneasy about this treasure, as he had some reason to fear that the Cretans were intending to seize it. He must contrive, then, some stratagem to enable him to get this gold away. The plan he adopted was this:

His Plan for Securing Them

He filled a number of earthen jars with lead, covering the tops of them with gold and silver. These he carried, with great appearance of caution and solicitude, to the Temple of Diana, a very sacred edifice, and deposited them there, under very special guardianship of the Cretans, to whom, as he said, he entrusted all his treasures. They received their false deposit with many promises to keep it safely, and then Hannibal went away with his real gold cast in the centre of hollow statues of brass, which he carried with him, without suspicion, as objects of art of very little value.

Hannibal's Unhappy Condition

Hannibal fled from kingdom to kingdom, and from province to province, until life became a miserable burden. The determined hostility of the Roman senate followed him everywhere, harassing him with continual anxiety and fear, and destroying all hope of comfort and peace. His mind was a prey to bitter recollections of the past, and still more dreadful forebodings for the future. He had spent all the morning of his life in inflicting the most terrible injuries on the objects of his implacable animosity and hate, although they had never injured him, and now, in the evening of his days, it became his destiny to feel the pressure of the same terror and suffering inflicted upon *him*. The hostility which he had to fear was equally merciless with that which he had exercised; perhaps it was made still more intense by being mingled with what they who felt it probably considered a just resentment and revenge.

Hannibal Fails in His Attempt to Escape – He Poisons Himself

When at length Hannibal found that the Romans were hemming him in more and more closely, and that the danger increased of his falling at last into their power, he had a potion of poison prepared, and kept it always in readiness, determined to die by his own hand rather than to submit to be given up to his enemies. The time for taking the poison at last arrived.

The wretched fugitive was then in Bithynia, a kingdom of Asia Minor. The King of Bithynia sheltered him for a time, but at length agreed to give him up to the Romans. Hannibal learning this, prepared for flight. But he found, on attempting his escape, that all the modes of exit from the palace which he occupied, even the secret ones which he had expressly contrived to aid his flight, were taken possession of and guarded. Escape was, therefore, no longer possible, and Hannibal went to his apartment and sent for the poison. He was now an old man, nearly 70 years of age, and he was worn down and exhausted by his protracted anxieties and sufferings. He was glad to die. He drank the poison, and in a few hours ceased to breathe.

Chapter XII
The Destruction of Carthage, 146–145 BC

Destruction – The Third Punic War

THE CONSEQUENCES of Hannibal's reckless ambition, and of his wholly unjustifiable aggression on Roman rights to gratify it, did not end with his own personal ruin. The flame which he had kindled continued to burn until at last it accomplished the entire and irretrievable destruction of Carthage. This was affected in a third and final war between the Carthaginians and the Romans, which is known in history as the Third Punic War. With a narrative of the events of this war, ending, as it did, in the total destruction of the city, we shall close this history of Hannibal.

Chronological Table of the Punic Wars

It will be recollected that the war which Hannibal himself waged against Rome was the second in the series, the contest in which Regulus figured so prominently having been the first. The one whose history is now to be given is the third. The reader will distinctly understand the chronological relations of these contests by the following table:

Date BCE	Events	Punic Wars
264	War commenced in Sicily	
262	Naval battles in the Mediterranean	I.
249	Regulus sent prisoner to Rome	24 years
241	Peace concluded	
	Peace for 24 years	
218	Hannibal attacks Saguntum	
217	Crosses the Alps	II.
216	Battle of Cannae	17 years
205	Is conquered by Scipio	
200	Peace concluded	
	Peace for 52 years	
148	War declared	III.
145	Carthage destroyed	3 years

Character of the Punic Wars – Intervals Between Them

These three Punic wars extended, as the table shows, over a period of more than 100 years. Each successive contest in the series was shorter, but more violent and desperate, than its predecessor, while the intervals of peace were longer. Thus, the First Punic War continued for 24 years, the Second about 17, and the Third only three or four. The interval, too, between the First and Second was 24 years, while between the Second and Third there was a sort of peace for about 50 years. These differences were caused, indeed, in some degree, by the accidental circumstances on which the successive ruptures depended, but they were not entirely owing to that cause. The longer these belligerent relations between the two countries continued, and the more they both experienced the awful effects and consequences of their quarrels, the less disposed they were to renew such dreadful struggles, and yet, when they did renew them, they engaged in them with redoubled energy of determination and fresh intensity of hate. Thus, the wars followed each other at greater intervals, but the conflicts, when they came, though shorter in duration, were more and more desperate and merciless in character.

Animosities and Dissensions

We have said that, after the close of the Second Punic War, there was a sort of peace for about 50 years. Of course, during this time, one generation after another of public men arose, both in Rome and Carthage, each successive group, on both sides, inheriting the suppressed animosity and hatred which had been cherished by their predecessors. Of course, as long as Hannibal had lived, and had continued his plots and schemes in Syria, he was the means of keeping up a continual irritation among the people of Rome against the Carthaginian name. It is true that the government at Carthage disavowed his acts and professed to be wholly opposed to his designs; but then it was, of course, very well known at Rome that this was only because they thought he was not able to execute them. They had no confidence whatever in Carthaginian faith or honesty, and, of course, there could be no real harmony or stable peace.

Numidia – Numidian Horsemen

There arose gradually, also, another source of dissension. To the west of Carthage was a country called Numidia. This country was 100 miles or more in breadth and extended back several hundred miles into the interior. It was a very rich and fertile region, and contained many powerful and wealthy cities. The inhabitants were warlike, too, and were particularly celebrated for their cavalry. The ancient historians say that they used to ride their horses into the field without saddles, and often without bridles, guiding and controlling them by their voices, and keeping their seats securely by the exercise of great personal strength and consummate skill. These Numidian horsemen are often alluded to in the narratives of Hannibal's campaigns, and, in fact, in all the military histories of the times.

Masinissa

Among the kings who reigned in Numidia was one who had taken sides with the Romans in the Second Punic War. His name was Masinissa. He became involved in some struggle for power with a neighbouring monarch named Syphax, and while he, that is, Masinissa, had allied himself to the Romans, Syphax had joined the Carthaginians, each chieftain hoping, by this means, to gain assistance from his allies in conquering the other. Masinissa's patrons proved to be the strongest, and at the end of the Second Punic War, when the conditions of peace were made, Masinissa's dominions were enlarged, and the undisturbed possession of them confirmed to him, the Carthaginians being bound by express stipulations not to molest him in any way.

Parties at Rome and Carthage – Their Differences

In commonwealths like those of Rome and Carthage, there will always be two great parties struggling against each other for the possession of power. Each wishes to avail itself of every opportunity to oppose and thwart the other, and they consequently almost always take different sides in all the great questions of public policy that arise. There were two such parties at Rome, and they disagreed in respect to the course which should be pursued in regard to Carthage, one being generally in favour of peace, the other perpetually calling for war. In the same manner there was at Carthage a similar dissension, the one side in the contest being desirous to propitiate the Romans and avoid collisions with them, while the other party were very restless and uneasy under the pressure of the Roman power upon them, and were endeavouring continually to foment feelings of hostility against their ancient enemies, as if they wished that war should break out again. The latter party were not strong enough to bring the Carthaginian state into an open rupture with Rome itself, but they succeeded at last in getting their government involved in a dispute with Masinissa, and in leading out an army to give him battle.

Masinissa Prepares for War

Fifty years had passed away, as has already been remarked, since the close of Hannibal's war. During this time, Scipio – that is, the Scipio who conquered Hannibal – had disappeared from the stage. Masinissa himself was very far advanced in life, being over 80 years of age. He, however, still retained the strength and energy which had characterized him in his prime. He drew together an immense army, and mounting, like his soldiers, bareback upon his horse, he rode from rank to rank, gave the necessary commands and matured the arrangements for battle.

Hasdrubal – Carthage Declares War

The name of the Carthaginian general on this occasion was Hasdrubal. This was a very common name at Carthage, especially among the friends and family of Hannibal. The bearer of it, in this case, may possibly have received it from his parents in commemoration of the brother of Hannibal, who lost his head in descending into Italy from the Alps, inasmuch as during the 50 years of peace which had elapsed, there was ample time for a child born after that event to grow up to full maturity. At any rate, the new Hasdrubal inherited the inveterate hatred to Rome which characterized his namesake, and he and his party had contrived to gain a temporary ascendency in Carthage, and they availed themselves of their brief possession of power to renew, indirectly at least, the contest with Rome. They sent the rival leaders into banishment, raised an army and, Hasdrubal himself taking the command of it, they went forth in great force to encounter Masinissa.

Parallel Between Hannibal and Hasdrubal

It was in a way very similar to this that Hannibal had commenced his war with Rome, by seeking first a quarrel with a Roman ally. Hannibal, it is true, had commenced his aggressions at Saguntum, in Spain. Hasdrubal begins in Numidia, in Africa, but, with the exception of the difference of geographical locality, all seems the same, and Hasdrubal very probably supposed that he was about to enter himself upon the same glorious career which had immortalized his great ancestor's name.

There was another analogy between the two cases, viz., that both Hannibal and Hasdrubal had strong parties opposed to them in Carthage in the incipient stages of their undertakings. In the present instance, the opposition had been violently suppressed, and the leaders of it sent into banishment; but still the elements remained, ready, in case of any disaster to Hasdrubal's arms, or any other occurrence tending to diminish his power, to rise at once and put him down. Hasdrubal had therefore a double enemy to contend against: one before him, on the battlefield, and the other, perhaps still more formidable, in the city behind him.

Battle with Masinissa – Defeat of the Carthaginians

The parallel, however, ends here. Hannibal conquered at Saguntum, but Hasdrubal was entirely defeated in the battle in Numidia. The battle was fought long and desperately on both sides, but the Carthaginians were obliged to yield, and they retreated at length in confusion to seek shelter in their camp. The battle was witnessed by a Roman officer who stood upon a neighbouring hill and looked down upon the scene with intense interest all the day. It was Scipio – the younger Scipio – who became afterward the principal actor in the terrible scenes which were enacted in the war which followed. He was then a distinguished officer in the Roman army and was on duty in Spain. His commanding general there had sent him to Africa to procure some elephants from Masinissa for the use of the army. He came to Numidia, accordingly, for this purpose, and as the battle between Masinissa and Hasdrubal came on while he was there, he remained to witness it.

The Younger Scipio – A Spectator of the Battle

This second Scipio was not, by blood, any relative of the other, but he had been adopted by the elder Scipio's son, and thus received his name; so that he was, by adoption, a grandson. He was, even at this time, a man of high consideration among all who knew him, for his great energy and efficiency of character, as well as for his sound judgment and practical good sense.

He occupied a very singular position at the time of this battle, such as very few great commanders have ever been placed in; for, as he himself was attached to a Roman army in Spain, having been sent merely as a military messenger to Numidia, he was a neutral in this contest, and could not, properly, take part on either side. He had, accordingly, only to take his place upon the hill, and look down upon the awful scene as upon a spectacle arranged for his special gratification.

He speaks of it as if he were highly gratified with the opportunity he enjoyed, saying that only two such cases had ever occurred before, where a general could look down, in such a way, upon a great battlefield, and witness the whole progress of the fight, himself a cool and disinterested spectator. He was greatly excited by the scene, and he speaks particularly of the appearance of the veteran Masinissa, then 84 years old, who rode all day from rank to rank, on a wild and impetuous charger, without a saddle, to give his orders to his men, and to encourage and animate them by his voice and his example.

Negotiations for Peace – Scipio Made Umpire

Hasdrubal retreated with his forces to his camp as soon as the battle was over, and entrenched himself there while Masinissa advanced with his army, surrounded the encampment and hemmed the imprisoned fugitives in. Finding himself in extreme and imminent danger, Hasdrubal sent to Masinissa to open negotiations for peace, and he proposed that Scipio should act as a sort of umpire or mediator between the two parties, to arrange the terms.

Scipio was not likely to be a very impartial umpire; but still, his interposition would afford him, as Hasdrubal thought, some protection against any excessive and extreme exorbitances on the part of his conqueror. The plan, however, did not succeed. Even Scipio's terms were found by Hasdrubal to be inadmissible. He required that the Carthaginians should accord to Masinissa a certain extension of territory. Hasdrubal was willing to assent to this. They were to pay him, also, a large sum of money. He agreed also to this. They were, moreover, to allow Hasdrubal's banished opponents to return to Carthage. This, by putting the party opposed to Hasdrubal once more into power in Carthage, would have been followed by his own fall and ruin; he could not consent to it. He remained, therefore, shut up in his camp, and Scipio, giving up the hope of effecting an accommodation, took the elephants which had been provided for him, and returned across the Mediterranean to Spain.

Hasdrubal Surrenders – Terms Imposed by Masinissa

Soon after this, Hasdrubal's army, worn out with hunger and misery in their camp, compelled him to surrender on Masinissa's own terms. The men were allowed to go free, but most of them perished on the way to Carthage. Hasdrubal himself succeeded in reaching some place of safety, but the influence of his party was destroyed by the disastrous result of his enterprise, and his exiled enemies being recalled in accordance with the treaty of surrender, the opposing party was immediately restored to power.

Carthaginian Embassy to Rome

Under these new councils, the first measure of the Carthaginians was to impeach Hasdrubal on a charge of treason, for having involved his country in these difficulties, and the next was to send a solemn embassy to Rome, to acknowledge the fault of which their nation had been guilty, to offer to surrender Hasdrubal into their hands, as the principal author of the deed, and to ask what further satisfaction the Romans demanded.

Their Mission Fruitless

In the meantime, before these messengers arrived, the Romans had been deliberating what to do. The strongest party were in favour of urging on the quarrel with Carthage and declaring war. They had not, however, come to any positive decision. They received the deputation, therefore, very coolly, and made them no direct reply. As to the satisfaction which the Carthaginians ought to render to the

Romans for having made war upon their ally contrary to the solemn covenants of the treaty, they said that that was a question for the Carthaginians themselves to consider. They had nothing at present to say upon the subject. The deputies returned to Carthage with this reply, which, of course, produced great uneasiness and anxiety.

Another Embassy

The Carthaginians were more and more desirous now to do everything in their power to avert the threatened danger of Roman hostility. They sent a new embassy to Rome, with still more humble professions than before. The embassy set sail from Carthage with very little hope, however, of accomplishing the object of their mission. They were authorized, nevertheless, to make the most unlimited concessions, and to submit to any conditions whatever to avert the calamity of another war.

The Romans Declare War

But the Romans had been furnished with a pretext for commencing hostilities again, and there was a very strong party among them now who were determined to avail themselves of this opportunity to extinguish entirely the Carthaginian power. War had, accordingly, been declared by the Roman senate very soon after the first embassy had returned, a fleet and army had been raised and equipped and the expedition had sailed. When, therefore, the embassy arrived in Rome, they found that the war, which it was the object of their mission to avert, had been declared.

Negotiations for Peace — The Romans Demand Hostages

The Romans, however, gave them audience. The ambassadors expressed their willingness to submit to any terms that the senate might propose for arresting the war. The senate replied that they were willing to make a treaty with the Carthaginians on condition that the latter were to surrender themselves entirely to the Roman power, and bind themselves to obey such orders as the consuls, on their arrival in Africa with the army, should issue; the Romans, on their part, guaranteeing that they should continue in the enjoyment of their liberty, their territorial possessions and their laws. As proof, however, of the Carthaginian honesty of purpose in making the treaty, and security for their future submission, they were required to give up to the Romans 300 hostages. These hostages were to be young persons from the first families in Carthage, the sons of the men who were most prominent in society there, and whose influence might be supposed to control the action of the nation.

The ambassadors could not but consider these as very onerous terms. They did not know what orders the consuls would give them on their arrival in Africa, and they were required to put the commonwealth wholly into their power. Besides, in the guarantee which the Romans offered them, their *territories* and their *laws* were to be protected, but nothing was said of their cities, their ships or their arms and munitions of war. The agreement there, if executed, would put the Carthaginian commonwealth wholly at the mercy of their masters, in respect to all those things which were in those days most valuable to a nation as elements of power. Still, the ambassadors had been instructed to make peace with the Romans on any terms, and they accordingly acceded to these, though with great reluctance. They were especially averse to the agreement in respect to the hostages.

Cruelty of the Hostage System

This system, which prevailed universally in ancient times, of having the government of one nation surrender the children of the most distinguished citizens to that of another as security for the fulfilment of its treaty stipulations, was a very cruel hardship to those who had to suffer the separation; but it would seem that there was no other security strong enough to hold such lawless powers as governments were in those days, to their word. Stern and rough as the men of those warlike nations often were, mothers were the same then as now, and they suffered quite as keenly in seeing their children sent away from them to pine in a foreign land, in hopeless exile, for many years; in danger, too, continually, of the most cruel treatment, and even of death itself, to revenge some alleged governmental wrong.

Return of the Ambassadors – Consternation in Carthage

Of course, the ambassadors knew, when they returned to Carthage with these terms, that they were bringing heavy tidings. The news, in fact, when it came, threw the community into the most extreme distress. It is said that the whole city was filled with cries and lamentations. The mothers, who felt that they were about to be bereaved, beat their breasts, tore their hair and manifested by every other sign their extreme and unmitigated woe. They begged and entreated their husbands and fathers not to consent to such cruel and intolerable conditions. They could not, and they would not give up their children.

Its Deplorable Condition

The husbands and the fathers, however, felt compelled to resist all these entreaties. They could not now undertake to resist the Roman will. Their army had been well-nigh destroyed in the battle with Masinissa; their city was consequently defenceless, the Roman fleet had already reached its African port and the troops were landed. There was no possible way, it appeared, of saving themselves and their city from absolute destruction, but entire submission to the terms which their stern conquerors had imposed upon them.

The hostages were required to be sent, within 30 days, to the island of Sicily, to a port on the western extremity of the island called Lilybaeum. Lilybaeum was the port in Sicily nearest to Carthage, being perhaps at a distance of 100 miles across the waters of the Mediterranean Sea. A Roman escort was to be ready to receive them there and conduct them to Rome. Although 30 days were allowed to the Carthaginians to select and send forward the hostages, they determined not to avail themselves of this offered delay, but to send the unhappy children forward at once, that they might testify to the Roman senate, by this their promptness, that they were very earnestly desirous to propitiate their favour.

Selecting the Hostages – The Hour of Parting – Grief and Despair

The children were accordingly designated, one from each of the leading families in the city, 300 in all. The reader must imagine the heart-rending scenes of suffering which must have desolated these 300 families and homes when the stern and inexorable edict came to each of them that one loved member of the household must be selected to go. And when, at last, the hour arrived for their departure, and they assembled upon the pier, the picture was one of intense and unmingled suffering.

The poor exiles stood bewildered with terror and grief, about to part with all that they ever held dear – their parents, their brothers and sisters and their native land – to go they knew not whither, under the care of iron-hearted soldiers, who seemed to know no feelings of tenderness or compassion for their woes. Their disconsolate mothers wept and groaned aloud, clasping the loved ones who were about to be torn forever from them in their arms, in a delirium of maternal affection and irrepressible grief; their brothers and sisters, and their youthful friends stood by, some almost frantic with emotions which they did not attempt to suppress, others mute and motionless in their sorrow, shedding bitter tears of anguish, or gazing wildly on the scene with looks of despair; while the fathers, whose stern duty it was to pass through this scene unmoved, walked to and fro restlessly, in deep but silent distress, spoke in broken and incoherent words to one another, and finally aided, by a mixture of persuasion and gentle force, in drawing the children away from their mothers' arms, and getting them on board the vessels which were to convey them away.

The vessels made sail and passed off slowly from the shore. The mothers watched them until they could no longer be seen, and then returned, disconsolate and wretched, to their homes; and then the grief and agitation of this parting scene was succeeded by the anxious suspense which now pervaded the whole city to learn what new dangers and indignities they were to suffer from the approaching Roman army, which they knew must now be well on its way.

Advance of the Roman Army – Surrender of Utica

The Roman army landed at Utica. Utica was a large city to the north of Carthage, not far from it, and upon the same bay. When the people of Utica found that another serious collision was to take place between Rome and Carthage, they had foreseen what would probably be the end of the contest, and they had decided that, in order to save themselves from the ruin which was plainly impending over the sister city, they must abandon her to her fate, and make common cause with Rome. They had, accordingly, sent deputies to the Roman senate, offering to surrender Utica to their power. The Romans had accepted the submission, and had made this city, in consequence, the port of debarkation for their army.

As soon as the news arrived at Carthage that the Roman army had landed at Utica, the people sent deputies to inquire what were the orders of the consuls, for it will be recollected they had bound themselves by the treaty to obey the orders which the consuls were to bring. They found, when they arrived there, that the bay was covered with the Roman shipping. There were 50 vessels of war, of three banks of oars each, and a vast number of transports besides. There was, too, in the camp upon the shore, a force of 80,000 foot soldiers and 4,000 horse, all armed and equipped in the most perfect manner.

Demands of the Romans

The deputies were convinced that this was a force which it was in vain for their countrymen to think of resisting. They asked, trembling, for the consuls' orders. The consuls informed them that the orders of the Roman senate were, first, that the Carthaginians should furnish them with a supply of corn for the subsistence of their troops. The deputies went back to Carthage with the demand.

The Carthaginians Comply

The Carthaginians resolved to comply. They were bound by their treaty and by the hostages they had given, as well as intimidated by the presence of the Roman force. They furnished the corn.

The consuls, soon after this, made another demand of the Carthaginians. It was, that they should surrender to them all their vessels of war. They were more unwilling to comply with this requisition than with the other; but they assented at last. They hoped that the demands of their enemies would stop here, and that, satisfied with having weakened them thus far, they would go away and leave them; they could then build new ships again when better times should return.

The Romans Demand All the Munitions of War – Their Great Number

But the Romans were not satisfied yet. They sent a third order, that the Carthaginians should deliver up all their arms, military stores and warlike machines of every kind, by sending them into the Roman camp. The Carthaginians were rendered almost desperate by this requisition. Many were determined that they would not submit to it, but would resist at all hazards. Others despaired of all possibility of resisting now, and gave up all as lost; while the 300 families from which the hostages had gone, trembled for the safety of the captive children, and urged compliance with the demand. The advocates for submission finally gained the day. The arms were collected and carried in an immensely long train of wagons to the Roman camp. There were 200,000 complete suits of armour, with darts and javelins without number, and 2,000 military engines for hurling beams of wood and stones. Thus, Carthage was disarmed.

Brutal Demands of the Romans – Carthage to Be Destroyed

All these demands, however unreasonable and cruel as the Carthaginians deemed them, were only preliminary to the great final determination, the announcement of which the consuls had reserved for the end. When the arms had all been delivered, the consuls announced to their now defenceless victims that the Roman senate had come to the determination that Carthage was to be destroyed. They gave orders, accordingly, that the inhabitants should all leave the city, which, as soon as it should be thus vacated, was to be burned. They might take with them such property as they could carry; and they were at liberty to build, in lieu of this their fortified seaport, an inland town, not less than 10 miles' distance from the sea, only it must have no walls or fortifications of any kind. As soon as the inhabitants were gone, Carthage, the consuls said, was to be destroyed.

Desperation of the People – Preparations for Defence

The announcement of this entirely unparalleled and intolerable requisition threw the whole city into a frenzy of desperation. They could not, and would not, submit to this. The entreaties and remonstrances of the friends of the hostages were all silenced or overborne in the burst of indignation and anger which arose from the whole city.

The gates were closed. The pavements of the streets were torn up, and buildings demolished to obtain stones, which were carried up upon the ramparts to serve instead of weapons. The slaves were all liberated and stationed on the walls to aid in the defence. Everybody that could work at a forge was employed in fabricating swords, spearheads, pikes and such other weapons as could be formed with the greatest facility and dispatch. They used all the iron and bronze that could be obtained, and then melted down vases and statues of the precious metals and tipped their spears with an inferior pointing of silver and gold.

In the same manner, when the supplies of flax and hempen twine for cordage for their bows failed, the beautiful sisters and mothers of the hostages cut off their long hair, and twisted and braided it into cords to be used as bowstrings for propelling the arrows which their husbands and brothers made. In a word, the wretched Carthaginians had been pushed beyond the last limit of human endurance, and had aroused themselves to a hopeless resistance in a sort of frenzy of despair.

Hasdrubal – Destruction of the Roman Fleet

The reader will recollect that, after the battle with Masinissa, Hasdrubal lost all his influence in Carthage, and was, to all appearance, hopelessly ruined. He had not, however, then given up the struggle. He had contrived to assemble the remnant of his army in the neighbourhood of Carthage. His forces had been gradually increasing during these transactions, as those who were opposed to these concessions to the Romans naturally gathered around him. He was now in his camp, not far from the city, at the head of 20,000 men.

Finding themselves in so desperate an emergency, the Carthaginians sent to him to come to their succour. He very gladly obeyed the summons. He sent around to all the territories still subject to Carthage, and gathered fresh troops, and collected supplies of arms and of food. He advanced to the relief of the city. He compelled the Romans, who were equally astonished at the resistance they met with from within the walls, and at this formidable onset from without, to retire a little, and entrench themselves in their camp, in order to secure their own safety. He sent supplies of food into the city.

He also contrived to fit up, secretly, a great many fire ships in the harbour, and, setting them in flames, let them drift down upon the Roman fleet, which was anchored in supposed security in the bay. The plan was so skilfully managed that the Roman ships were almost all destroyed. Thus, the face of affairs was changed. The Romans found themselves disappointed for the present of their prey. They confined themselves to their encampment and sent home to the Roman senate for new re-enforcements and supplies.

Horrors of the Siege

In a word, the Romans found that, instead of having only to effect, unresisted, the simple destruction of a city, they were involved in what would, perhaps, prove a serious and a protracted war. The war did, in fact, continue for two or three years – a horrible war, almost of extermination, on both sides. Scipio came with the Roman army, at first as a subordinate officer; but his bravery, his sagacity and the success of some of his almost romantic exploits, soon made him an object of universal regard. At one time, a detachment of the army, which he succeeded in releasing from a situation of great peril in which they had been placed, testified their gratitude by platting a crown of *grass*, and placing it upon his brow with great ceremony and loud acclamations.

Heroic Valour of the Carthaginians

The Carthaginians did everything in the prosecution of this war that the most desperate valour could do; but Scipio's cool, steady and well-calculated plans made irresistible progress, and hemmed them in at last, within narrower and narrower limits, by a steadily increasing pressure, from which they found it impossible to break away.

Battering Engines – Attempt to Destroy Them

Scipio had erected a sort of mole or pier upon the water near the city, on which he had erected many large and powerful engines to assault the walls. One night a large company of Carthaginians took torches, not lighted, in their hands, together with some sort of apparatus for striking fire, and partly by wading and partly by swimming, they made their way through the water of the harbour toward these machines. When they were sufficiently near, they struck their lights and set their torches on fire. The Roman soldiers who had been stationed to guard the machines were seized with terror at seeing all these flashing fires burst out suddenly over the surface of the water, and fled in dismay. The Carthaginians set the abandoned engines on fire, and then, throwing their now useless torches into the flames, plunged into the water again, and swam back in safety. But all this desperate bravery did very little good. Scipio quietly repaired the engines, and the siege went on as before.

The City Stormed – A Desperate Struggle – The People Retreat to the Citadel

But we cannot describe in detail all the particulars of this protracted and terrible struggle. We must pass on to the closing scene, which, as related by the historians of the day, is an almost incredible series of horrors. After an immense number had been killed in the assaults which had been made upon the city, besides the thousands and thousands which had died of famine and of the exposures and hardships incident to such a siege, the army of Scipio succeeded in breaking their way through the gates and gaining admission to the city.

Some of the inhabitants were now disposed to contend no longer, but to cast themselves at the mercy of the conqueror. Others, furious in their despair, were determined to fight to the last, not willing to give up the pleasure of killing all they could of their hated enemies, even to save their lives. They fought, therefore, from street to street, retreating gradually as the Romans advanced, till they found refuge in the citadel.

One band of Scipio's soldiers mounted to the tops of the houses, the roofs being flat, and fought their way there, while another column advanced in the same manner in the streets below. No imagination can conceive the uproar and din of such an assault upon a populous city – a horrid mingling of the vociferated commands of the officers, and of the shouts of the advancing and victorious assailants, with the screams of terror from affrighted women and children, and dreadful groans and imprecations from men dying maddened with unsatisfied revenge and biting the dust in an agony of pain.

The City Fired – Hasdrubal's Wife

The more determined of the combatants, with Hasdrubal at their head, took possession of the citadel, which was a quarter of the city situated upon an eminence, and strongly fortified. Scipio advanced to the walls of this fortification and set that part of the city on fire which lay nearest to it. The fire burned for six days, and opened a large area which afforded the Roman troops room to act. When the troops were brought up to the area thus left vacant by the fire, and the people within the citadel saw that their condition was hopeless, there arose, as there always does in such cases, the desperate struggle within the walls whether to persist in resistance or to surrender in despair.

There was an immense mass, not far from 60,000, half women and children, who were determined on going out to surrender themselves to Scipio's mercy and beg for their lives. Hasdrubal's wife, leading her two children by her side, earnestly entreated her husband to allow her to go with them. But he refused. There was a body of deserters from the Roman camp in the citadel, who, having no possible hope of escaping destruction except by desperate resistance to the last, Hasdrubal supposed would never yield. He committed his wife and children, therefore, to their charge, and these deserters, seeking refuge in a great temple within the citadel, bore the frantic mother with them to share their fate.

Hasdrubal Surrenders

Hasdrubal's determination, however, to resist the Romans to the last, soon after this gave way, and he determined to surrender. He is accused of the most atrocious treachery in attempting thus to save himself, after excluding his wife and children from all possibility of escaping destruction. But the confusion and din of such a scene, the suddenness and violence with which the events succeed each other, and the tumultuous and uncontrollable mental agitation to which they give rise, deprive a man who is called to act in it of all sense and reason, and exonerate him, almost as much, from moral responsibility for what he does, as if he were insane. At any rate, Hasdrubal, after shutting up his wife and children with a furious gang of desperadoes who could not possibly surrender, surrendered himself, perhaps hoping that he might save them after all.

The Citadel Fired – Resentment and Despair of Hasdrubal's Wife

The Carthaginian soldiers, following Hasdrubal's example, opened the gates of the citadel, and let the conqueror in. The deserters were now made absolutely desperate by their danger, and some of them, more furious than the rest, preferring to die by their own hands rather than to give their hated enemies the pleasure of killing them, set the building in which they were shut up in on fire. The miserable inmates ran to and fro, half suffocated by the smoke and scorched by the flames. Many of them reached the roof.

Hasdrubal's wife and children were among the number. She looked down from this elevation, the volumes of smoke and flame rolling up around her, and saw her husband standing below with the Roman general – perhaps looking, in consternation, for his wife and children, amid this scene of horror. The sight of the husband and father in a position of safety made the wife and mother perfectly furious with resentment and anger. 'Wretch!' she screamed, in a voice which raised itself above the universal din, 'is it thus you seek to save your own life while you sacrifice ours? I cannot reach you in your own person, but I kill you hereby in the persons of your children.' So saying, she stabbed her affrighted sons with a dagger, and hurled them down, struggling all the time against their insane mother's frenzy, into the nearest opening from which flames were ascending, and then leaped in after them herself to share their awful doom.

Carthage Destroyed – Its Present Condition

The Romans, when they had gained possession of the city, took most effectual measures for its complete destruction. The inhabitants were scattered into the surrounding country, and the whole territory was converted into a Roman province. Some attempts were afterward made to rebuild the city, and it was for a long time a place of some resort, as men lingered mournfully there in huts that they built among the ruins. It, however, was gradually forsaken, the stones crumbled and decayed, vegetation regained possession of the soil, and now there is nothing whatever to mark the spot where the city lay.

War and Commerce – Antagonistic Principles

War and commerce are the two great antagonistic principles which struggle for the mastery of the human race, the function of the one being to preserve, and that of the other to destroy. Commerce causes cities to be built and fields to be cultivated, and diffuses comfort and plenty, and all the blessings of industry and peace. It carries organization and order everywhere; it protects property and life; it disarms pestilence, and it prohibits famine. War, on the other hand, *destroys*. It disorganizes the social state. It ruins cities, depopulates fields, condemns men to idleness and want, and the only remedy it knows for the evils which it brings upon man is to shorten the miseries of its victims by giving pestilence and famine the amplest commission to destroy their lives. Thus, war is the great enemy, while commerce is the great friend of humanity. They are antagonistic principles, contending continually for the mastery among all the organizations of men.

Hannibal's Greatness as a Military Hero

When Hannibal appeared upon the stage, he found his country engaged peacefully and prosperously in exchanging the productions of the various countries of the then-known world, and promoting everywhere the comfort and happiness of mankind. He contrived to turn all these energies into the new current of military aggression, conquest and war. He perfectly succeeded.

We certainly have in his person and history all the marks and characteristics of a great military hero. He gained the most splendid victories, devastated many lands, embarrassed and stopped the commercial intercourse which was carrying the comforts of life to so many thousand homes, and spread, instead of them, everywhere, privation, want and terror, with pestilence and famine in their train. He kept the country of his enemies in a state of incessant anxiety, suffering and alarm for many years, and overwhelmed his own native land, in the end, in absolute and irresistible ruin. In a word, he was one of the greatest military heroes that the world has ever known.

The Histories by Polybius

THE HISTORIES BY POLYBIUS is a vitally important – and arguably the best – source about Hannibal and his war to survive from the Ancient World.

The Greek word Ἱστορίαι ('*Historiae*') means 'Inquiries'. The title of his work is apt. Polybius was painstaking in his historical research. He wrote: 'The peculiar function of history is to discover, in the first place, the words actually spoken, whatever they were, and next to ascertain the reason why what was done or spoken led to failure or success. For the mere statement of fact may interest us but is of no benefit to us: but when we add the cause of it, study of history becomes fruitful.' Polybius often discloses his sources of information, such as inscriptions he found on his research trips. He frequently finds fault with the conclusions of other historians. He is now regarded highly for his objectivity and critical reasoning.

These extracts – taken from the translation by H.J. Edwards (1922) – set out the background to Hannibal's siege of Saguntum; describe Hannibal's crossing of the Pyrenees; explain how his army forded the Rhône River; and details the perilous march through the Alps – a journey Polybius says he himself made in the course of conducting his research several decades after the historic event.

From the First Book

Chapter I
Historian's Introduction

CHRONICLERS neglected to speak in praise of history in general, it might perhaps have been necessary for me to recommend everyone to choose for study and welcome such treatises as the present, since men have no more ready corrective of conduct than knowledge of the past. But all historians, one may say without exception, and in no half-hearted manner, but making this the beginning and end of their labour, have impressed on us that the soundest education and training for a life of active politics is the study of History, and that surest and indeed the only method of learning how to bear bravely the vicissitudes of fortune, is to recall the calamities of others.

Evidently therefore no one, and least of all myself, would think it his duty at this day to repeat what has been so well and so often said. For the very element of unexpectedness in the events I have chosen as my theme will be sufficient to challenge and incite everyone, young and old alike, to peruse my systematic history. For who is so worthless or indolent as not to wish to know by what means and under what system of polity the Romans in less than 53 years have succeeded in subjecting nearly the whole inhabited world to their sole government – a thing unique in history? Or who again is there so passionately devoted to other spectacles or studies as to regard anything as of greater moment than the acquisition of this knowledge?

From the Third Book

Chapter VI
Start of the Second Punic War

SOME OF THOSE AUTHORS who have dealt with Hannibal and his times, wishing to indicate the causes that led to the above war between Rome and Carthage, allege as its first cause the siege of Saguntum by the Carthaginians and as its second their crossing, contrary to treaty, the river whose native name is the Iber. I should agree in stating that these were the beginnings of the war, but I can by no means allow that they were its causes, unless we call Alexander's crossing to Asia the cause of his war against Persia and Antiochus' landing at Demetrias the cause of his war against Rome, neither of which assertions is either reasonable or true.

For who could consider these to be *causes* of wars, plans and preparations for which, in the case of the Persian war, had been made earlier, many by Alexander and even some by Philip during his life, and in the case of the war against Rome by the Aetolians long before Antiochus arrived? These are pronouncements of men who are unable to see the great and essential distinction between a beginning and a cause or purpose, these being the first origin of all, and the beginning coming last.

By the beginning of something I mean the first attempt to execute and put in action plans on which we have decided, by its causes what is most initiatory in our judgements and opinions, that is to say our notions of things, our state of mind, our reasoning about these and everything through which we reach decisions and projects.

Chapter XIII
Hannibal Assumes Command

The Carthaginians could ill bear their defeat in the war for Sicily, and, as I said above, they were additionally exasperated by the matter of Sardinia and the exorbitance of the sum they had been last obliged to agree to pay. Therefore, when they had subjugated the greater part of Iberia, they were quite ready to adopt any measures against Rome which suggested themselves.

On the death of Hasdrubal, to whom after that of Hamilcar they had entrusted the government of Iberia, they at first waited for a pronouncement on the part of the troops, and when news reached them from their armies that the soldiers had unanimously chosen Hannibal as their commander, they hastened to summon a general assembly of the commons, which unanimously ratified the choice of the soldiers.

Hannibal, on assuming the command, at once set forth with the view of subduing a tribe called the Olcades, and arriving before their most powerful city Althaea, encamped there and soon made himself master of it by a series of vigorous and formidable assaults, upon which the rest of the tribe were overawed and submitted to the Carthaginians. After exacting tribute from the towns and possessing himself of a considerable sum, he retired to winter quarters at New Carthage. By the generosity he now displayed to the troops under his command, paying them in part and promising further payment, he inspired in them great goodwill to himself and high hopes of the future.

Chapter XIV
Battle of the Tagus River

Next summer he made a fresh attack on the Vaccaei, assaulted and took Hermandica at the first onset, but Arbacala being a very large city with a numerous and brave population, he had to lay siege to it and only took it by assault after much pain. Subsequently on his return he unexpectedly found himself in great peril, the Carpetani, the strongest tribe in the district gathering to attack him and being joined by the neighbouring tribes, all incited to this by the fugitive Olcades, and also by those who had escaped from Hermandica.

Had the Carthaginians been obliged to meet all this host in a pitched battle, they would assuredly have suffered defeat; but, as it was, Hannibal very wisely and skilfully faced about and retreated so as to place the river Tagus in his front, and remained there to dispute the crossing, availing himself of the aid both of the river and of his elephants, of which he had about 40, so that everything went as he had calculated and as no one else would have dared to expect. For when the barbarians tried to force a crossing at various points, the greater mass of them perished in coming out of the river, the elephants following its bank and being upon them as soon as they landed. Many also were cut down in the stream itself by the cavalry, as the horses could bear up better against the current, and the mounted men in fighting had the advantage of being higher than the unmounted enemy. Finally, Hannibal in his turn crossed the river and attacked the barbarians, putting to flight a force of more than 100,000.

After their defeat, none of the peoples on that side of the Ebro ventured lightly to face the Carthaginians, with the exception of the Saguntines. Hannibal tried as far as he could to keep his hands off this city, wishing to give the Romans no avowed pretext for war, until he had secured his possession of all the rest of the country, following in this his father Hamilcar's suggestions and advice.

Chapter XV
Saguntines Seek Help from Rome

But the Saguntines sent repeated messages to Rome, as on the one hand they were alarmed for their own safety and foresaw what was coming, and at the same time they wished to keep the Romans informed how well things went with the Carthaginians in Spain. The Romans, who had more than once paid little attention to them, sent on this occasion legates to report on the situation. Hannibal at the same time, having reduced the tribes he intended, arrived with his forces to winter at New Carthage, which was in a way the chief ornament and capital of the Carthaginian empire in Spain. Here he found the Roman legates, to whom he gave audience and listened to their present communication. The Romans protested against his attacking Saguntum, which they said was under their protection, or crossing the Ebro, contrary to the treaty engagements entered into in Hasdrubal's time.

Hannibal, being young, full of martial ardour, encouraged by the success of his enterprises, and spurred on by his long-standing enmity to Rome, in his answer to the legates affected to be guarding the interests of the Saguntines and accused the Romans of having a short time previously, when there was a party quarrel at Saguntum and they were called in to arbitrate, unjustly put to death some of the leading men. The Carthaginians, he said, would not overlook this violation of good faith for it was from of old the principle of Carthage never to neglect the cause of the victims of injustice. To Carthage, however, he sent, asking for instructions, since the

Saguntines, relying on their alliance with Rome, were wronging some of the peoples subject to Carthage.

Being wholly under the influence of unreasoning and violent anger, he did not allege the true reasons, but took refuge in groundless pretexts, as men are wont to do who disregard duty because they are prepossessed by passion. How much better would it have been for him to demand from the Romans the restitution of Sardinia, and at the same time of the tribute which they had so unjustly exacted, availing themselves of the misfortunes of Carthage, and to threaten war in the event of refusal!

But as it was, by keeping silent as to the real cause and by inventing a non-existing one about Saguntum, he gave the idea that he was entering on the war not only unsupported by reason but without justice on his side. The Roman legates, seeing clearly that war was inevitable, took ship for Carthage to convey the same protest to the government there. They never thought, however, that the war would be in Italy, but supposed they would fight in Spain with Saguntum for a base.

Chapter XVI
Roman Miscalculation

Consequently, the senate, adapting their measures to this supposition, decided to secure their position in Illyria, as they foresaw that the war would be serious and long and the scene of it far away from home. It so happened that at that time in Illyria, Demetrius of Pharos, oblivious of the benefits that the Romans had conferred on him, contemptuous of Rome because of the peril to which she was exposed first from the Gauls and now from Carthage, and placing all his hopes in the Royal House of Macedon owing to his having fought by the side of Antigonus in the battles against Cleomenes, was sacking and destroying the Illyrian cities subject to Rome, and, sailing beyond Lissus, contrary to the terms of the treaty, with 50 boats, had pillaged many of the Cyclades.

The Romans, in view of those proceedings and of the flourishing fortunes of the Macedonian kingdom, were anxious to secure their position in the lands lying east of Italy, feeling confident that they would have time to correct the errors of the Illyrians and rebuke and chastise Demetrius for his ingratitude and temerity. But in this calculation, they were deceived; for Hannibal forestalled them by taking Saguntum, and, as a consequence, the war was not waged in Spain but at the very gates of Rome and through the whole of Italy. However, the Romans now moved by these considerations dispatched a force under Lucius Aemilius just before summer in the first year of the 140th Olympiad [220 BCE] to operate in Illyria.

Chapter XVII
Hannibal Advances on Saguntum

Hannibal at the same time quitted New Carthage with his army and advanced towards Saguntum. This city lies on the seaward foot of the range of hills connecting Iberia and Celtiberia, at a distance of about seven stades from the sea. The territory of the Saguntines yields every kind of crop and is the most fertile in the whole of Iberia.

Hannibal, now encamping before the town, set himself to besiege it vigorously, foreseeing that many advantages would result from its capture. First of all he thought that he would thus deprive the Romans of any prospect of a campaign in Iberia, and secondly, he was convinced that by this blow he would inspire universal terror, and render the Iberian tribes who had already submitted more orderly and those who were still independent more cautious, while above all he would be enabled to advance safely with no enemy left in his rear. Besides, he would then have abundant funds and supplies for his projected expedition, he would raise the spirit of his troops by the booty distributed among them and would conciliate the Carthaginians at home by the spoils he would send them.

From all these considerations he actively pursued the siege, now setting an example to the soldiers by sharing personally the fatigue of the battering operations, now cheering on the troops and exposing recklessly to danger. At length after eight months of hardship and anxiety he took the city by storm. A great booty of money, slaves and property fell into his hands. The money, as he had determined, he set aside for his own purposes, the slaves he distributed among his men according to rank and the miscellaneous property he sent off at once to Carthage.

The result did not deceive his expectations, nor did he fail to accomplish his original purpose; but he both made his troops more eager to face danger and the Carthaginians more ready to accede to his demands on them, while he himself, by setting aside these funds, was able to accomplish many things of much service to him.

Chapter XX
Romans React to the Fall of Saguntum

The Romans, when the news of the fall of Saguntum reached them, did not assuredly hold a debate on the question of the war, as some authors allege, even setting down the speeches made on both sides – a most absurd proceeding. For how could the Romans, who a year ago had announced to the Carthaginians that their entering the territory of Saguntum would be regarded as a casus belli, now when the city itself had been taken by assault, assemble to debate whether to go to war or not? How is it that on the one hand these authors draw a wonderful picture of the gloomy aspect of the senate and on the other tell us that fathers brought their sons from the age of 12 upwards to the senate house, and that these boys attended the debate but divulged not a syllable even to any of their near relatives?

Nothing in this is the least true or even probable, unless, indeed, Fortune has bestowed on the Romans among other gifts that of being wise from their cradles. No further criticism, indeed, of such works as those of Chaereas and Sosylus is necessary; they rank in authority, it seems to me, not with history, but with the common gossip of a barber's shop.

The Romans, on hearing of the calamity that had befallen Saguntum, at once appointed ambassadors and sent them post-haste to Carthage, giving the Carthaginians the option of two alternatives, the one of which, if they accepted it, entailed disgrace and damage, while the other would give rise to extreme trouble and peril. Either they must give up Hannibal and the members of his council, or war would be declared. On the Roman envoys arriving and appearing before the senate and delivering their message, the Carthaginians listened with indignation to this choice of alternatives, but putting up their most able member to speak, they entered upon their justification.

Chapter XXI
Romans' Diplomatic Overtures

They said not a word of the treaty with Hasdrubal, considering it as not existent, or if existent, as not concerning them, since it was made without their approval. Here they quoted the precedent of the Romans themselves, alleging that the treaty made in the war for Sicily under Lutatius, though agreed to by Lutatius, had been repudiated by the Romans as having been made without their approval.

In all their plea of justification they founded and insisted on the treaty at the end of the war for Sicily, in which they said there was no mention of Iberia, but it was expressly set down that the allies of each power should be secure from attack by the other. They pointed out that at that time the Saguntines were not the allies of Rome, and to prove their point they read aloud several extracts from the treaty.

The Romans refused definitely to discuss the matter of justification, saying that while Saguntum still stood unharmed matters admitted of a plea of justification and it was possible to reach a decision on the disputed points by argument, but now that the treaty had been broken by the seizure of the city either they must give up the culprits, which would make it clear to all that they had no share in the wrong, but that it had been done without their approval, or if they refused to do so and thus confessed that they were participators in the misdeed they must accept war.

On this occasion the question was dealt with in more or less general terms, but I think it necessary for myself not to neglect it, so that neither those whose duty and interest it is to be accurately informed about this may deviate from the truth in critical debates, nor students, led astray by the ignorance or partisanship of historians, acquire mistaken notions on the subject, but that there may be some survey generally recognized as accurate of the treaties between Rome and Carthage up to our own time.

Chapter XXIX
Roman Demands

I have already stated what the Carthaginians alleged and will now give the reply of the Romans – a reply, indeed, which they did not make at the time owing to their indignation at the loss of Saguntum, but it has been given on many occasions and by many different people at Rome.

In the first place, they contend that the treaty with Hasdrubal should not be ignored, as the Carthaginians had the audacity to say; for there was no conditioning clause at the end as in the treaty made by Lutatius: 'This treaty shall be valid if the Roman people also agree to it,' but Hasdrubal finally and unconditionally made the agreement in which was the clause, 'The Carthaginians shall not cross the Ebro in arms.' Again, in the treaty about Sicily there was, as the Carthaginians admit, the clause: 'The allies of either party are to be secure from attack by the other,' and this does not mean 'those who were allies at that time,' as the Carthaginians interpret it;

for in that case there would have been a further clause to the effect that neither party should enter into other alliances than their existing ones or that those subsequently received into alliance should not be admitted to the benefits of the treaty. But since neither of these clauses was appended, it is evident that each party undertook that all allies of the other, both those then existing and those subsequently admitted to alliance, should be secure from attack.

This indeed seems a quite reasonable view; for, surely, they would never have made a treaty by which they deprived themselves of the freedom to admit into alliance from time to time any peoples whose friendship seemed to be of advantage to them, nor, having taken such under their protection, was it to be supposed that they would ignore injuries done to them by certain people. But the chief meaning of the treaty to both parties when they made it was that they should each leave unmolested the existing allies of the other and in no way admit any of those into their own alliance, whereas, regarding subsequent alliances, to which this clause particularly applies, they undertook not to enlist soldiers or levy contributions in the provinces of each or in countries allied to each, and that all allies of each in general should be secure from attack by the other.

Chapter XXX
Causes of the Second Punic War

This being so, it is an acknowledged fact that the Saguntines, a good many years before the time of Hannibal, placed themselves under the protection of Rome. The surest proof of this, and one accepted by the Carthaginians themselves, is that when a civil disturbance broke out at Saguntum they did not call in the mediation of the Carthaginians, although they were close at hand and already concerning themselves with Spanish matters, but that of the Romans, and with their help set right the affairs of the state.

Therefore, if we take the destruction of Saguntum to be the cause of the war we must allow that the Carthaginians were in the wrong in beginning the war, both in view of the treaty of Lutatius, in which it was stipulated that the allies of each should be secure from attack by the other, and in view of the convention made with Hasdrubal, by which the Carthaginians undertook not to cross the Ebro in arms. If, however, we take the cause of the war to have been the robbery of Sardinia and the tribute then exacted, we must certainly confess that they had good reason for entering on the Hannibalic war, since having yielded only to circumstances, they now availed themselves of circumstances to be avenged on those who had injured them.

Chapter XXXIII
Carthaginian Response

I interrupted my narrative to enter on this digression at the point where the Roman ambassadors were at Carthage. After listening to the Carthaginians' statement of their case, they made no other reply but the following.

The oldest member of the embassy, pointing to the bosom of his *toga*, told the senate that it held both war and peace for them: therefore, he would let fall from it and leave with them whichever of the two they bade him. The Carthaginian Suffete bade him let fall whichever the Romans chose, and when the envoy said he would let fall war, many of the senators cried out at once, 'We accept it.' The ambassadors and the senate parted on these terms.

Hannibal, who was wintering in New Carthage, in the first place dismissed the Iberians to their own cities hoping thus to make them readily disposed to help in the future; next he instructed his brother Hasdrubal how to manage the government of Spain and prepare to resist the Romans if he himself happened to be absent; in the third place he took precautions for the security of Africa, adopting the very sensible and wise policy of sending soldiers from Africa to Spain, and vice versa, binding by this measure the two provinces to reciprocal loyalty.

The troops who crossed to Africa were supplied by the Thersitae, Mastiani, Iberian Oretes and Olcades, and numbered 1,200 horse and 13,870 Balearians, a popular appellation, derived from *ballein*, 'to throw', and meaning slingers, given to them owing to their skill with this weapon and extended to their nation and islands. He stationed most of these troops at Metagonia in Libya and some in Carthage itself.

From the socalled Metagonian towns he sent 4,000 foot to Carthage to serve both as a reinforcement and as hostages.

In Spain he left with his brother Hasdrubal 50 quinqueremes, two quadriremes and all the triremes being fully manned. He also gave him as cavalry Liby-Phoenicians and Libyans to the number of 450, 300 Ilergetes and 1,800 Numidians drawn from the Masylii, Masaesylii, Maccoei and Maurusi, who dwell by the ocean, and as infantry 11,850 Libyans, 300 Ligurians and 500 Balearians, as well as 21 elephants.

No one need be surprised at the accuracy of the information I give here about Hannibal's arrangements in Spain, an accuracy which even the actual organizer of the details would have some difficulty in attaining, and I need not be condemned off hand under the idea that I am acting like those authors who try to make their misstatements plausible. The fact is that I found on the Lacinian promontory a bronze tablet on which Hannibal himself had made out these lists during the time he was in Italy, and thinking this an absolutely first-rate authority, decided to follow the document.

Chapter XXXIV
Hannibal Prepares for War with Rome

Hannibal, after taking all precautions for the safety of Africa and Spain, was anxiously awaiting the arrival of the messengers he expected from the Celts. He had informed himself accurately about the fertility of the land at the foot of the Alps and near the river Po, the denseness of its population, the bravery of the men in war and above all their hatred of Rome ever since that former war with the Romans which I described in the preceding Book to enable my readers to follow all I am about to narrate. He therefore cherished high hopes of them, and was careful to send messengers with unlimited promises to the Celtic chiefs both on this side of the Alps and in the mountains themselves, thinking that the only means of carrying the war against the Romans into Italy was, after surmounting, if possible, the difficulties of the route, to reach the above country and employ the Celts as co-operators and confederates in his enterprise.

When the messengers arrived and reported that the Celts consented and awaited him, at the same time saying that the crossing of the Alps was very toilsome and difficult, but by no means impossible, he drew out his troops from their winter quarters in the early spring. As the news of what had happened in Carthage had just reached him, his spirits were now high, and trusting in the favourable disposition of the citizens, he now called openly on his men to join him in the war against Rome, impressing upon them the demand of the Romans that he and all his principal officers should be given up to them, and pointing out at the same time the wealth of the country they were bound for and the friendly feelings of the Gauls who would be their allies. When he saw that the soldiers listened gladly and were as eager as himself to be off, he commended their alacrity and after ordering them to be ready on the day fixed for his departure, dismissed the meeting.

Chapter XXXV
Hannibal's Expeditionary Army

Having completed the arrangements I mentioned above during the winter and thus assured the security of Africa and Spain, he advanced on the day he had fixed with an army of about 90,000 foot and 12,000 horse. Crossing the Ebro, he set about subduing the tribes of the Ilurgetes, Bargusii, Aerenosii and Andosini as far as the Pyrenees, and having reduced them all and taken some cities by assault, with unexpected rapidity indeed, but after many severe engagements and with great loss, he left Hanno in command of all the country on this side of the river, placing the Bargusii under his absolute rule, as he mistrusted them most, owing to their friendly sentiments toward Rome. He assigned to Hanno out of his own army 10,000 foot and 1,000 horse, and he left with him all the heavy baggage of the expeditionary force.

He dismissed at the same time an equal number of troops to their homes, with the view of leaving them well disposed to himself and encouraging the hope of a safe return in the rest of the Spaniards, not only those who were serving with him, but those who remained at home, so that if he ever had to call on them for reinforcements, they might all readily respond.

With the rest of his force, thus lightened of its *impedimenta* and consisting now of 50,000 foot and about 9,000 horse, he advanced throughout the Pyrenees towards the crossing of the Rhône, having now an army not so strong in number as serviceable and highly trained owing to the unbroken series of wars in Spain.

Chapter XXXIX
Scale of the Logistical Challenge

At the time of which we are speaking the Carthaginians were masters of all that part of Africa which looks towards the Mediterranean from the Altars of Philaenus on the Greater Syrtis as far as the Pillars of Hercules.

The length of this coastline is more than 16,000 *stades*. Crossing the straits at the Pillars of Hercules they had similarly subdued all Iberia as far as the point on the coast of the Mediterranean where the Pyrenees, which separate the Celts from the Iberians, end. This spot is about 8,000 *stades* distant from the mouth of this sea at the Pillars of Hercules, the distance being 3,000 *stades* from the

Pillars to New Carthage, from which place Hannibal started for Italy, 2,600 *stades* from hence to the Ebro, and from the Ebro to Emporium 1,600 *stades*. From Emporium to Narbo it is about 600 *stades*, and from Narbo to the passage of the Rhône about 1,600, this part of the road having now been carefully measured by the Romans and marked with milestones at every eighth *stade*. From the passage of the Rhône, following the bank of the river in the direction of its source as far as the foot of the pass across the Alps to Italy, the distance is 1,400 stades, and the length of the actual pass which would bring Hannibal down into the plain of the Po, about 1,200. So that to arrive there he had, starting from New Carthage, to march about 9,000 *stades*.

Of this, as far as distance goes, he had nearly traversed the half, but if we look to difficulty far the largest part lay before him.

Chapter XL
Romans Evaluate Their Options

While Hannibal was thus attempting to cross the Pyrenees, in great fear of the Celts owing to the natural strength of the passes, the Romans, having received from the envoys they had sent to Carthage an account of the decision arrived at, and the speeches made there, and on news reaching them sooner than they had expected that Hannibal had crossed the Ebro with his army, determined to send, with their legions, the consuls Publius Cornelius Scipio to Spain and Tiberius Sempronius Longus to Africa. While occupied in enrolling the legions and making other preparations, they were pushing on the project of establishing in Cisalpine Gaul the colonies on which they had decided. They took active steps to fortify the towns, and ordered the colonists, who were about 6,000 in number for either city, to be on the spot within 30 days.

The one city they founded on this side of the Po, calling it Placentia, the other, which they named Cremona, on the far side. Scarce had both these colonies been established when the Boii Gauls, who had been for long as it were lying in wait to throw off their allegiance to Rome, but had hitherto found no opportunity, elated now by the messages they received assuring them of the near arrival of the Carthaginians, revolted from Rome, abandoning the hostages they gave at end of the former war which I described in my last Book. Calling on the Insubres to join them, whose support they easily gained owing to their long-standing rancour against

Rome, they overran the lands which the Romans had allotted to their colonies and on the settlers taking to flight, pursued them to Mutina, a Roman colony, and there besieged them.

Among those shut up there were three men of high rank who had been sent to carry out the partitionment of the country, Gaius Lutatius, a former consul, and two former praetors. On these three requesting a parley with the Boii, the latter consented, but when they came out for the purpose, they treacherously made them prisoners, hoping by means of them to get back their own hostages. When the Praetor Lucius Manlius, who with his troops was occupying an advanced position in the neighbourhood, heard of this, he hastened up to give help.

The Boii had heard of his approach and, posting ambuscades in a certain forest, attacked him from all sides at once as soon as he reached the wooded country, and killed many of the Romans. The remainder at first took to flight, but on getting to higher ground rallied just enough to give their retreat an appearance of order. The Boii following at their heels shut this force too up in the place called Vicus Tannetis.

When the news reached Rome that the fourth legion was surrounded by the Boii and besieged, they instantly sent off the legions destined for Publius under the command of a Praetor to its assistance, ordering Publius to enroll other legions from the allies.

Chapter XLI
The Romans Pursue Hannibal

The condition and course of Celtic affairs from the outset up to the arrival of Hannibal were such as I have narrated here and in the previous Book.

The two Roman consuls, having made all preparations for their respective enterprises, set sail early in summer to take in hand the operations determined on, Publius bound for Iberia with 60 ships and Tiberius Sempronius for Africa with a 160 quinqueremes. With these he threatened such a redoubtable expedition and made such vast preparations at Lilybaeum, collecting all kinds of forces from everywhere, that it seemed as if he expected to sail up to Carthage and at once lay siege to it. Publius, coasting along Liguria, reached the neighbourhood of Marseilles from Pisa in five days, and coming to anchor off the first mouth of the Rhône, known as the Massaliotic mouth, disembarked his forces there, having heard that Hannibal was already crossing the Pyrenees, but convinced that he was still at a distance of many days' march owing to the difficulty of the country and the numbers of Celtic tribes between them.

Hannibal, however, who had bribed some of the Celts and forced others to give him passage, unexpectedly appeared with his army at the crossing of the Rhône, having marched with the Sardinian Sea on his right. Publius, when the arrival of the enemy was reported to him, being partly incredulous owing to the cupidity of their advance and partly desirous of ascertaining the exact truth – while he himself was refreshing his troops after their voyage and consulting with his Tribunes in what place it would be wisest to offer battle to the enemy – sent out 300 of his bravest cavalry, giving them as guides and supports certain Celts who were in the service of the Massaliots as mercenaries.

Chapter XLII
Hannibal Prepares to Cross the Rhône River

Hannibal, on reaching the neighbourhood of the river, at once set about attempting to cross it where the stream is single at a distance of about four days' march from the sea. Doing his best to make friends with the inhabitants of the bank, he bought up all their canoes and boats, amounting to a considerable number, since many of the people on the banks of the Rhône engage in maritime traffic. He also got from them the logs suitable for making the canoes, so that in two days he had an innumerable quantity of ferryboats, everyone doing his best to dispense with any assistance and relying on himself for his chance of getting across.

In the meantime, a large force of barbarians had gathered on the opposite bank to prevent the Carthaginians from crossing. Hannibal observing this and concluding that as things stood it was neither possible to force a crossing in face of such a strong hostile force nor to put it off, lest he should find himself attacked on all sides, sent off on the third night after his arrival a portion of his army, giving them native guides and placing them under the command of Hanno, the son of Bomilcar the Suffete. Advancing up the bank of the river for 200 *stades* they reached a place at which the stream divides, forming an island, and here they stopped. Using the timber they found ready to hand and either nailing or lashing logs together they soon constructed a number of rafts sufficient for their present need, and on these they crossed in safety, meeting with no opposition.

Occupying a post of some natural strength they remained there for that day to rest after their exertions and at the same time to prepare for the movement, which they had been ordered to execute. Hannibal, moreover, with the part of the army that remained behind with him, was similarly occupied. The question that caused him the greatest embarrassment was how to get the elephants, 37 in number, across.

Chapter XLIII
Hannibal's Men Attacked While Crossing the Rhône River

On the fifth night, however, the force which had already crossed began a little before dawn to advance along the opposite bank against the barbarians there, while Hannibal had got his soldiers ready and was waiting until the time for crossing came. He had filled the boats with his light horse and the canoes with his lightest infantry. The large boats were placed highest upstream and the lighter ferryboats farther down, so that the heavier vessels receiving the chief force of the current, the canoes should be less exposed to risk in crossing. They hit on the plan of towing the horses astern of the boats swimming, one man at each side of the stern guiding three or four horses by their leading reins, so that a considerable number were got across at once in the first batch.

The barbarians, seeing the enemy's project, poured out of their camp, scattered and in no order, feeling sure that they would easily prevent the Carthaginians from landing. Hannibal, as soon as he saw that the force he had previously sent across was near at hand on the opposite bank, they having announced their approach by a smoke signal as arranged, ordered all in charge of the ferryboats to embark and push up against the current. He was at once obeyed, and now with the men in the boats shouting as they vied with one another in their efforts and struggled to stem the current, with the two armies standing on either bank at the very brink of the river, the Carthaginians following the progress of the boats with loud cheers and sharing in the fearful suspense, and the barbarians yelling their war cry and challenging to combat, the scene was in the highest degree striking and thrilling.

At this moment, the barbarians having deserted their tents, the Carthaginians on the far bank attacked suddenly and unexpectedly, and while some of them set fire to the enemy's encampment, the larger portion fell upon the defenders of the passage. The barbarians, taken quite by surprise, rushed some of them to save their tents, while others defended themselves against their assailants. Hannibal, all falling out favourably as he had purposed, at once marshalled those of his men who were the first to land, and after addressing some words of exhortation to them, led them to meet the barbarians, upon which the Celts, owing to their disordered condition and to their being taken by surprise, soon turned and took to flight.

Chapter XLIV
Hannibal Placates the Gauls

The Carthaginian general, having thus made himself master of the passage and defeated the enemy, at once occupied himself in fetching over the men who had been left on the other bank and, having in a very short time brought his whole army across, encamped for that night beside the river.

Next morning, hearing that the Roman fleet was anchored off the mouths of the Rhône, he selected 500 of his Numidian horse and sent them off to observe the whereabouts and number of the enemy and what they were about. At the same time, he set the proper men to the task of bringing the elephants across and then called a meeting of his soldiers and, introducing Magilus and the other chieftains who had come to him from the plain of the Po, made the troops acquainted through an interpreter with what they reported to be the decision of their tribes.

What encouraged the soldiers most in their address was firstly the actual and visible presence of those Gauls who were inviting them to Italy and promising to join them in the war against Rome, and secondly the reliance they placed on their promise to guide them by a route which would take them without their being exposed to any privations, rapidly and safely to Italy. In addition to this the Gauls dwelt on the richness and extent of the country they were going to, and the eager spirit of the men by whose side they were about to face the armies of Rome.

The Celts, after speaking in this sense, withdrew, and Hannibal himself now came forward and began by reminding them of their achievements in the past: though, he said, they had undertaken many hazardous enterprises and fought many a battle they had never met with ill success when they followed his plans and counsels. Next, he bade them be of good heart considering that the hardest part of their task was now accomplished, since they had forced the passage of the river and had the testimony of their own eyes and ears to the friendly sentiments and readiness to help of their allies. He begged them therefore to be at their ease about details which were his own business, but to obey orders and behave like brave men and in a manner worthy of their own record in the past.

When the men applauded him, exhibiting great enthusiasm and ardour, he commended them and, after offering a prayer to the gods on behalf of all, dismissed them, bidding them get everything ready expeditiously as they would start on their march next day.

Chapter XLV
Romans in Hot Pursuit

After the assembly had broken up, the Numidian scouts who had been sent out to reconnoitre returned, the greater part of the force lost and the remainder in headlong flight. Not far from their own camp they had fallen in with the Roman cavalry sent out by Publius on the same errand, and both forces had shown such heroism in the engagement that the Romans and Celts lost about 140 horsemen and the Numidians more than 200.

Afterwards, the Romans carried their pursuit close-up to the Carthaginian camp, and having surveyed it, turned and hastily rode off to report to the consul the arrival of the enemy, and on reaching their camp did so. Publius at once put his baggage on board the ships and started with his whole army marching up the riverbank with the view of encountering the Carthaginians.

Hannibal, on the day after the assembly, advanced his cavalry in the direction of the sea to act as a covering force and then moved his infantry out of the camp and sent them off on their march, while he himself waited for the elephants and the men who had been left with them. The way they got the elephants across was as follows.

Chapter XLVI
Hannibal's Elephants the Cross the Rhône River

They built a number of very solid rafts and lashing two of these together fixed them very firmly into the bank of the river, their united width being about 50 feet. To these they attached others on the farther side, prolonging the bridge out into the stream. They secured the side of it which faced the current by cables attached to the trees that grew on the bank, so that the whole structure might remain in place and not be shifted by the current.

When they had made the whole bridge or pier of rafts about 200 feet long they attached to the end of it two particularly compact ones, very firmly fastened to each other, but so connected with the rest that the lashings could easily be cut. They attached to these several towing lines by which boats were to tow them, not allowing them to be carried downstream, but holding them up against the current, and thus were to convey the elephants which would be in them across. After this they piled up a quantity of earth on all the line of rafts, until the whole was on the same level and of the same appearance as the path on shore leading to the crossing.

The animals were always accustomed to obey their drivers up to the water, but would never enter it on any account, and they now drove them along over the earth with two females in front, whom they obediently followed. As soon as they set foot on the last rafts the ropes which held these fast to the others were cut, and the boats pulling taut, the towing lines rapidly tugged away from the pile of earth the elephants and the rafts on which they stood. Hereupon the animals becoming very alarmed at first turned round and ran about in all directions, but as they were shut in on all sides by the stream, they finally grew afraid and were compelled to keep quiet.

In this manner, by continuing to attach two rafts to the end of the structure, they managed to get most of them over on these, but some were so frightened that they threw themselves into the river when halfway across. The drivers of these were all drowned, but the elephants were saved, for owing to the power and length of their trunks they kept them above the water and breathed through them, at the same time spouting out any water that got into their mouths and so held out, most of them passing through the water on their feet.

Chapter XLVII
Hannibal Approaches the Alps

After the elephants had been put across, Hannibal, taking them and his cavalry and forming these into a rearguard, advanced up the riverbank away from the sea in an easterly direction as though making for the centre of Europe.

The Rhône rises north-west of the head of the Adriatic on the northern slope of the Alps, and running in a south-westerly direction, falls into the Sardinian Sea. A great part of its course is through a deep valley, to the north of which lives the Celtic tribe of the Ardyes, while on the south it is bounded for its whole extent by the northern spurs of the Alps. The plain of the Po which I described above at length is separated from the Rhône valley by the lofty main chain of these mountains, which starting from Marseilles extends to the head of the Adriatic. It is this chain which Hannibal now crossed to enter Italy from the Rhône valley.

Some of the writers who have described this passage of the Alps, from the wish to impress their readers by the marvels they recount of these mountains, are betrayed into two vices ever most alien to true history; for they are compelled to make both false statements and statements which contradict each other. While on the one hand introducing Hannibal as a commander of unequalled courage and foresight, they incontestably represent him to us as entirely wanting in prudence, and again, being unable to bring their series of falsehoods to any close or issue they introduce gods and the sons of gods into the sober history of the facts. By representing the Alps as being so steep and rugged that not only horses and troops accompanied by elephants, but even active men on foot would have difficult in passing, and at the same time picturing to us the desolation of the country as being such, that unless some god or hero had met Hannibal and showed him the way, his whole army would have gone astray and perished utterly, they unquestionably fall into both the above vices.

Chapter XLVIII
Hannibal's Genius

For, in the first place, can we imagine a more imprudent general or a more incompetent leader than Hannibal would have been, if with so large an army under his command and all his hopes of ultimate success resting on it, he did not know the roads and the country, as these writers say, and had absolutely no idea where he was marching or against whom, or in fact if his enterprise were feasible or not?

What they would have us believe is that Hannibal, who had met with no check to diminish his high hopes of success, ventured on a course that no general, even after a crushing defeat and utterly at his wits' end, would take, to march, that is, into a country as to which he had no information.

Similarly, in what they say about the loneliness, and the extreme steepness and difficulty of the road, the falsehood is manifest. For they never took the trouble to learn that the Celts who live near the Rhône not on one or on two occasions only before Hannibal's arrival but often, and not at any remote date but quite recently, had crossed the Alps with large armies and met the Romans in the field side by side with the Celts who inhabit the plain of the Po (as I narrated in an earlier Book) nor are they aware that there is a considerable population in the Alps themselves; but in entire ignorance of all this they tell us that some hero appeared and showed the road. The natural consequence is that they get into the same difficulties as tragic dramatists all of whom, to bring their dramas to a close, require a *deus ex machina*, as the data they choose on which to found their plots are false and contrary to reasonable probability.

These writers are necessarily in the same spirit and invent apparitions of heroes and gods, since the beginnings on which they build are false and improbable; for how is it possible to finish conformably to reason what has been begun in defiance of it? Of course, Hannibal did not act as these writers describe, but conducted his plans with sound practical sense. He had ascertained by careful inquiry the richness of the country into which he proposed to descend and the aversion of the people to the Romans, and for the difficulties of the route he employed as guides and pioneers, natives of the country, who were about to take part in his adventure.

On these points I can speak with some confidence as I have inquired about the circumstances from men present on the occasion and have personally inspected the country and made the passage of the Alps to learn for *myself* and see.

Chapter XLIX
The Romans Arrive to Find Hannibal Already Gone

Now the Roman Consul Publius arrived at the crossing of the river three days after the departure of the Carthaginians, and finding the enemy gone was in the highest degree astonished, as he had been convinced that they would never venture to march on Italy by this route owing to the number and unruly character of the native inhabitants. On seeing that they had done so he returned with all speed to his ships and began to embark his forces. Sending his brother to conduct the campaign in Spain, he himself turned back and made sail for Italy with the design of marching rapidly through Etruria and reaching the foot of the pass over the Alps before the enemy.

Hannibal, marching steadily from the crossing place for four days, reached a place called the 'Island', a populous district producing abundance of corn and deriving its name from its situation; for the Rhône and Isère running along each side of it meet at its point. It is similar in size and shape to the Egyptian Delta; only in that case the sea forms the base line uniting the two branches of the Nile, while here the base line is formed by a range of mountains difficult to climb or penetrate, and, one may say, almost inaccessible.

On arriving there he found two brothers disputing the crown and posted over against each other with their armies, and on the elder one making overtures to him and begging him to assist in establishing him on the throne, he consented, it being almost a matter of certainty that under present circumstances this would be of great service to him. Having united with him therefore to attack and expel the other, he derived great assistance from the victor; for not only did he furnish the army with plenty of corn and other provisions, but he replaced all their old and worn weapons by new ones, thus freshening up the whole force very opportunely. He also supplied most of them with warm clothing and footwear, things of the greatest possible service to them in crossing the mountains. But the most important of all was that for the Carthaginians, being not at all easy on the subject of their passage through the territory of the Allobroges, he protected them in the rear with his own forces and enabled them to reach the foot of the pass in safety.

Chapter L
Hannibal Begins to Ascend the Alps

After a 10 days' march of 800 stades along the bank of the Isère, Hannibal began the ascent of the Alps and now found himself involved in very great difficulties. For as long as they had been in flat country, the various chiefs of the Allobroges had left them alone, being afraid both of the cavalry and of the barbarians who were escorting them. But when the latter had set off on their return home, and Hannibal's troops began to advance into the difficult region, the Allobrogian chieftains got together a considerable force and occupied advantageous positions on the road by which the Carthaginians would be obliged to ascend.

Had they only kept their project secret, they would have utterly annihilated the Carthaginian army, but, as it was, it was discovered, and though they inflicted a good deal of damage on Hannibal, they did more injury to themselves; for the Carthaginian general having learnt that the barbarians had seized on these critical positions, encamped himself at the foot of the pass, and remaining there sent on in advance some of his Gaulish guides, to reconnoitre and report on the enemy's plan and the whole situation. His orders were executed, and on learning that the enemy remained most strictly at their post during the daytime, but retired at night to a neighbouring township, he adapted his measures to this intelligence and arranged the following plan. He advanced openly with his whole army, and on approaching the difficult points he encamped not far from the enemy.

As soon as it was night, he ordered the fires to be lit, and leaving the greater part of his forces there, took the men most fitted for the enterprise, whom he had lightened of their accoutrements, and passing through the narrow part of the road occupied the posts abandoned by the enemy, who had retired as usual to the town.

Chapter LI
Hannibal Attacked, Suffers Losses of Pack Animals

At daylight, the enemy observed what had happened and at first desisted from their project, but afterwards on seeing the long string of pack animals and horsemen slowly and with difficulty winding up the narrow path, they were tempted by this to molest their march.

On their doing so and attacking at several different points, the Carthaginians suffered great loss chiefly in horses and pack mules, not so much at the hands of the barbarians as owing to the ground. For the road up the pass being not only narrow and uneven but precipitous, the least movement or disturbance caused many of the animals to be pushed over the precipice with their packs. It was chiefly the horses on being wounded which caused the disturbance, some of them, terrified by the pain, turning and meeting the pack animals and others rushing on ahead and pushing aside in the narrow path everything that came in their way, thus creating a general confusion.

Hannibal, on seeing this and reflecting that there would be no chance of safety even for those who escaped from the battle if the pack train were destroyed, took with him the men who had occupied the heights at night and hastened to render assistance to the head of the marching column. He inflicted great loss on the Allobroges, as he was charging from higher ground, but the loss was equally heavy among his own troops, since the column on the march was thrown into further confusion in both directions at once owing to the shouting and struggling of those taking part in this combat.

It was only when he had put the greater part of the Allobroges to the sword and compelled the rest to take to flight and run for their own land that the remainder of the pack train and the horses got slowly and with great difficulty over the dangerous part, and he himself rallying as many troops as he could after the fight, attacked the town from which the enemy had issued to make their onslaught.

He found it nearly deserted, as all the inhabitants had been tempted out by hope of pillage, and seized on it. This proved of great service to him for the future as well as the present; for not only did he recover a number of pack animals and horses and the men who had been captured together with them, but he got a supply of corn and cattle amply sufficient for two or three days, and in addition to this he struck such terror into the next tribes that none of those in the neighbourhood of the ascent were likely to venture to molest him.

Chapter LII
Hannibal Ponders Alliances with the Natives

For the present, he encamped here, and after a stay of one day resumed his march. For the following days he conducted the army in safety up to a certain point, but on the fourth day he was again placed in great danger.

The natives near the pass conspired together and came out to meet him with treacherous intentions, holding olive branches and wreaths, which nearly all the barbarians use as tokens of friendship, just as we Greeks use the herald's staff. Hannibal, who was a little suspicious of such proffer of alliance, took great pains to ascertain what their project and general motives were. When they told him that they knew all about the capture of the city and the destruction of those who had attempted to do him wrong, and assured him that for this reason they were come to him, as they neither wished to inflict nor to suffer any injury, and on their promising to give him hostages from among themselves, he for long hesitated, distrusting their word. But, reflecting that if he accepted their offers, he might perhaps make them charier of attacking him and more pacific, but that if he refused, they would certainly be his declared enemies, he finally agreed to their proposals, and feigned to accept their friendship.

Upon the barbarians now delivering the hostages and providing him with cattle in abundance, and altogether putting themselves unreservedly into his hands, he trusted them in so far as to employ them as guides for the next difficult part of the road. But after two days march these same barbarians, collecting and following on the heels of the Carthaginians, attacked them as they were traversing a certain difficult and precipitous gorge.

Chapter LIII
Hannibal's Column Assaulted

On this occasion Hannibal's whole army would have been utterly destroyed had he not still been a little apprehensive and, foreseeing such a contingency, placed the pack train and cavalry at the head of the column and the heavy infantry in the rear. As the latter now acted as a covering force, the disaster was less serious, the infantry meeting the brunt of the attack.

But in spite of all this, a great many men, pack animals and horses were lost. For the enemy being on higher ground skirted along the slopes and either by rolling rocks down or by hurling stones from the hand threw the Carthaginians into such extreme peril and confusion that Hannibal was compelled to pass the night with half his force at a certain place defended by bare rocks and separated from his horses and pack train, whose advance he waited to cover, until after a whole night's labour they managed to extricate themselves from the defile.

Next day, the enemy having taken their departure, he joined the cavalry and pack animals and advanced to the summit of the pass, encountering no longer any massed force of barbarians, but molested from time to time and in certain places by some of them who took advantage of the ground to attack him either from the rear or from the front and carry off some of the pack animals. In these circumstances, the elephants were of the greatest service to him; for the enemy never dared to approach that part of the column in which these animals were, being terrified by the strangeness of their appearance.

After an ascent of nine days, Hannibal reached the summit and, encamping there, remained for two days to rest the survivors of his army and wait for stragglers. During this interval a good many of the horses, which had broken away in terror and a number of those sumpter animals which had thrown off their packs returned strangely enough, having followed the track of the march, and came into the camp.

Chapter LIV
Hazards on the Descent

As it was now close on the setting of the Pleiades, snow had already gathered on the summit, and noticing that the men were in bad spirits owing to all they had suffered up to now and expected to suffer he summoned them to a meeting and attempted to cheer them up, relying chiefly for this purpose on the actual view of Italy, which lies so close under these mountains, that when both are viewed together the Alps stand to the whole of Italy in the relation of a citadel to a city. Showing them, therefore, the plain of the Po, and reminding them of the friendly feelings of the Gauls inhabiting it, while at the same time pointing out the situation of Rome itself, he to some extent restored their spirits.

Next day he broke up his camp and began the descent. During this he encountered no enemy, except a few skulking marauders, but owing to the difficulties of the ground and the snow his losses were nearly as heavy as on the ascent. The descending path was very narrow and steep, and as both men and beasts could not tell on what they were treading owing to the snow, all that stepped wide of the path or stumbled were dashed down the precipice. This trial, however, they put up with, being by this time familiar with such sufferings, but they at length reached a place where it was impossible for either the elephants or the pack animals to pass owing to the extreme narrowness of the path, a previous landslip having carried away about one and a half *stades* of the face of the mountain and a further landslip having recently occurred, and here the soldiers once more became disheartened and discouraged. The Carthaginian general at first thought of avoiding the difficult part by a detour, but as a fresh fall of snow made progress impossible, he had to abandon this project.

Chapter LV
Hannibal Encamps on the Ridge

The state of matters was altogether peculiar and unusual. The new snow which had fallen on the top of the old snow remaining since the previous winter, was itself yielding, both owing to its softness, being a fresh fall, and because it was not yet very deep, but when they had trodden through it and set foot on the congealed snow beneath it, they no longer sunk in it, but slid along it with both feet, as happens to those who walk on ground with a coat of mud on it. But what followed on this was even more trying.

As for the men, when, unable to pierce the lower layer of snow, they fell and then tried to help themselves to rise by the support of their knees and hands, they slid along still more rapidly on these, the slope being exceedingly steep. But the animals, when they fell, broke through the lower layer of snow in their efforts to rise, and remained there with their packs as if frozen into it, owing to their weight and the congealed condition of this old snow.

Giving up this project, then, Hannibal encamped on the ridge, sweeping it clear of snow, and next set the soldiers to work to build up the path along the cliff, a most toilsome task. In one day he had made a passage sufficiently wide for the pack train and horses; so he at once took these across and encamping on ground free of snow, sent them out to pasture, and then took the Numidians in relays to work at building up the path, so that with great difficulty in three days he managed to get the elephants across, but in a wretched condition from hunger; for the summits of the Alps and the parts near the tops of the passes are all quite treeless and bare owing to the snow lying there continuously both winter and summer, but the slopes halfway up on both sides are grassy and wooded and on the whole inhabitable.

Chapter LVI
Cost in Lives of Hannibal's March

Hannibal, having now got all his forces together, continued the descent, and in three days' march from the precipice just described reached flat country. He had lost many of his men by the hands of the enemy in the crossing of rivers and on the march in general, and the precipices and difficulties of the Alps had cost him not only many men, but a far greater number of horses and pack animals.

The whole march from New Carthage had taken him five months, and he had spent 15 days in crossing the Alps, and now, when he thus boldly descended into the plain of the Po and the territory of the Insubres, his surviving forces numbered 12,000 African and 8,000 Iberian foot, and not more than 6,000 horse in all, as he himself states in the inscription on the column at Lacinium relating to the number of his forces.

About the same time, as I stated above, Publius Scipio, leaving his forces with his brother Cnaeus with orders to conduct operations in Spain and vigorously combat Hasdrubal, arrived by sea at Pisa with a small following. Marching through Etruria and taking over from the praetors the frontier legions which were engaged with the Boii, he reached the plain of the Po, and encamping there, waited for the enemy, being anxious to give him battle.

Chapter LX
Hannibal Arrives in Italy

I have already stated the strength of Hannibal's army when he entered Italy. Once arrived there he at first encamped at the very foot of the Alps to refresh his forces. For his men had not only suffered terribly from the toil of ascent and descent of the passes and the roughness of the road but they were also in wretched condition owing to the scarcity of provisions and neglect of their persons, many having fallen into a state of utter despondency from prolonged toil and want of food.

For it had been impossible to transport over such ground a plentiful supply of provisions for so many thousand men, and with the loss of the pack animals the greater part of what they were carrying perished. So that while Hannibal started from the passage of the Rhône with 38,000 foot and more than 8,000 horse he lost in crossing the passes, as I said above, about half his whole force, while the survivors, owing to the continued hardships they had suffered, had become in their external appearance and general condition more like beasts than men. Hannibal, therefore, made every provision for carefully attending to the men and the horses likewise until they were restored in body and spirit.

After this, his forces having now picked up their strength, when the Taurini who live at the foot of the mountains quarrelled with the Insubres and showed no confidence in the Carthaginians, he at first made overtures for their friendship and alliance, but on their rejecting these he encamped round their chief city and reduced it in three days. By massacring those who had been opposed to him he struck such terror into the neighbouring tribes of barbarians that they all came in at once and submitted to him. The remaining Celtic inhabitants of the plains were impatient to join the Carthaginians, as had been their original design, but as the Roman legions had advanced beyond most of them and cut them off, they kept quiet, some even being compelled to serve with the Romans. Hannibal, in view of this, decided not to delay, but to advance and try by some action to encourage those who wished to take part in his enterprise.

The History of Rome by Livy

FROM THE FOUNDATION OF THE CITY (a.k.a. *The History of Rome*) by Livy gives an unmistakably Roman perspective on Hannibal and his war. His narrative has largely established the historical Hannibal for the ages.

Hannibal is the wily adversary of the story, for years managing to outwit the Roman commanders sent to defeat him. They constantly underestimate his abilities, grit and determination. While the consuls play politics, Hannibal gets on with the business of war. Finally in Scipio, the Romans find a man who will save them from the invader – and from themselves.

Livy provides dramatic depictions of the Roman army in the thick of battle and succumbing to Hannibal's superior forces and strategies, resulting in panic among the citizens when news of the army's defeat reaches the city. He also reveals the inner workings of Roman politics and how religion played a role in it, with the consuls and Senate consulting the colleges of priests to decide their courses of action.

These extracts, from the translation by Rev. Canon Roberts (1912), portray Hannibal's character, strengths and weaknesses as the Romans perceived them, and describe his campaign in Italy, including the battles of Lake Trasimene and Cannae, and the immediate aftermath.

From the Twenty-First Book

Chapter I
Historian's Introduction

I CONSIDER MYSELF at liberty to commence what is only a section of my history with a prefatory remark such as most writers have placed at the very beginning of their works, namely, that the war I am about to describe is the most memorable of any that have ever been waged, I mean the war which the Carthaginians, under Hannibal's leadership, waged with Rome.

No states, no nations ever met in arms greater in strength or richer in resources; these powers themselves had never before been in so high a state of efficiency or better prepared to stand the strain of a long war; they were no strangers to each other's tactics after their experience in the First Punic War; and so variable were the fortunes and so doubtful the issue of the war that those who were ultimately victorious were in the earlier stages brought nearest to ruin.

And yet, great as was their strength, the hatred they felt towards each other was almost greater. The Romans were furious with indignation because the vanquished had dared to take the offensive against their conquerors; the Carthaginians bitterly resented what they regarded as the tyrannical and rapacious conduct of Rome. The prime author of the war was Hamilcar. There was a story widely current that when, after bringing the African War to a close, he was offering sacrifices before transporting his army to Spain, the boy Hannibal, nine years old, was coaxing his father to take him with him, and his father led him up to the altar and made him swear with his hand laid on the victim that as soon as he possibly could he would show himself the enemy of Rome. The loss of Sicily and Sardinia vexed the proud spirit of the man, for he felt that the cession of Sicily had been made hastily in a spirit of despair, and that Sardinia had been filched by the Romans during the troubles in Africa, who, not content with seizing it, had imposed an indemnity as well.

THE HISTORY OF ROME

Chapter II
Hamilcar's Treaty with Rome

Smarting under these wrongs, he made it quite clear from his conduct of the African War which followed immediately upon the conclusion of peace with Rome, and from the way in which he strengthened and extended the rule of Carthage during the nine years' war with Spain, that he was meditating a far greater war than any he was actually engaged in, and that had he lived longer it would have been under his command that the Carthaginians effected the invasion of Italy, which they actually carried out under Hannibal. The death of Hamilcar, occurring as it did most opportunely, and the tender years of Hannibal delayed the war.

Hasdrubal, coming between father and son, held the supreme power for eight years. He is said to have become a favourite of Hamilcar's owing to his personal beauty as a boy; afterwards he displayed talents of a very different order, and became his son-in-law. Through this connection he was placed in power by the influence of the Barcine party, which was unduly preponderant with the soldiers and the common people, but his elevation was utterly against the wishes of the nobles. Trusting to policy rather than to arms, he did more to extend the empire of Carthage by forming connections with the petty chieftains and winning over new tribes by making friends of their leading men than by force of arms or by war.

But peace brought him no security. A barbarian whose master he had put to death murdered him in broad daylight, and when seized by the bystanders he looked as happy as though he had escaped. Even when put to the torture, his delight at the success of his attempt mastered his pain and his face wore a smiling expression. Owing to the marvellous tact he had shown in winning over the tribes and incorporating them into his dominions, the Romans had renewed the treaty with Hasdrubal. Under its terms, the river Ebro was to form the boundary between the two empires, and Saguntum, occupying an intermediate position between them, was to be a free city.

Chapter III
Hannibal's Youth

There was no hesitation shown in filling his place. The soldiers led the way by bringing the young Hannibal forthwith to the palace and proclaiming him their commander-in-chief amidst universal applause. Their action was followed by the plebs [common people].

Whilst little more than a boy, Hasdrubal had written to invite Hannibal to come to him in Spain, and the matter had actually been discussed in the Senate. The Barcines wanted Hannibal to become familiar with military service; Hanno, the leader of the opposite party, resisted this.

'Hasdrubal's request,' he said, 'appears a reasonable one, and yet I do not think we ought to grant it.' This paradoxical utterance aroused the attention of the whole Senate. He continued: 'The youthful beauty which Hasdrubal surrendered to Hannibal's father he considers he has a fair claim to ask for in return from the son. It ill becomes us, however, to habituate our youths to the lust of our commanders, by way of military training. Are we afraid that it will be too long before Hamilcar's son surveys the extravagant power and the pageant of royalty which his father assumed, and that there will be undue delay in our becoming the slaves of the despot to whose son-in-law our armies have been bequeathed as though they were his patrimony? I, for my part, consider that this youth ought to be kept at home and taught to live in obedience to the laws and the magistrates on an equality with his fellow citizens; if not, this small fire will someday or other kindle a vast conflagration.'

Chapter IV
Hannibal's Character

Hanno's proposal received but slight support, though almost all the best men in the council were with him, but as usual, numbers carried the day against reason. No sooner had Hannibal landed in Spain than he became a favourite with the whole army. The veterans thought they saw Hamilcar restored to them as he was in his youth; they saw the same determined expression the same piercing eyes, the same cast of features. He soon showed, however, that it was not his father's memory that helped him most to win the affections of the army. Never was there a character more capable of the two tasks so opposed to each other of commanding and obeying; you could not easily make out whether the army or its general were more attached to him.

Whenever courage and resolution were needed Hasdrubal never cared to entrust the command to anyone else; and there was no leader in whom the soldiers placed more confidence or under whom they showed more daring. He [Hannibal] was fearless in exposing himself to danger and perfectly self-possessed in the presence of danger. No amount of exertion could cause him either bodily or mental fatigue; he was equally indifferent to heat and cold; his eating and drinking were measured by the needs of nature, not by appetite; his hours of sleep were not determined by day or night, whatever time was not taken up with active duties was given to sleep and rest, but that rest was not wooed on a soft couch or in silence, men often saw him lying on the ground amongst the sentinels and outposts, wrapped in his military cloak. His dress was in no way superior to that of his comrades; what did make him conspicuous were his arms and horses. He was by far the foremost both of the cavalry and the infantry, the first to enter the fight and the last to leave the field.

But these great merits were matched by great vices – inhuman cruelty, a perfidy worse than Punic, an utter absence of truthfulness, reverence, fear of the gods, respect for oaths, sense of religion. Such was his character: a compound of virtues and vices. For three years he served under Hasdrubal, and during the whole time he never lost an opportunity of gaining by practice or observation the experience necessary for one who was to be a great leader of men.

From the Twenty-Second Book

Chapter I
Omens and Religious Rites Observed at Rome

Spring was now coming on; Hannibal accordingly moved out of his winter quarters. His previous attempt to cross the Apennines had been frustrated by the insupportable cold; to remain where he was would have been to court danger. The Gauls had rallied to him through the prospect of booty and spoil, but when they found that instead of plundering other people's territory their own had become the seat of war and had to bear the burden of furnishing winter quarters for both sides, they diverted their hatred from the Romans to Hannibal.

Plots against his life were frequently hatched by their chiefs, and he owed his safety to their mutual faithlessness, for they betrayed the plots to him in the same spirit of fickleness in which they had formed them. He guarded himself from their attempts by assuming different disguises, at one time wearing a different dress, at another putting on false hair. But these constant alarms were an additional motive for his early departure from his winter quarters.

About the same time Cn. Servilius entered upon his consulship at Rome, on the 15th of March. When he had laid before the senate the policy which he proposed to carry out, the indignation against C. Flaminius broke out afresh. 'Two consuls had been elected, but as a matter of fact they only had one. What legitimate authority did this man possess? What religious sanctions? Magistrates only take these sanctions with them from home, from the altars of the state, and from their private altars at home after they have celebrated the Latin Festival, offered the sacrifice on the Alban Mount, and duly recited the vows in the capitol. These sanctions do not follow a private citizen, nor if he has departed without them can he obtain them afresh in all their fulness on a foreign soil.'

To add to the general feeling of apprehension, information was received of portents having occurred simultaneously in several places. In Sicily several of the soldiers' darts were covered with flames; in Sardinia the same thing happened to the staff in the hand of an officer who was going his rounds to inspect the sentinels on the wall; the shores had been lit up by numerous fires; a couple of shields had sweated blood; some soldiers had been struck by lightning; an eclipse of the sun had been observed; at Praeneste there had been a shower of red-hot stones; at Arpi shields had been seen in the sky and the sun had appeared to be fighting with the moon; at Capena two moons were visible in the daytime; at Caere the waters ran mingled with blood, and even the spring of Hercules had bubbled up with drops of blood on the water; at Antium the ears of corn which fell into the reapers' basket were bloodstained; at Falerii the sky seemed to be cleft asunder as with an enormous rift and all over the opening there was a blazing light; the oracular tablets shrank and shrivelled without being touched and one had fallen out with this inscription, 'MARS IS SHAKING HIS SPEAR'; and at the same time the statue of Mars on the Appian Way and the images of the wolves sweated blood. Finally, at Capua the sight was seen of the sky on fire and the moon falling in the midst of a shower of rain.

Then credence was given to comparatively trifling portents, such as that certain people's goats were suddenly clothed with wool, a hen turned into a cock and a cock into a hen. After giving the details exactly as they were reported to him and bringing his informants before the Senate, the consul consulted the House as to what religious observances ought to be proclaimed. A decree was passed that to avert the evils which these portents foreboded, sacrifices should be offered, the victims to be both full-grown animals and sucklings and also that special intercessions should be made at all the shrines for three days. What other ceremonial was necessary was to be carried out in accordance with the instructions of the decemvirs [board of 10 magistrates] after they had inspected the Sacred Books and ascertained the will of the gods.

On their advice it was decreed that the first votive offering should be made to Jupiter in the shape of a golden thunderbolt weighing 50 pounds, gifts of silver to Juno and Minerva and sacrifices of full-grown victims to Queen Juno on the Aventine and Juno Sospita at Lanuvium, whilst the matrons were to contribute according to their means and bear their gift to Queen Juno on the Aventine. A *lectisternium* was to be held, and even the freedwomen were to contribute what they could for a gift to the temple of Feronia. When these instructions had been carried out the decemvirs sacrificed full-grown victims in the forum at Ardea, and finally in the middle of December there was a sacrifice at the Temple of Saturn, a *lectisternium* [sacred meal for the gods] was ordered (the senators prepared the couch), and a public banquet. For a day and a night, the cry of the Saturnalia resounded through the city, and the people were ordered to make that day a festival and observe it as such forever.

Chapter II
Travails of Marching Through Italy; Hannibal Loses Sight in One Eye

While the consul was occupied in these propitiatory ceremonies and also in the enrolment of troops, information reached Hannibal that Flaminius had arrived at Arretium, and he at once broke up his winter quarters.

There were two routes into Etruria, both of which were pointed out to Hannibal; one was considerably longer than the other but a much better road. The shorter route, which he decided to take, passed through the marshes of the Arno, which was at the time in higher flood than usual. He ordered the Spaniards and Africans, the main strength of his veteran army, to lead, and they were to take their own baggage with them, so that, in case of a halt, they might have the necessary supplies; the Gauls were to follow so as to form the centre of the column; the cavalry were to march last, and Mago and his Numidian light horse were to close up the column, mainly to keep the Gauls up to the mark in case they fell out or came to a halt through the fatigue and exertion of so long a march, for as a nation they were unable to stand that kind of thing. Those in front followed wherever the guides led the way, through the deep and almost bottomless pools of water, and though almost sucked in by the mud through which they were half-wading, half-swimming, still kept their ranks.

The Gauls could neither recover themselves when they slipped nor when once down had they the strength to struggle out of the pools; depressed and hopeless they had no spirits left to keep up their bodily powers. Some dragged their worn-out limbs painfully along, others gave up the struggle and lay dying amongst the baggage animals which were lying about in all directions. What distressed them most of all was want of sleep, from which they had been suffering for four days and three nights. As everything was covered with water and they had not a dry spot on which to lay their wearied bodies, they piled up the baggage in the water and lay on the top, whilst some snatched a few minutes' needful rest by making couches of the heaps of baggage animals which were everywhere standing out of the water.

Hannibal himself, whose eyes were affected by the changeable and inclement spring weather, rode upon the only surviving elephant so that he might be a little higher above the water. Owing, however, to want of sleep and the night mists and the malaria from the marshes, his head became affected, and as neither place nor time admitted of any proper treatment, he completely lost the sight of one eye.

Chapter III
Hannibal Taunts the Romans

After losing many men and beasts under these frightful circumstances, he at last got clear of the marshes, and as soon as he could find some dry ground he pitched his camp. The scouting parties he had sent out reported that the Roman army was lying in the neighbourhood of Arretium.

His next step was to investigate as carefully as he possibly could all that it was material for him to know – what mood the consul was in, what designs he was forming, what the character of the country and the kind of roads it possessed and what resources it offered for the obtaining of supplies. The district was amongst the most fertile in Italy; the plains of Etruria, which extend from Faesulae to Arretium, are rich in corn and livestock and every kind of produce.

The consul's overbearing temper, which had grown steadily worse since his last consulship, made him lose all proper respect and reverence even for the gods, to say nothing of the majesty of the Senate and the laws, and this self-willed and obstinate side of his character had been aggravated by the successes he had achieved both at home and in the field. It was perfectly obvious that he would not seek counsel from either God or man, and whatever he did would be done in an impetuous and headstrong manner. By way of making him show these faults of character still more flagrantly, the Carthaginian prepared to irritate and annoy him. He left the Roman camp on his left, and marched in the direction of Faesulae to plunder the central districts of Etruria. Within actual view of the consul, he created as widespread a devastation as he possibly could, and from the Roman camp they saw in the distance an extensive scene of fire and massacre.

Flaminius had no intention of keeping quiet even if the enemy had done so, but now that he saw the possessions of the allies of Rome plundered and pillaged almost before his very eyes, he felt it to be a personal disgrace that an enemy should be roaming at will through Italy and advancing to attack Rome with none to hinder him. All the other members of the council of war were in favour of a policy of safety rather than of display; they urged him to wait for his colleague, that they might unite their forces and act with one mind on a common plan and, pending his arrival, they should check the wild excesses of the plundering enemy with cavalry and the light-armed auxiliaries.

Enraged at these suggestions, he dashed out of the council and ordered the trumpets to give the signal for march and battle; exclaiming at the same time: 'We are to sit, I suppose, before the walls of Arretium, because our country and our household gods are here. Now that Hannibal has slipped through our hands, he is to ravage Italy, destroy and burn everything in his way till he reaches Rome, while we are not to stir from here until the Senate summons C. Flaminius from Arretium as they once summoned Camillus from Veii.' During this outburst, he ordered the standards to be pulled up with all speed and at the same time mounted his horse.

No sooner had he done so than the animal stumbled and fell and threw him over its head. All those who were standing round were appalled by what they took to be an evil omen at the beginning of a campaign, and their alarm was considerably increased by a message brought to the consul that the standard could not be moved though the standard-bearer had exerted his utmost strength. He turned to the messenger and asked him: 'Are you bringing a despatch from the Senate, also, forbidding me to go on with the campaign? Go, let them dig out the standard if their hands are too benumbed with fear for them to pull it up.' Then the column began its march.

The superior officers, besides being absolutely opposed to his plans, were thoroughly alarmed by the double portent, but the great body of the soldiers were delighted at the spirit their general had shown; they shared his confidence without knowing on what slender grounds it rested.

Chapter IV
Hannibal Lays a Trap at Lake Trasimene

In order still further to exasperate his enemy and make him eager to avenge the injuries inflicted on the allies of Rome, Hannibal laid waste with all the horrors of war the land between Cortona and Lake Trasimene. He had now reached a position eminently adapted for surprise tactics, where the lake comes up close under the hills of Cortona. There is only a very narrow road here between the hills and the lake, as though a space had been purposely left for it. Further on there is a small expanse of level ground flanked by hills, and it was here that Hannibal pitched camp, which was only occupied by his Africans and Spaniards, he himself being in command. The Balearics and the rest of the light infantry he sent behind the hills; the cavalry, conveniently screened by some low hills, he stationed at the mouth of the defile, so that when the Romans had entered it they would be completely shut in by the cavalry, the lake and the hills. Flaminius had reached the lake at sunset.

The next morning, in a still uncertain light, he passed through the defile, without sending any scouts on to feel the way, and when the column began to deploy in the wider extent of level ground the only enemy they saw was the one in front, the rest were concealed in their rear and above their heads. When the Carthaginian saw his object achieved and had his enemy shut in between the lake and the hills with his forces surrounding them, he gave the signal for all to make a simultaneous attack, and they charged straight down upon the point nearest to them.

The affair was all the more sudden and unexpected to the Romans because a fog which had risen from the lake was denser on the plain than on the heights; the bodies of the enemy on the various hills could see each other well enough, and it was all the easier for them to charge all at the same time. The shout of battle rose round the Romans before they could see clearly from whence it came, or become aware that they were surrounded. Fighting began in front and flank before they could form line or get their weapons ready or draw their swords.

Chapter V
Battle of Lake Trasimene Begins

In the universal panic, the consul displayed all the coolness that could be expected under the circumstances. The ranks were broken by each man turning towards the discordant shouts; he re-formed them as well as time and place allowed and, wherever he could be seen or heard, he encouraged his men and bade them stand and fight. 'It is not by prayers or entreaties to the gods that you must make your way out,' he said, 'but by your strength and your courage. It is the sword that cuts a path through the middle of the enemy, and where there is less fear there is generally less danger.'

But such was the uproar and confusion that neither counsel nor command could be heard, and so far was the soldier from recognizing his standard or his company or his place in the rank, that he had hardly sufficient presence of mind to get hold of his weapons and make them available for use, and some who found them a burden rather than a protection were overtaken by the enemy. In such a thick fog, ears were of more use than eyes; the men turned their gaze in every direction as they heard the groans of the wounded and the blows on shield or breastplate, and the mingled shouts of triumph and cries of panic. Some who tried to fly ran into a dense body of combatants and could get no further; others who were returning to the fray were swept away by a rush of fugitives.

At last, when ineffective charges had been made in every direction and they found themselves completely hemmed in by the lake and the hills on either side, and by the enemy in front and rear, it became clear to every man that his only hope of safety lay in his own right hand and his sword. Then each began to depend upon himself for guidance and encouragement, and the fighting began afresh, not the orderly battle with its three divisions of *principes*, *hastati* and *triarii*, where the fighting line is in front of the standards and the rest of the army behind, and where each soldier is in his own legion and cohort and maniple. Chance massed them together, each man took his place in front or rear as his courage prompted him, and such was the ardour of the combatants, so intent were they on the battle, that not a single man on the field was aware of the earthquake which levelled large portions of many towns in Italy, altered the course of swift streams, brought the sea up into the rivers and occasioned enormous landslips amongst the mountains.

Chapter VI
Hannibal Victorious at Lake Trasimene

For almost three hours the fighting went on; everywhere a desperate struggle was kept up, but it raged with greater fierceness around the consul. He was followed by the pick of his army, and wherever he saw his men hard pressed and in difficulties he at once went to their help.

Distinguished by his armour he was the object of the enemy's fiercest attacks, which his comrades did their utmost to repel, until an Insubrian horseman who knew the consul by sight – his name was Ducarius – cried out to his countrymen, 'Here is the man who slew our legions and laid waste our city and our lands! I will offer him in sacrifice to the shades of my foully murdered countrymen.' Digging spurs into his horse he charged into the dense masses of the enemy, and slew an armour-bearer who threw himself in the way as he galloped up lance in rest, and then plunged his lance into the consul; but the *triarii* protected the body with their shields and prevented him from despoiling it.

Then began a general flight; neither lake nor mountain stopped the panic-stricken fugitives, they rushed like blind men over cliff and defile, men and arms tumbled pell-mell on one another. A large number, finding no avenue of escape, went into the water up to their shoulders; some in their wild terror even attempted to escape by swimming, an endless and hopeless task in that lake. Either their spirits gave way and they were drowned, or else finding their efforts fruitless, they regained with great difficulty the shallow water at the edge of the lake and were butchered in all directions by the enemy's cavalry who had ridden into the water. About 6,000 men who had formed the head of the line of march cut their way through the enemy and cleared the defile, quite unconscious of all that had been going on behind them. They halted on some rising ground, and listened to the shouting below and the clash of arms, but were unable, owing to the fog, to see or find out what the fortunes of the fight were.

At last, when the battle was over and the sun's heat had dispelled the fog, mountain and plain revealed in the clear light the disastrous overthrow of the Roman army and showed only too plainly that all was lost. Fearing lest they should be seen in the distance and cavalry be sent against them, they hurriedly took up their standards and disappeared with all possible speed. Maharbal pursued them through the night with the whole of his mounted force, and on the morrow, as starvation, in addition to all their other miseries, was threatening them, they surrendered to Maharbal, on condition of being allowed to depart with one garment apiece. This promise was kept with 'Punic faith' by Hannibal – and he threw them all into chains.

Chapter VII
Roman Casualties at Lake Trasimene; Dismay in Rome

This was the famous battle at Trasimene, and a disaster for Rome memorable as few others have been. Fifteen thousand Romans were killed in action; 1,000 fugitives were scattered all over Etruria and reached the city by diverse routes; 2,500 of the enemy perished on the field, many in both armies afterwards of their wounds. Other authors give the loss on each side as many times greater, but I refuse to indulge in the idle exaggerations to which writers are far too much given, and what is more, I am supported by the authority of Fabius, who was living during the war.

Hannibal dismissed without ransom those prisoners who belonged to the allies and threw the Romans into chains. He then gave orders for the bodies of his own men to be picked out from the heaps of slain and buried; careful search was also made for the body of Flaminius that it might receive honourable interment, but it was not found.

As soon as the news of this disaster reached Rome, the people flocked into the Forum in a great state of panic and confusion. Matrons were wandering about the streets and asking those they met what recent disaster had been reported or what news was there of the army. The throng in the Forum, as numerous as a crowded Assembly, flocked towards the Comitium and the Senate-house and called for the magistrates.

At last, shortly before sunset, M. Pomponius, the praetor, announced, 'We have been defeated in a great battle.' Though nothing more definite was heard from him, the people, full of the reports which they had heard from one another, carried back to their homes the information that the consul had been killed with the greater part of his army; only a few survived, and these were either dispersed in flight throughout Etruria or had been made prisoners by the enemy. The misfortunes which had befallen the defeated army were not more numerous than the anxieties of those whose relatives had served under C. Flaminius, ignorant as they were of the fate of each of their friends, and not in the least knowing what to hope for or what to fear.

The next day and several days afterwards, a large crowd, containing more women than men, stood at the gates waiting for someone of their friends or for news about them, and they crowded round those they met with eager and anxious inquiries, nor was it possible to get them away, especially from those they knew, until they had got all the details from first to last. Then as they came away from their informants you might see the different expressions on their faces, according as each had received good or bad news, and friends congratulating or consoling them as they wended their way homewards.

The women were especially demonstrative in their joy and in their grief. They say that one who suddenly met her son at the gate safe and sound expired in his arms, whilst another who had received false tidings of her son's death and was sitting as a sorrowful mourner in her house, no sooner saw him returning than she died from too great happiness.

For several days the praetors kept the Senate in session from sunrise to sunset, deliberating under what general or with what forces they could offer effectual resistance to the victorious Carthaginian.

Chapter VIII
Romans Appoint Fabius as Dictator

Before they had formed any definite plans, a fresh disaster was announced; 4,000 cavalry under the command of C. Centenius, the propraetor, had been sent by the consul Servilius to the assistance of his colleague. When they heard of the Battle of Trasimene they marched into Umbria, and here they were surrounded and captured by Hannibal. The news of this occurrence affected men in very different ways. Some, whose thoughts were preoccupied with more serious troubles, looked upon this loss of cavalry as a light matter in comparison with the previous losses; others estimated the importance of the incident not by the magnitude of the loss but by its moral effect.

Just as where the constitution is impaired, any malady, however slight, is felt more than it would be in a strong robust person, so any misfortune which befell the state in its present sick and disordered condition must be measured not by its actual importance but by its effect on a state already exhausted and unable to bear anything which would aggravate its condition. Accordingly, the citizens took refuge in a remedy which for a long time had not been made use of or required, namely the appointment of a dictator.

As the consul by whom alone one could be nominated was absent, and it was not easy for a messenger or a despatch to be sent through Italy, overrun as it was by the arms of Carthage, and as it would have been contrary to all precedent for the people to appoint a dictator, the Assembly invested Q. Fabius Maximus with dictatorial powers and appointed M. Minucius Rufus to act as his Master of the Horse. They were commissioned by the Senate to strengthen the walls and towers of the city and place garrisons in whatever positions they thought best, and cut down the bridges over the various rivers, for now it was a fight for their city and their homes, since they were no longer able to defend Italy.

Chapter IX
While Hannibal Ravages Umbria, Roman Senate Seeks Divine Guidance

Hannibal marched in a straight course through Umbria as far as Spoletum, and after laying the country round utterly waste, he commenced an attack upon the city which was repulsed with heavy loss. As a single colony was strong enough to defeat his unfortunate attempt, he was able to form some conjecture as to the difficulties attending the capture of Rome, and consequently diverted his march into the territory of Picenum, a district which not only abounded in every kind of produce but was richly stored with property which the greedy and needy soldiers seized and plundered without restraint.

He remained in camp there for several days during which his soldiers recruited their strength after their winter campaigns and their journey across the marshes, and a battle which though ultimately successful was neither without heavy loss nor easily won. When sufficient time for rest had been allowed to men who delighted much more in plundering and destroying than in ease and idleness, Hannibal resumed his march and devastated the districts of Praetutia and Hadria, then he treated in the same way the country of the Marsi, the Marrucini and the Peligni and the part of Apulia which was nearest to him, including the cities of Arpi and Luceria.

Cn. Servilius had fought some insignificant actions with the Gauls and taken one small town, but when he heard of his colleague's death and the destruction of his army, he was alarmed for the walls of his native city and marched straight for Rome that he might not be absent at this most critical juncture. Q. Fabius Maximus was now dictator for the second time.

On the very day of his entrance upon office he summoned a meeting of the Senate and commenced by discussing matters of religion. He made it quite clear to the senators that C. Flaminius' fault lay much more in his neglect of the auspices and of his religious duties than in bad generalship and foolhardiness. The gods themselves, he maintained, must be consulted as to the necessary measures to avert their displeasure, and he succeeded in getting a decree passed that the decemvirs should be ordered to consult the Sibylline Books, a course which is only adopted when the most alarming portents have been reported.

After inspecting the Books of Fate, they informed the Senate that the vow which had been made to Mars in view of that war had not been duly discharged, and that it must be discharged afresh and on a much greater scale. The Great Games must be vowed to Jupiter, a temple to Venus Erycina and one to Mens; a *lectisternium* must be held and solemn intercessions made; a Sacred Spring must also be vowed. All these things must be done if the war was to be a successful one and the republic remain in the same position in which it was at the beginning of the war. As Fabius would be wholly occupied with the necessary arrangements for the war, the Senate with the full approval of the pontifical college ordered the praetor, M. Aemilius, to take care that all these orders were carried out in good time.

Chapter X
Roman People Consulted on the
'Sacred Spring' Question

After these resolutions had been passed in the Senate, the praetor consulted the pontifical college as to the proper means of giving effect to them, and L. Cornelius Lentulus, the Pontifex Maximus, decided that the very first step to take was to refer to the people the question of a 'Sacred Spring', as this particular form of vow could not be undertaken without the order of the people.

The form of procedure was as follows: 'Is it,' the praetor asked the [People's] Assembly, 'your will and pleasure that all be done and performed in manner following? That is to say, if the Commonwealth of the Romans and the *Quirites* [citizens] be preserved, as I pray it may be, safe and sound through these present wars – to wit, the war between Rome and Carthage and the wars with the Gauls now dwelling on the hither side of the Alps – then shall the Romans and *Quirites* present as an offering whatever the spring shall produce from their flocks and herds, whether it be from swine or sheep or goats or cattle, and all that is not already devoted to any other deity shall be consecrated to Jupiter from such time as the Senate and people shall order.

'Whosoever shall make an offering let him do it at whatsoever time and in whatsoever manner he will, and howsoever he offers it, it shall be accounted to be duly offered. If the animal which should have been sacrificed die, it shall be as though unconsecrated, there shall be no sin. If any man shall hurt or slay a consecrated thing unwittingly, he shall not be held guilty. If a man shall have stolen any such animal, the people shall not bear the guilt, nor he from whom it was stolen. If a man offer his sacrifice unwittingly on a forbidden day, it shall be accounted to be duly offered. Whether he do so by night or day, whether he be slave or freeman, it shall be accounted to be duly offered. If any sacrifice be offered before the Senate and people have ordered that it shall be done, the people shall be free and absolved from all guilt therefrom.'

To the same end, the Great Games were vowed at a cost of 333,333 1/3 *ases* [low denomination bronze coins], and in addition 300 oxen to Jupiter, and white oxen and the other customary victims to a number of deities. When the vows had been duly pronounced a litany of intercession was ordered, and not only the population of the city but the people from the country districts, whose private interests were being affected by the public distress, went in procession with their wives and children.

Then a *lectisternium* was held for three days under the supervision of the 10 keepers of the Sacred Books. Six couches were publicly exhibited: one for Jupiter and Juno, another for Neptune and Minerva, a third for Mars and Venus, a fourth for Apollo and Diana, a fifth for Vulcan and Vesta and the sixth for Mercury and Ceres. This was followed by the vowing of temples. Q. Fabius Maximus, as dictator, vowed the temple to Venus Erycina, because it was laid down in the Books of Fate that this vow should be made by the man who possessed the supreme authority in the State. T. Otacilius, the praetor, vowed the temple to Mens.

Chapter XI
Dictator Fabius Takes Charge

After the various obligations towards the gods had thus been discharged, the dictator referred to the Senate the question of the policy to be adopted with regard to the war, with what legions and how many the senators thought he ought to meet their victorious enemy.

They decreed that he should take over the army from Cneius Servilius, and further that he should enroll from amongst the citizens and the allies as many cavalry and infantry as he considered requisite; all else was left to his discretion to take such steps as he thought desirable in the interests of the Republic. Fabius said that he would add two legions to the army which Servilius commanded; these were raised by the Master of the Horse and he fixed a day for their assembling at Tibur.

A proclamation was also issued that those who were living in towns and strongholds that were not sufficiently fortified should remove into places of safety, and that all the population settled in the districts through which Hannibal was likely to march should abandon their farms, after first burning their houses and destroying their produce, so that he might not have any supplies to fall back upon.

He then marched along the Flaminian Road to meet the consul. As soon as he caught sight of the army in the neighbourhood of Ocriculum near the Tiber, and the consul riding forward with some cavalry to meet him, he sent an officer to tell him that he was to come to the dictator without his lictors. He did so, and the way they met produced a profound sense of the majesty of the dictatorship amongst both citizens and allies, who had almost by this time forgotten that greatest of all offices.

Shortly afterwards a despatch was handed in from the city stating that some transports which were carrying supplies for the army in Spain had been captured by the Carthaginian fleet near the port of Cosa. The consul was thereupon ordered to man the ships which were lying off Rome or at Ostia with full complements of seamen and soldiers, and sail in pursuit of the hostile fleet and protect the coast of Italy. A large force was raised in Rome, even freedmen who had children and were of the military age had been sworn in. Out of these city troops, all under 35 years of age were placed on board the ships, the rest were left to garrison the city.

Chapter XXXVI
Roman Military Resources

The armies were increased, but as to what additions were made to the infantry and cavalry, the authorities vary so much, both as to the numbers and nature of the forces, that I should hardly venture to assert anything as positively certain. Some say that 10,000 recruits were called out to make up the losses; others, that four new legions were enrolled so that they might carry on the war with eight legions. Some authorities record that both horse and foot in the legions were made stronger by the addition of 1,000 infantry and 100 cavalry to each, so that they contained 5000 infantry and 300 cavalry, whilst the allies furnished double the number of cavalry and an equal number of infantry.

Thus, according to these writers, there were 87,200 men in the Roman camp when the Battle of Cannae was fought. One thing is quite certain; the struggle was resumed with greater vigour and energy than in former years, because the dictator had given them reason to hope that the enemy might be conquered. But before the newly raised legions left the city the decemvirs were ordered to consult the Sacred Books owing to the general alarm which had been created by fresh portents.

It was reported that showers of stones had fallen simultaneously on the Aventine in Rome and at Aricia; that the statues of the gods amongst the Sabines had sweated blood, and cold water had flowed from the hot springs. This latter portent created more terror, because it had happened several times. In the colonnade near the Campus [Martius] several men had been killed by lightning. The proper expiation of these portents was ascertained from the Sacred Books. Some envoys from Paestum brought golden bowls to Rome. Thanks were voted to them as in the case of the Neapolitans, but the gold was not accepted.

Chapter XXXVIII
Departing Roman Troops Swear an Oath

After completing the enrolment, the consuls waited a few days for the contingents furnished by the Latins and the allies to come in. Then a new departure was made; the soldiers were sworn in by the military tribunes.

Up to that day there had only been the military oath binding the men to assemble at the bidding of the consuls and not to disband until they received orders to do so.

It had also been the custom among the soldiers, when the infantry were formed into companies of 100, and the cavalry into troops of 10, for all the men in each company or troop to take a voluntary oath to each other that they would not leave their comrades for fear or for flight, and that they would not quit the ranks save to fetch or pick up a weapon, to strike an enemy or to save a comrade. This voluntary covenant was now changed into a formal oath taken before the tribunes.

Before they marched out of the city, Varro delivered several violent harangues in which he declared that the war had been brought into Italy by the nobles, and would continue to feed on the vitals of the republic if there were more generals like Fabius; he, Varro, would finish off the war the very day he caught sight of the enemy.

His colleague, Paulus, made only one speech, in which there was much more truth than the people cared to hear. He passed no strictures on Varro, but he did express surprise that any general, whilst still in the city before he had taken up his command, or become acquainted with either his own army or that of the enemy, or gained any information as to the lie of the country and the nature of the ground, should know in what way he should conduct the campaign and be able to foretell the day on which he would fight a decisive battle with the enemy.

As for himself, Paulus said that he would not anticipate events by disclosing his measures, for, after all, circumstances determined measures for men much more than men made circumstances subservient to measures. He hoped and prayed that such measures as were taken with due caution and foresight might turn out successful; so far rashness, besides being foolish, had proved disastrous. He made it quite clear that he would prefer safe to hasty counsels and, in order to strengthen him in this resolve, Fabius is said to have addressed him on his departure in the following terms:

Chapter XXXIX
Fabius' Speech

'L. Aemilius, if you were like your colleague or, if you had a colleague like yourself – and I would that it were so – my address would be simply a waste of words. For if you were both good consuls, you would, without any suggestions from me, do everything that the interests of the state or your own sense of honour demanded; if you were both alike bad, you would neither listen to anything I had to say, nor take any advice which I might offer. As it is, when I look at your colleague and consider what sort of a man you are, I shall address my remarks to you.

'I can see that your merits as a man and a citizen will affect nothing if one half of the commonwealth is crippled and evil counsels possess the same force and authority as good ones. You are mistaken, L. Paulus, if you imagine that you will have less difficulty with C. Terentius than with Hannibal; I rather think the former will prove a more dangerous enemy than the latter. With the one you will only have to contend in the field, the opposition of the other you will have to meet everywhere and always.

'Against Hannibal and his legions you will have your cavalry and infantry, when Varro is in command he will use your own men against you. I do not want to bring ill luck on you by mentioning the ill-starred Flaminius, but this I must say that it was only after he was consul and had entered upon his province and taken up his command that he began to play the madman, but this man was insane before he stood for the consulship and afterwards while canvassing for it, and now that he is consul, before he has seen the camp or the enemy he is madder than ever. If he raises such storms amongst peaceful civilians as he did just now by bragging about battles and battlefields, what will he do, think you, when he is talking to armed men – and those young men – where words at once lead to action. And yet if he carries out his threat and brings on an action at once, either I am utterly ignorant of military science, of the nature of this war, of the enemy with whom we are dealing, or else some place or other will be rendered more notorious by our defeat than even Trasimene.

'As we are alone, this is hardly a time for boasting, and I would rather be thought to have gone too far in despising glory than in seeking it, but as a matter of fact, the only rational method of carrying on war against Hannibal is the one which I have followed. This is not only taught us by experience – experience the teacher of fools – but by reasoning, which has been and will continue to be unchanged as long as the conditions remain the same. We are carrying on war in Italy, in our own country on our own soil, everywhere around us are citizens and allies, they are helping us with men, horses, supplies, and they will continue to do so, for they have proved their loyalty thus far to us in our adversity; and time and circumstance are making us more efficient, more circumspect, more self-reliant.

'Hannibal, on the other hand, is in a foreign and hostile land, far from his home and country, confronted everywhere by opposition and danger; nowhere by land or sea can he find peace; no cities admit him within their gates, no fortified towns; nowhere does he see anything which he can call his own, he has to live on each day's pillage: he has hardly a third of the army with which he crossed the Ebro; he has lost more by famine than by the sword, and even the few he has cannot get enough to support life. Do you doubt then, that if we sit still we shall get the better of a man who is growing weaker day by day, who has neither supplies nor reinforcements nor money? How long has he been sitting before the walls of Gereonium, a poor fortress in Apulia, as though they were the walls of Carthage? But I will not sound my own praises even before you. See how the late consuls, Cn. Servilius and Atilius, fooled him.

'This, L. Paulus, is the only safe course to adopt, and it is one which your fellow citizens will do more to make difficult and dangerous for you than the enemy will. For your own soldiers will want the same thing as the enemy; Varro though he is a Roman consul will desire just what Hannibal the Carthaginian commander desires. You must hold your own single-handed against both generals. And you will hold your own if you stand your ground firmly against public gossip and private slander, if you remain unmoved by false misrepresentations and your colleague's idle boasting. It is said that truth is far too often eclipsed but never totally extinguished. The man who scorns false glory will possess the true. Let them call you a coward because you are cautious, a laggard because you are deliberate, unsoldierly because you are a skilful general. I would rather have you give a clever enemy cause for fear than earn the praise of foolish compatriots. Hannibal will only feel contempt for a man who runs all risks, he will be afraid of one who never takes a rash step.

'I do not advise you to do nothing, but I do advise you to be guided in what you do by common sense and reason and not by chance. Never lose control of your forces and yourself; be always prepared, always on the alert; never fail to seize an opportunity favourable to yourself, and never give a favourable opportunity to the enemy. The man who is not in a hurry will always see his way clearly; haste blunders on blindly.'

Chapter XL
Paulus Responds; Hannibal Gloats

The consul's reply was far from being a cheerful one, for he admitted that the advice given was true, but not easy to put into practice. If a dictator had found his Master of the Horse unbearable, what power or authority would a consul have against a violent and headstrong colleague?

'In my first consulship,' he said, 'I escaped, badly singed, from the fire of popular fury. I hope and pray that all may end successfully, but if any mischance befalls us I shall expose myself to the weapons of the enemy sooner than to the verdict of the enraged citizens.' With these words Paulus, it is said, set forward, escorted by the foremost men amongst the patricians; the plebeian consul was attended by his plebeian friends, more conspicuous for their numbers than for the quality of the men who composed the crowd.

When they came into camp the recruits and the old soldiers were formed into one army, and two separate camps were formed, the new camp, which was the smaller one, being nearer to Hannibal, while in the old camp the larger part of the army and the best troops were stationed. M. Atilius, one of the consuls of the previous year, pleaded his age and was sent back to Rome; the other, Geminus Servilius, was placed in command of the smaller camp with one Roman legion and 2,000 horse and foot of the allies.

Although Hannibal saw that the army opposed to him was half as large again as it had been he was hugely delighted at the advent of the consuls. For not only was there nothing left out of his daily plunder, but there was nothing left anywhere for him to seize, as all the corn, now that the country was unsafe, had been everywhere stored in the cities. Hardly 10 days' rations of corn remained, as was afterwards discovered, and the Spaniards were prepared to desert, owing to the shortness of supplies, if only the Romans had waited till the time was ripe.

Chapter XLI
Hannibal Lays Another Trap

An incident occurred which still further encouraged Varro's impetuous and headstrong temperament. Parties were sent to drive off the foragers; a confused fight ensued owing to the soldiers rushing forward without any preconcerted plan or orders from their commanders, and the contest went heavily against the Carthaginians. As many as 1,700 of them were killed, the loss of the Romans and the allies did not amount to more than 100.

The consuls commanded on alternate days, and that day happened to be Paulus' turn. He checked the victors who were pursuing the enemy in great disorder, for he feared an ambuscade. Varro was furious, and loudly exclaimed that the enemy had been allowed to slip out of their hands, and if the pursuit had not been stopped the war could have been brought to a close.

Hannibal did not very much regret his losses; on the contrary, he believed that they would serve as a bait to the impetuosity of the consul and his newly raised troops, and that he would be more headstrong than ever. What was going on in the enemy's camp was quite as well known to him as what was going on in his own; he was fully aware that there were differences and quarrels between the commanders, and that two-thirds of the army consisted of recruits.

The following night he selected what he considered a suitable position for an ambuscade and marched his men out of camp with nothing but their arms, leaving all the property, both public and private, behind in the camp. He then concealed the force behind the hills which enclosed the valley, the infantry to the left and the cavalry to the right, and took the baggage train through the middle of the valley, in the hope of surprising the Romans whilst plundering the apparently deserted camp and hampered with their plunder. Numerous fires were left burning in the camp in order to create the impression that he wished to keep the consuls in their respective positions until he had traversed a considerable distance in his retreat. Fabius had been deceived by the same stratagem the previous year.

Chapter XLII
Romans Discover Hannibal's Trap

As it grew light the pickets were seen to have been withdrawn, then on approaching nearer the unusual silence created surprise. When it was definitely learnt that the camp was empty, the men rushed in a body to the commanders' quarters with the news that the enemy had fled in such haste that they left the tents standing, and to secure greater secrecy for their flight had also left numerous fires burning.

Then a loud shout arose demanding that the order should be given to advance, and that the men should be led in pursuit and that the camp should be plundered forthwith. The one consul behaved as though he were one of the clamorous crowd; the other, Paulus, repeatedly asserted the need of caution and circumspection. At last, unable to deal with the mutinous crowd and its leader in any other way, he sent Marius Statilius with his troop of Lucanian horse to reconnoitre.

When he had ridden up to the gates of the camp he ordered his men to halt outside the lines. He himself with two of his troopers entered the camp and after a careful and thorough examination he brought back word that there was certainly a trick somewhere, the fires were left on the side of the camp which fronted the Romans, the tents were standing open with all the valuables exposed to view, in some parts he had seen silver lying about on the paths as though it had been put there for plunder. So far from deterring the soldiers from satisfying their greed, as it was intended to do, this report only inflamed it, and a shout arose that if the signal was not given they would go on without their generals. There was no lack of a general, however, for Varro instantly gave the signal to advance.

Paulus, who was hanging back, received a report from the keeper of the sacred chickens that they had not given a favourable omen, and he ordered the report to be at once carried to his colleague as he was just marching out of the camp gates. Varro was very much annoyed, but the recollection of the disaster which overtook Flaminius and the naval defeat which the consul Claudius sustained in the First Punic War made him afraid of acting in an irreligious spirit.

It seemed as though the gods themselves on that day delayed, if they did actually do away, the fatal doom which was impending over the Romans. For it so happened that whilst the soldiers were ignoring the consul's order for the standards to be carried back into camp, two slaves, one belonging to a trooper from Formiae, the other to one from Sidicinum, who had been captured with the foraging parties when Servilius and Atilius were in command, had that day escaped to their former masters. They were taken before the consul and told him that the whole of Hannibal's army was lying behind the nearest hills. The opportune arrival of these men restored the authority of the consuls, though one of them in his desire to be popular had weakened his authority by his unscrupulous connivance at breaches of discipline.

Chapter XLIII
Discontent in Hannibal's Camp

When Hannibal saw that the ill-considered movement, which the Romans had commenced, was not recklessly carried out to its final stage, and that his ruse had been detected, he returned to camp.

Owing to the want of corn, he was unable to remain there many days, and fresh plans were continually cropping up, not only amongst the soldiers, who were a medley of all nations, but even in the mind of the general himself. Murmurs gradually swelled into loud and angry protests as the men demanded their arrears of pay, and complained of the starvation which they were enduring, and in addition, a rumour was started that the mercenaries, chiefly those of Spanish nationality, had formed a plot to desert. Even Hannibal himself, it is said, sometimes thought of leaving his infantry behind and hurrying with his cavalry into Gaul.

With these plans being discussed and this temper prevailing amongst the men, he decided to move into the warmer parts of Apulia, where the harvest was earlier and where, owing to the greater distance from the enemy, desertion would be rendered more difficult for the fickle-minded part of his force. As on the previous occasion, he ordered campfires to be lighted and a few tents left where they could be easily seen, in order that the Romans, remembering a similar stratagem, might be afraid to move.

However, Statilius was again sent to reconnoitre with his Lucanians, and he made a thorough examination of the country beyond the camp and over the mountains. He reported that he had caught a distant view of the enemy in line of march, and the question of pursuit was discussed. As usual, the views of the two consuls were opposed, but almost all present supported Varro, not a single voice was given in favour of Paulus, except that of Servilius, consul in the preceding year. The opinion of the majority of the council prevailed, and so, driven by destiny, they went forward to render Cannae famous in the annals of Roman defeats.

It was in the neighbourhood of this village that Hannibal had fixed his camp with his back to the Sirocco which blows from Mount Vultur and fills the arid plains with clouds of dust. This arrangement was a very convenient one for his camp, and it proved to be extremely advantageous afterwards, when he was forming his order of battle, for his own men, with the wind behind them, blowing only on their backs, would fight with an enemy who was blinded by volumes of dust.

Chapter XLIV
Discontent Among the Roman Consuls

The consuls followed the Carthaginians, carefully examining the roads as they marched, and when they reached Cannae and had the enemy in view, they formed two entrenched camps separated by the same interval as at Gereonium, and with the same distribution of troops in each camp. The river Aufidus, flowing past the two camps, furnished a supply of water which the soldiers got as they best could, and they generally had to fight for it. The men in the smaller camp, which was on the other side of the river, had less difficulty in obtaining it, as that bank was not held by the enemy.

Hannibal now saw his hopes fulfilled that the consuls would give him an opportunity of fighting on ground naturally adapted for the movements of cavalry, the arm in which he had so far been invincible, and accordingly he placed his army in order of battle, and tried to provoke his foe to action by repeated charges of his Numidians. The Roman camp was again disturbed by a mutinous soldiery and consuls at variance, Paulus bringing up against Varro the fatal rashness of Sempronius and Flaminius, Varro retorting by pointing to Fabius as the favourite model of cowardly and inert commanders, and calling gods and men to witness that it was through no fault of his that Hannibal had acquired, so to speak, a prescriptive right to Italy; he had had his hands tied by his colleague; his soldiers, furious and eager for fight, had had their swords and arms taken away from them.

Paulus, on the other hand, declared that if anything happened to the legions flung recklessly and betrayed into an ill-considered and imprudent action, he was free from all responsibility for it, though he would have to share in all the consequences. 'See to it,' he said to Varro, 'that those who are so free and ready with their tongues are equally so with their hands in the day of battle.'

Chapter XLV
Hannibal's Cavalry Taunt the Romans

Whilst time was thus being wasted in disputes instead of deliberation, Hannibal withdrew the bulk of his army, who had been standing most of the day in order of battle, into camp. He sent his Numidians, however, across the river to attack the parties who were getting water for the smaller camp. They had hardly gained the opposite bank when with their shouting and uproar they sent the crowd flying in wild disorder and, galloping on as far as the outpost in front of the rampart, they nearly reached the gates of the camp. It was looked upon as such an insult for a Roman camp to be actually terrorized by irregular auxiliaries that one thing, and one thing alone, held back the Romans from instantly crossing the river and forming their battle line – the supreme command that day rested with Paulus.

The following day Varro, whose turn it now was, without any consultation with his colleague, exhibited the signal for battle and led his forces drawn up for action across the river. Paulus followed, for though he disapproved of the measure, he was bound to support it. After crossing, they strengthened their line with the force in the smaller camp and completed their formation. On the right, which was nearest to the river, the Roman cavalry were posted, then came the infantry; on the extreme left were the cavalry of the allies, their infantry was between them and the Roman legions. The javelin men with the rest of the light-armed auxiliaries formed the front line. The consuls took their stations on the wings, Terentius Varro on the left, Aemilius Paulus on the right.

Chapter XLVI
Hannibal Prepares for the Battle of Cannae

As soon as it grew light Hannibal sent forward the Balearics and the other light infantry. He then crossed the river in person and as each division was brought across he assigned it its place in the line. The Gaulish and Spanish horse he posted near the bank on the left wing in front of the Roman cavalry; the right wing was assigned to the Numidian troopers.

The centre consisted of a strong force of infantry, the Gauls and Spaniards in the middle, the Africans at either end of them. You might fancy that the Africans were for the most part a body of Romans from the way they were armed, they were so completely equipped with the arms, some of which they had taken at the Trebia, but the most part at Trasimene. The Gauls and Spaniards had shields almost of the same shape their swords were totally different, those of the Gauls being very long and without a point, the Spaniard, accustomed to thrust more than to cut, had a short handy sword, pointed like a dagger. These nations, more than any other, inspired terror by the vastness of their stature and their frightful appearance: the Gauls were naked above the waist, the Spaniards had taken up their position wearing white tunics embroidered with purple, of dazzling brilliancy. The total number of infantry in the field was 40,000, and there were 10,000 cavalry.

Hasdrubal was in command of the left wing, Maharbal of the right; Hannibal himself with his brother Mago commanded the centre. It was a great convenience to both armies that the sun shone obliquely on them, whether it was that they had purposely so placed themselves, or whether it happened by accident, since the Romans faced the north, the Carthaginans the South. The wind, called by the inhabitants the Vulturnus, was against the Romans, and blew great clouds of dust into their faces, making it impossible for them to see in front of them.

Chapter XLVII
Battle of Cannae Begins

When the battle shout was raised the auxiliaries ran forward, and the battle began with the light infantry. Then the Gauls and Spaniards on the left engaged the Roman cavalry on the right; the battle was not at all like a cavalry fight, for there was no room for manoeuvring, the river on the one side and the infantry on the other hemming them in, compelled them to fight face to face. Each side tried to force their way straight forward, until at last the horses were standing in a closely pressed mass, and the riders seized their opponents and tried to drag them from their horses. It had become mainly a struggle of infantry, fierce but short, and the Roman cavalry was repulsed and fled. Just as this battle of the cavalry was finished, the infantry became engaged, and as long as the Gauls and Spaniards kept their ranks unbroken, both sides were equally matched in strength and courage.

At length after long and repeated efforts the Romans closed up their ranks, echeloned their front, and by the sheer weight of their deep column bore down the division of the enemy, which was stationed in front of Hannibal's line, and was too thin and weak to resist the pressure. Without a moment's pause they followed up their broken and hastily retreating foe till they took to headlong flight. Cutting their way through the mass of fugitives, who offered no resistance, they penetrated as far as the Africans who were stationed on both wings, somewhat further back than the Gauls and Spaniards who had formed the advanced centre. As the latter fell back the whole front became level, and as they continued to give ground it became concave and crescent-shaped, the Africans at either end forming the horns.

As the Romans rushed on incautiously between them, they were enfiladed by the two wings, which extended and closed round them in the rear. On this, the Romans, who had fought one battle to no purpose, left the Gauls and Spaniards, whose rear they had been slaughtering, and commenced a fresh struggle with the Africans. The contest was a very one-sided one, for not only were they hemmed in on all sides, but wearied with the previous fighting they were meeting fresh and vigorous opponents.

Chapter XLVIII
Deception of Hannibal's Numidian Cavalry

By this time the Roman left wing, where the allied cavalry were fronting the Numidians, had become engaged, but the fighting was slack at first owing to a Carthaginian stratagem. About 500 Numidians, carrying, besides their usual arms and missiles, swords concealed under their coats of mail, rode out from their own line with their shields slung behind their backs as though they were deserters, and suddenly leaped from their horses and flung their shields and javelins at the feet of their enemy. They were received into their ranks, conducted to the rear, and ordered to remain quiet. While the battle was spreading to the various parts of the field they remained quiet, but when the eyes and minds of all were wholly taken up with the fighting they seized the large Roman shields which were lying everywhere amongst the heaps of slain and commenced a furious attack upon the rear of the Roman line. Slashing away at backs and hips, they made a great slaughter and a still greater panic and confusion.

Amidst the rout and panic in one part of the field and the obstinate but hopeless struggle in the other, Hasdrubal, who was in command of that arm, withdrew some Numidians from the centre of the right wing, where the fighting was feebly kept up, and sent them in pursuit of the fugitives, and at the same time sent the Spanish and Gaulish horse to the aid of the Africans, who were by this time more wearied by slaughter than by fighting.

Chapter XLIX
Romans Suffer Terrible Casualties

Paulus was on the other side of the field. In spite of his having been seriously wounded at the commencement of the action by a bullet from a sling, he frequently encountered Hannibal with a compact body of troops, and in several places restored the battle. The Roman cavalry formed a bodyguard round him, but at last, as he became too weak to manage his horse, they all dismounted. It is stated that when someone reported to Hannibal that the consul had ordered his men to fight on foot, he remarked, 'I would rather he handed them over to me bound hand and foot.'

Now that the victory of the enemy was no longer doubtful, this struggle of the dismounted cavalry was such as might be expected when men preferred to die where they stood rather than flee, and the victors, furious at them for delaying the victory, butchered without mercy those whom they could not dislodge. They did, however, repulse a few survivors exhausted with their exertions and their wounds. All were at last scattered, and those who could regained their horses for flight.

Cn. Lentulus, a military tribune, saw, as he rode by, the consul covered with blood sitting on a boulder. 'Lucius Aemilius,' he said, 'the one man whom the gods must hold guiltless of this day's disaster, take this horse while you have still some strength left, and I can lift you into the saddle and keep by your side to protect you. Do not make this day of battle still more fatal by a consul's death, there are enough tears and mourning without that.'

The consul replied: 'Long may you live to do brave deeds, Cornelius, but do not waste in useless pity the few moments left in which to escape from the hands of the enemy. Go, announce publicly to the Senate that they must fortify Rome and make its defence strong before the victorious enemy approaches, and tell Q. Fabius privately that I have ever remembered his precepts in life and in death. Suffer me to breathe my last among my slaughtered soldiers, let me not have to defend myself again when I am no longer consul, or appear as the accuser of my colleague and protect my own innocence by throwing the guilt on another.'

During this conversation a crowd of fugitives came suddenly upon them, followed by the enemy, who, not knowing who the consul was, overwhelmed him with a shower of missiles. Lentulus escaped on horseback in the rush.

Then there was flight in all directions; 7,000 men escaped to the smaller camp, 10,000 to the larger, and about 2,000 to the village of Cannae. These latter were at once surrounded by Carthalo and his cavalry, as the village was quite unfortified. The other consul, who either by accident or design had not joined any of these bodies of fugitives, escaped with about 50 cavalry to Venusia; 45,500 infantry, 2,700 cavalry – almost an equal proportion of Romans and allies – are said to have been killed. Amongst the number were both the quaestors attached to the consuls, L. Atilius and L. Furius Bibulcus, 29 military tribunes, several ex-consuls, ex-praetors and ex-aediles (amongst them are included Cn. Servilius Geminus and M. Minucius, who was Master of the Horse the previous year and, some years before that, consul), and in addition to these, 80 men who had either been senators or filled offices qualifying them for election to the Senate and who had volunteered for service with the legions. The prisoners taken in the battle are stated to have amounted to 3,000 infantry and 1,500 cavalry.

Chapter L
Leaderless Roman Survivors Debate What to Do

Such was the Battle of Cannae, a battle as famous as the disastrous one at the Allia; not so serious in its results, owing to the inaction of the enemy, but more serious and more horrible in view of the slaughter of the army. For the flight at the Allia saved the army though it lost the city, whereas at Cannae hardly 50 men shared the consul's flight, nearly the whole army met their death in company with the other consul.

As those who had taken refuge in the two camps were only a defenceless crowd without any leaders, the men in the larger camp sent a message to the others asking them to cross over to them at night when the enemy, tired after the battle and the feasting in honour of their victory, would be buried in sleep. Then they would go in one body to Canusium. Some rejected the proposal with scorn. 'Why,' they asked, 'cannot those who sent the message come themselves, since they are quite as able to join us as we to join them? Because, of course, all the country between us is scoured by the enemy and they prefer to expose other people to that deadly peril rather than themselves.' Others did not disapprove of the proposal, but they lacked courage to carry it out.

P. Sempronius Tuditanus protested against this cowardice. 'Would you,' he asked, 'rather be taken prisoners by a most avaricious and ruthless foe and a price put upon your heads and your value assessed after you have been asked whether you are a Roman citizen or a Latin ally, in order that another may win honour from your misery and disgrace? Certainly not, if you are really the fellow countrymen of L. Aemilius, who chose a noble death rather than a life of degradation, and of all the brave men who are lying in heaps around him. But, before daylight overtakes us and the enemy gathers in larger force to bar our path, let us cut our way through the men who in disorder and confusion are clamouring at our gates. Good swords and brave hearts make a way through enemies, however densely they are massed. If you march shoulder to shoulder you will scatter this loose and disorganised force as easily as if nothing opposed you. Come then with me, all you who want to preserve yourselves and the state.' With these words he drew his sword, and with his men in close formation marched through the very midst of the enemy.

When the Numidians hurled their javelins on the right, the unprotected side, they transferred their shields to their right arms, and so got clear away to the larger camp. As many as 600 escaped on this occasion, and after another large body had joined them they at once left the camp and came through safely to Canusium. This action on the part of defeated men was due to the impulse of natural courage or of accident rather than to any concerted plan of their own or any one's generalship.

Chapter LI
Hannibal Enjoys His Victory, but Fails to Use It

Hannibal's officers all surrounded him and congratulated him on his victory, and urged that after such a magnificent success he should allow himself and his exhausted men to rest for the remainder of the day and the following night. Maharbal, however, the commandant of the cavalry, thought that they ought not to lose a moment. 'That you may know,' he said to Hannibal, 'what has been gained by this battle I prophesy that in five days you will be feasting as victor in the capitol. Follow me; I will go in advance with the cavalry; they will know that you are come before they know that you are coming.'

To Hannibal the victory seemed too great and too joyous for him to realize all at once. He told Maharbal that he commended his zeal, but he needed time to think out his plans. Maharbal replied: 'The gods have not given all their gifts to one man. You know how to win victory, Hannibal, you do not know how to use it.' That day's delay is believed to have saved the city and the empire.

The next day, as soon as it grew light, they set about gathering the spoils on the field and viewing the carnage, which was a ghastly sight even for an enemy. There all those thousands of Romans were lying, infantry and cavalry indiscriminately as chance had brought them together in the battle or the flight. Some covered with blood raised themselves from amongst the dead around them, tortured by their wounds which were nipped by the cold of the morning, and were promptly put an end to by the enemy. Some they found lying with their thighs and knees gashed but still alive; these bared their throats and necks and bade them drain what blood they still had left. Some were discovered with their heads buried in the earth, they had evidently suffocated themselves by making holes in the ground and heaping the soil over their faces.

What attracted the attention of all was a Numidian who was dragged alive from under a dead Roman lying across him; his ears and nose were torn, for the Roman with hands too powerless to grasp his weapon had, in his mad rage, torn his enemy with his teeth, and while doing so expired.

Chapter LII
Remaining Romans Surrender to Hannibal

After most of the day had been spent in collecting the spoils, Hannibal led his men to the attack on the smaller camp and commenced operations by throwing up a breastwork to cut off their water supply from the river. As, however, all the defenders were exhausted by toil and want of sleep, as well as by wounds, the surrender was affected sooner than he had anticipated. They agreed to give up their arms and horses, and to pay for each Roman 300 'chariot pieces' [high denomination silver coins], for each ally 200, and for each officer's servant 100, on condition that after the money was paid they should be allowed to depart with one garment apiece. Then they admitted the enemy into the camp and were all placed under guard, the Romans and the allies separately.

Whilst time was being spent there, all those in the larger camp, who had sufficient strength and courage, to the number of 4,000 infantry and 200 cavalry, made their escape to Canusium, some in a body, others straggling through the fields, which was quite as safe a thing to do. Those who were wounded and those who had been afraid to venture surrendered the camp on the same terms as had been agreed upon in the other camp.

An immense amount of booty was secured, and the whole of it was made over to the troops with the exception of the horses and prisoners and whatever silver there might be. Most of this was on the trappings of the horses, for they used very little silver plate at table, at all events when on a campaign.

Hannibal then ordered the bodies of his own soldiers to be collected for burial; it is said that there were as many as 8,000 of his best troops. Some authors state that he also had a search made for the body of the Roman consul, which he buried. Those who had escaped to Canusium were simply allowed shelter within its walls and houses, but a high-born and wealthy Apulian lady, named Busa, assisted them with corn and clothes and even provisions for their journey. For this munificence the Senate, at the close of the war, voted her public honours.

Chapter LVIII
Hannibal Ransoms Roman Captives

After his great success at Cannae, Hannibal made his arrangements more as though his victory were a complete and decisive one than as if the war were still going on. The prisoners were brought before him and separated into two groups; the allies were treated as they had been at the Trebia and at Trasimene, after some kind words they were dismissed without ransom; the Romans, too, were treated as they had never been before, for when they appeared before him he addressed them in quite a friendly way. He had no deadly feud, he told them, with Rome, all he was fighting for was his country's honour as a sovereign power. His fathers had yielded to Roman courage, his one object now was that the Romans should yield to his good fortune and courage.

He now gave the prisoners permission to ransom themselves; each horseman at 500 'chariot pieces' and each foot soldier at 300, and the slaves at 100 per head. This was somewhat more than the cavalry had agreed to when they surrendered, but they were only too glad to accept any terms. It was settled that they should elect 10 of their number to go to the Senate at Rome, and the only guarantee required was that they should take an oath to return. They were accompanied by Carthalo, a Carthaginian noble, who was to sound the feelings of the senators, and if they were inclined towards peace, he was to propose terms.

When the delegates had left the camp, one of them, a man of an utterly un-Roman temper, returned to the camp, as if he had forgotten something, and in this way hoped to free himself from his oath. He re-joined his comrades before nightfall. When it was announced that the party were on their way to Rome a *lictor* was despatched to meet Carthalo and order him in the name of the dictator to quit the territory of Rome before night.

The Foreign Wars
by Appian

THE FOREIGN WARS, by Appian of Alexandria, is one of the most complete sources about Hannibal, his life and military career.

Appian wrote in Greek in a clear, unembellished style. Not a historian like Polybius or Livy who wrote chronologically, instead Appian's work is ethnographical, explaining, by region, the Romans' conflicts with other peoples and themselves. Thus, Hannibal appears in *The Iberian Wars*, *The Punic Wars*, *The Hannibalic Wars*, *The Sicilian Wars* and *The Syrian Wars*.

These extracts explain the grounds for the recall of Hannibal by the Carthaginians and the diplomatic negotiations for peace with the Romans; describe the Battle of Zama in which Hannibal was finally defeated by Scipio; describe Hannibal's last stand in Africa; explain how Hannibal came to serve Antiochus; report on the extraordinary face-to-face meeting and conversation between Hannibal and Scipio; and offer one explanation for how he died.

This selection is taken from the translation by Horace White (1899).

From The Sicilian Wars

Chapter VI
Hannibal Evades Capture

THE CARTHAGINIANS, depressed by their ill success, chose Hannibal as their commanding general and sent an admiral with ships to hasten his coming. At the same time, they sent ambassadors to Scipio to negotiate for peace, thinking to gain one of two things, either peace or a delay until Hannibal should arrive.

Scipio consented to an armistice, and having thus gained sufficient supplies for his army allowed them to send their ambassadors to Rome. They did so, but they were received there as enemies and required to lodge outside the walls. When the Senate gave them audience, they asked pardon. Some of the senators adverted to the faithlessness of the Carthaginians, and told how often they had made treaties and broken them, and what injuries Hannibal had inflicted on the Romans and their allies in Spain and Italy. Others represented that the Carthaginians were not more in need of peace than themselves, Italy being exhausted by so many wars; and they showed how much danger was to be feared from the great armies moving together against Scipio, that of Hannibal from Italy, that of Mago from Liguria and that of Hanno at Carthage.

The Senate was not able to agree but sent counsellors to Scipio with whom he should advise, and then do whatever he should deem best. Scipio made peace with the Carthaginians on these terms: That Mago should depart from Liguria forthwith, and that hereafter the Carthaginians should hire no mercenaries; that they should not keep more than 30 long galleys; that they should restrict themselves to the territory within the so-called Phoenician trenches; that they should surrender to the Romans all captives and deserters, and that they should pay 6,000 talents of silver within a certain time; also that Masinissa should have the kingdom of the Massylians and as much of the dominion of Syphax as he could take. Having made this agreement, ambassadors on both sides set sail, some to Rome to take the oaths of the consuls, and others from Rome to Carthage to receive those of the Carthaginian magistrates. The Romans gave to Masinissa, as a reward for his alliance, a crown of gold, a signet ring of gold, a chair of ivory, a purple robe, a horse with gold trappings and a suit of armour.

In the meantime, Hannibal set sail for Africa against his will, knowing the untrustworthy character of the people of Carthage, their bad faith toward their magistrates and their general recklessness. He did not believe that a treaty would be made, and if made he well knew that it would not last long. He landed at the city of Hadrumetum, in Africa, and began to collect corn and buy horses. He made an alliance with the chief of a Numidian tribe called the Areacidae. He slew with arrows 4,000 horsemen who had come to him as deserters. These had formerly been Syphax's men and afterward Masinissa's, and he suspected them. He gave their horses to his own army.

Mesotulus, another chieftain, came to him with 1,000 horse; also Verminia, another son of Syphax, who ruled the greater part of his father's dominions. He gained some of Masinissa's towns by surrender and some by force. He took the town of Narce by stratagem in this way. Dealing in their market he sent to them as to friends, and when he thought the time had come to spring the trap, he sent in a large number of men carrying concealed daggers, and ordered them not to do any harm to the traders until the trumpet should sound, and then to set upon all they met, and hold the gates for him. In this way was Narce taken.

The common people of Carthage, although the treaty had been so lately concluded, and Scipio was still there, and their own ambassadors had not yet returned from Rome, plundered some of Scipio's stores that had been driven into the port of Carthage by a storm, and put the carriers in chains, in spite of the threats of their own council and of their admonitions not to violate the treaty so recently made. The people found fault with the treaty and said that hunger was more dangerous to them than treaty breaking.

Scipio did not deem it best to renew the war after the treaty, but he demanded reparation as from friends who were in the wrong. The people attempted to seize his messengers, intending to hold them until their own ambassadors should return from Rome, but Hanno the Great and Hasdrubal Eriphus ['the Kid'] rescued them from the mob and sent them away in two galleys. Some others, however, sent word to Hasdrubal, the admiral, who was moored near the promontory of Apollo, that when the escort should leave them, he should set upon Scipio's galleys. This he did, and some of the messengers were killed with arrows. The others were wounded, and the rowers darted into the harbour of their own camp and sprang from the ship which was just being seized. So narrowly did they escape being taken prisoners.

When the Romans at home learned these things they ordered the Carthaginian ambassadors, who were still there treating for peace, to depart immediately as enemies. They accordingly set sail and were driven by a tempest to Scipio's camp. To his admiral, who asked what he should do with them, Scipio said: 'We shall not imitate Carthaginian bad faith; send them away unharmed.' When the Carthaginian Senate learned this, they chided the people for the contrast between their behaviour and Scipio's, and advised them to beg Scipio to adhere to the agreement and to accept reparation for the Carthaginian wrongdoing. But the people had been finding fault with the Senate a long time for their ill success, because they had not sufficiently foreseen what was for their advantage and, being pushed on by demagogues and excited by vain hopes, they summoned Hannibal and his army.

Hannibal, in view of the magnitude of the war, asked them to call in Hasdrubal and the force he had in hand. Hasdrubal was accordingly forgiven for his offence, and he delivered his army over to Hannibal. Yet he did not dare to show himself to the Carthaginians but concealed himself in the city. Now Scipio blockaded Carthage with his fleet and cut off their supplies by sea, while from the land they were poorly supplied by reason of the war. About this time there was a cavalry engagement between the forces of Hannibal and those of Scipio near Zama, in which the latter had the advantage. On the succeeding days they had sundry skirmishes until Scipio, learning that Hannibal was very short of supplies and was expecting a convoy, sent the military tribune, Thermus, by night to attack the supply train. Thermus took a position on the crest of a hill at a narrow pass, where he killed 4,000 Africans, took as many more prisoners, and brought the supplies to Scipio.

Hannibal, being reduced to extremity for want of provisions and considering how he might arrange for the present, sent messengers to Masinissa reminding him of his early life and education at Carthage, and asking that he would persuade Scipio to renew the treaty, saying that the former infractions of it were the work of the common people, and of fools who had stirred them up. Masinissa, who had in fact been brought up and educated at Carthage, and who had a high respect for the dignity of the city, and was the friend of many of the inhabitants, besought Scipio to comply, and brought them to an agreement on the following terms: That the Carthaginians should surrender the men and ships bringing provisions to the Romans, which they had taken, also all plunder, or the value of it, which Scipio would estimate, and pay 1,000 talents as a penalty for the wrong done. These things were agreed upon. An armistice was concluded until the Carthaginians should be made acquainted with the details; and thus, Hannibal was saved in an unexpected way.

Chapter VII
Battle of Zama

The Carthaginian council warmly welcomed the agreement and exhorted the people to adhere to its terms, explaining all their misfortunes and their immediate want of soldiers, money and provisions. But the people, like a mere mob, behaved like fools. They thought that their generals had made this arrangement for their own private ends, so that, relying upon the Romans, they might hold the power in their own country.

They said that Hannibal was doing now what had been done before by Hasdrubal, who had betrayed his camp to the enemy by night, and a little later wanted to surrender to Scipio, having approached him for that purpose, and was now concealed in the city. Thereupon there was a great clamour and tumult, and some of them left the assembly and went in search of Hasdrubal. He had anticipated them by taking refuge in his father's tomb, where he destroyed himself with poison. But they pulled his corpse out, cut off his head, put it on a pike and carried it about the city. Thus was Hasdrubal first banished unjustly, next falsely slandered by Hanno, and then driven to his death by the Carthaginians and loaded with indignities after his death.

Then the Carthaginians ordered Hannibal to break the truce and begin war against Scipio, and to fight as soon as possible on account of the scarcity of provisions. Accordingly, he sent word that the truce was at an end. Scipio marched immediately and took the great city of Partha and encamped near Hannibal. The latter moved off, but he sent three spies into the Roman camp who were captured by Scipio. The latter did not put them to death, however, according to the custom of dealing with spies, but ordered that they should be taken around and shown the camp, the arsenals, the engines and the army under review. He then set them free so that they might inform Hannibal concerning all these things.

The latter deemed it advisable to have a parley with Scipio, and when it was granted, he said that the Carthaginians had rejected the former treaty on account of the money indemnity. If he would remit that, and if the Romans would content themselves with Sicily, Spain and the islands they now held, the agreement would be lasting. 'Hannibal's escape from Italy would be a great gain to him,' said Scipio, 'if he could obtain these terms in addition.' He then forbade Hannibal to send any more messages to him. After indulging in some mutual threats, they departed, each to his own camp.

The town of Cilla was in the neighbourhood and near it was a hill well adapted for a camp. Hannibal, perceiving this, sent a detachment forward to seize it and lay out a camp. Then he started and moved forward as though he were already in possession of it. Scipio having anticipated him and seized it beforehand, Hannibal was cut off in the midst of a plain without water and was engaged all night digging wells. His army, by toiling in the sand, with great difficulty obtained a little muddy water to drink, and so they passed the night without food, without care for their bodies and some of them without removing their arms. Scipio, mindful of these things, moved against them at daylight while they were exhausted with marching, with want of sleep and want of water.

Hannibal was troubled, since he did not wish to join battle in that plight. Yet he saw that if he should remain there his army would suffer severely from want of water, while if he should retreat the enemy would take fresh courage and fall upon his rear. For these reasons it was necessary for him to fight. He speedily put in battle array about 50,000 men and 80 elephants. He placed the elephants in the front line at intervals in order to strike terror into the enemy's ranks. Next to them he placed the third part of his army, composed of Celts and Ligurians, and mixed with them everywhere Moorish and Balearic archers and slingers. Behind these was his second line, composed of Carthaginians and Africans. The third line consisted of Italians who had followed him from their own country, in whom he placed the greatest confidence, since they had the most to apprehend from defeat. The cavalry was placed on the wings. In this way Hannibal arranged his forces.

Scipio had about 23,000 foot and 1,500 Italian and Roman horse. He had as allies Masinissa with a large number of Numidian horse, and another prince, named Dacamas, with 1,600 horse. He drew up his infantry, like those of Hannibal, in three lines. He placed all his cohorts in straight lines with open spaces so that the cavalry might readily pass between them. In front of each cohort he stationed men armed with heavy stakes two cubits long, mostly shod with iron, for the purpose of assailing the oncoming elephants by hand, as with catapult bolts. He ordered these and the other foot soldiers to avoid the impetus of these beasts by turning aside and continually hurling javelins at them, and by darting around them to hamstring them whenever they could. In this way Scipio disposed his infantry.

He stationed his Numidian horse on his wings because they were accustomed to the sight and smell of elephants. As the Italian horse were not so, he placed them all in the rear, ready to charge through the intervals of the foot soldiers when the latter should have checked the first onset of the elephants. To each horseman was assigned an attendant armed with plenty of darts with which to ward off the attack of these beasts. In this way was his cavalry disposed. Laelius commanded the right wing and Octavius the left. In the middle both Hannibal and himself took their stations, out of respect for each other, each having a body of horse in order to send reinforcements wherever they might be needed. Of these Hannibal had 4,000 and Scipio 2,000, besides the 300 Italians whom he had armed in Sicily.

When everything was ready each one rode up and down encouraging his soldiers. Scipio, in the presence of his army, invoked the gods, whom the Carthaginians had offended by their frequent violation of treaties. He told the soldiers not to think of the numbers of the enemy but of their own valour, by which previously these same enemies, in even greater numbers, had been overcome in this same country. If fear, anxiety and doubt oppress those who have hitherto been victorious, how much more, he said, must these feelings weigh upon the vanquished. Thus did Scipio encourage his forces and console them for their inferiority in numbers.

Hannibal reminded his men of what they had done in Italy, their great and brilliant victories won, not over Numidians, but over those who were all Italians, and throughout Italy. He pointed out, in plain sight, the smallness of the enemy's force, and exhorted them not to show themselves inferior to a less numerous body in their own country. Each general magnified to his own men the consequences of the coming engagement. Hannibal said that the battle would decide the fate of Carthage and all Africa; if vanquished, they would be enslaved forthwith, if victorious, they would have universal supremacy hereafter. Scipio said that there was no safe refuge for his men if they were vanquished, but if victorious there would be a great increase of the Roman power, a rest from their present labours, a speedy return home and glory forever after.

Having thus exhorted their men they joined battle. Hannibal ordered the trumpet to sound, and Scipio responded in like manner. The elephants began the fight decked out in fearful panoply and urged on with goads by their riders. The Numidian horse flying around them incessantly thrust darts into them. Being wounded and put to flight and having become unmanageable, their drivers took them out of the combat. This is what happened to the elephants on both wings. Those in the centre trampled down the Roman infantry, who were not accustomed to that kind of fighting and were not able to avoid or to pursue them easily on account of their heavy armour, until Scipio brought up the Italian cavalry, who were in the rear and more lightly armed, and ordered them to dismount from their frightened horses and run around and stab the elephants. He was himself the first to dismount and wound the front-tramping elephant. The others were encouraged by his example, and they inflicted so many wounds upon the elephants that these also withdrew.

The field being cleared of these beasts the battle was now waged by men and horses only. The Roman right wing, where Laelius commanded, put the opposing Numidians to flight, and Masinissa struck down their prince, Massathes, with a dart, but Hannibal quickly came to their rescue and restored the line of battle. On the left wing, where Octavius commanded and where the hostile Celts and Ligurians were stationed, a doubtful battle was going on. Scipio sent the tribune Thermus thither with a reinforcement of picked men, but Hannibal, after rallying his left wing, flew to the assistance of the Ligurians and Celts, bringing up at the same time his second line of Carthaginians and Africans. Scipio, perceiving this, brought his second line in opposition. When the two greatest generals of the world thus met, in hand-to-hand fight, there was, on the part of the soldiers of each, a brilliant emulation and reverence for their commanders, and no lack of zeal on either side in the way of sharp and vehement fighting and cheering.

As the battle was long and undecided, the two generals had compassion on their tired soldiers, and rushed upon each other in order to bring it to a speedier decision. They threw their javelins at the same time. Scipio pierced Hannibal's shield. Hannibal hit Scipio's horse. The horse, smarting from the wound, threw Scipio over backwards. He quickly mounted another and again hurled a dart at Hannibal, but missed him and struck another horseman near him. At this juncture, Masinissa, hearing of the crisis, came up, and the Romans seeing their general not only serving as a commander but fighting also as a common soldier, fell upon the enemy more vehemently than before, routed them and pursued them in flight.

Nor could Hannibal, who rode by the side of his men and besought them to make a stand and renew the battle, prevail upon them to do so. Therefore, despairing of these, he turned to the Italians who had come with him, and who were still in reserve and not demoralized. These he led into the fight, hoping to fall upon the Romans in disorderly pursuit. But they perceived his intention, and speedily called one another back from the pursuit and restored the line of battle. As their horse were no longer with them and they were destitute of missiles, they now fought sword in hand in close combat. Great slaughter ensued and innumerable wounds, mingled with the shouts of the combatants and the groans of the dying, until, finally, the Romans routed these also and put them to flight. Such was the brilliant issue of this engagement.

Hannibal in his flight seeing a mass of Numidian horse collected together, ran up and besought them not to desert him. Having secured their promise, he led them against the pursuers, hoping still to turn the tide of battle. The first whom he encountered were the Massylians, and now a single combat between Masinissa and Hannibal took place. Rushing fiercely upon each other, Masinissa drove his spear into Hannibal's shield, and Hannibal wounded his antagonist's horse. Masinissa, being thrown, sprang towards Hannibal on foot, and struck and killed a horseman who was advancing towards him in front of the others. At the same time, he received in his shield – made of elephant's hide – several darts, one of which he pulled out and hurled at Hannibal; but, as it happened, it struck another horseman who was near and killed him. While he was pulling out another, he was wounded in the arm, and withdrew from the fight for a brief space.

When Scipio learned this, he feared for Masinissa and hastened to his relief, but he found that the latter had bound up his wound and returned to the fight on a fresh horse. Thus, the battle continued doubtful and very severe, the soldiers on either side having the utmost reverence for their commanders, until Hannibal, discovering a body of Spanish and Celtic troops on a hill nearby, dashed over to them to bring them into the fight. Those who were still engaged, not knowing the cause of his going, thought that he had fled. Accordingly, they abandoned the fight of their own accord and broke into disorderly rout, not following after Hannibal, but helter skelter. This band having been dispersed, the Romans thought that the fight was over and pursued them in a disorderly way, not perceiving Hannibal's purpose.

Presently, Hannibal returned, accompanied by the Spanish and Celtic troops from the hill. Scipio hastened to recall the Romans from the pursuit, and formed a new line of battle much stronger than those who were coming against him, by which means he overcame them without difficulty. When this last effort had failed, Hannibal despaired utterly, and fled in plain sight. Many horsemen pursued him, and among others Masinissa, although suffering from his wound, pressed him hard, striving eagerly to take him prisoner and deliver him to Scipio. But night came to his rescue and under cover of darkness, with 20 horsemen who had alone been able to keep pace with him, he took refuge in a town named Thon.

Here he found many Bruttian and Spanish horsemen who had fled after the defeat. Fearing the Spaniards because they were fickle barbarians, and apprehending that the Bruttians, as they were Scipio's countrymen, might deliver him up in order to secure pardon for their transgression against Italy, he fled secretly with one horseman in whom he had full confidence. Having accomplished about 3,000 *stades* in two nights and days, he arrived at the seaport of Hadrumetum, where a part of his army had been left to guard his supplies. Here he began to collect forces from the adjacent country and from those who had escaped from the recent engagement, and to prepare arms and engines of war.

Chapter VII
Scipio Imposes Terms on the Carthaginians

Now Scipio, having gained this splendid victory, girded himself as for a sacrifice and burned the less valuable spoils of the enemy, as is the custom of the Roman generals. He sent to Rome 10 talents of gold, 2,500 talents of silver, a quantity of carved ivory and many distinguished captives in ships, and Laelius to carry news of the victory. The remainder of the spoils he sold, and divided the proceeds among the troops. He also made presents for distinguished valour, and crowned Masinissa again. He also sent out expeditions and gathered in more cities.

Such was the result of the engagement between Hannibal and Scipio, who here met in combat for the first time. The Roman loss was 2,500 men, that of Masinissa rather more. That of the enemy was 25,000 killed, and 8,500 taken prisoners. Three hundred Spaniards deserted to Scipio, and 800 Numidians to Masinissa.

Before the news reached either Carthage or Rome, the former sent word to Mago, who was collecting Gallic mercenaries, to invade Italy if possible, and if not, to set sail with his forces for Africa. These letters being intercepted and brought to Rome, another army, together with horses, ships and money, was despatched to Scipio. The latter had already sent Octavius by the land route to Carthage, and was going thither himself with his fleet. When the Carthaginians learned of Hannibal's defeat they sent ambassadors to Scipio on a small fast-sailing ship, of whom the principal ones were Hanno the Great and Hasdrubal Eriphus, who bore a herald's staff aloft on the prow and stretched out their hands toward Scipio in the manner of suppliants. He directed them to come to the camp, and when they had arrived he attended to their business in high state. They threw themselves on the ground weeping, and when the attendants had lifted them up and bade them say what they wished, Hasdrubal Eriphus spoke as follows:

'For myself, Romans, and for Hanno here, and for all sensible Carthaginians, let me say that we are guiltless of the wrongs which you lay at our door. For when the same men, driven by hunger, did violence to your legates, we rescued them and sent them back to you. You ought not to condemn all the people of Carthage who so recently sought peace, and when it was granted eagerly took the oath to support it. But cities are easily swayed to their hurt, because the masses are always controlled by what is pleasing to their ears. We have had experience of these things, having been unable either to persuade or to restrain the multitude by reason of those who slandered us at home and who have prevented us from making ourselves understood by you.

'Romans, do not judge us by the standard of your own discipline and good counsel. If anyone esteems it a crime to have yielded to the persuasions of these rabble-rousers, consider the hunger and the necessity that was upon us by reason of suffering. For it could not have been a deliberate intention on the part of our people, first to ask for peace, and give such a large sum of money to obtain it, and deliver up all their galleys except a few, and surrender the bulk of their territory, swear to these things, and send an embassy to Rome with the ratifications, and then wantonly to violate the agreement before our embassy had returned. Surely some god misled them and the tempest that drove your supplies into Carthage; and besides the tempest, hunger carried us away, for people who are in want of everything do not form the best judgments respecting other people's property. It would not be reasonable to punish with severity a multitude of men so disorganized and unfortunate.

'But if you consider us more guilty than unfortunate, we confess our fault and ask pardon for it. Justification belongs to the innocent, entreaty to those who have offended. And much more readily will the fortunate extend pity to others, when they observe the mutability of human affairs, and see people craving mercy today who yesterday were carrying things with a high hand. Such is the condition of Carthage, the greatest and most powerful city of Africa, in ships and money, in elephants, in infantry and cavalry and in subject peoples, which has flourished 700 years and held sway over all Africa and so many other nations, islands and seas, standing for the greater part of this time on an equality with yourselves, but which now places her hope of safety not in her dominion of the sea, her ships, her horses, her subjects (all of which have passed over to you), but in you, whom we have heretofore shamefully treated.

'Contemplating these facts, Romans, it is fit that you should beware of the Nemesis which has come upon them and should use your good fortune mercifully, to do deeds worthy of your own magnanimity and of the former fortunes of Carthage, and to deal with the changes which Providence has ordered in our affairs without reproach, so that your conduct may be blameless before the gods and win the praises of all mankind.

'There need be no fear that the Carthaginians will change their minds again, after being subjected to such repentance and punishment for their past folly. Wise men are prevented from wrongdoing by their wisdom, the wicked by their suffering and repentance. It is reasonable to suppose that those who have been chastised will be trustier than those who have not had such experience. Be careful that you do not imitate the cruelty and the sinfulness that you lay at the door of the Carthaginians. The misfortunes of the miserable are the source of fresh transgressions arising from poverty. To the fortunate the opportunity for clemency exists in the abundance of their means. It will be neither to the glory nor to the advantage of your government to destroy so great a city as ours, instead of preserving it. Still, you are the better judges of your own interests. For our safety we rely on these two things: the ancient dignity of the city of Carthage and your well-known moderation, which, together with your arms, has raised you to so great dominion and power. We must accept peace on whatever terms you grant. It is, needless to say, that we place everything in your hands.'

At the conclusion of his speech Eriphus burst into tears. Then Scipio dismissed them and consulted with his officers a long time. After he had come to a decision, he called the Carthaginian envoys back and addressed them thus:

'You do not deserve pardon, you who have so often violated your treaties with us, and only lately abused our envoys in such a public and heaven-defying manner that you can neither excuse yourselves nor deny that you are worthy of the severest punishment. But what is the use of accusing those who confess? And now you take refuge in prayers, you who would have wiped out the very name of Rome if you had conquered. We did not imitate your bad example. When your ambassadors were at Rome, although you had violated the agreement and maltreated our envoys, the city allowed them to go free, and when they were driven into my camp, although the war had been recommenced, I sent them back to you unharmed. Now that you have condemned yourselves, you may consider whatever terms are granted to you in the light of a gain. I will tell you what my views are, and our Senate will vote upon them as it shall think best.

'We will yet grant you peace, Carthaginians, on condition that you surrender to the Romans all your warships except 10, all your elephants, the plunder you have lately taken from us, or the value of what has been lost, of which I shall be the judge, all prisoners and deserters and those whom Hannibal led from Italy. These conditions to be fulfilled within 30 days after peace is declared. Mago to depart from Liguria within 60 days, and your garrisons to be withdrawn from all cities beyond the Phoenician trenches and their hostages to be surrendered. You to pay to Rome the sum of 250 Euboic talents per annum for 50 years. You shall not recruit mercenaries from the Celts or the Ligurians, nor wage war against Masinissa or any other friend of Rome, nor permit any Carthaginians to serve against them with consent of your people. You to retain your city and as much territory inside the Phoenician trenches as you had when I sailed for Africa. You to remain friends of Rome and be her allies on land and sea; all this, if the Senate please, in which case the Romans will evacuate Africa within 150 days. If you desire an armistice until you can send ambassadors to Rome, you shall forthwith give us 150 of your children as hostages whom I shall choose. You shall also give 1,000 talents in addition for the pay of my army, and provisions likewise. When the treaty is ratified we will release your hostages.'

Chapter IX
Hannibal's Last Stand in Africa

When the Carthaginians were continually beaten by Scipio in Africa, those of the Bruttians who heard of it revolted from Hannibal, some of them slaying their garrisons and others expelling them. Those who were not able to do either of these things sent messengers to Rome secretly to explain the necessity under which they had acted and to declare their goodwill.

Hannibal came with his army to Petelia, which was not now occupied by the Petelians, as he had expelled them and given the town to the Bruttians. He accused the latter of sending an embassy to Rome. When they denied it, he pretended to believe them, but in order, as he said, that there might be no ground for suspicion, he delivered their principal citizens over to the Numidians, who were ordered to guard each one of them separately. He also disarmed the people, armed the slaves and stationed them as guards over the city. He did the same to the other cities that he visited. He removed 3,000 citizens of Thurii, who were particularly friendly to the Carthaginians, and 500 others from the country, but gave the goods of the remainder as spoils to his soldiers. Leaving a strong garrison in the city he settled these 3,500 people at Croton, which he found to be well situated for his operations and where he established his magazines and his headquarters against the other towns.

When the Carthaginians summoned him to hasten to the aid of his own country, which was in danger from Scipio, and sent Hasdrubal, their admiral, to him that there might be no delay, he lamented the perfidious and ungrateful conduct of the Carthaginians toward their generals, of which he had had long experience. Moreover, he had apprehensions for himself touching the cause of this great war, which had been begun by himself in Spain. Nevertheless, he recognized the necessity of obeying, and accordingly he built a fleet, for which Italy supplied abundant timber.

Despising the cities still allied to him now as foreigners, he resolved to plunder them all, and thus, by enriching his army, render himself secure against his calumniators in Carthage. But being ashamed of such a breach of faith, he sent Hasdrubal, the admiral, about, on pretence of inspecting the garrisons. The latter, as he entered each city, ordered the inhabitants to take what things they and their slaves could carry, and move away. Then he plundered the rest. Some of them, learning of these proceedings before Hasdrubal came, attacked the garrisons, overcoming them in some places and being overcome by them in others. Indiscriminate slaughter, accompanied by the violation of wives and the abduction of virgins, and all the horrors that usually take place when cities are captured, ensued.

Hannibal himself, knowing that the Italians in his army were extremely well-drilled soldiers, sought to persuade them by lavish promises to accompany him to Africa. Those of them who had been guilty of crimes against their own countries willingly expatriated themselves and followed him. Those who had committed no such wrong hesitated. Collecting together those who had decided to remain, as though he wished to say something to them, or to reward them for their services, or to give them some command as to the future, he surrounded them with his army unexpectedly, and directed his soldiers to choose from among them such as they would like to have for slaves. Some made their selections accordingly. Others were ashamed to reduce their comrades in so many engagements to servitude. All the rest Hannibal put to death with darts in order that the Romans might not avail themselves of such a splendid body of men. With them he slaughtered also about 4,000 horses and a large number of pack animals, which he was not able to transport to Africa.

Thereupon he embarked his army and waited for a wind, having left a few garrisons on the land. These the Petalini and other Italians set upon, slew some of them, and then ran away. Hannibal passed over to Africa, having devastated Italy for 16 successive years, and inflicted countless evils upon the inhabitants, and reduced Rome several times to the last extremity, and treated his own subjects and allies with contumely as enemies. For, just as he had made use of them for a time, not from any goodwill but from necessity, so now that they could be of no further service to him he scorned them and considered them enemies.

When Hannibal had departed from Italy the Senate pardoned all the Italian peoples who had sided with him, and voted a general amnesty except as to the Bruttians, who remained most zealous for him to the end. From these they took away a considerable part of their land, also their arms, if there were any that Hannibal had not taken. They were also forbidden to be enrolled in the military forces thereafter, as being no longer free persons, and they were required to attend as servants upon the consuls and praetors who went about inspecting the affairs of government and the public works of the provinces. Such was the end of Hannibal's invasion of Italy.

From The Syrian Wars

Chapter II
Hannibal Serves Antiochus; Meets Scipio; Poisoned by Prusias

Antiochus (the son of Seleucus and grandson of Antiochus), king of the Syrians, the Babylonians, and other nations, was the sixth in succession from that Seleucus who succeeded Alexander in the government of the Asiatic countries around the Euphrates. He invaded Media and Parthia, and other countries that had revolted from his ancestors, and performed many exploits, from which he was named Antiochus the Great.

Elated by his successes, and by the title which he had derived from them, he invaded Coele-Syria and a portion of Cilicia and took them away from Ptolemy Philopator [Epiphanes], king of Egypt, who was still a boy. As there was nothing small in his views, he marched among the Hellespontines, the Aeolians, and the Ionians as though they belonged to him as the ruler of Asia; and, indeed, they had been formerly subjects of the Asiatic kings. Then he crossed over to Europe, brought Thrace under his sway, and reduced by force those who would not obey him. He fortified Chersonesus and rebuilt Lysimacheia, which Lysimachus, who ruled Thrace in the time of Alexander, built as a stronghold against the Thracians themselves, but which they destroyed after his death. Antiochus repeopled it, calling back the citizens who had fled, redeeming those who had been sold as slaves, bringing in others, supplying them with cattle, sheep, and agricultural implements, and omitting nothing that might contribute to its speedy completion as a stronghold; for the place seemed to him to be admirably situated to hold all of Thrace in subjection, and a convenient base of supplies for other operations that he contemplated.

Here the open disagreements between him and the Romans began, for as he passed among the Greek cities thereabout most of them joined him and received his garrisons because they feared capture by him. But the inhabitants of Smyrna and Lampsacus, and some others who still resisted, sent ambassadors to [Titus Quinctius] Flamininus, the Roman general, who had lately overthrown Philip the Macedonian in a great battle in Thessaly; for the affairs of the Macedonians and of the Greeks were closely linked together at certain times and places, as I have shown in my Grecian history. Accordingly, certain embassies passed between Antiochus and Flamininus and tested each other to no purpose. The Romans and Antiochus had been suspicious of each other for a long time, the former surmising that he would not keep quiet because he was so much puffed up by the extent of his dominions and the acme of fortune that he had reached.

Antiochus, on the other hand, believed that the Romans were the only people who could put a stop to his increase of power and prevent him from passing over to Europe. Still, there was no outward cause of enmity between them until ambassadors came to Rome from Ptolemy Philopator complaining that Antiochus had taken Syria and Cilicia away from him. The Romans gladly seized this occasion as one well-suited to their purposes, and sent to Antiochus ostensibly to bring about a reconciliation between him and Ptolemy, but really to find out his designs and to check him as much as they could.

Cnaeus, the chief of the embassy, demanded that Antiochus should allow Ptolemy, who was a friend of the Roman people, to rule over all the countries that his father had left to him, and that the cities of Asia that had been part of the dominions of Philip should be independent, for it was not right that Antiochus should usurp powers of which the Romans had deprived Philip. 'We are wholly at a loss to know,' he said, 'why Antiochus should come from Media bringing such a fleet and such an army from the upper country to the Asiatic coast, make an incursion into Europe, build cities there and subdue Thrace, unless these are the preparations for another war.'

Antiochus replied that Thrace had belonged to his ancestors, that it had fallen away from them when they were occupied elsewhere, and that he had resumed possession because he had leisure to do so. He had built Lysimacheia as the future seat of government of his son Seleucus. He would leave the Greek cities of Asia independent if they would acknowledge the gratitude therefor as due to himself and not to the Romans. 'I am a relative of Ptolemy,' he said, 'and I shall be his father-in-law, although I am not so now, and I will see to it that he renders gratitude to you. I am at a loss to know by what right you meddle with the affairs of Asia when I never interfere with those of Italy.' And so they separated without coming to any understanding, and both sides broke into more open threats.

A rumour having spread abroad that Ptolemy Philopator was dead, Antiochus hastened to Egypt in order to seize the country while bereft of a ruler. While on this journey Hannibal the Carthaginian met him at Ephesus. He was now a fugitive from his own country on account of the accusations of his enemies, who reported to the Romans that he was hostile to them, that he wanted to bring on a war and that he could never enjoy peace. This was a time when the Carthaginians were leagued with the Romans by treaty. Antiochus received Hannibal in a magnificent manner on account of his great military reputation, and kept him near himself. At Lycia he learned that Ptolemy was alive. So, he gave up the idea of seizing Egypt and turned his attention to Cyprus, hoping to take it instead of Egypt, and sailed thither with all speed. Encountering a storm at the mouth of the river Sarus and losing many of his ships, some of them with his soldiers and friends, he sailed back to Seleucia in Syria to repair his damaged fleet. There he celebrated the nuptials of his children, Antiochus and Laodice, whom he had joined together in marriage.

Now, determining no longer to conceal his intended war with the Romans, he formed alliances by marriage with the neighbouring kings. To Ptolemy in Egypt he sent his daughter Cleopatra, surnamed Syra, giving with her Coele-Syria as a dowry, which he had taken away from Ptolemy himself, thus flattering the young king in order to keep him quiet during the war with the Romans. To Ariarathes, king of Cappadocia, he sent his daughter Antiochis, and the remaining one to Eumenes, king of Pergamus. But the latter, seeing that Antiochus was about to engage in war with the Romans and that he wanted to form a marriage connection with him on this account, refused her. To his brothers, Attalus and Philetaerus, who were surprised that he should decline marriage relationship with so great a king, who was also his neighbour and who made the first overtures, he showed that the coming war would be of doubtful issue at first, but that the Romans would prevail in the end by their courage and perseverance. 'If the Romans conquer,' said he, 'I shall be firmly seated in my kingdom. If Antiochus is the victor, I may expect to be stripped of all my possessions by my powerful neighbour, or, if I am allowed to reign, to be ruled over by him.' For these reasons he rejected the proffered marriage.

Then Antiochus went down to the Hellespont and crossed over to Chersonesus and possessed himself of a large part of Thrace by conquest or surrender. He freed the Greeks who were under subjection to the Thracians, and conciliated the Byzantines in many ways, because their city was admirably situated at the outlet of the Euxine Sea. By gifts and by fear of his warlike preparations he brought the Galatians into his alliance, because he considered them formidable by reason of their bodily size. Then he went back to Ephesus and sent as ambassadors to Rome Lysias, Hegesianax and Menippus. They were sent really to find out the intentions of the Senate, but for the sake of appearances Menippus said, 'King Antiochus, while strongly desirous of the friendship of the Romans and willing to be their ally if they wish, is surprised that they urge him to give up the cities of Ionia and to remit tribute for certain states, and not to interfere with certain of the affairs of Asia and to leave Thrace alone, though it has always belonged to his ancestors. Yours are not the exhortations of friends, but resemble orders given by victors to the vanquished.'

The Senate, perceiving that the embassy had come to make a test of their disposition, replied curtly, 'If Antiochus will leave the Greeks in Asia free and independent, and keep away from Europe, he can be the friend of the Roman people if he desires.' Such was the answer of the Romans, and they gave no reason for their rejoinder.

As Antiochus intended to invade Greece first and thence begin his war against the Romans, he communicated his design to Hannibal. The latter said that as Greece had been wasted for a long time, the task would be easy; but that wars which were waged at home were the hard ones to bear, by reason of the scarcity which they caused, and that those which took place in foreign territory were much easier to endure. Antiochus could never vanquish the Romans in Greece, where they would have plenty of homegrown corn and all needed material. Hannibal urged him to occupy some part of Italy and make his base of operations there, so that the Romans might be weakened both at home and abroad. 'I have had experience of Italy,' he said, 'and with 10,000 men I can occupy some convenient place and write to my friends in Carthage to stir up the people to revolt. As they are already discontented with their condition, and harbour ill will toward the Romans, they will be filled with courage and hope if they hear that I am ravaging Italy again.' Antiochus listened eagerly to this advice, and as he considered a Carthaginian accession a great advantage (as it would have been) for his war, directed him to write to his friends at once.

Hannibal did not write the letters, since he did not consider it yet safe to do so, as the Romans were searching out everything and the war was not yet openly declared, and he had many opponents in Carthage, and the city had no fixed or sound policy – the very lack of which caused its destruction, not long afterward. But he sent Aristo, a Tyrian merchant, to his friends, on the pretext of trading, to tell them that when he should invade Italy they should rouse Carthage to avenge her wrongs. Aristo did this, but when Hannibal's enemies learned that he was in the city they raised a tumult as though a revolution was impending, and searched everywhere to find him.

In order that Hannibal's friends might not be particularly accused, he posted letters in front of the Senate-chamber secretly by night, saying that Hannibal exhorted the whole Senate to rescue the country with the help of Antiochus. Having done this he sailed away. In the morning, the friends of Hannibal were relieved of their fears by this afterthought of Aristo, which implied that he had been sent to the whole Senate. The city was filled with all kinds of tumult, the people feeling bitterly toward the Romans, but despairing of accomplishing anything indirectly. Such was the situation of affairs in Carthage.

In the meantime, Roman ambassadors, and among them Scipio, who had humbled the Carthaginian power, were sent, like those of Antiochus, to ascertain his designs and to form an estimate of his strength. Learning that the king had gone to Pisidia, they waited for him at Ephesus. There they entered into frequent conversations with Hannibal, Carthage being then at peace with them and war with Antiochus not yet declared. They reproached Hannibal for flying his country when the Romans had nothing to complain against him, or against the other Carthaginians, under the terms of the last treaty. They did this in order to cast suspicion on Hannibal in the mind of the king by the protracted conversations and intercourse. Hannibal, although a most profound military genius, did not perceive their design, but the king, when he learned what had been going on, did suspect him, and was more reluctant to give him his confidence thereafter. There was also some jealousy and envy added, lest Hannibal should carry off the glory of the exploits.

It is said that at one of their meetings in the gymnasium Scipio and Hannibal had a conversation on the subject of generalship, in the presence of a number of bystanders, and that Scipio asked Hannibal whom he considered the greatest general, to which the latter replied, 'Alexander of Macedon'. To this Scipio assented since he also yielded the first place to Alexander. Then he asked Hannibal whom he placed next, and he replied, 'Pyrrhus of Epirus', because he considered boldness the first qualification of a general; 'for it would not be possible,' he said, 'to find two kings more enterprising than these.' Scipio was rather nettled by this, but nevertheless he asked Hannibal to whom he would give the third place, expecting that at least the third would be assigned to him; but Hannibal replied, 'To myself; for when I was a young man I conquered Spain and crossed the Alps with an army, the first after Hercules. I invaded Italy and struck terror into all of you, laid waste 400 of your towns, and often put your city in extreme peril, all this time receiving neither money nor reinforcements from Carthage.'

As Scipio saw that he was likely to prolong his self-laudation he said, laughing, 'Where would you place yourself, Hannibal, if you had not been defeated by me?' Hannibal, now perceiving his jealousy, replied, 'In that case I should have put myself before Alexander.' Thus, Hannibal continued his self-laudation, but flattered Scipio in a delicate manner by suggesting that he had conquered one who was the superior of Alexander.

At the end of this conversation Hannibal invited Scipio to be his guest, and Scipio replied that he would be so gladly if Hannibal were not living with Antiochus, who was held in suspicion by the Romans. Thus, did they, in a manner worthy of great commanders, cast aside their enmity at the end of their wars. Not so Flamininus, for, at a later period when Hannibal had fled after the defeat of Antiochus and was wandering around Bithynia, Flamininus sent an embassy to King Prusias on other matters, and, although he had no grievance against Hannibal, and had no orders from the Senate, and Hannibal was no longer formidable to them, Carthage having fallen, he caused Prusias to put him to death by poison.

There was a story that an oracle had once said: 'Libyssan earth shall cover Hannibal's remains.' So, he believed that he should die in Libya. But there is a river Libyssus in Bithynia, and the adjoining country takes the name of Libyssa from the river. These things I have placed side by side as memorials of the magnanimity of Hannibal and Scipio and of the smallness of Flamininus.